ATTRITION
WORLD OF ANTHRAX
#5

Attrition

World of Anthrax Book 5

ISBN: 9798854674331

Editing by Marti Lynch
Cover concept by S.Marko
Cover & Interior design by Adrienne Lecter

www.adriennelecter.com

Give feedback on the book at:
adrienne@adriennelecter.com

Twitter: @AdrienneLecter

First Edition August 2023
Produced and published by Barbara Klein, Vienna, Austria

To M

Just because.

CHAPTER 1

What exactly do you do after waking up and realizing you've spent the last however many hours as a homicidal cannibal? Or a zombie—although I really wasn't sure if that changed anything about the matter at hand, or whether it made the situation better or worse.

Pondering such questions full of philosophical, existential dread while you're still packed up in layers upon layers of brain fog? It didn't make the situation any easier, that much was for sure.

What I was also sure of was that I needed to think, and doing so from a vantage point high off the ground seemed pertinent, particularly since the ground was, if not lava, then layers of gore.

Gore that I had—quite possibly—been responsible for producing.

Or maybe the reason I found myself climbing up onto the roof of the black SUV was to prevent myself from hurling myself—snarling and salivating—at the still-feeding zombies and chasing them away from my kill so I could continue gorging myself on it. After all, I had wasted an entire stomach full of good meat by vomiting it all up once the realization of what I'd done had hit me like a freight train.

My stomach was still upset over that.

Both over emptying itself and being empty.

Because between the massive waves of revulsion, hunger still ebbed and swelled, making me feel like a toddler sitting in front of her birthday cake.

ME WANTS!!

So, so much.

No! Bad Callie! No savaged Marines for you!

Only once did a cackle wrench itself from my throat, giving voice to the madness still rolling through my brain. That, of course, made the six zombies—my pack!—stop immediately as they jerked around, all filmed-over, bloodshot eyes on me.

Yeah, how about not creating a repeat performance of that? If anything, I needed to get rid of them, not make them even more aware of my presence.

At least none of them had gotten it into their rotten brains to attack me, but the sore muscles all over my body—particularly my arms and back—told me plainly why.

Not that I remembered. Not exactly. Certainly not in a coherent, movie-like way, as memories were supposed to work. More like snapshots, almost random. But if I tried hard enough, I could make sense of them—or at least form some kind of order of occurrence.

The last thing I clearly remembered was stumbling along a road in the dark when bright lights suddenly blinded me.

After I'd jumped out of a speeding car because Jared was an asshole of epic proportions—

And my, wasn't that a can of worms I was very much aware I would have to deal with very soon. But right now, I had to be selfish and deal with more pressing matters.

But before I got to that, I needed to spend some more time sitting here, in the first rays of the late September sun somewhere in South Carolina, and get a grip on urges that I absolutely refused to follow.

There was something inherently meditative about watching my pack feed.

Damnit! I had to snap out of whatever this fucked-up headspace was where I felt almost… possessive of them. But I was ninety percent sure from my snapshot memory flashes that I'd been the one who'd killed the four Marines whose corpses the pack was almost done devouring. I also had a vague sense that the first of them I'd put in their place was the aggressive female who snapped at me when I'd returned to the scene of carnage before she'd backed down. I'd kind of made her my… lieutenant, for lack of a better word. That was why she'd defended me from the equally aggressive male. He could have wiped the floor with both of us—but only one-on-one. I must have injured him somehow, and she'd been quick to climb past him in the pack's pecking order. The other four had never posed a problem, content to follow whoever was the leader right then and provided a fresh kill for them to gorge on.

When I looked at them—and really concentrated—they were little more than somewhat well-fed zombies. But it was when my thoughts drifted off and my mind got cloudy that all the knowledge and certainty snapped back into my head; like instinct or muscle memory.

I must have been up on my perch a good twenty minutes when I realized that simply waiting didn't change anything about my situation. Sure, awareness and intellect had increased little by little the first minutes after waking up, but now it seemed to have gotten stuck somewhere around the halfway point to what I thought was my full mental capacity. Not that I could be sure, because the only certainty I had was that if I didn't concentrate hard, the urges started crawling back up my spine to take root in my brain stem, and then it was just a matter of jumping off the vehicle and chasing them away so I could feed—

If hoping for deliverance wasn't doing shit, maybe putting some distance between me and my birthday cake would do the trick?

I should also look for some clothes, it occurred to me.

I wasn't cold, exactly, and there was nobody around who would appreciate my state of nakedness, but just maybe this was something I should take care of. Also, cleaning up, because the entire upper half of my body was layered in grime to the point that I wasn't sure I actually looked naked —and the mud that had dried all along my back and ass was the least of it. I'd deliberately avoided looking at my face in any of the reflective surfaces of the car, but it couldn't be pretty.

With not just a hint of macabre mirth, I regretted not having a phone at hand so I could take a selfie to later show Jared. How would that fit into his little fantasies, huh?

Thinking of him again kicked off an avalanche of emotions that I quickly put a lid on. That, I would deal with later. Right now, I was more than at capacity with planning the simple tasks of cleaning up and getting dressed.

First things first.

If my mind had actually been working well, I would have searched the tent first, but since that wasn't the case, base-brain reasoning sent me scurrying over to the small creek I could hear gurgling on the other side of the clearing, away from the carnage and where I'd woken up. I walked the short distance there, which felt both good and utterly wrong, as if my body had to re-learn to be strictly bipedal instead of spending a good portion of my time crouching or hunched over.

Who would have thought that being a zombie was good for your quads?

I was still fighting another cackle when the ice-cold water gave me a good shock to the system when I dunked myself straight into a shallow pool close to a bend in the creek. The pool was barely deep enough that the water completely covered my thighs when my ass hit the bottom, but that was more than enough to splash water everywhere if I just rolled around in it like a dog. Which was exactly what I did.

It sure woke me up, but it did little for actual clarity of mind.

It made me miss coffee, though, which might have done the trick. Or not.

Even in the now muddy water—thanks to my vigorous motions—I saw clouds of grime come off me. I kept going until that stopped, then spent an extra minute scrubbing my face and upper torso, particularly my chin, neck, and upper chest.

Apparently, I'd been quite the messy eater.

Who'd have thunk it?

With little feeling left in my fingers, I finally made it back onto the shore and sauntered across the clearing again. Six blood-smeared faces lifted and followed my progress with rapt attention, but when they saw I went for the tent rather than made as if to join them, they ignored me once more. The urge to do so was rekindled when the overwhelming scent of blood hit my nostrils, but I managed.

Was I deluding myself, or had that gotten just a little easier?

Not enough to make me relax, so I distracted myself by rooting through what I found in the partly fallen-in tent.

My flash-flashbacks sadly didn't reveal anything about the tent. Had it already been there? Had the Marines erected it when they made camp? Had I ever been in there, staring hopelessly at the tarp above or the isolation mats below? No clue. All I had to go on was the heap of rags that used to be my clothes. I checked what used to be my jeans briefly, finding them ripped rather than cut. No guessing who'd been responsible for that—me, or someone else.

Since my sneakers were still usable, I put them on, my toes unfamiliar with the sensation of no longer being in contact with the bare ground.

There were two packs in the tent, still unopened. Three more I found inside the car after needing a laughably long time to open the doors to the back row and the trunk. Rooting through them, I found ten MREs altogether, some assorted other food, and enough moderately clean clothes to look like I was having a slumber party in my brother's PJs. It wasn't perfect, but I was now covered from neck to elbows and knees—decent, for lack of a better word.

I also found the car's key fob stashed in the cup holder, so once I dared take the next step and try my addled brain at vehicular control, I was set. There were also three full cans of gas in the trunk, making me guess the SUV would start without a hitch.

Since I didn't quite feel like leaving yet, I returned to my perch up on the roof. To think, and just maybe to have a better overview of what my undead minions were getting up to since a thread of unease started weaving itself around the back of my mind.

It was probably smart to stop relying on the certainty that they wouldn't attack me—and if so, that I would easily come out on top of that altercation.

I had the sneaking suspicion that if that happened, my mind would immediately snap back into survival mode and make exactly that happen, but there was no way to be certain about it. Even if it made sense that I would no longer have to worry about infection, they could still do a hell of a lot of damage—and I had no clue from how much damage I could recover.

That those two things were connected I felt reasonably certain of now, even though I couldn't begin to guess at how or why. With the surface-level reasoning I was capable of, it made zero sense. They were essentially rotting sacks of meat. How did super-fast healing fit into that concept?

And looking down on them now—particularly the four weaker ones—I could clearly see the signs of deterioration all across their partly clothed bodies, matching what I'd seen way too many times on way too many animated bodies everywhere over the past four months. The bruises that were too dark with little yellowing, if at all. Broken bones—sometimes even sticking out of the scabbed-over wounds that had created them. Pieces of flesh, muscle, and viscera exposed, turned gangrenous. Those creepy, filmed-over eyes that shouldn't have been working anymore. Even the way they were moving as they were feeding was somehow inherently wrong.

But if I looked from them to the two stronger, better-fed ones, the signs were still there but on a much reduced level, and not just because they were far less injured. Their bruises were still healing, their wounds either fresh but mending, or already scarred over.

Just like my own scars, on the right side of my torso and right thigh. I knew they were only roughly nine weeks old from when those assholes on the Catawba River had shot at us—and hit, in my case and Blake's. I didn't need to check on them to know they looked years old, even faded in some places, almost as barely visible as the cutting scars on my arms and legs. That those hadn't completely disappeared yet struck me as weird all of a sudden. Because that was what I needed to concern myself with now, of all things.

It was when one of the weaker ones moved back to one of the previously savaged bodies and almost fell over a discarded rifle that I realized I had a different reason than ungodly nutrition to maybe check on the dead Marines one last time.

Since the zombies had not just eaten the bodies but essentially torn them apart in doing so, it took some time to find where what the Marines had been wearing had ended up. The boots—with gnawed-off feet still securely laced into them except for one single boot—were easy to find. The rest was harder, but everything they'd had fastened to the outside of the clothes was easier to find since what was left of the rags had ended up wrapped around themselves. More specifically, their carbines, handguns, knives, and assorted things stashed on the outside of their plate carriers.

It took some gingerly moving around the clearing so as not to disturb the feeding too much, but I ended up with nine things that went boom and three things for slicy-slicy or stabby-stabby in the end, plus some ammo and a med kit. The magazines in the carbines were half-empty, making me wonder if the Marines had shot at me and the zombies before dying, or hadn't reloaded after the last time they'd used them, probably to conserve ammo—or whatever. Even fully aware, I wouldn't have known what was standard practice for these people. Now, that was way beyond me.

The watch I'd found next to one bundle of rags—thankfully without a hand or wrist still attached—read 8:39 by the time I decided that there was little sense in lingering here.

The fact that I felt ever so slightly resentful at the idea of leaving my trusty pack of undead behind made me want to scurry behind the steering wheel and peel out of there at Jared's preferred driving speed.

Thinking of him made something in my chest seize up.

I almost laughed when I realized what was missing in that snarl of entangled emotions.

Fear.

Looked like whatever that damn brain fog did to my mind was still heavily affecting my amygdala—the center in my brain responsible for that whole fear-flight-fight response. While I didn't exactly feel like I was jonesing for a fight—which had been my primary impulse just after waking up—the rest was still very much dormant. It was a twisted mess of resentment, betrayal, and longing that made me want to pound my chest hard enough to make it stop. Not the urge to run until I reached the end of the world.

It seemed like a good idea to leave rumination for when I was on the move—and yes, that meant I was still deliberately stalling as I got behind the wheel and then checked what I found stuffed into the passenger-side glove compartment.

Maps. A whole stack of maps. One in particular was interesting, since it was scrawled all over with marks.

Studying it for a while, I did my best to find the handful of towns that we had visited, at least those of which I had a vague sense of where they were. The one close to where we'd spent most of the summer—Josh's territory near Lancaster—was struck out after having gotten circled red previously; or at least, I presumed that was the order of things. All the other ones were still there, although Geek Central was also marked in red. I was glad to see that the little paradise close to the coast that Dwayne and Grace called their home was only marked as existing, nothing else.

Of course, thinking of that came with a wave of resentment—resentment for my own stupidity, although now I realized that most of that likely hadn't been my fault, or only as far as to blindly traipse into Jared's trap.

After that, we'd hit that town close to Tim's farm—where what little innocence my cold, dead heart had managed to hold on to had gotten stomped out of existence.

Staring at the map for a second, I wondered where the three assholes had ended up.

North of that town, there was only a single other marked in what I figured was a day or night's drive nowadays, roughly forty miles northeast, toward the North Carolina border. Of course, they could have driven on in any possible direction, but that was only a short distance away from what looked like the best route along the road we must have taken out of town. Where I'd then jumped out of the car and ended up... wherever the fuck I was.

Still musing, I reached for the seatbelt to buckle myself in and then started the car, wincing at the loud sound of the engine roaring to life.

In the side mirror, I caught two of the weaker zombies bolting up and for the trees. When I turned my head to look their way, I saw that the others were following, only the female lingering.

She was staring straight at me, clearly seeing me sitting inside the car.

Her expression remained blank, which was almost disappointing. But what had I expected? Grief that I was leaving her? Happiness that she was the new leader of the pack?

Since none of them made a move to come for me, I forced myself to look forward, at the road, then over at the center console of the dashboard. The touchscreen display was conveniently set to GPS—that looked like it was still working, from what I could tell.

Following a hunch that my mind couldn't quite puzzle out, I checked the last destinations programmed into the system. The second-to-last had been Grace's town. The last one, the one to the northeast. Without hesitation, I tipped my finger—grime still encrusted under my torn, ragged fingernail—at the last destination, watching a blue band spring into existence that let me know where I was going.

Then it was just a matter of forcing my mind to go through the motions of driving the car—which was hard for the first mile even though it wasn't even a stick shift—and I was on my way.

To where and to what end, I would hopefully puzzle out before I got there.

And if not? Winging it sounded like a good-enough plan.

CHAPTER 2

Thinking while driving? Not that great of an idea. Not necessarily because I threatened to total the car twice within the first five miles. That happened mostly because I got distracted by something moving in the bushes or running across a field. No, it kind of made me zone out immediately, and it was damn hard not to flip back into must-eat-anything-I-can-get-my-hands-on mode before I could catch myself. The second time I caught myself tearing through a box of crackers blindly snatched from the open pack on the passenger seat with the car idling in the middle of the road, I decided that multitasking just wasn't happening today.

So I found a convenient place where I could park the car out of sight of the road, got first one, then a second full MRE hydrated for convenient eating, snarfed down an entire pack of nuts while I waited impatiently for them to be done, and then pigged out completely.

Driving while no longer ravenously hungry was slightly better, but as soon as I thought about a certain asshole…

For that, I'd have to take some extra time, I figured.

Also, I should maybe be looking for more food and better-suited clothes than some dead Marine's comically huge shirt and boxer shorts. Socks would have been nice, too.

It didn't take long for the first house to appear near the road. I wasn't even close to the gravel driveway leading there yet when I got an overwhelmingly bad feeling about it. It was weird, disorienting, but about as plain as two similarly poled magnets rejecting each other, however much you tried to snap them together.

I drove right on without even slowing down.

It happened again close to the next house.

This time, when I looked in the rearview mirror, I saw something moving by the barn next to the house.

So apparently I couldn't concentrate for shit, but I'd somehow acquired a new danger radar. Or at least a this-is-some-other-pack's-lair radar.

The third house—or cluster of buildings—turned out to be an emotional wasteland, so that was where I sent my trusty horse made of plastic and steel.

Grabbing one of the carbines I'd liberated from the Marines—and wincing at the intact carrying sling still slightly sticky with blood—I got out of the car to do a first quick tour around the most promising building that looked like it might have housed a larger family, or maybe even two. The doors were standing open and several windows were broken, but I didn't get more than the faintest hint of decay as I carefully sniffed my way around the corners and close to the entrances.

When I finally dared to enter, I found the interior ransacked, but all biological spills were old—blood crusty and flaking off, some food or drink liquids long since dried up and no longer sticky. Judging from the open cupboard doors and emptied drawers—including some ripped out and on the floor—I wouldn't find anything edible in there, but the bedrooms yielded a good assortment of clothes. I'd had better in the past, but also worse. Socks and moderately fitting jeans were a bonus, even if I had to go with a tight tank top instead of a bra. Still better than Buff Marine Bro's T-shirt.

I avoided all mirrors or other reflective surfaces, but before exiting, I forced myself to check myself out in the bathroom mirror.

I looked remarkably normal, if one ignored the matted mass that was my hair, which was easily remedied by forcing it into a sloppy bun and putting on a ball cap. I could possibly have used the water left in the toilet reservoir and the shampoo left untouched in the shower to remedy that, but I quite frankly lacked the patience—and ripping out half my hair with a bad hairbrush wouldn't help make me look any more presentable, I figured.

It was kind of a relief to see that I looked more indifferent than sporting that thousand-yard stare I'd expected—and was way too familiar with. I tried myself at a smile, but that quickly turned into a violent grimace. Yeah, not feeling the happy-times golden glow inside right now. I even tried thinking of food—and when that didn't help, of that alternate source of nutrition I shouldn't have been considering—but all that did was make me salivate, which in turn got me looking a lot more feral than relaxed.

So resting-bitch-face calm it was. Fine with me. If that meant nobody would bother me and inadvertently provoke a very different reaction than they were likely going for, all the better.

Still staring deep into my eyes—and getting a little lost in there, I had to admit—I tried to force my mind to tackle the question at hand.

What would I do if I found the others in that town?

As much as I hadn't really been thinking much at all, a certain set of truths had started to congeal in the back of my mind. Truths that my little solo ransacking of this house had hammered down.

I couldn't hack it on my own for much longer out here in the wilderness.

Sure, I had weapons, ammo, and a car. I also had the strength and energy to run and quite possibly fight. I probably stood the best chance with small zombie packs that I could either avoid or intimidate, with the idiotic possibility tempting to take them over and become their vicious alpha-queen bitch. Against trained soldiers like the Marines, I didn't stand much of a chance. I still couldn't remember how I'd taken them out, but I'd obviously surprised them, and I couldn't count on that working even a second time, let alone for it to become my survival strategy.

Strength in numbers was key.

The problem was, I didn't really trust myself around the numbers part of that truth.

Right now, I was calm and collected. I had a feeling that larger gatherings like the wake at Grace's town would already make me anxious. A huge gathering of people like the Enclave made me start to tense up just considering that.

I also had no idea how I'd react to the different kinds of people I would encounter in towns. Would I go for the jugular of the first stupid man who stared at my ass? Would I try to tear apart a child because it was a helpless, easy kill? And all that was ignoring the fact that I was likely a walking, talking infection risk for them.

Talk about Jared's Typhoid Mary taunts becoming the bitter truth.

Thinking of him was enough to raise my pulse a good twenty points, most of that connected to a hairline trigger promising violence. But not all of my instincts ran this way, because apparently I was a million ways fucked up, even knowing what I knew now.

Although it stood to reason, what did I actually know?

What he'd told me. And as far as I knew, he'd killed a single man in that alley.

Okay, two if I counted Tony's execution.

Four or five if I counted the other survivors he'd supposedly shot at the triage tents in Charlotte.

Six with Armando, because why should he have claimed that death if he hadn't actually killed him?

Add to that countless disappearances...

I didn't need to write down that list to realize it was getting longer and longer and very much pointed to the fact that Jared hadn't been lying about his... proclivities.

And Blake and Axel's lack of a reaction had pretty much confirmed it, too.

Just how fucked up did someone have to be to want to hang out with a serial killer?

It's not the hanging-out-with part you're conflicted about, my mind was happy to taunt.

Yeah. That, too.

Although, in all honesty, that was something I was less concerned about. Sex wasn't among the urges my mind currently had issues with keeping under wraps. That might change once I felt a little more like myself, but I still had the sense that between humping Jared and tearing his face off, right now it was at least an even split, leaning heavily toward the latter the more I thought about it.

And who would be insane enough to want to fuck a zombie?

It was disturbing how much that question kept popping up in my life of late.

Even more disturbing that I had a feeling I could still come up with two names on that list, only one of them reciprocal.

Which sadly made it very obvious which way reality was pointing where a solution for my problem was concerned.

Four people were just enough to make surviving out there possible—and except for Axel's reaction, I was pretty sure I knew how the other two idiots would react to my recent… changes.

And if worse came to worst, I doubted Jared would have a problem with executing me in cold blood if he had to. He'd probably regret it, but for a different reason than someone else would have. Probably something to do with missed chances, boredom, and his fucked-up fantasies.

I almost laughed when I realized I was smiling. It wasn't big, and it certainly wasn't nice, but that was definitely a smile.

Yeah, take that, you sadistic bastard—my utter and heartfelt lack of fear. And none of that was his doing. Ha!

I could probably have spent the entire day standing there, amusing myself with the crap my brain was coming up with, but since I now had my answer, there was little sense in wasting time and potentially risking my life if I was wrong about my fighting prowess—or managed to once more run into the assholes who had nothing better to do than to want to drag me off to the next mad scientist's lab to do whatever the fuck with me next. I had a strong feeling that my momentary… condition was directly connected to what these fucked-up quacks had done to me, but I absolutely didn't hunger for payback.

Actually, what I was really hungering for was food, and if I couldn't have a juicy, rare steak, another MRE would have to do.

I was only thirty miles from the town, the sat nav let me know. At the rate I was going, my food would last me just long enough to get there if I didn't dawdle too much.

So back behind the wheel it was after another quick snack.

As I was driving, I idly wondered what would happen to me if I couldn't get enough food. It made sense that my mega-quick healing was the cause for needing upward of three times as many calories now. Would my body start eating itself if it didn't get outside nourishment? Or would the healing rate slow down until it stopped and natural decay took over…

That opened up another question: was I dead?

I didn't feel like it, although I had zero experience in that, I had to admit. I still had a heartbeat, and while my mind was sluggish at times, everything seemed to be working like it should.

Including my internal plumbing, as I found out twenty miles into my journey in the middle of a thick stretch of wood when my GI tract informed me that a bowel movement was happening, and it was going to happen right fucking now.

Way to hurl yourself out of a car and your pants in the middle of nowhere in hopes of avoiding that special kind of unpleasant accident. Although, was that really worse than throwing up half-chewed male reproductive organs?

At least my sense of humor was very much alive.

Also, my morbid curiosity when I didn't simply hobble back to the car once I was done, but tentatively studied what had come out the other end. Not that I was usually prone to doing that, but the smell was just… weird, so it felt pertinent to check.

Considering how fast the evacuation process had happened—and with virtually no sticky residues—I wasn't that surprised to find the consistency compact, if smelling to the high heavens. It was also very… dark, for lack of a better word. Old, congealed-blood dark, although I was sure that I was just making that up. I tried to remember what happened to blood when humans digested it, but could only come up with that one compound—bilirubin—and kidney issues.

Whatever. Not that it mattered. But it looked like what I'd digested hadn't been full of fiber, and my body had done a good job absorbing all the nutrients from it that it could.

I chose not to complete the thought about the implications and instead went back to the car to continue my journey.

A few times, roaming packs of the undead forced me to pause—or on two occasions backtrack—but since that weird sense of danger got the back of my mind tingling every single time, it wasn't that hard to make good progress. There generally seemed to be less of them around than I was used to, probably because of the geography.

Good. One less issue I had to deal with.

Honestly, the living ones were a much more pressing concern to me right now—or what I'd do if I didn't find those three idiots soon. I was almost in sight of my destination when I realized that was a very valid possibility—that they'd either not gone to that town or had already moved on. I was sure that with some sweet-talking, I'd get the radio operators to have a look out for a band of three men roaming alone, but it was anyone's guess how well that would work. The four of us hadn't exactly been stealthy, but even so, it must have been impossible to track us.

I spent a moment considering the hilarity of imagining me chasing Jared across the country for months and months.

Yeah, that wasn't happening. Either I found him within a week, or I was going to look for other options. Grace still sounded like the best one to me. I was sure that if I went full-on repentant sinner, she'd find it in her heart to forgive me.

And it wasn't like I had access to drugs anymore.

That made me briefly consider returning to our lake house near Lancaster. I had everything there I needed to cook up several batches more, and I knew where to get more supplies. Also, the idea of maybe finding out why Josh was no longer operating his radio station was tantalizing. Not that I'd grown overly fond of him, but Oliver and Kay had been okay, and at least knowing whether they were still alive or not would be neat.

Then again, there was always the option of sneaking back into the Enclave and finding out what had happened after Jared had dragged me off. I was sure I could lie my way back in if things hadn't turned too bad—and really, what were they going to do to me now? Dancing tango with the undead kind of nixed a lot of worse-case scenarios that had haunted my day-to-day for months.

They can lock you up in a cell. Again.

Or dissect you while you're still alive. Who knows how far those healing abilities go? I had a feeling I knew some scientists who'd be burning to find out.

Ah, no. That wasn't going to be happening.

First things first. Before I could look for the guys—or even decide what to do next—I had to get into that town. While more presentable, I was still a messed-up-looking woman on her own with a borderline insane stack of weapons in her car. That sounded mighty suspicious.

Then I realized I was a woman alone with a stack of weapons. Unless I absolutely had to hold on to them all, getting into the settlement would hardly be an issue. One convenient lie, and they'd admit me with open arms.

Problem was, I hardly had the brain capacity to work out plans that went beyond eating the last two of my MREs that had miraculously survived the journey until now—probably because thinking about what to do kept me just distracted enough to forget about being so damn hungry for five seconds at a time. Intricate lies? Not so much.

The town finally came into view, smack in the middle of a gently rolling plateau. At a first glance, it looked like the worst position imaginable, with mobs of thousands of zombies able to swarm it from all sides. But I could see where that also meant they pretty much had a 360-degree killing field all around that had made barricading themselves possible—and judging from the heaps of shipping containers and trucks piled up generously around the center of the town, that was exactly what they had done. How, I had no clue. That must have taken weeks to assemble, possibly raiding several cargo terminals to get everything here.

Somebody had been very smart about their defenses. I had a feeling that simply sneaking in at night wouldn't work.

As I sat there, staring, I realized that maybe I was looking at this from the wrong perspective.

As in, coming from the wrong road.

Maybe a mile away from my current position, I saw a long string of vehicles close in on one of the heavily fortified gates, at least twenty cars and three trucks driving at a moderate speed. Ahead of me, there was even a small connector road that would lead me right to where the end of the convoy would be when I got there…

And that was exactly what I did, only having to wait for the last three cars to slowly trundle past me before I could fall in line behind them.

For a good minute, my paranoia was screaming at me that this could never work, not in a million years. Someone from the convoy would shoot at me, or the guards that must have watched me join the convoy so late would for sure bar my way.

Yet no shots were fired, and when I finally crawled through the gates twenty minutes later, the only notice I got was a harried guard signaling me to go faster so they could close up their gate once more.

Getting into town had been barely an inconvenience.

But that was about when I realized I'd run out of luck, as far as convenience went, at least.

The town was swarming with people. Even sitting in the car just inside the gate, I felt crowded and claustrophobic—or would that be agoraphobic instead since the car was my happy little cage? And yes, thinking about cages absolutely triggered the usual unease, only times a million as I watched no less than fifty people already exiting the vehicles, and twice that many coming over to check up on them.

Casting around frantically, I tried to decide what to do. Simply vaulting out of the car and running into the streets sounded like the best idea—the only idea, really—but I was well aware that would get me attention that I didn't want.

Also, a good fifth of the people around showed up on my nifty new danger radar, making my instincts go absolutely haywire. Whatever the fuck was going on with that, now was not the time to puzzle that out.

More out of opportunity than planning, I slowly maneuvered the car around the closest cluster of vehicles and people, simply to put some distance between myself and them.

That was when I saw it—the semi-beat-up SUV that Dwayne had handed to us to bring the generator to Tim before things had come to a head. The very same car I'd vaulted out of last night, although that felt like a million years ago.

Feeling ever so slightly smug—even with my mind screaming at me to do a million things to get myself out of here—I parked my black SUV right in front of the other, making sure to completely close it in between the barn wall behind and the vehicles left and right of it.

So much for possibly ditching me.

Of course, they could have left the car here and otherwise moved on, but I didn't think that was very likely. The car had a few dents and scrapes more than I last remembered, but was still fully operational. No way the Asshole would leave behind a car in still working condition if he could total it instead.

My momentary satisfaction lasted for exactly ten seconds. Then I grabbed one of the packs and locked the car, heading for the next small thoroughfare to squeeze in between houses and get the fuck away from the masses.

I ended up in a small, artificial alleyway, created by yet more shipping containers arrayed left and right along the road, squeezed in right up to the houses. They all had their doors open, letting me see racks with stuff inside but also open space with sleeping bags rumpled on the floor. What exactly was going on here, I didn't know, but there were only two men in sight, ignoring me after a brief glance. Both looked burly and strong, but my danger radar completely disregarded them.

Leaning against the rusty wall of one of the containers, I allowed myself a few deep breaths while I dug into my pack for my last bag of nuts to chew on while I tried to force my addled thoughts into order.

If I just concentrated hard enough, I could still feel all those blips on my mental landscape move in the open space behind me. And way more, off to the right, where most of the town was. Easily a hundred, if not more. Some stationary, some moving slowly, others fast. It was all very confusing, and it sure had my teeth on edge—

And then there was one among them that felt stronger, brighter somehow. Like all the others were tiny candles compared to a beacon lit in the night.

I had a very strong suspicion who that might be.

But how?

Had my mind fucking imprinted on him or some shit, straight out of a bad romance novel?

Then again, it made sense that I could feel him if my theory was right and it was the fucking zombie blood they'd infected us with that gave me these abilities somehow. He was—at best—a step behind me then.

A random thought whizzed through my brain. Could it be that the reason he hadn't gone full native on us yet was that since he was already a homicidal maniac, he had a hell of a lot more control over his urges?

Now that was a sobering thought.

Also utterly inconsequential somehow.

But what was going on with all the others? If this had been the Enclave, maybe I could have bought that over a hundred people had gone through the same ordeal as we had. But judging from the markings on the map—and the utter lack of any signs of any military unit around here—I figured this was a free town. Yes, the Marines had been here, but maybe just as simple visitors. Or maybe only to lurk around. Or infiltrate the town for a later strike or whatnot. Which, in hindsight, explained how they had such an easy time overrunning the Enclave. They must have had plenty of spies already inside.

Still not the point now, I reminded myself.

Why the fuck were there potentially a hundred half-zombies—or whatever the hell I was now—in this town?

"Miss? You might want to get that checked out."

I jerked as an unfamiliar voice called out close to me. Not froze—that would have been too easy. I actually had to deliberately lock my muscles to keep myself from attacking the man who was standing maybe twenty feet away from me. He'd joined the other two workers further down the road.

I must have stared at him for several seconds straight before my mind finally kicked in. Certainly long enough to make him grow uncomfortable, and that was never a good thing.

I forced my stare to drop away from him, incidentally to my right arm. He must have been referring to the huge bruise still visible above my wrist, although since I had woken up it had already gone down from vivid purple to sickly yellow-green. But he, of course, didn't know that, which was a good thing.

"It's nothing," I muttered, my voice hoarse and low—presumably from disuse and a lot of angry shouting.

Considering my healing rate, that must have been quite a lot of shouting.

"You should still see the doctor," he advised. "You came in with the caravan just now, huh? The doc actually set some extra time aside for you." He smiled, although it was only a wan gesture, probably because I was yet again staring at him. "It's free of charge, if you're worried about that. One great thing about the damn undead—no more filing for medical bankruptcy."

I realized that must have been a joke. I tried smiling but then thought better of it, remembering my grimace in the mirror. Instead, I nodded, hoping against hope that I came across as grateful.

The man wasted another second looking at me, then gave himself a visible shake and disappeared down one of the other streets.

I tried to decide what to do next—which got incidentally harder as I felt the supposedly-Jared blip move closer to the open space by the gate. So he was still looking for me, maybe checking if I'd hitched a ride with this group?

Of course he was. I was honestly surprised I hadn't found him randomly strutting into the clearing this morning. Giving me space was the last thing I'd expected him to do. He probably regretted that already.

How about giving him something to regret even more?

But no. Not with my mind still running this way and that and hardly able to concentrate on watching the men work and chewing my nuts all at the same time. That conversation I was only going to enter with my wits once more at full capacity.

I wondered what might get me there. More food sounded good. It was only early afternoon—still time to grab lunch, and most towns had been happy to feed us visitors. Yes, food sounded like a very good idea.

Food, and maybe I should drop by that doctor, if I could somehow verify that it wasn't one of the insane ones I'd had to deal with in the past.

When I passed them, both workers gave me weird looks but didn't approach me. Good for them.

Navigating the town wasn't that hard since the area wasn't that large—maybe five by five blocks before they had boarded it up however possible. It was those shipping containers that turned it into kind of a maze, but right now, that worked to my advantage. It made it very easy to get lost or find ways around larger groups of people. I did my best to avoid them in general, not just the groups where I felt more than one blip ahead. All the while, the beacon that was supposedly Jared kept annoying the back of my mind, like an itch screaming to be scratched. I had, of course, no idea where he was going, but after a while I felt him head off in a different direction— nowhere near my position, which was just as well.

Finding the communal kitchen and the doctor's office turned out to be easy—both because they were right next to each other and because people immediately started pointing me in that direction when they saw me looking around as if searching for something. That said "something" was an open space didn't matter. Not having to talk much was a relief, though.

I was almost at my destination—judging from the heavenly scents in the air—when I realized that the looks they gave me were full of sympathy.

So, just maybe, I did look way worse than I felt.

At least being a scrawny, bruised woman got me a bowl of soup with some semi-stale bread in no time, again with little to no talking.

It was lukewarm and there were way too many vegetables and rice in it, but I still inhaled it in record time. I would have gone for seconds, but just then the Jared blip started heading my way, and I chose to go hide inside the doctor's office, mostly because it was the next best open door to an enclosed space he couldn't easily look into.

The waiting room was small and cramped, looking more like the reception area of an office. The entire building didn't look like it had started out as any kind of medical facility, really. Two patients were already sitting there, both with visible injuries, the bandages fresh.

I hesitated before I stepped up to the makeshift nurse's station—a simple table with an empty chair behind it. There was no paperwork to fill out anywhere in sight, but that made sense.

And there I'd already been afraid of what to do about the fact that I hadn't had any ID with me for four months straight.

While I was still glancing uneasily back toward the entrance—wondering just how out of sight I was—the door next to the desk opened and out stepped two people in scrubs with paw-print patterns on them. More veterinarians, but that wasn't much of a surprise, really. It also didn't matter, since I hardly needed anything from them.

Except... there was something I was still wondering about. Not that I was sure with my healing rate there was anything left to find or diagnose.

I would have intuitively figured that the older, African-American woman was the doctor and not the tall, going on gangly Hispanic man, his cheeks still sporting the last wave of late-teen acne, but I would have been wrong. She quickly introduced herself as Nurse Keira and him as Doctor Marco—probably not the first time anyone had mistaken her age for seniority. I still bet she knew way more than what must have been a vet student earlier in the year, but none of that mattered now.

One look at me, and I got another round of sympathy glances, although they both tried to behave absolutely professionally about it.

"Sweetie, come let us look at you," Nurse Keira said, already stepping aside to lead me down a corridor that looked very much like an office hallway. Maybe this had been a realtor's office, or something like that?

She brought me into the last room on the right, furnished only with what looked like a foldable massage table and two chairs, one of them occupied by a yellow legal pad. There was also a small cart with medical supplies—and a box of latex gloves.

I still wondered how I should go about pointing out I wouldn't let either of them touch me without gloves when the doctor snapped them on. Maybe the seconds of staring had given away my feelings about that, even though they couldn't have had a clue why.

Before I could stop myself, the first thing connected to that was already out of my mouth.

"Have you heard about anyone turning into a zombie and then snapping back to human?"

The doctor and nurse glanced at each other, her expression definitely on the cautioning side. The doctor licked his lips as he focused on me.

"Not exactly. No. Has that happened to your group? That one of you turned and attacked the others?"

The way his attention dropped down to my arm made it obvious that he thought he'd just heard the cause for my bruises.

I was about to shake my head, but then forced myself to nod. "Something like that." Maybe if I kept my sentences short, they'd think I was still in shock, or something? "Do they ever… turn back?"

"Oh sweetie," the nurse almost cooed, sympathy heavy in her voice as she put a gentle hand on my shoulder. "No. They don't. They're dead for good. I know this is hard to stomach when it happens to a loved one. We all hope that everyone we love is safe and won't catch it. But it has already happened and is way too late for them."

I had a feeling I wasn't going to discuss my newfound sensory range with them anytime soon.

Good. I had more pressing matters to discuss. Or better yet, for them to check.

Maybe including more bullet holes I wasn't aware of, I realized. The idea of asking Jared to do that still skeeved me out, even if my fear response seemed to be centered on masses of people only—and mostly because I didn't trust myself around them, not because I was afraid of what they could do to me, if I was honest.

They took my silence for grief, which was just as well.

"Do you want us to check out those bruises?" the nurse said next, doing her best to gently nudge me along. She didn't comment on the fact that I didn't have a jacket with me, which was stupid—on her and my own account. But honestly, wearing clothes still felt weird. I'd been too distracted by everything when I'd gotten out of the car to take care of that.

I really had to snap out of this quickly, or else I'd never stand to be around Jared, not for a single minute. He'd probably die laughing his ass off at me in my current state.

And good riddance to that.

"When's the last time you ate?" the doctor asked, reaching for something on his cart. "We don't have much equipment here, but enough to check your vitals and blood sugar. You seem a little distracted. That could easily be because of hypoglycemia."

The nurse didn't even wait for my answer as she pulled something out of her scrubs pocket.

"Here, sweetie. Have some of that and you'll feel better immediately."

I stared stupidly at the white squares in her hand, my mouth instantly starting to salivate. I wolfed down the dextrose squares as soon as I got the cellophane off them. Eating them with the plastic on didn't sound like a smart move.

And, wouldn't you know it, I kind of did feel better a minute later, even though something deep in my memory supplied that it would take a little longer for the sugar to hit my bloodstream.

The doctor took my blood pressure next and did a quick check on my lungs with his stethoscope pressed to my back. The way I heard him inhale sharply, I must have had quite some additional bruises on my back. No questions about bullet wounds, though, so I figured I was good in that quadrant of my body.

"Your pulse and blood pressure are low, lungs are clear," he offered a couple of minutes later. "Judging from your vitals, I'd say you're doing just fine."

The nurse glared at him, which made him shrink away from her just a little.

She turned back to me.

"Do you want to tell us what happened, sweetie? Or do you want to tell just me, with the doctor waiting outside for a minute?"

Part of my mind wondered why she suggested that, since it made no sense to keep a medical professional out of this conversation.

The other part—the part already riding the sugar high—sadly took over before my mind had a chance to catch up with the words spurting out of me.

"It hardly makes sense to do a rape kit when you can't do DNA comparison and have no access to a database, huh? Not that we even know who's still alive or not."

I would have been pissed at someone snapping at me like that. Nurse Keira was all compassion and calm, though. Considering her bar for patient misdemeanor was probably around being bitten in the face... not that I should have done that now because that, for sure, would have been bad.

Although I was kind of curious if I was contagious now, including but not limited to my saliva.

What if this conversion thing was dose dependent? I would have very much liked to know if coming in contact with any of my bodily fluids would send Jared over the edge when it came to that... and with the sugar coursing through my veins, not just my higher brain functions seemed to be returning.

Because acting like a hormonal teenager was exactly what I needed now!

Still patient with me, the nurse gave my arm another pat. I had to work hard not to tense—not because the contact was uncomfortable but because below the intellectual bitchiness, the urge to fight was still roiling around.

To put it mildly, they were both very easy targets. Temptingly easy.

I briefly wondered if that was another pro point for Team Assholes. If there was any kind of rational component to my aggression, it should have been lower around Blake and Jared for sure, and quite possibly Axel as well.

Unless, of course, they'd need all of a minute to make a game out of provoking me.

At least no innocents would die in that fight.

I very much felt like grinning in anticipation.

Stupid brain! Heel!

Forcing myself to calm down again, I tried to find the words the nurse wanted to hear—because that was what lying was all about.

"I... I don't know what happened. Not exactly," I hedged. "I'm having some serious trouble remembering. Not sure if I hit my head—"

As soon as the words were out of my mouth, a bright light already seared my retinas, making me recoil violently.

So much for staying civil.

The doctor excused himself profoundly, but didn't back up. He went through the whole "follow the light" and then "follow the finger" thing, annoying me on several levels.

"I don't think you have a concussion," he mused. "But something's going on with your eyes. Did you notice any changes in your eyesight?"

I was about to snap at him that this wasn't why I was here, but then caught myself.

Actually, I'd had trouble focusing this morning, but by the time I'd washed up—including vigorously scrubbing my face—that had cleared up.

Just a guess, but exactly how long would it take for filmed-over eyes to recover to my normal, almost 20:20 eyesight?

That very idea creeped me out. That my eyes had been just like theirs.

Oh, and the eyeball-biting memory as well.

Ick.

"What is it you do remember?" the nurse prodded gently.

"Not much," I lied—or not, because the part she was fishing for was the part I was still mostly in the dark about. "I'm not sure what they did."

Well, didn't that sound exactly like an intimidated trauma victim? Only too bad that I knew I could have done so much better if my damn brain had finally started working.

Next chance I got, I would find myself an entire pack of sugar cubes and finish it in one go. Maybe that would jump-start the useless waste of space inside my skull.

"Are you hurt?"

I hesitated at her next question, which probably gave her more answers than any words could have. Not my intention, but I didn't mind things working out in my favor.

"We can do a quick checkup," she offered. "To see if there's any damage or bruising. We don't have any Plan B left, but one of the towns to the east still has some if you think you'd need it."

It was probably a stupid question, but I still had to ask it.

"What if there's no bruising?" Because even my addled brain knew what else they'd find.

The nurse almost winced before she caught herself.

"We might still be able to find something independent of that. The smell," she added when I must have looked like a useless oaf.

Oh. Right. That I could have thought of myself.

I was very tempted to decline her offer, but just then the annoying blip in the back of my mind came closer still, for sure lurking outside by the kitchen next door. I couldn't leave yet. Might as well make the best of their offer—even if I damn well hoped that what else was going on with my mind wouldn't make this too embarrassing. At least that might make things go a little more smoothly—

And I damn well hoped they weren't working with the horse equipment, or this wasn't going to end well.

I had to fight hard not to laugh at that absolutely terrible joke as I pulled down my pants and plonked my ass down on the very edge of the massage table. The fact that it had been days since I'd last washed with warm water and soap certainly wouldn't make that a laughing matter for the poor doctor.

I had to admit, he was handling himself well and was very professional. He also seemed so much more at ease than I expected, until I realized he was doing well whenever he could roll out his medical expertise. It was the dealing with the patient part itself that he mostly needed Nurse Keira's support for. Not because he was a vet, but because he was a twenty-one-year-old who hadn't had time to acquire a good bedside manner yet.

Nobody found any half-healed bullet or bite wounds on my legs while they were exposed, so that was good.

"Inconclusive at best," the doctor finally said. "I'd even go as far as to say it's a probable negative."

I felt myself heave a sigh of relief, but it came with a certain amount of ambiguity. Sure, was I glad that the Marines—likely—hadn't acted like complete asswipes? Yes, but that meant I'd killed four men practically unprovoked. Not that I could be sure about that, either, but it looked more and more like that.

That wasn't the most comforting thought ever.

At least the blip had moved on by the time they were done with assuring me I could come back any time I wanted some painkillers for my many bruises and possible sprains.

I quickly hightailed it out of there after that before I could take them up on that offer.

On my way past the kitchen, I snatched up a piece of apple pie, quickly wolfing it down as I stepped into the alley running behind the building.

I wasn't even halfway done yet when it became impossible not to notice that a certain eternal nuisance was honing in on me, currently walking across the open space in front of the kitchen.

So much for evading him.

Before he reached the alley, I was around the next corner, wanting to linger but forcing myself not to.

Looked like this conversation was happening, whether my mind was back to its usual snappy self or not.

The least I could do was try to do it somewhere we were mostly alone—so that if I really couldn't control myself either way, I wouldn't have to leave a trail of witnesses on top of a body.

My, but my innuendos really weren't up to par yet.

I certainly had to work on that.

I briefly considered running, but then nixed that idea on the spot.

If my aggressive skittishness with the nurse was any indicator, I absolutely couldn't stay in town on my own—not this town, and even less so Grace's town, where I'd spent enough time with the people there that I'd know all my possible future victims at least passingly. That, I really didn't need on my conscience.

Looked like I had only a single alternative, unless I wanted to head back to my pack—who'd at least been loyal to me after I'd showed them who was boss.

I had a feeling the same wouldn't work twice.

Oh, well. I'd long since learned to live with the cards I had been dealt with. Now was absolutely no different.

Fuck, but I really hoped that was true. Else, the next few hours weren't going to be pleasant—and I had a feeling I would remember every fucking second this time.

CHAPTER 3

I let Jared catch up to me five small alleys later. Twice, I'd deliberately hung back just long enough to verify that it was indeed him who was coming after me.

Stalking me, really.

By the time I rounded a last corner and set myself up, leaning casually against the wall, the grin on my face was a bright and real one.

Did he really think I hadn't noticed him—or was stupid enough to deliberately slink deeper and deeper into the less populated part of the town, far away from the gate and the large gathering space by the kitchen? I got he was likely rocking a serious superiority complex, but that was just fucking stupid.

He rounded the last corner with his usual smirk firmly in place—plus an extra dash of that special kind of glee he'd dumped on me that last time the two of us had ended up in an alley, all on our own. The only thing that was different was the lack of dead bodies nearby—and the fact that while something deep inside of me snapped to attention, it was very much only in a "hi there" way, without the deep-seated knowledge that I was going to end up as the next cooling body on the floor.

We stared at each other for several seconds straight. Which was good because staring was absolutely something that I excelled at right now.

It was a little disappointing that he looked just the same as yesterday. Monsters shouldn't look like normal people.

Then again, considering who was thinking that thought…

The triumph in his expression dimmed ever so slightly as he seemed to realize that I wasn't frozen in terror but staring back with challenge clear in every line of my body.

When he didn't say anything, I decided I might as well jump into the ring and throw the first punch.

"Took you long enough to track me down. You completely missed me by the gate, and I had enough time for an entire meal from the kitchen. Really, after your little show there yesterday, I would have expected more."

He didn't visibly draw up short, but I could see from the calculating quality his gaze took on that he was quickly assessing the changes in the situation and working a way around them.

Damn, I wished my mind would have been up for that challenge right now.

Why had I never noticed that what I'd thought was him being very flexible in any given situation was his superior skill at manipulating me and everyone else?

"Yesterday, huh?" he drawled, playfully cocking his head to the side. "I was going to retort something like 'took you long enough to come crawling back to me,' but now I'm curious about how you lost an entire fucking day."

My turn to draw up short.

I did a quick—or not so quick—calculation in my mind. It must have been around eleven when I'd thrown myself out of the car. Two or three when I'd happened on the Marine patrol since the sky had still been fully dark. I thought I'd come to at roughly six or seven this morning, but then again it made sense that it took seven zombies more than maybe two hours to completely eat two beefy humans and reduce the other two to picked-apart heaps of gore. And my stomach had been full to bursting when I'd vomited up all that good nutritious fat and protein...

But at least now I had my timeline straight again. Some of the memory flashes hadn't made that much sense in hindsight. Adding an entire twenty-four hours aligned a few things better. Like that it had been broad daylight when I'd chewed off...

Yeah. That of all things I could remember.

Still nothing clear about the killing itself, but I was happy to ignore that for now—and fucking forever, too.

"I was busy," I told him, proud that it came out like a taunt. "Must have lost track of time. That happens when you're having fun." And that wasn't even a lie. Whatever was in those flashes or outside of them, filling myself to bursting sure hadn't felt bad.

Annoyance crossed Jared's face, clearly at my reactions not fitting what he'd been expecting.

"Are you still on something? You don't look stoned, but I have to admit, you have a remarkable ability to overplay that." He leaned closer, as if to intimidate me—but instead took a deep inhale, quickly moving back out of my personal space. "And fuck, you reek."

I couldn't help but flash him another bright, real smile. "The best things in life come with lots of sweat and body odor involved."

It was hilarious to watch him try to work with that. If I hadn't known what was lurking underneath his mask of civility, I would have said that was a thread of uncertainty I could see, if only for a second. Couldn't be that he, of all people, was getting insecure now?

"You sure don't smell like booze. Or sex." His usual smirk resurfaced. "Because I sure am very familiar with you smelling of both."

If he thought he could intimidate me like that, he had a surprise coming.

Clearly, me not reacting at all to his taunt and just staring back at him annoyed him. That he was incapable of hiding his annoyance spoke volumes. It would have been nice to actually feel superior because of this—if only for a second—but my brain wasn't up for having such complicated emotions yet.

As it was, it annoyed the hell out of me that while intellectually, I was very much riding the wave of "you fucking asshole betrayed me and want to do God knows what shit to me!" my body was all "oh, I like you, you make me feel good! Let's have more of that, and right now, please!" like an untrained puppy tearing at the leash.

That I managed to get anything coherent out was bordering on a miracle!

Then again, not running scared from him was definitely a bonus. For me, not for him. That much was obvious. Ha!

I wondered for a moment if I should straight up lie to him, but the thing was, I didn't want to. I also wasn't sure if I could have pulled it off. This was the Asshole we were talking about, after all. Maybe I should have changed that moniker for him, now that I knew what I knew... but it was hard to change now that I had gotten so used to it.

Was it actual complacency that would end making me compliant? Now that was some food for thought.

"Did you just zone out on me?"

The indignation heavy in Jared's tone made me flash him a quick smile before I could rein in my expression. It just felt like... such a relief to be getting under his skin. My mind also wasn't up for full-on gloating right now, but there was a part of me that definitely wanted to get back at him, seeing as avoiding him wasn't in the cards.

Cocking my head to the side, I tried to decide how to best go about this.

"Do you want the chronological version or how I experienced it?"

If anything, his irritation with me only increased.

"If you think that being verbose now pisses me off, you're right." He leaned into my personal space, as if that should have scared me somehow. "And trust me, you don't want to piss me off."

It was too easy to hold his gaze. It was obvious that my reaction wasn't normal; there was definitely something missing from my usual emotional range. Maybe that should have given me some pause, but right then, it didn't.

"I'm not afraid of you."

His eyes narrowed with malicious glee that was kind of new but also wasn't about to break through, but then he paused.

"You really aren't. Huh."

Far was it from me to point out that his eloquence was rivaling mine right now, which was a new low for both of us.

"I know. Must be so disappointing."

"It actually is," he admitted, briefly laughing as if to himself. Then his intense gaze zeroed in on me once more, boring deep into my eyes. "Trust me, I'll find a way to change that."

Honestly, his boasting was getting a little tedious. Not that I doubted his words; I didn't. But none of that mattered now, and it was already hard enough to concentrate on the important stuff.

Like food. I really could have done with some more food.

Preferably meat, and not necessarily well done.

Ick, my mind supplied... after quite the noticeable lag time.

Huh.

Since Jared looked about ready to wring my neck if I kept this up, I got to the point.

"I woke up this morning in a puddle of mud next to a clearing where I found six zombies savaging the bodies of four Marines that I killed—yesterday, I think, although to me it all still feels like we last saw each other last night before I jumped out of the car. They got a little aggressive, so I got aggressive right back, re-establishing pack hierarchy. Then the brain fog cleared up a little, which made me barf up an entire stomach full of partially digested Marine. Hence, my theory that I did it. Oh, and I'm having these random, violent flashbacks that very much establish that I did. I still don't know why I was completely naked, but that's besides the point."

Jared stared at me—and kept on staring, as if that would make me either provide more, or go completely back on my story.

Yeah, I kind of got that.

There just wasn't much more I could add to that.

"You really expect me to believe that?" he finally said when my silence stretched to well over thirty seconds.

"It's the truth," I offered. "I honestly don't give a fuck whether you believe me or don't. But if it happens again, it would be stupid of you not to be prepared and know how to act."

"When what happens again?"

I stared at him as if he was stupid, because clearly, he was—or at least acting like it.

"When I turn into a zombie again," I said, my voice surprisingly even. Then again, why not? This was a fact of life now for me. Better accept it and move on than the alternative.

For just a moment, my brain fog lifted further, giving me just a glimpse of something deep inside of me screaming…

I quickly put a lid on that and the wave of confusing emotions it came with.

Not going to deal with that yet if I could avoid it for a little longer.

I expected him not to believe me—or outright laugh in my face now—but all Jared did was visibly shrug.

So much for that.

Clearly, this encounter was disappointing for both of us, it seemed.

I could tell he was getting ready to deliver the next, without a doubt scintillating volley when something inside of me made me snap to attention.

Something weird.

Something dangerous.

Another blip had appeared on my mental map.

I realized it had been there for a while, but now it was definitely coming closer. Not yet quite honing in on us, but now that it had separated from the fray I knew was the open space by the gate, it was impossible to ignore. Maybe it had been present much longer, but concentrating on my little cat-and-mouse game with Jared must have distracted me.

"You're doing it again."

Yes, I could see where my brief moment of inattention must be galling to Jared, since all but my entire rapt attention on him alone was likely not cutting it.

I wondered why exactly I'd been so afraid of him in that alley and afterward. As it was, I was pretty sure I was safe from his proclivities as they were, since he would simply have deprived himself if he killed me, and that was very unlike him.

Maybe if I kept annoying him like this... but I could tell his curiosity was piqued, which likely gave me some leeway.

The blip moved closer at an alarming rate and with enough accuracy that I dared judge he was now actually coming for us.

Color me jaded, but I didn't think for a second that was a good thing.

"I think we should take this elsewhere, possibly even discuss it another time."

Jared looked less than pleased at my suggestion.

"You are going exactly nowhere," he growled, leaning closer.

I held his gaze evenly.

"Do you really think you can stop me when four Marines couldn't?"

"If you killed them," he taunted. "If they're even dead."

My ego wanted to grouse at that, but I quickly dropped the impulse to argue. No sense in that.

Jared seemed utterly disappointed when I didn't further pursue the point.

"Something's coming. Or someone. And I have a feeling we don't want to hang around by the time they get here."

As I said that, I realized it hadn't just been a slip of the tongue. I could actually feel several blips converging on us—and not all of them falling in behind the main one. That... sensation for lack of a better term was weird enough to leave me transfixed all over again... until it was too late.

Turning in slow motion, I looked back over my shoulder at the exact moment the blip in my mind turned into a real person stepping around the corner, coming into sight.

It was the commander of the Marines that had taken over the Enclave, directly responsible for Dharma's death and chief bloodhound of the insane scientists who had killed Kas.

Just like I recognized him, his narrowing eyes let me know that he knew exactly who we were, only a moment's surprise passing over his features.

Busted.

Maybe I should have been surprised to see him here, but I wasn't. Intellectually, maybe, but the same sure gut feeling that had known it was Jared must have already identified him before he'd come close.

Apparently, that was quite the smart radar.

Question was, did it work the same for him as well? Had he known it was us? Had he been hunting us? Or had he just happened randomly on us and now decided to investigate?

Whatever the answers to all these questions were, I only cared about one thing: to stop occupying the same space as him... and his

Marines who came surging toward us from front, back, and the side street that I had walked down to get here.

Before I could do anything dramatic, like shout "run!" Jared's hand grabbed my arm and he started pulling me down the street, barreling right through the two unsuspecting Marines there who clearly hadn't counted on us running right through them.

The front of my mind lit up with fear and paranoia-driven scenarios, but that was tantalizingly easy to ignore. Instead, my lizard brain was aglow with glee. Finally some action! And she was quite happy to have Jared right beside her, while Front Brain was still on the fence about his presence.

The rush of adrenaline that hit my veins didn't exactly make any of this less confusing. Either I needed more sugar and food to be able to think clearly, or much less to let instinct alone get into the driver's seat. This yes-no-maybe-I'm-afraid was just no fun.

Drugs would make it more fun, my mind noted. Drugs that Jared very likely still had in his possession. A very good reason to stick around him.

No, I reminded myself, quite firmly. That was how this entire shitshow had started. This was not how I would let myself slide into even deeper layers of excrement.

At the end of the alley, Jared pulled me around a hard right corner, then right into another one, sending us down the parallel alley to the one we'd been in. Two houses down, he finally let go of me as we had to squeeze through the gap between two shipping containers. Then, alongside the wall of a warehouse, he pulled me through a small door, not bothering with closing it as he took off across the cramped floor of the building, narrowly avoiding crashing into stacks of… stuff. Out through another door, down another alley, through yet another gap, into yet another building—previously a shop, judging from the large, open spaces between aisles of shelves. I followed him without question as he aimed for a small door in the back, stepping into what used to be an employee locker room. There was a door leading back outside right there, but rather than push on, Jared only cracked it to peer outside. I waited impatiently next to him, equally winded but uniquely keyed up, hard-pressed to keep from bouncing up and down on the balls of my feet.

"Looks like we shook them off."

I took a moment to pause and listen—or would that be feel?

"Nope. They're about to home in on us again."

He cast an irritated glare my way. I couldn't tell if that was because of me doubting his wisdom or the bad news.

"How would you possibly be able to tell? You haven't been here long enough to get the lay of the land. Or town, in this case."

That was true.

It was also true that I hadn't had a chance to share my newfound superpower with him yet.

"I can feel them. Some of them," I amended. "The asshole in charge, and maybe a fifth of his people?"

Jared looked at me as if I'd gone insane.

"Okay, maybe closer to a fourth," I admitted. "Way more among the Marines than the townspeople."

He was still staring at me. I huffed with annoyance.

"Just like the zombies?" I suggested. "Of course, I feel all of them. Obviously." I narrowed my eyes at him. "When exactly did you get so dense?"

The corner of his mouth quivered, his usual smirk appearing, if only for a second.

"We really need to have a long talk about this," he said—and dropped the point, going back to looking at our surroundings. "The road's still clear outside?"

"How should I know? I can mostly tell you that the asshole in charge is about to head into this building the way we came in."

"Good enough," Jared grunted and stepped outside, strolling down the street without any care in the world. We'd spent just about enough time catching our breaths to maybe pull it off.

"Relax," he drawled. "And stop looking over your shoulder. They are looking for someone running. Not casually strolling away. You wouldn't believe how blind people get when they are relying on patterns."

I doubted that would work on their commander—since I was pretty sure he could feel us, too—but it might confuse his burly boys and girls. And there was hoping he'd lose us in the background static of the town.

Jared continued his erratic path, turning my already addled sense of direction completely useless.

"I presume you know where we're heading?"

His lips pursed for a second.

"I think it's time that we leave. I wasn't done here yet, but this town's getting too hot."

It took me several seconds to realize the hinted-at implications—and several more for my mind to supply the appropriate horror and disgust, if at a very low level.

When the next random turn got us stepping into the alley behind where I'd left the car, I realized something else.

"You've cased this joint to make sure you have a quick exit route."

All I got was a "duh" sidelong glance.

We had to pause for a second to let two people pass—riding horses. I found myself staring after the animals, way too transfixed. Now that's what I call lunch…

My stomach growled, pulling me back to the here and now. Jared was still looking around before he noticed my expression. His confusion made it obvious that he had no fucking clue why I'd just started salivating.

"We should go," I muttered under my breath, forced to suppress a shudder.

Then another.

Raising my hand, I stared at it, watching it tremble ever so slightly. That same jittery feeling was spreading throughout my body, my stomach cramping up again.

Oops. Looked like I was about to slam into a sugar crash.

We were just stepping out onto the parking lot when loud cursing made my head whip to the side, where my attention had naturally been straying to, anyway. Blake was standing next to the car, glaring at my new ride with disdain.

"Motherfucker blocked us in!" he shouted across the vehicle to where Axel was looking none too impressed.

Jared cast a sidelong glance my way.

I shrugged. "If I decide I have to put up with you, it doesn't really do if you drive off before I can find you."

He didn't respond, but his self-satisfied smile didn't go unnoticed.

How the fuck had I missed that he was such a constant attention whore? He must have been toning down some of that. Or he was simply overdoing it now. It didn't really matter, but not knowing irked me.

I hadn't been talking that loudly, but apparently the sound of my voice was enough to make both Blake and Axel whip around, eyes wide. It took Blake all of a second to throw his head back and let out a ripping roar of laughter. So much for that. Axel managed the feat of looking both relieved and disappointed. He got a sarcastic smile from me for that.

"I think we've already established that I'm not known for making the smartest decisions," I said in a way of greeting. I left it to him to figure out whether I meant coming back to them or jumping out of the car in the first place.

My mind was addled enough that I wasn't quite sure what the real answer was.

"It's good to see you're okay," Axel offered, then frowned. Possibly at the loud growl my stomach let out; maybe he meant the bruises. "You are okay, right?"

Okay, but ravenous.

Sadly, I didn't get to say that since Jared just had to cut me off.

"As much as I'd love to celebrate our reunion, we really need to go."

It was only when I followed where he was looking that I noticed two things. First, several Marines had stormed into the parking lot, one of them frantically talking to—or mostly yelling at—the gate guards. And second, that one of the men standing off to the side was gesturing wildly at Jared, looking frantic.

That made zero sense until I noticed Jared's smirk. I still felt like I had to ask for clarification.

"Why exactly is that guy gesturing you to haul ass?"

He shrugged, although it was obvious that he very much knew why.

"It would be presumptuous of me to say I know—"

"Oh, please. Presumptuous is your middle name," I taunted.

He actually snorted.

"Could be because he asked me to take care of his brother-in-law, and considering the Marines are likely calling for a lockdown, that would mean there's someone still around to not just confess to taking care of said problem but who specifically put him up to it, I think it's safe to say he'll hold that gate open for as long as he can." His smile was a bright one. "I think we should oblige the poor man's wish."

I needed to physically shake myself to keep my brain from rattling around inside my skull.

"Is that how you do it? You just ask around to see if someone needs a hitman?"

Jared's answering smile was a wry one.

"Ask Axel just how well that has been working for him." The smile brightened. "And for how long."

The man in question looked a second away from hitting someone with a hard object. Jared and me as well, I might add.

"Could you, for once in your life, show an ounce of self preservation? Both of you!" The last thing was clearly directed at me.

I was well aware that he was right, but it was still hard not to bicker back.

Hunger was clearly making me stupid.

Reaching inside my pants, I got out the key fob, glancing at Jared. "Do you want to drive? Stupid question. Of course you do. It's probably for the best if you do."

He caught the fob with alacrity as we both marched for the car, quickly switching places to end up on the right sides.

"Not that I'm protesting your sudden realization that I am, indeed, the better driver, but what gives?"

I smiled sweetly at him.

"I get distracted easily. Like a dog when a rabbit suddenly takes off in front of him. Not sure I should be driving with that kind of attention span. It was hard enough to get here."

As if to underline my point, my mind ground to a sudden halt, my full attention torn away from Jared and the car to across the lot... where the commander had just stepped out from between the houses. He was looking toward the gate, seemingly oblivious to our presence off to the side.

How was that possible? We were right there, easy to pick out between the maybe thirty other people milling around the cars...

That was when I realized our radars must not be working in sync. While I could blindly pick him out in a crowd, to him we must have faded into the background. I could feel a good third of the people present, so that made sense. I still had no clue why both he and Jared continued to be beacons in the night while Axel was practically a black hole and I only got the vaguest echo from Blake, but right now I didn't really give a shit.

Ah, it was good not to be special. And that was definitely not something I should say out loud where Jared could hear it.

Jared paused when he saw what was spread out all over the back row of the car. Right. Maybe I should have covered up the weapons with something.

"Where did you get all that from?" he asked while already reaching inside to hand off parts of the loot to Blake, who looked very much like a small child in a candy store. Neither man seemed to mind the dried blood flaking off the weapons.

I gave Jared a flat stare.

"The Marines, maybe? I told you I killed four of them."

Jared took that with a simple shrug. It was almost offensive that he clearly hadn't believed me, and likely still didn't. Not completely. Blake—on the other hand—guffawed. "So, this is all your fault?" He clearly meant the Marines swarming the town.

I shook my head after a moment of consideration.

"I highly doubt that they found them. Or what's left of them. They have no reason to connect any of that to me, and since they aren't swarming all over the car yet, I doubt they know where I got it from. Mere coincidence." Something occurred to me then. I glared at Jared. "Makes much more sense that they're here because you killed the wrong asshole."

Jared shrugged, as if that was neither here nor there. Blake was satisfied with my answer, now returning to the other car with his hands full of weapons. Only Axel remained rooted in the spot, staring at me with confusion and mounting horror.

"Callie, what the fuck did you do while you were gone?"

There was a lot I could have said, but I left it at a tight smile when I noticed how heated the debate at the gate was getting.

"It's a long story." Of course I couldn't leave it at that, so after a moment, I added, "He might be the monster you know. I'm still more of a wild card."

Jared gave me another of those "we need to talk about this" looks that I was happy to ignore.

It was only when I saw the gigantic heap of discarded food wrappers all over the passenger side that I thought of something, turning back to Axel.

"I need food. Like Blake-on-a-bad-day amounts of food. Please tell me you have some provisions in your car?"

Axel kept staring at me for another second before he ducked into the back seat, coming up with a pack full to bursting that he lugged over to me and exchanged it for two more of the looted weapons, now equaling their distribution among us.

That would do. At least for the next hour or so.

As soon as my ass hit the seat, Jared revved the engine and sent the car toward the gate, leaving civilians and Marines alike to scramble out of the way. Axel was right behind him, showing none of his usual caution.

I had a moment to see the commander recognize us, his icy glare promising nothing good. Then we were flying through the closing gate, the second car narrowly missing getting hit in the rear bumper by it. We blasted right by the column of Humvees and other larger vehicles waiting outside, heavily armed men and women staring stupidly after us.

I had a feeling the inertia among them wouldn't last long.

After making sure that I was securely buckled in, I reached into the back and pulled the provisions pack forward, narrowly avoiding hitting Jared in the shoulder with it. Lots of it was cans, which was fine with me as long as they had tabs. I grabbed the first one I saw and tore it open, blindly guzzling the contents without even checking what they were.

Beans, of course, and they were kind of disgusting.

I followed that up with some cherries, sticky with syrup. Now we were talking! At least as far as my brain was concerned, letting me root through the pack with a little more distinction as I checked what else was there.

And maybe consider something besides where my next rush of calories was coming from.

In the rearview mirror, I caught sight of the Marines starting to turn their column around in pursuit while three smaller SUVs were already coming after us. We had maybe five minutes on them, ten max.

"Where are we going?" I asked Jared, then remembered something. "The Marines also had a map with them, presumably with their allies penciled in. It's right there in the center console."

Jared grimaced as if to say he could hardly check on that now, but still pulled out the neatly folded piece of paper, pinning it with his thumbs to the steering wheel. I munched two cans of peas while he alternated between staring at the road and the map before he put it away.

At the intersection up ahead, he took a sharp right turn, momentarily bringing us closer to the column of our pursuers, but then quickly heading away as he turned onto a gravel path.

It was only a mile or so later that I noticed Jared kept glancing into the mirrors whenever the road would let him.

"They're still after us," I notified him. "And gaining, from what I can tell. I don't think we can shake that many."

He glanced at me, but not totaling the car took up too much of his attention to allow for more.

"You're sounding awfully relaxed about this."

I considered that. He was probably right.

"It's kind of inevitable, seeing as the asshole commander already tracked us down in town. He must have a reason for coming after us full force now."

It took Jared's actual sneer to realize his mood had flipped.

"Did you fucking betray us? Sell us out to these assholes?"

The idea was ludicrous enough to make me laugh. I had a feeling he took the next turn deliberately too fast to make my body slam into the seatbelt. My own ire quickly disappeared as I kept munching on some crackers.

"They killed two of the only people in the world I still give a shit about. I'd rather die than cooperate, let alone actively help them." I shot him a mirthless smile that hopefully looked feral. "They easily surpass any and all misgivings I have about you."

Jared was still on the fence.

"You're taking all this exceptionally lightly. Hence my suspicion. Also would explain where you got the car and weapons, and why they were right there after you supposedly tracked us down."

Two more crackers, and I could see where he had a point.

"I told you about my brain fog, right? Fear center's still mostly offline. I'd say that's convenient, but it's likely cutting down my chances of survival hard. Also taking all the fun out of me being back for you, huh? Must be so frustrating when what you most get off on is my fear of what you could do to me?"

It was fun watching his profile as he gnashed his teeth and didn't find a chance to glare at me for a good fifteen seconds. By the time he managed, he'd sadly reined in whatever true emotion I'd caused, offering a wry smile.

"That part is disappointing."

"It might come back if you feed me enough. Or at least if I eat enough sugar. That seems to make a difference," I noted.

It was only then that he noticed I'd eaten my way through half of the rations.

"Just how starved are you? I know you can pack it away like nobody's business, but this is an obscene amount of food."

I shrugged.

"Not sure. I barfed up my last stomach full of Marine, but considering you told me I've lost an entire day, I probably managed to digest two or three times that before. Since I woke up, I've eaten ten MREs and maybe four packs of nuts on the way to town, and two meals' worth in town before we met. And now… eight cans and a box of crackers." I did a quick calculation in my head. "Maybe eight thousand calories today? Might be closer to ten. The pack and I were pretty much done with the Marines, so that's four times eighty thousand calories divided by seven, minus maybe five thousand that I couldn't hold down…"

Jared let out a fake chuckle. "Now you're just fucking with me."

"Wish I was. Would be so much easier to have options."

"Wait. That's the reason you came back? Because your delusions tell you you're stuck with me?"

I considered laying off the food simply to let him find out what happened when I got really hungry. Not that I knew for sure. Maybe that wasn't the worst idea, considering what would happen to us once the Marines caught up to us. I wasn't sure I needed to be mentally clocked in for that.

"I don't really want to risk snapping back to being in control of my actions with my hands inside the savaged ribcage of a child."

Jared chuckled, still highly amused.

"No worries," he told me, catching my gaze for a moment. "I'd still tap that if that happens."

That opened up an entirely new concern to fret about. What exactly were my triggers? Fear and aggression made sense. But what about other high-emotion states of mind? Not that I would be too heartbroken right now if I accidentally killed him during sex, even if it might turn out to be inconvenient…

Several blips becoming noticeable in front of us derailed that train of thought, likely for the best.

"There's a group of zombies up ahead. Likely in that copse of trees over there. At least five strong ones and twenty possible lurkers, right next to the road. You should avoid them."

Jared said nothing—and did nothing when he could have sent the car into a wide circle around that stretch of the road, going through the high grass to the other side.

I still couldn't see them, but once we were within a hundred feet of them, I could perfectly feel them snapping to attention, going from baseline awareness into high-aggression mode.

"Now you've done it—"

And all five of them were on us, tackling the car as if it was a large, lumbering herbivore.

Jared cursed, fighting the bucking car for several seconds as he crashed into two of the somewhat less aggressive ones. A lot of swerving was needed to finally shake them off for good. Axel managed to avoid most of it, going through the grass just as I'd suggested. As we sped away, I could feel the lurkers emerge from the trees, patiently waiting while the stronger ones took apart the heavily wounded ones. I might have gotten a little lost in that until the Marines barging right through the killing field made the zombies scamper away once more.

Our car was decidedly more noisy than before, even if it was still moving.

"Told you so," I quipped, quite satisfied… until I found the last of the crackers gone. Damnit.

Jared was gnashing his teeth for a good minute before he responded. My guess was he was annoyed both because I'd been right, and by me being able to feel them for real killed his theory about me being a spy.

"Let me know next time."

As if I hadn't just done that, but I didn't gloat. Being right was enough, fucked up as it was.

It occurred to me that sneaking through the world on foot had gotten tantalizingly easier for me. The cars were loud and fast, both drawing attention and closing distances too quickly. Walking, I'd have none of these problems. But it made carrying stuff harder and meant I'd have to go hunt for food pretty much nonstop.

Not the worst idea, my mind noted, my mouth already salivating.

Yeah, maybe not, unless I was ready to give up for good.

Two more times, I managed to give Jared a heads-up. And he actually listened. Not much time passed before I got aware of several strings of blips moving in too much coordination to be roaming bands of zombies—and they were homing in on us with deadly precision.

I was just about to warn Jared and explain what I thought was going on when we went around another bend in the road, and all four tires of the car blew as he drove right over two strips of spike traps, going too fast to avoid them.

I had a single "oh shit!" second as the car went off the road, gravity punching us in the face and elsewhere. My adrenaline spiked—

And my mind was gone again, waving goodbye to my intellect as instinct took over.

Not this again.

CHAPTER 4

I didn't completely black out this time, although control wasn't exactly something I retained. Not in the sense of actually being mistress of the actions my addled brain cooked up and my body swiftly enforced. In no way was what I kept even close to coherent, but it was a more cohesive reel than what had happened with the Marines in the forest.

And I'd have Jared to later fill me in on the details I missed.

The first points in the sequence still made some sense.

My body getting flung around as the car went off the road, somersaulting into the underbrush.

Me hanging upside down, caught in my seatbelt until Jared cut me free.

Running.

Shots, coming from a distance, followed by return fire directly next to me.

I really didn't like that. Both the sonic assault on my unprotected ears, but mostly the running. Running away, that was. I definitely wanted to run after something. Hunt down whoever was giving chase.

Then, pain. Lots of pain, sharp and hot and impossible to ignore. Low across my back, and high up on my right shoulder.

More pain, but this was different. Good pain. Pain from using my body for what it was made: to hunt; to fight. Muscles ached and bones shuddered under blunt force trauma, both on the giving and receiving end.

The metallic taste of blood in my mouth

First, my own. Then lots more—someone else's. Gushing freely, covering me in the warm nectar of the gods.

I got a little distracted there, the impressions going hazy, but I knew for sure that the sharp gnawing in my stomach lessened.

My mind cleared up after that a little, not that it needed to.

I was locked in somewhere, metal around me, my wrists and ankles chafed raw from not being free. I didn't like that, being locked in and not being able to move. Jared was there, but that was little relief.

He told me to keep it together.

The constant lurching and rocking stopped.

Hope flared as sunlight hit my eyes, the stink of human bodies hitting my nostrils.

Someone punched my shoulder hard—the hurt one, feeling much better now.

Reason disappeared as searing pain raced through my ankles and wrists as I broke through my bonds.

Freedom, fresh and sweet.

More physical something. Running, punching, clawing.

I heard myself scream but didn't feel the pain anymore.

I heard myself roar, feeling powerful, raw, and free.

One more fight, the hunger getting worse, my thoughts jumbled…

And then sweet, sweet salvation, washing away that confusing annoyance.

Satisfaction.

All needs met and wants slaked.

And sadly, reason, roaring back with a vengeance even though every part of me was fighting against it.

Unlike last time, I didn't snap back into a body that was just about to wake up. It also wasn't a gradual thing. On some level, I must have been fighting for control since regaining it felt good… for all of a single second. There was also no disorientation. I was immediately aware of what I was doing—and continued to do, since my body was running on autopilot, apparently.

I was hunched over the dead, bloody, absolutely savaged torso of a Marine, one hand still thrust into the cavernous hole in his abdomen, the other raised to my mouth where I was holding a cooling hunk of meat that I was currently chewing on as if my life depended on it

Liver, probably.

My mind wanted to immediately flip into panic mode, but something held me back. The same something that kept me tearing off chunks with my teeth and swallowing greedily while I should have stopped, been utterly horrified, and started purging my stomach as quickly as possible.

While the horror was definitely present—and almost overwhelming whatever else was going on inside my mind—reason cut through that, not quite cold and calculating, but impossible to ignore.

The hunger was gone. Ignoring the overwhelming sense of disgust, I actually felt like myself for the first time since I'd woken up... or quite possibly since that damn alley and Jared's little revelation. There was no way of knowing for sure, but it felt like a certainty that this was connected. Also, the guy was already dead, and there must have been a reason why my instinct kept me going.

How nice to realize that pragmatism was turning me into a ravenous cannibal. But I guessed that came with the territory.

While I wouldn't—couldn't—make myself stop eating, the least I could do was to expand my awareness. Checking up on the body first was the obvious next step. His face was oddly untouched, only splattered with blood. Male African-American, early twenties, buff with a solid layer of fat that hinted at good, regular nutrition—not a given in the apocalypse. He was wearing the same fatigues I'd seen all the Marines wear. No obvious hint of what exactly had killed him, except for, well, me.

Unbidden, pieces of the puzzle that were my memory flashes fell into place. He'd been a part of... the convoy that had brought us here; wherever here was beyond grassland next to the woods, with water close enough that I could smell it, even over the overwhelming scent of blood.

He'd tried bashing me in the side of my head with the stock of his carbine.

He'd been quiet—unlike some of the others—and quick to follow orders.

He'd let out a gurgling scream as I ripped out his throat—

Enough of that. I didn't need to know more. It was enough to be sure I hadn't gone for a random, innocent man. Still didn't mean he'd deserved it, but that wasn't something I was going to hash out now.

I looked from his body to what was nearby, tearing off another hunk of liver as I kept chewing.

Several more bodies. Seven—make that eight—Marines, all bloody and dead but not desecrated. I couldn't tell the exact cause of their deaths, but most looked like bullet wounds had done the job. No vehicles in sight, but I knew there would be three not far from here—a small transport and two chaperones.

Stupid, stupid, stupid. They'd had us pinned down with their overwhelming numbers, only to give us the perfect chance to escape. One could even say they'd absolutely deserved what had happened to them.

No, not that. But they'd sure had it coming.

I didn't know if it was those thoughts or an actual sound he made, but I became aware that I wasn't alone. Off to my left, I found Jared sitting on a log, knife in hand, two rifles propped up beside him. He was hunched over, forearms on his knees, and he was laughing softly to himself as he was watching me.

Of course he was. Some things never change.

Something must have shifted in my body language to alert him to the fact that I was back among the intellectually thinking part of the populace because he sat up, his expression adjusting, never mind that I was still munching on my liver. Before, he'd simply been the amused observer. Now the taunting asshole was back.

It was probably my instant negative reaction to the latter that made me utter a guttural growl and switch into a more aggressive crouch, not his movement. While I didn't consider him harmless for a second, my instinct still put him firmly in the to-be-trusted category, which wasn't something my newly regained intellect would have, not even for a second. But just as I found myself incapable of stopping my feasting, I also didn't want to attack him. That growl had been a warning. Mine. Just mine. Get yourself your own juicy hunk of meat.

It was baffling when Jared read my reaction better than I could have.

"Easy there. Not gonna intrude on your dinner. But I have to say, you are a thing of deadly efficient beauty, very much surpassing my expectations. Which isn't that hard since I didn't believe a word you said until you tore into the first two idiots with guns that didn't stand a chance, but still. I absolutely underestimated you, and for that, I'm sorry. It won't happen again."

I had no fucking clue how to respond to that, so I just kept on chewing.

Talking was overrated, even if I could have offered some witty banter now. I simply didn't want to. I was oddly content with the way things were.

Jared shifted as if to get up, which got me surging several inches toward him, my bloody prize still clutched in one hand but the other free now to put to good use. He immediately relaxed back onto his log, raising both hands placatingly, the knife still in one of them.

"Down, girl. Message received. I have nowhere to go, anyway, so might as well stay here. But, just saying, you could show a smidgen more gratitude. Who do you think was it that cut open his abdomen and tore out the intestines so you could more easily get to the good stuff?"

I didn't exactly remember it that way. To me, it had felt like an unnecessary delay, and one that had almost cost him his life when I'd been considering making it nine dead bodies to get rid of the distraction.

"You're welcome," he said, taking my continuing silence as acquiescence. "Once I got my mind wrapped around that new kind of reality we're now living in—and let me tell you, I'm not at all used to me being the one who has to do that—I figured I should help you along, right? It's in both our best interests. You're fed and no longer want to make a meal out of me, and I get front-row seats to whatever gore-fest shitshow this is going to turn into. That made me think about the incoherent parts you've been yapping on about, and I realized, girl needs some quality nutrition to keep functioning! Something full of vitamins, and the liver in particular should be great with its glycogen stores if you actually do need sugar for your brain to properly function. Although, I don't mind the base program running, either. As I said, highly entertaining and very efficient. Didn't think of that when I was delivering my grand speech to you, but I'll take a vicious, homicidal sidekick if you can't reconcile your good girl bullshit act with the magnificent woman you could be."

I might have torn off the next hunk with a little more emphasis than necessary, my gaze still holding his.

All Jared did was laugh, with way too much glee drenching his tone.

He wasn't acting. That was a genuine reaction. I knew that should have freaked me out, but my mind had already shut that away with everything else I was ignoring right now. Which was a lot.

I really didn't look forward to the moment when that stopped working and I'd get buried under my own immense heap of shit.

Keep calm and carry on. Wasn't that what people said in situations like this? So I kept on chewing, finally finishing my dark-red, somewhat chewy treat.

I was just about to swallow that last bite when rustling in the underbrush made me perk up. Not just raise my state of alertness, but I felt my mind get ready to fold back under, how it had been for the past... however many hours that had passed. Not too many since the sun was still up in the sky, but the shadows were markedly lengthening.

I realized I was incapable of stopping that from happening when I had to work hard to tear myself away from zoning out right then and there while my body was readying for a fight.

Jared kept watching me closely, his interest clearly piqued. I tried to keep myself grounded by glaring at him, but that only added anger to the mix, which felt like someone had just tried to douse a campfire with rocket fuel.

"There you are!" a familiar, loud voice hollered from between the trees behind Jared, the noise of branches breaking and leaves rustling drawing closer.

Blake, I realized.

A brief wave of disappointment washed through me. Not hostile, so no fighting for me. No fresh food. Sure, there were still the other bodies, but they were cold now. And some of them had a weird scent to them. Good enough if I was starving, but not worth the trouble otherwise…

To tide myself over my momentary moroseness, I thrust my right hand into the open cavity in front of me and tore off a hunk of skin, the inside nicely coated with half an inch of fat. My mouth watered as I bit into it, doing my best to get the juicy, yellowish stuff off and down my gullet.

Maybe I should switch food sources in the future. To something that was less muscle and way more fat. I didn't mind the harder kills with the fitter people, but this stuff was so good…

"What the everlasting fuck?"

I glanced up from where I'd been studying the corpse underneath me, trying to determine where most of the remaining fatty tissue was and how to best get there. Maybe asking Jared to filet it for me was a good idea, the wry, nasty voice in the back of my mind suggested. Since he'd already been so concerned about me getting enough minerals…

My mind came to a screeching halt when the dumbstruck looks on Blake and Axel's faces registered, Axel being mostly horrified.

It cost me a lot to drop the wad of fat in my hand because I really didn't want it to go to waste.

Jared's slightly insane-sounding chuckle helped ground me further.

"You missed the best parts, but this is still pretty hilarious. Just don't make any sudden movements, particularly not toward her kill. Clearly, she's not in a sharing mood right now."

I gave him the indignant glare that deserved before looking back to the other men. The memory flashes supplied that they'd been around the first minutes after Jared had totaled the car but had taken off before the Marines managed to wrestle both Jared and me into submission and dragged us into that transport. There was a lot of confusing, extra information connected to that, like people shouting orders and my mind not making sense of the sounds, but that wasn't important now. They'd gotten away, sending the Marines on a merry chase as they'd forced them to split up. Clearly, they'd escaped and had miraculously found us. How, I didn't even start to question. That was well beyond me.

"Took you long enough," I grated out, my voice hoarse from disuse, or possibly screaming. Probably both.

Now all three of them were staring at me, perplexed.

I slowly came to my feet, already feeling a little more like myself now that I was physically mimicking that mode. The fat cravings were still present but started fading into the background.

"Well," Blake started, then laughed. "I got nothing. Probably a first for me, so don't get used to it."

I glanced at the bloody corpses strewn all across the clearing. I had a feeling this wasn't going to be the last time this happened, so he'd get another chance for that witty comeback.

Fuck.

Axel once again proved that he was the only one present with at least a sense of normal human behavior.

"Callie, are you okay?" he asked, his tone very much stating that this was obviously not the case.

"I will be. I think." That sounded better than to spread my arms wide and ask, "Does this look like okay to you?"

Jared, of course, had to rain on my parade. Nothing unusual there.

"She got shot at least three or four times and her left shoulder's probably dislocated. Ankle hurt maybe as well. That was harder to tell. They never stood a chance against her in full attack mode, but she's still only one hundred and twenty pounds, even if it's all voracious violence. The only reason she got the upper hand was because they had orders to keep her alive and clearly showed some hesitation executing a pretty young thing like that at point blank range. She had no such reservations. Obviously, neither did I."

Obviously.

From my higher vantage point standing up now, I got a better look at the Marines. Not all of them had died from blunt force trauma or bullets, it seemed. At least two had their throats slit, and who knew how many stab wounds the others had sustained.

It said a lot about my state of mind that I checked that first before taking stock of my own body. It wasn't exactly like the pain came roaring back now that Jared had mentioned my possible injuries, but I definitely felt them now.

Looking down at my blood-soaked clothes, I couldn't help but think, yeah, that fit. Messy eater I might be, but not that messy. And it wasn't like I couldn't feel the pain. Now that I was searching for it, it became a lot harder to ignore. But I could ignore it, which was disconcerting. Convenient, but disconcerting.

"We should maybe get you cleaned up," Axel suggested.

"So I won't stain the car seats too badly?" I quipped.

He actually looked disturbed, likely at my humor. Nothing new about that.

"That, too," he muttered, avoiding my gaze. Or looking at me in general, I realized. Maybe that should have given me some pause. It sure made me realize that while I felt pretty much like myself again, I wasn't quite there yet.

Before I could head for the water nearby, Jared stopped me, his lopsided smile too nice and genuine to be a good sign.

"Should we, maybe, pack some trail rations for you?"

And because that wasn't obvious enough yet, he pointedly nudged the leg of a dead Marine with the tip of his boot.

I glared at him, although I couldn't quite muster the level of ire that deserved.

"No, thanks. I'm good."

His grin broadened. It wasn't a nice one anymore.

"I don't mind providing… sustenance for you. Might actually work really well for both of us. Just saying."

He paused, as if giving me a chance to blow up in his face. I just gave him a level stare, letting his taunt fizzle out. Not that he cared, quickly shrugging it off.

"Just one thing to consider. There's no guessing at how much time will pass until we come across a useful… individual. Not sure how picky you are, but there's plenty left you can eat for, say, a day or two, even without cooling." He smirked. "If you even mind rotting meat—"

I couldn't quite hold back a growl that seemed to surprise both of us. It took me a second to realize where that had come from.

"I actually care," I offered with a sweet smile.

He snorted. "Your good girl act again? How disappointing."

The reality of what was actually going on should have made me feel guilty, but considering everything else, that was easy to ignore.

"No. The meat's not fresh anymore. I could still eat it, but it's turned from delicious steak right off the grill into yesterday's overcooked leftovers. Besides, half of them smell weird." I took a deep breath through my nose as I stepped up to him. He didn't budge an inch, staring straight into my eyes. "Just like you smell weird; only worse than most of them. I might be wrong, but I think that's the reason the strong ones always go for the humans and only the weak ones have to feast amongst themselves. They can smell the difference. And it is a huge difference."

Which explained why I'd survived our trip way back when to the Militia HQ—and maybe many other close calls before that as well. I'd already been the less savory option for them.

My, wasn't that a revelation.

"But be sure to pack some extra normal-people food for me, just in case," I offered sweetly.

Jared grinned, although it had a dark edge to it. Blake chuckled. Axel sighed.

Looked like we were back to business as usual.

While the men set to cleaning out what useful gear the dead Marines had on their bodies and inside their vehicles, I found the creek close by, only having to hunt for a basin on the side deep enough to dunk myself in for a couple minutes. It was only after the cool water had washed away most of the grime and blood that I realized I should maybe have brought spare clothes with me first. But then they would have been dirty from my bloody hands at the very least, so it was just as well.

I wasn't surprised to find my old pack sitting next to a log on the shore, with my pair of haphazardly cleaned up sneakers beside it. Axel's doing, if I had to guess, because Jared would have remained standing there, watching me.

I still didn't get what was so damn interesting about me that he continued doing so, but I had a feeling that wouldn't change now, seeing as today I'd proven to be quite prone to turning into a spectacle.

At the very edge of my mind, I was aware of a fleeting feeling of guilt skipping around, but I quickly ignored that. If I could stall beating myself up over what I'd done when I'd been ten degrees out of my mind just a little longer, I'd take it. That made me wonder if I could maybe push that moment out indefinitely if I just kept myself not quite fully fed.

I was also very much aware of how my vocabulary had changed, and that was another hornet's nest I was unwilling to poke.

There was also a bottle of shampoo, which was definitely Axel's doing and the opposite of a subtle hint. Since the water wasn't that cold, I slogged back into the basin and started lathering up my hair, then gave myself a good full-body scrub.

Jared had been right about the shots. I found three bullet wounds myself and there were two more parts on my back that felt equally sore. They'd already closed up but were clearly fresh, and when I poked them enough, I could feel the deformed bullets lodged underneath. They also decreased my range of motion, including the damage to the surrounding tissues. They still didn't hurt as much as I knew they should have, but then my toes were now numb from the cool water and that didn't hurt much, either. That was also something I didn't look forward to changing.

After submerging myself fully one last time—and staying under for at least a minute to check that my lungs were indeed starting to scream for air—I slogged back out onto the riverbank, only to find Blake standing between the trees a short distance away, staring at me, quite unabashedly so. I stared right back, only after a few moments wondering if I should have felt weird about being naked. He was obviously ogling me, but that seemed more of a perk than the main reason for his actions.

"Are you checking up on me to make sure I don't run off?"

He flashed me a big grin.

"Something like that," he muttered. "Axel expressed his concern about leaving you alone in the woods. For when something might attack you. He didn't want to stand guard himself because he has some really weird hangups about your privacy."

"It's called common decency, I think."

He guffawed, not the least bit chastised.

"Honestly, I was hoping for that to happen, really. I got some glimpses of you in action before we had to split, and that was mighty impressive. Obviously, I've missed out on the best parts back over there."

I didn't know what to make of that. Vague embarrassment briefly came up, but it disappeared right with the other emotions I refused to deal with right now.

"And seeing me buck-ass naked had nothing to do with it, huh?"

Blake grinned and gave me a bona fide leer, but his attention kept snagging to the bullet wounds in my side and abdomen. That almost made me burst out laughing. I allowed myself a small smile and went to go through my pack, seeing if there was anything useful left in there.

Blake waited until I was done, and we returned to the car together.

Axel and Jared had been busy stowing everything in the car in the meantime. I was a little surprised they didn't consider taking at least one of the other vehicles as well, until Jared noted acerbically, "They likely track them somehow."

Good point.

It felt both familiar and oddly different to slide into the passenger seat, noting with curiosity that for once, none of the usual backseat drivers spoke up. When I cast a curious glance into the back row, Blake was only too happy to enlighten me, although Axel's pinched face told me all I needed to know.

"Jared's the only one insane enough to dare being that close to you, at least until we know what exactly is going on."

I cast a sidelong glance at the madman in question, who, of course, had a salacious smile ready for me.

Oh well. At least I wouldn't take down anyone innocent with me if my calculations were wrong about what triggered me, and whether I'd be safe for now.

The very ridiculousness of that idea made me chuckle to myself.

"You're not having another mental breakdown, right?" Jared more jeered than asked.

I didn't even bother getting annoyed, or setting his presumption about my decision to leave straight. My silence was apparently enough.

I had a feeling that would only be a short respite, because if anything, I'd gotten more interesting to him than less.

Well, fuck.

CHAPTER 5

We drove well into the night, aided by the map we now had in our possession. It was anyone's guess whether we were actually on the run, or at least if anyone was currently chasing us. From what Axel relayed, around half of the Marines must have survived their ambush, the consequent split, and how I'd ended things. Not just me since Jared had quite the role in that as well, but it had sure been a major distraction capable of causing quite a fallout.

Sticking to small roads only, we didn't get that far distance-wise, but with Jared for once only driving like half a jackass, it was a mostly uneventful journey. When I pointed out a roaming group of undead in the dusk veering close to where we would be crossing a larger road, he actually listened and sent the car into a more generous circle around the wrecks where a few lurkers were lying in wait.

That actually surprised me. Not so much that he used it as a conversation starter.

"So how exactly does this zombie radar of yours work?"

It was impossible to ignore the tension ratcheting up in the back row. Apparently, my recent status update was a reason for concern after all.

"No clue," I admitted. "But when I'm close enough, I get a pretty good sense of their strength and level of aggression. My guess is that this is how they establish their hierarchies. The top dogs still sort out the details mano-a-mano, but the others seem to know pretty well who not to underestimate."

"And you got that knowledge how, exactly?" Axel inquired.

I allowed myself a mirthless grin as I looked back over my shoulder at him.

"By waking up in the middle of the forest, buck-ass naked, and then chasing away my handy little zombie pack from my recent kills."

After that, it was only fair to relay the remaining details of my journey, or at least what little coherent chunks I actually remembered. Now that my mind was running pretty much back on track, it was weirdly harder to make sense of the memory flashes than when it had barely been functioning.

Blake, of course, found all this hilarious, although I got the sense I'd risen several rungs on his internal ladder of esteem, or maybe danger. Axel looked vaguely sick. Also perfectly understandable. I could feel more conflicting emotions wanting to go toe to toe with my intellect, but I kept pushing them away. It was much too soon to deal with that.

Jared asked the pertinent question next. "So you think your level of deliberate action and thinking depends on how much quality calories you get to eat?"

I had been wondering about that, particularly the specifics. That we were even discussing this in a detached, almost clinical way was disturbing, but it also fit right in with the company I kept.

"I don't know. What makes sense is that if I want higher cognitive function, I need more food. Or maybe special food. It stands to reason that I regained consciousness after eating enough to get me out of whatever state I was in before. Then ate more food, and yet more at the town. When they gave me sugar at the clinic, it definitely gave me a cognitive boost, but I was still pretty out of it when we met. I've only felt moderately like myself since, well…"

I didn't even know why I trailed off there. It wasn't like they didn't tolerate Jared's… proclivities.

"Are you hungry now?" he asked.

I took a moment to listen into my body, but while I could have eaten something, that mad hunger still lay dormant. I didn't delude myself into thinking that it was completely gone.

"Not particularly, no."

A grin appeared on Jared's face. I had a feeling I already knew what was coming.

"As for choice of nutrition," he started, actually glancing over to where I was already glaring at him. "Any particular preference, or was it just a matter of getting the best bioavailable calories that were on hand right there?"

Fuck if I knew the answer to that, but I sure knew the answer I wanted to give.

"I don't think any one of them gives a shit whether the meat they eat comes from animals or humans."

Jared smirked. "The ultimate proof that we are indeed all just animals."

"And you're still a gigantic asshole," I griped.

Of course, he laughed that off.

Axel took it upon himself to keep digging, because at least one person in this car was able to keep track of the important stuff.

"You let us know well ahead of time when you get hungry again, right? We'll try to stock up on as much food as we can find so we can keep you well supplied."

"You mean sane and not on the fast track to killing everything in sight?" I asked sweetly.

Axel pointedly didn't answer. Blake laughed, because why wouldn't he?

"Actually, I think your friend versus foe sense still works quite well even when your higher cognitive functions go out the window," Jared remarked. "I admit, I was a little concerned during the initial ambush when you flew right off the handle, but you didn't even attack me once. The only time you growled and snapped at me was when I eviscerated that body for you so you could more easily get to the good parts."

Of course, he had to repeat that. Never let a good deed go uncelebrated.

What a mental picture his words painted. Most of that was even there in my fainter memories, more like a film with a filter on than mere snapshots.

"Yeah, that was because you were actively trying to keep me from feeding," I snapped, very much aware of how awful that sentence was in every possible sense. "And don't let that get to your head. I didn't seriously attack the zombies in my pack, either. Just enough to reestablish dominance."

Of course, Jared had to smirk at that and give me one of those insane "mrow" fake kitty-cat roars.

What exactly had I done to deserve this?

Lots, and lots more today, it seemed.

Still.

"Don't worry about the food thing," Jared offered. "One way or another, we'll keep you fed."

That had sounded much more comforting coming from Axel.

"Don't even think for a second you can use me as your garbage disposal," I growled.

Jared's answering smile was nothing shy of beatific.

"But it's the perfect deal! You don't go hungry and eventually attack us when reason goes completely out of the window, and I never get stuck again with having to drag the corpses somewhere they can get savaged by actual zombies! Plus, nobody will suspect you, and it will cause so much confusion that we can make a lazy getaway. Either way you look at it, it's the perfect solution."

I didn't bother responding to that. It was just too... I wanted to say ludicrous, but I had to admit, he wasn't completely wrong.

Axel's displeasure was palpable. "You're not going to drag her down with you."

Jared chuckled, not even offended. "She doesn't need my active participation to hit rock bottom. She can get there all by herself well enough."

Sheesh, wasn't that a vote of confidence! What I hated even more was that it was true, and it showed how well he knew me. But then that was par for the course, considering how long and well he'd been manipulating me.

Fucking asshole.

It was absolutely disconcerting how conflicted that realization made me feel. The fact that there was dissent inside of my mind. Because rationally, intellectually, there was nothing shy of hatred for him in my mind. But underneath that lurked another layer that I hated even more, that had already forgiven him and simply accepted that he was, in all things that counted, my perfect match. All the beast cared about was that he knew how to fuck and feed me, and that was more than enough for her.

I very much wanted to blame that on my recent switch into debatable alive status, but I was afraid that had been present way longer than those damn bacteria. Only now that so many layers of learned behavior had been peeled away was she back in the light of day.

"You can't just let her run around, killing people at random because she gets hungry," Axel griped.

Jared looked terribly amused by that notion. I had to admit, I agreed with Axel, but his tone still irritated me.

"Why not?" I asked, only half joking. "Can that misogynist crap. You've been watching from the sidelines while he's killed how many people? But if I fight for my life and maybe do it a little more efficiently than everyone thinks I'm capable of, it's suddenly a huge no-go?"

More laughter from Blake and Jared now. Axel seemed chastised for a moment, but then he grimaced.

"Normally, I'd say you have a point, but that wasn't what I meant. The issue with him is that he can absolutely control himself, but he usually doesn't want to. Can you say the same about yourself? What happens when the next asshole in town makes a move on you? Or if something else tips you off? Scares you? Because correct me if I'm wrong, but you just told us you decided to go after us because you're afraid you'll accidentally kill innocents in a town, but you're sure that between the three of us, we will handle you, and if worse comes to worst, that includes killing you. That doesn't sound like you trust yourself much. That doesn't work at all with giving you free rein to kill as you please."

Fuck, I hated it when someone used my own sound reasoning against me. Mostly because of that, but also because I really didn't know what to offer in my defense, I remained quiet.

Until I felt the next group of mental blips appear ahead of us.

Another sobering fact that I couldn't particularly ignore any longer now was Axel's way of referring to Jared's favorite pastime. While I hadn't exactly doubted him after what he'd pulled in that alley, there had been a small part of me that held out hope he was just screwing with me. Or that I was missing some vital parts of the picture. But what Axel didn't say—more what he offered—quenched that hope more and more. I had a feeling I'd get the chance soon to ask the homicidal asshole in question about all of that simply because he seemed to delight in laying it all out for me, but that didn't mean I had to like anything about that.

Even if it might be convenient if it turned out I couldn't keep myself fed, sane, and calm with noodles and rice anymore.

Fuck.

It was close to midnight when we finally stopped to crash in a lone house set back from the road, somewhere along the border between North and South Carolina. One advantage my new zombie radar had: no more surprise lurkers in dwellings or close by. The men still took pains to case the joint before they informed me that the air was clear. I would have helped, but my muscles had started locking up, and I definitely felt the discomfort and massively reduced range of motion caused by my freakishly healed injuries. It was a surprisingly large house with at least four bedrooms—plenty of space to separate while still remaining hunkered down together.

Zero surprise that Jared followed me into the room I'd chosen to crash in upstairs. It was obvious that sleep wasn't in my near future, either.

Conflicting emotions threatened to well up inside of me until I noticed what he was carrying—a first-aid kit and disinfectant. Looked like getting physical was about to happen, but not in the way that involved sweat and voluntary moans.

"I presume there's no chance we can postpone this until morning?"

He gave me a curious look. "I figured you'd want to get this over with now so you can be all healed up and ready to go in the morning." An almost cruel twist came to his lips. "Plus, correct me if I'm wrong, but judging from the fact that you're not moving extremely gingerly while suppressing constant sounds of pain, your pain response isn't quite up to par yet. Presuming that your body continues to heal, that might change come morning."

I hadn't even considered that. It freaked me out on some level, but with everything else going on, not howling with agony right now was a bonus.

I had a feeling he was about to test the limits of that, anyway.

"So you're graciously offering to cut the bullets out of me, huh?"

He smiled. It even reached his eyes. That was damn creepy and did little to alleviate my unease.

"You know I'll do a good, thorough job. Like the last several times I've patched you up."

How could I forget? Of course I hadn't. But feeling the downright eagerness coming off him in waves was very different to me now that I knew where it likely stemmed from.

"You did warn me not to want to know how you know what you know how to do," I noted, incapable of keeping a certain level of accusation out of my tone.

Jared put his stuff on a nearby table without responding, likely hiding a smile.

"Get undressed. I'll grab some towels from the bathroom. And then let's see how much I can make you bleed."

Knowing that he was fucking with me did little to staunch the apprehension rising further inside of me. While he was rummaging around, I considered ditching just the most important parts of my clothing, but then I realized I was being stupid. Plus, what could he possibly do to me, big, bad zombie that I was?

Only that I wasn't sure if that descriptor even fit, and I was very much aware that he could inflict so much horror on me, and that wasn't even counting the scalpel he'd left on top of the other things.

So when Jared returned, he found me naked, waiting for him, ready to take the towels, spread them on the faded hardwood floors, and plant my ass on them, my back turned toward him.

I wished I was the praying kind, because this would have been so much easier to deal with asking for deliverance from some deity or other.

Just maybe, gorging myself on Private Unlucky's innards had been a bad idea. My mind had been much more at ease before that.

"Want something to numb the pain beforehand? Not sure that shit still works on you now, but there's half a bottle of painkillers left."

Such a tempting offer… and definitely not one I was going to take. On principle. Because I'd rather suffer through the worst physical pain now than the mental anguish of being weak and pathetic and little more than his pawn.

"Just go for it," I told him.

No surprise, that was all the invitation Jared needed.

Until I flinched violently the moment the scalpel sliced into my flesh. It didn't even hurt that much, but my reaction was a visceral one.

Jared's eyes found mine, and after a silent moment of us staring at each other, he got out a sterile syringe from his med kit and a small bottle of local anesthetic. I tried to watch calmly as he injected it with perfect precision, feeling the area go numb—for all of seconds compared to minutes or even hours, as should have been the case.

He paused again, considering. I was just about to tell him that if he suggested to go for a nerve block next, I'd kill him, but instead, he shrugged off his momentary concern and did exactly what I'd told him.

He went for it.

As all the times before, his motions were sure and precise, limiting both the pain he inflicted and the time spent working on me because he didn't hesitate, flinch, or dawdle. I'd greatly appreciated that before. I still did so now because even though the sensation of pain caused was bearable rather than driving me insane, it was still what it was—damn fucking uncomfortable.

What was way worse was realizing just how excited he got.

Had I been too blind to notice that before? Not that I'd been looking for it because, nakedness aside, it was damn hard for any man to sustain a boner while being knuckles deep in someone's flesh and bones. I suspected he'd been good at hiding it. Now, he no longer cared for that.

Or, knowing Jared, he did it to deliberately antagonize me.

Yeah, that sounded much more plausible.

I tried to keep quiet, but then pain slowly turned to agony, and I did the next best thing to distract myself.

"You really get off on that? Cutting me up? Digging out the bullets from my muscles? Stitching me back together?"

He never stopped what he was doing, but his low chuckle held a world of darkness.

"I like the look of blood," he mused. "Scent, too. Taste, even more, but the risk of infection is too high for that."

The laugh that wrenched itself from my throat wasn't exactly sane.

"Infection for you or me? Because I hate to break it to you, but I doubt there's anything going on in my body that you haven't been exposed to before. Actually, there's a good chance you're right behind me. Say, a week? Or maybe a month?"

He didn't reply to that, and I was surprised that his motions remained deft but gentle. For that taunt, I'd expected at least a harder squeeze or two.

"When did you catch it?" I asked when something suddenly made sense. "This new fucked-up strain of anthrax. That's why you had such an easy time guessing what I could and couldn't do when we first met. You've been through the same."

His chuckle held no surprise, but it certainly sounded delighted.

"Took you long enough to figure that out," he teased. "But, so far, you're the only one who did, so maybe I'm too harsh on you. Yes, I got it. Symptoms not unlike yours, although my lungs weren't that badly affected. Got the worst muscle cramps, though. Way to feel like I finally had to repent for my sins."

That made little sense. He'd been in top physical condition back in Charlotte. Unless…

"You got sick before the rest of us!"

I didn't even know why I exclaimed that. It simply felt like some kind of triumph to me.

He chuckled. "Way before. Some time around mid February. Still not quite sure who the carrier was. I was aware that I'd been running a high risk for catching something eventually that would kill me, but didn't expect that."

It took me a little longer to figure that one out—although he'd been the one to give me the clue. Or clues, rather. Just now, and his proficiency with a blade, plus licking that dead man's blood off my cheek—

"Trophies," I whispered, mostly to myself. "You're taking fucking trophies from your kills." Because my mind refused to utter the word "victim," for whatever reason. Maybe because I didn't want to become the next in a long, long line.

It was also impossible not to see Private Unlucky's savaged gut right in front of my eyes.

Fucking hypocrite.

"Gold star for my star pupil," he jeered—and this time did squeeze a little harder than felt necessary.

The rest of his response was postponed by him digging out the second bullet, this one much more painful than the first. It must have struck the top of my pelvis in the back, because even when it was gone, I felt my very bones aching.

"It's a smart choice, of course," Jared prattled on as he sewed me back up. "And just so we're clear here, I don't mean just a quick lick of blood off the knife I kill them with. I take a piece from each of them. Something that has meaning. Or sometimes just what I'm in the mood for. Not the brain, because the chance of getting prions from that has always been too dicey for me. Inner organs are easiest. Doesn't even require messing up the body much to hide that. I've tried the whole butcher-cuts route once, even frying up a small steak in a pan, but that's just overly complicated. Plus, it leaves so much more to clean up and make sure not to leave DNA evidence, so why bother with that? It's about the symbolism, not some gourmet chef bullshit. And voila, ten hours later it's all digested, two days later the last of it gets shit out, and there's no way for anyone to find anything and pin it on me. Only amateurs leave collections that their wives can stumble upon."

That was without a doubt the most fucked up thing anyone had ever told me and it was a million times made worse by the fact that I could see the cold underlying logic to it.

There was nothing I could have said to that, so I remained mute.

Jared would have none of that, of course.

"If what you told me is true—and I have no reason to doubt you anymore—you have one on me there, actually. Well, two, because I've never seen the sense in chewing off some guy's dick. But eyeball? That's an interesting choice. It kind of irks me that you know how it feels to bite into one and I don't."

I couldn't help but laugh. It definitely came out strained.

"If I could, I'd trade that to you for cheap. Or even give it to you for free." I was tempted to joke that he'd better not think about using one of mine for the experience, but thought better of it. The last thing he needed was a new idea or some encouragement.

His good-natured laugh was creepy as fuck. I was surprised when he simply moved on without trying to freak me out more.

Then again, right now I must have been a seven-course meal for him, anyway. Gluttony didn't become him.

"Just if you missed that detail, I caught the shit two and a half months before the first reported cases. Three months before the general outbreak that almost put an end to your delightful existence."

I hadn't missed that. I'd just gotten sidetracked.

"Does anyone know about that?" An old suspicion came filtering back into my mind. "Is that why you know so much about that shit?

Because you've been working with people who've had time to learn to deal with it?"

He chuckled softly.

"You mean like our favorite homicidal scientists? Sorry to disappoint you, but no. I couldn't exactly go to the next hospital to get treated. Both because of what else they might have found, but mostly because I haven't had insurance in years. Too much surveillance for my liking. I've had one of my contacts run a few blood panels on me, and he found both anthrax bacteria and antibodies against them." He chuckled. "Over time, I've built up an impressive amount of antibodies and resistances against all kinds of shit. You don't really survive constant contact with quite possibly deadly shit in bodily fluids for long unless you do. Mostly drugs, but once in a while, something else, too."

The idea that he got a literal contact high from a drugged victim almost made me laugh. It did explain why he could almost keep up with me... or had, before my change.

The other implications shut me up for good.

Done taping a bandage over the wound, Jared moved to the side. I hesitated before I turned over and stretched out on my back, with him now looming over me. I did my best to give him only a level stare, but of course he saw right through me.

"Do I make you uncomfortable, Callie?" he teased.

"A lot less than you'd probably like," I shot back.

He offered me a disappointed grimace but already, his usual smirk broke through.

"Doesn't really matter. I'm still getting something out of this." He flattened his palm over my ribcage and readied his knife after swabbing half my torso down with antiseptic. "And no. I'm not concerned about contracting anything from you. I highly doubt my saliva contains anything that's not already in your body, but let's not get all my hard work undone by being deliberately stupid."

Wasn't that peachy?

Shifting, I had to work hard to suppress a groan of pain. Whatever kept my pain receptors partly offline was wearing off, and we were nowhere near done. The anesthetic he injected was next to useless, my body absolutely churning through that like nobody's business.

"I'm so sorry I'm raining on your parade," I told him between sharp inhales and winces. "Must be horrible for you, how I'm waltzing all over your daydreams and fantasies."

The only emotion Jared showed until he was done with his current task was the hint of a smile curling his lips up.

"Don't flatter yourself. I'll learn to deal with the unexpected changes. Besides, this isn't half bad." And because he simply couldn't leave it at that, he added, "I can ask one or both of the guys to hold you down, if you prefer not to be alone with me. Or, you know, for moral support."

"Thanks, but no thanks."

Of course he found that funny.

I tried to keep quiet, but that was pretty much impossible, particularly when one of the bullets turned out to be lodged somewhat deeply inside of my lower torso. I could only guess at how much it must have damaged going that far in, but my body seemed to be working just fine... if that was the right term for it.

Talking sure helped keep my mind from spinning off in interesting directions.

"Do you see anything different in there? I mean, how my body reacts to..."

"Being cut open?" Jared grinned. Because of course he did. I would have sighed if I didn't have to grit my teeth to keep from hissing constantly. After a pregnant pause, he took some pity on me and answered. "The fresh cuts, not so much. You still bleed like a stuck pig. You clearly have a pulse. And I have enough time to get the work done and close the wounds up, as they should get closed up before anything weird happens. I'm obviously not a surgeon, but I've had to dig my fair share of bullets out of myself over the years. Yours now all look like you got shot weeks or even months ago, the tissue completely closed and healed around them. If you're not concerned about lead poisoning, I could almost leave them in."

There was a lot about that I could have questioned. I left it at a very weak shake of my head. "No, keep going."

"Your blood coagulates much faster," he observed as he kept working. "That's different. But it was already different when I had to push out those massive blood clots from your leg. In hindsight, that should have given me some pause."

"It didn't?"

He even paused to flash me that grin, his eyes too bright. "Was already hard enough not to get distracted."

That idea made me shudder. All I remembered from that was the massive ick factor of watching all that nasty, dark-red gunk come out of me.

Better not to think too much about that.

Particularly since it made quite a lot of very bloody, recent memories come up in my mind.

"I don't think I died," I mused. When Jared paused to look at my face, I elaborated. "I mean, I don't know for sure. And I do have a hole in my memory from when the headlights of the car blinded me to when I was mid-fight with the Marines, about to kill the first one. But I don't think I died."

Jared shrugged, surprisingly indifferent about that one detail that irked me to no end.

"Does it matter?"

"Ultimately? No. But I'd really like to know." I paused. "Maybe I'll find out when you bite it?"

"Who says I will?"

I couldn't help but smirk. "Eventually, we're all going to die, one way or another."

He chuckled. "Was that your unintentional declaration of wanting to stick it out with me until the bitter end of my life? Could easily be another fifty years or so."

I couldn't help but laugh. That wasn't a good idea, considering the state of my entire torso.

"Oh, please. We'll all be lucky to make it five years, let alone what used to be a normal human lifespan. We probably won't make it through the winter."

If anything, he was amused by that notion.

"I don't think I'll worry about old age just yet."

Silence fell. I absolutely didn't like that.

"You really think you're different from me?" I asked. "You got sick. Then you got better. Then you got shot up with zombie gunk. Same, same, if you ask me."

"Well, there's a difference. I wasn't some mad scientist's guinea pig twice. Or maybe even three times. You that sure the good doctor didn't shoot you up with something while you were having the time of your life, rocking withdrawal, in that cell?"

I was surprised that he knew about the quarantine tent, but then again, I maybe shouldn't have been. Jared had done a phenomenal job hoovering up any and all details he could have possibly found about me anywhere. And he definitely had a point with what had happened in the cell. I didn't have any clearer memories about that than before I'd woken up in a puddle of mud this morning.

"Could be," I admitted. "But wouldn't that have been a reason to keep me locked up somewhere? They were convincingly indifferent about me in general."

His lips quirked up at that. "Doesn't that grate? Being utterly replaceable?"

Another pained chuckle wrenched itself out of me. "Compared to what?" When he simply kept on staring at me, that turned into a full laugh. "Oh, you mean compared to all the attention I'm getting from you? Thanks, but I can do without an obsessive stalker."

Jared grimaced as if that hurt him deeply, but I doubted that was the case.

Thankfully, he went back to cutting. I hadn't expected to ever think along those lines, but yes, that was better than whatever else might come up if we kept going on that tangent.

"You stress the fact a lot that you're a ruthless killer," I finally said, not sure if it was wise to broach that subject. "As in, not a vigilante."

Even studying him closely, I didn't notice even a hint of tension or apprehension in his body language. If anything, his tone was conversational as he replied.

"That's because I don't want to set expectations," Jared offered. "I kill because I want to. Yeah, sure, sometimes it feels like I need to, but I could control that."

"If you wanted to."

"Exactly." He chuckled. "It's a choice of convenience to go after the worst elements of society rather than the easiest, like frail women and innocent children."

"Plus, no challenge there, huh?" I presumed.

He flashed me a grin. "Also true. But I care less about that than you probably assume, seeing as you think I have a gigantic ego. Among other things."

I hated that this made me laugh again, although it had a certain hitch to it. The situation for sure wasn't ideal to have this conversation, seeing as I wasn't just naked, prone right in front of him, but he already had his bloody fingers inside my body cavity.

"So, it's convenient," I prompted when nothing more came from him. That surprised me. I would have expected him to keep gushing, considering how important that topic must have been to him. Apparently, if he couldn't make me cringe or go full dear-in-headlights frozen, he wasn't that interested in talking.

"Sure is. Nobody really tries hard to find out what happened to some asshole gangbanger, provided he's no longer useful for the information he might have. Which is where Axel came in, which you were likely already guessing. A fountain of knowledge, that man with his manila folders. That whole thing with nobody giving a shit doesn't really work if I kill their informant or someone they've been working on for ages."

I realized something else. "Plus, with you masquerading as a bail bondsman, you had all the details you needed, like home addresses and shit."

He nodded without looking up from his work.

"Exactly. And you wouldn't believe what a bad job I often did, getting them to their court dates."

I could imagine.

"How were you able to afford to live like that?"

Now he did glance my way, looking a little disappointed. Maybe it was a stupid question after he'd already divulged that he hadn't had insurance.

"You've been running in crime circles for years. Do I really need to spell out how I got my grubby little hands on enough dough to make rent?"

Good point.

"Drugs and ammo aplenty as well," he went on. "Food and clothes, too. I couldn't really sell much of that, but thankfully, crime still involves good old dollar bills rather than card payments. And I didn't exactly have need of much else."

"Isn't that a kind of empty life?"

Jared snorted. "Because sweating your ass off, working minimum wage to afford frothy lattes and makeup was that rewarding for you? I'll take having the power over someone's life in my literal hands any day over that."

I hated that he kind of had a point—and probably not just for his... tastes.

"Don't knock it until you've tried it," I shot back. That came out way more defensive than intended. "Plus, I got as many lattes free for myself as I wanted."

He grinned. "I still can't believe you thought that was what you wanted out of life. Being a drone—whether as a fast-food worker or data-sheet cruncher. How can you give up on life that young?"

As before, his criticism of what had forever felt like my shot at redemption and a second chance in life still grated.

"Well, maybe that was my one passion in life? You kill people. I hunt down errors in decimal places."

He actually paused to look at me.

"Is it?"

He waited until I responded. It must have been only in my imagination that he was deliberately pressing harder on the pulsing knot of agony low in my abdomen.

"Fuck, no! But that's life, right? That sometimes you have to do shit you don't want to!"

He held my gaze for another second before he went back to work—actually getting the last suture ready.

"Is it? I've never bought into that lie. If you don't have a choice, sure. But condemn yourself to boredom for the rest of your life? Please. That's pathetic."

Not much I could add to that.

Shit, but I hated that I kind of agreed with him.

At least it had been a life with a lot less physical discomfort than I was living with now—and the mental strain had been quite different, too.

I couldn't quite quell a few more hisses and groans as he finished up. Mostly to distract myself, I watched his expression—intent but weirdly passive. I would have expected him to have a harder time hiding his glee at what he inflicted on me, but apparently, that was something he could deliberately switch on and off as well—or simply play-act for my benefit.

I didn't know what came over me, but I just had to ask. "That doing it for you, too? Hurting me?"

Rather than pause now, Jared finished his work, even taking the time to put on one last bandage. My torso now looked like a gruesome patchwork quilt.

"Hurting you doesn't do a thing for me," he finally said, sounding sincere. "Might sound weird, but the sadistic glee I derive from my actions is all centered on the emotional, psychological shit. Do I get a hard-on from scaring the living shit out of you? Definitely. The sheer power of deciding whether someone lives or dies? Pure deliciousness. But it's the same to me whether I do it quick and merciful, or torture someone for hours."

"Except for them going crazy with fear," I harped.

He smiled. Because of course he would. "Except for that."

I tried to get up—both to see how well my body was holding up now but mostly to get out of this position—but Jared wouldn't let me, one hand on my shoulder enough to push me down flat on my back. He leaned over me, crowding me, his intense eyes boring into mine.

This should have made me ten shades of uncomfortable.

While there was some residual discomfort coming from all parts of my body because of the injuries I'd sustained, I remained otherwise relaxed, the resistance in my mind feeling more like token protest than the actual need to get away from him.

I stared back at him, momentarily unsure how to proceed.

A slight smile started to curve his lips up as his eyes never left mine. "That's not a no," he remarked.

I said nothing, just kept on staring back.

His hand slid up the outside of my thigh and over my hip, ignoring the bandage he'd just slapped on there.

A hint of a triumphant smile flitted across his features.

Without stiffening—or even so much as tensing—I easily held his gaze and drawled, "Go fuck yourself, Jared."

His pause was a pregnant one, taking me more seriously than I'd been afraid he would. His hand remained on my bare hip, lingering as if he hadn't quite given up hope yet.

"Why not?" he asked, his self-assured tone remaining smack in place. "Why not let me make you feel good? Let me fuck you? You know I'm good for it."

Did I ever.

I was almost proud of myself for standing up to him.

"Well, I can't exactly claim I have high standards, as my recent choices have yet again proven," I said—and pointedly plucked his paw off me.

Half sitting up as I was, he was still close enough that if he'd exhaled sharply, I would have felt his breath waft over me. That was also close enough for me to easily grab him and launch myself at him.

I could tell that occurred to him—and yet, he made no move to leave my personal space, his eyes remaining zeroed in on mine.

"Fuck standards," he huffed.

"Let's try self-preservation?" I suggested.

His grin split into shit-eating territory—definitely not befitting the situation.

"Yours or mine?"

Excellent question. One I didn't have an answer to, I realized.

"You can't honestly think I'd let you touch me after the stunt you pulled in that alley."

His attention briefly dipped to the—admittedly impressive—stack of bloody gauze strewn all over.

"Isn't it a little late for that sentiment?"

"Sexually," I stressed. "Trust me, the only reason you're here instead of Axel or Blake is because I know you're good at this, and I don't trust Axel not to get all jittery with…" I trailed off, not quite sure how to put that.

Jared had no such qualms. "Yeah, shitting himself over both the risk of infection or what might happen if pain made you snap is truly inconvenient." His beginning smile spread. "One might even go so far as to say you owe me one for the service I just provided."

I couldn't help but snort, quite happy how derisive it came out.

"Really? You're actively telling me I owe you sex for quite possibly giving you the least sexual hard-on of your life?"

That smile flipped into a smirk. "Nothing non-sexual about that."

Didn't need to know that.

Also, that one I'd traipsed right into, eyes open and all that.

I ignored the very real flutter of anxiety finally starting up in the pit of my stomach, and the multitude of superficial, mostly fake embarrassment.

"Looks like you'll have to try harder next time. Now, get out. Unless you want to find out just how immune to my homicidal urges you really are."

I hated how considering his expression got.

Was he seriously going to provoke me just to see who would come out on top? That seemed incessantly foolhardy to me, even more so after he'd watched me completely destroy the Marines… and Private Unlucky.

It was only ten seconds into our staring match that I realized he must have been fucking with me, once more returning to the age-old argument that I'd admittedly flung into his face maybe one too many times for him showing exactly zero inclination ever where forcing me to do anything was concerned.

Damn, but I was fucking tired of this shit.

Maybe I should have argued with him. Scratch that—I absolutely should have. Because that would have been the mature thing to do. The Good Girl Callie thing to do.

Well, fuck her, too.

He must have felt me tense, but he was still too slow when I suddenly bolted up and gave him a hard-enough shove that sent him not just staggering back but right against the table still holding the first-aid paraphernalia. I'd put most, but not all, of my strength behind the motion. It was still enough to send the fragile-looking piece of furniture slamming back and against a cupboard, loud enough in the stillness of the house to raise the dead.

Hopefully not literally, but since my danger radar remained dormant, I figured I was on the safe side.

It sure was enough to make Jared freeze once he caught himself against the cupboard, giving me a calculating rather than baleful look.

Just to be sure, I got ready to follow that up with a punch, if he got any weird ideas.

I realized just how loud that crash must have been when a loud knock sounded on the door.

"Callie? You okay?" Axel's voice came filtering through the thick wood.

A salacious grin spread across Jared's face.

I frowned at him, very much a "don't you dare."

Of course, he ignored me. Why I'd expected anything different, I couldn't say.

"Yeah, I'd say she's doing all right!" he called, hard-pressed to hide a snicker—and infusing the sentence with just enough innuendo to make me groan.

Apparently that was the wrong answer, as became apparent twenty seconds later when the door flew inward as Blake kicked it in, hard enough for it to slam into the adjacent wall.

I had a feeling that nobody in this house had seriously expected for us to get it on tonight after all.

I waited for more of that embarrassment to come filtering through whatever kept my normal thoughts and reactions at bay, but that seemed to be reserved for self-flagellating thoughts only. Blake and Axel found me standing there, almost relaxed, for sure not scurrying for anything to cover myself with, all the bandages and mostly healed bruises in plain sight. And my ass and tits, as Blake's stare made quite obvious—after he'd assessed the distance between Jared and me, and also between me and him, judging I was well outside of where I could reach him before he could ready himself.

Smart man—to a very small point.

If we sank any lower, we could very well start an oil-drilling business.

Axel immediately averted his gaze and lowered his gun, already turning away. Blake kept on staring, even when I continued to make deliberate eye contact with him. It didn't even give him pause when I snarled at him, the sound coming out not entirely human anymore.

"And we'll never know if they came storming in to your rescue… or mine," Jared tittered as he picked up his tools in passing, making for the door. "You know where to find me, should you change your prudish mind."

I stared after Jared until he was out of sight, refusing to acknowledge the flutter of disappointment deep inside of me.

Just how low could I sink?

Tonight wasn't the night to answer that, I decided.

Axel muttered something apologetic under his breath as he pulled Blake out of the room, then had to duck back in once again to grab the door and pull it closed behind him.

I stared at the closed door for another second, then glanced at my discarded clothes and the bed. Most of them were dirty again, soaked with sweat, blood, and lymph. My instincts screamed to ignore them; to stretch out on the soft sheets naked instead and relish the sensation of freedom.

If anything, the men barging in was a good reminder that, unless I wanted to risk running around again buck-ass naked, I should probably put my clothes on.

Sighing loudly, I did what was smart over what felt good, telling myself this was all about getting dressed, and not at all about me rebuking Jared's… suggestion didn't quite seem to cut it. Even more so since I had no fucking clue exactly what he'd been offering.

Fuck.

Sleep was a long time coming, but at least stretching out on the bed and not moving for a while felt good. The actual sensation of feeling my flesh knit itself together, turning sutured cuts into red scars and then almost unblemished, barely marred pinkish skin was... disconcerting, but also comforting.

And yes, I checked on one bandage after the other, peeling them off once the skin was completely closed, the adhesive still way too fresh for my own good.

I would get to fight another day.

Right now, that was the only thing that mattered.

CHAPTER 6

I didn't sleep at all that night.

Not because of pain or stiffness, all but the very last, vague twinges of discomfort gone. Also, no guilt or worry, exactly. That was thankfully also still mostly suppressed. But my mind wouldn't shut up. I tried lying in bed for a good three hours before I gave up, my body feeling the intense need to move. It was still dark outside, so I grabbed a flashlight and went downstairs to go rummaging through all the cabinets I could find. Knowing that no lurkers were about to sneak up on us was very convenient, but I tried to keep my use of light to a minimum.

Not all bipedal potential attackers were zombies, after all, and now that I'd had time to think about it, most of the second group of Marines that had sprung the trap on us hadn't been on my radar. Which made sense, if their leader had the same ability as I did and could consequently pick his men and women for optimal stealth.

I tried to remember if he'd been part of the attack at all, or even better, if I'd gotten a chance to kill him, but my memories were too sketchy for that. Once my mind had flipped, it was all snapshot impressions, analysis pretty much impossible.

While I went through random packs of food, I started munching on them without much thought. It was only when Jared joined me an hour later that I realized I'd chowed down every single bite of food except for the soaking rice and pasta set aside for breakfast.

Jared gave the heap of wrappers and empty cans I'd mindlessly thrown in the sink one slightly disturbed look, but otherwise ignored it.

Of course he would, after his offer of… trail rations for me.

"I presume the hunger is back?"

I gave that some thought as I chewed the last mouthful of beans.

"Not as bad as when I woke up yesterday, or even when I got to the town. But I could definitely eat something."

Jared pointedly stared at the mess in the sink before he turned back to me.

If he was going to offer up a special protein source now, I was ready to scream.

Surprisingly, he went a completely different way.

"Have you taken a dump already?"

That wasn't a question I'd expected, nor one I particularly appreciated.

"None of your business," I harped. "But since the town? No."

"Let me know how that goes when you do."

I just stared at him. "Why?"

He shrugged. "In part morbid curiosity about how what you've eaten comes out the other end. But there's a very easy explanation for why you keep stuffing your face like that without it making much of a dent in your feeling of satiety."

"And what is that, pray tell?"

His grin had a nasty edge to it. Already, I knew I wouldn't like the answer.

"There's a chance your body can't digest any of this starchy vegetable shit anymore. And you know what that means for your meal plan."

I didn't like the implications—or why he was grinning like that.

"We've literally seen them eat each other. Do you really think their digestive system makes that much of a difference?"

"Humans—dead or alive—are still animals. Let me know before your cravings to take a literal bite out of me become uncontrollable."

Maybe that explained why he was abstaining from blowjob jokes?

Nah. That couldn't be it.

I ignored him in favor of pouring myself some of the black coffee that we'd kept soaking overnight. It was still too weak for my liking, but this morning even the strongest espresso might not have cut it. Not that I was tired. Just not... as alert as I'd been the previous evening.

I so didn't like the implications of that.

Axel and Blake joined us soon after, the sky still only barely lightening. Fall was in full swing now, at least where the length of day was concerned. The leaves were only just starting to turn for real, but up in the mountains, the first snow wasn't that far away anymore, I guessed.

Axel avoided looking my way like the plague, but Blake had no such qualms. When I ignored his salacious grin—as usual—he turned to Jared, who was listlessly poking at the noodles.

"Just so we're sure I didn't misread the room last night—you were absolutely trying to tap that!"

Jared flashed him a grin around his own coffee mug that was more appropriate to showing enthusiasm about normal hobbies... like car racing, or playing golf.

"Pains me to admit it, but you're a braver man than I am," Blake went on. "After what she told us about the eyeball and shit, I wouldn't have dared—"

He cut off when the can I threw at him hit the side of his arm.

After scooping up the spoils from the floor, Blake gave me a bright grin that I equally ignored, but at least that had shut him up.

Jared chuckled. "What do they say? You only live once."

"Yeah, but how much fun is that when she chews off your dick when she's jonesing for a snack?" Blake wanted to know.

There was no winning with these two.

That we hadn't actually had sex seemed to make no difference.

At least I was wearing clothes now, even if they felt restrictive as hell.

Sadly, the entire situation was my own fault, and I didn't even have Axel to silently commiserate with.

"I wouldn't have thought it possible, but somehow, me turning into a half zombie has completely trashed our high level of conversation," I complained.

"You sure about that?"

Blake's question made me raise my eyebrows at him.

"The finesse we trade words with?"

He rolled his eyes at me. "You being half a zombie. Because you look mighty alive, particularly last night."

He kind of had a point. Twice in one day, I'd given him a great chance to ascertain that my body was showing zero signs of decomposition.

"I'm still the same person, if you mean that," I pointed out. "And my body functions about the same. Only that my circadian rhythm is all fucked up, I feel maybe a tenth of the pain I should, I have a really unhealthily strong appetite, oh, and then there's that small detail of me absolutely losing it and turning into a flesh-eating monster. But all systems nominal except for that."

A hint of annoyance ghosted across Blake's face. "I meant, when have we ever seen them rutting around in the muck? Correct me if I'm wrong, but you didn't kick him out because you didn't want to ride his dick into oblivion. You're just sore because of the games he was playing with you."

"That's one way of putting it," I muttered, sending Jared the appropriate, much warranted glare—that he, of course, ignored.

"My point is, if anything makes you human, it's that. And don't we all go a little berserk sometimes?"

"No, we don't," I shot back. "And who, how, why, or if I fuck is still none of your business."

Blake grinned. "Hey, we weren't sure if you were fucking or trying to kill each other. The sounds could have meant either. Axel was so very concerned about your well-being that it was a given that I had to lend a hand—"

"I'm sure your concern for him and me were the only reasons you busted down that door," I said.

"Swear on my mother's grave. I had no ill intentions."

I shook my head and drank my coffee since no good could come of that, anyway.

"You sure she was sober? When she made that lunge for you." Blake turned to Jared next. "Because I've had to deal with my fair share of assholes high on meth, and all of them were behaving like super-strong lunatics. Just because she says that she lost her mind doesn't mean she's turning into one of the undead."

I couldn't help but cackle. "Don't you think I know the difference?"

I got a deadpan stare back. "Callie, you're an addict. You're the opposite of trustworthy or reliable."

That stung.

Also, because it was true.

Doubly so, since Jared had expertly used that against me.

"And where would I have gotten any meth from? My pack stayed with you when I jumped out of the car. I lost everything except my sneakers—and no, I didn't hide some spare pills in there for bad times. Besides, I can cook my own shit. I'm not stupid enough to take anyone else's."

Except for that one time at the power plant, and I was still regretting that, now more than ever.

Blake shook my reasoning off like droplets of water.

"Could be that those four Marines drugged you. Make you compliant, or just a little crazy? Some assholes are into that."

I did not need to see the sidelong glance he cast in Jared's direction.

I was ready to cast his reasoning off, but then paused. Could that have happened? Not necessarily meth—because I sure knew how that felt to the point of overdose, and that didn't fit with my memory flashes. But there were a lot of other drugs out there that messed with your mind—including some that completely wiped your short-term memory.

"Not saying that's it, but it would explain why I felt more and more like myself as my body had time to break down whatever chemicals were messing with my brain," I mused. "Still doesn't explain why I'm hungry now, and that pasta looks as enticing to me as cardboard."

Blake guffawed. "Because it also doesn't taste much better." He seemed to wait for someone to laugh at his joke. Everyone remained silent, not just Axel, who seemed to refuse to participate in us shooting the shit at all today.

"It's not the wildest theory out there," Jared finally said, sounding way too sincere.

"You can't be serious."

He shrugged off my dismissal.

"Might be worth investigating."

Was he for real?

No, that couldn't be. It made way more sense that he was punishing me for rejecting him.

Yes, that made a lot more sense—but didn't help me right now.

I shook my head. "I'm not going on a week-long bender with you just for 'science.'" I added the air quotes with my fingers.

Jared grimaced, as if he was truly disappointed. Maybe he even was.

"Then only you take the drugs. We wait and see what happens."

"Not going to happen," I insisted.

"Why not? Aren't you the least bit curious?"

I shook my head.

"Nope. Since we can't run a blood test on what potentially used to be in my bloodstream yesterday, I'm not."

Jared wasn't ready to drop it yet. "I'm sure there are still places where they can do that."

"Sure. We've been in one of them. I, for sure, am not going back there."

He made a face as if to protest, but then shrugged.

"Fine. You do you. But Blake's right. That's a hell of a lot more likely than your theory."

All I could do was to stare at him. Was this his idea of punishing me for that rejection?

"Excuse me? Do you think I want to turn into a flesh-eating monster? Do you have any idea how disgusting that is?"

He shrugged. "You looked quite eager when I cut up that Marine for you yesterday."

"Yes! Because my mind was running in zombie mode!"

"Or because whatever drugs they gave you were still in your system, and the adrenaline shock from the car going flying in the ambush got them to kick in one more time."

That was simply ludicrous.

"If anything, adrenaline is a great antagonist of a hell of a lot of drugs. That's why that entire family of chemicals is the shit they inject you with when you overdose or have a heart attack. It's a reset. Not an amplifier."

They both just stared at me. Axel got himself some coffee, still ignoring the entire lot of us.

"This is fucking insane!" I cried, ready to go full-on drama queen and throw my hands up, but my mug of coffee prevented me from such antics. "You all saw what I did to those Marines! How can you justify that with… with… fucking drugs!"

More staring, until finally, Axel decided to join the conversation.

"It's not been that long since you tried your very best to beat Jared to a bloody pulp," he remarked between gulps. "Even you have to admit, your recent behavior's not that different."

All I could do was stare at him.

"But I didn't try to fucking eat him!"

Blake snickered. Because he would. Both Jared and Axel looked less than impressed by my arguing.

Had they all collectively gone insane? Although it stood to reason that I should have counted myself among that as well, considering my recent changes in dietary habits…

I just couldn't let this go. Hard as it was to accept, I could swallow the bitter pill that was Jared's… everything, particularly if I had no other choice. But this? This was one step too far.

"How the fuck can you just accept me eating people?!"

Jared gave me a lazy smile. "Do you really want an answer from me on that topic?"

"Oh, shut the fuck up."

Surprisingly, he did.

Blake shook his head, chuckling, indicating that I wouldn't get any better from him. "First thing you did after returning to us was let him cut you up. I don't think that your most illogical action was turning full-on cannibal, if you're really that opposed to his urges as you pretend you are."

This was getting better and better.

"Excuse me if I was being rational about my injuries," I ground out.

Blake gave me a level stare. "Were you? I'd call that the actions of a psycho groupie."

On some level, I realized I'd brought most of this on myself because I hadn't shut up before, but them ganging up on me really didn't help. So I turned to Axel, usually my saving grace.

"Anything you got to say to that?"

He kept nursing his coffee as he must have planned his answer carefully. Never a good sign.

"Your behavior does reek of a psychotic break," he finally offered. "We all know you're damn resilient—and that's me saying this, fully knowing that you've only shared maybe a tenth of what you've had to live through. Everyone reaches their breaking point, eventually. It really pains me to say this, but I'm with Blake in this. Drugs make the most sense. You have proven—repeatedly—in the past that you don't get all mellow and giggly when you're high. Could your theory be true? Yes, but it's a hell of a lot more unlikely than that the assholes drugged you and raped you, which made something in your mind break for good, and you're right now running on some kind of… contingency program. That you feel more like yourself now, well. It's a shitty saying, but time heals all wounds. Clearly, your mind knows how to make you deal with shit and move on in record time."

I couldn't help but stare at him, having to work hard to keep my mouth from hanging open. What was even worse was the fact that listening to him made doubt creep up my spine. Jared, I could ignore easily right now since I was pretty sure he'd say the sky was green just to antagonize me. Blake thrived on fucked-up comebacks and wasn't much better. But Axel?

In the end, all I could say was a haughty, "Well, excuse me, but I know what it feels like to wake up the day after, and let me tell you, my body is functioning way different from that."

Axel shrugged, even looking a hint apologetic.

"We all know you have that weirdly accelerated wound healing going on. Add a day of that—"

I shook my head vehemently, annoyed.

Axel narrowed his eyes. Clearly, my stubbornness was rubbing him the wrong way.

"Are you still sore or tender from last night? Because whatever you two got into while he patched you up sounded like you were throwing furniture at each other—which wasn't that far off, as Blake and I sadly got to verify."

"Not sad about that in the least," Blake threw in.

All of us ignored him.

I couldn't help but feel heat creep into my cheeks, and not all of that was anger.

"As I said—"

"Nobody gives a shit about what you two get up to," Axel interjected before I could launch into my next tirade. "I'm afraid that even includes killing sprees, because that was exactly what that clearing looked like where we found you after the ambush. Feel free to think less of me, but I have decades under my belt of watching garbage people never getting their comeuppance. Those Marines likely didn't deserve that kind of end, but that's what you get when you go after the wrong kind of people. I know you don't want to accept that, but there's a good chance that you fully belong in that category. You can sure hold your own."

How was that for a backhanded compliment?

I would have loved to argue with all three of them for hours, but even I could see when I had lost. That pill was damn hard to swallow, almost worse than any of the others the universe had rammed down my throat since I'd gone on that fated cream-cheese-bagel run.

It wasn't even because, clearly, I was right, and these idiots were wrong.

No.

It meant I had to take responsibility for my actions, and I knew that once I accepted that, a tsunami of guilt would sooner or later break over me and sweep me away for good.

Sure, they had attacked me, but what exactly did someone have to do to warrant being bludgeoned to death, have their throat ripped out, and then their inner organs torn out and eaten?

I absolutely loathed to admit it, but maybe Axel had a point.

Jared's smile was insufferable as he took the coffee mug from my hand to refill it. Thankfully, he knew better than to say something, or things would have gotten physical.

And considering what Axel had said, there was now niggling doubt in the back of my head that made me wonder—had I inadvertently made myself into Jared's perfect match? All feminist, independent-woman grandstanding aside, I knew I had a certain... urge to conform to expectations. That was one of the reasons why I'd latched on to the girls like a barnacle—to surround myself with an air of purpose and career-minded striving, no frat parties and binge drinking allowed.

I quickly abandoned that train of thought before the usual wave of grief could come crashing through me.

A barrage of assault-rifle shots tearing through the kitchen made that remarkably easy.

CHAPTER 7

My body hit the floor before my brain fully computed what the fuck was going on. Miraculously uninjured, except for chunks of ceramic shards raining down on my head and back from where more bullets chewed through the entire faux-vintage mug collection. Axel lay right next to me, looking equally fine. Blake and Jared I couldn't see with the kitchen island inconveniently between us, but since nobody was screaming, I figured they hadn't been wounded too badly.

Of course they could have been dead as well, but I didn't think I'd get so lucky any time soon.

Who the fuck was stupid enough to sneak up on someone and then missed every single person present in the cramped kitchen?

The shots stopped for a second, making thinking infinitesimally easier, although with my head exploding with pain from my tortured ears, that wasn't a small feat. I waited for more shots to come, but either the shooter lay in wait now, or had run out of bullets. Judging from how they'd acted so far, I figured it was the latter.

Time to get moving!

Ignoring the chunks of ceramic that cut into my palms and knees, I scrambled under the nearby table and on toward the wall, silently praying that the seconds of exposed scrambling wouldn't get my entire body chewed up with yet more bullets. My guess was that the shooter was standing outside that very wall, so I was hopefully out of his field of vision now.

There, I halted, trying to make sense of my scattered thoughts.

I had no fucking clue where any of our weapons were. Clear as my thoughts might have been last night—at least compared to the morning before—but I'd been far too focused on getting patched up and what to do with Jared... or not. Either none of the three idiots had noticed my lapse in judgment, or they plain didn't care. In Jared's case, I'd even go as far as to say he'd deliberately "forgotten" to drop off a carbine for me nearby to force me to flip back into savage mode.

It took that thought for me to realize—and wonder—why I was even capable of coherent thought right now and wasn't already tearing through the flimsy windscreen of the door on my way to jumping our assailant. Or assailants, rather, my mind noticed belatedly, since the shots had come from two directions.

I felt nothing on my danger radar, but that didn't have to mean much. Or that had also just been a figment of my imagination, my scrambled thoughts drawing random connections based on clues my intellect had been too slow to make first.

Now was not the time to consider that.

Movement across the room drew my attention. In the gloom left by the flashlight that we'd been using before that had ended up behind the kitchen counter, I saw a tall, substantial figure stepping through the door into the room—a man in body armor, the barrel of his assault rifle sweeping this way and that. He looked capable, but not as coordinated as the Marines had been.

Or maybe that was simply wishful thinking.

Before I got more than a fleeting impression of him, Blake was suddenly there, barreling into him, both men going down in a tangle of limbs.

Using the immediate distraction, I reared up and sprinted for the door, somehow managing not to slip on the shards that were everywhere or stumble over the wrestling men on the floor.

Early morning cool greeted me, cold on my bare arms since I'd not just forgotten all about weapons but hadn't donned a jacket yet, either. Rather than look for more assailants, I dove for the bushes next to the driveway, hitting the high grass as soon as I felt the ground under my sneakers turn from gravel to earth.

I paused there for a moment, trying to orient myself and listen, but my ears were still ringing, making both attempts futile. So I blindly turned to my left and started crawling in what I hoped was a circle back toward the house.

Was I tempted to simply run off, hide, and leave this shitshow behind?

Yes, but these fuckers had shot at us, and the maddening anger rising inside of me was far stronger than my fear or sense of self-preservation.

After all, who could fault me for getting cannibalistically homicidal when they had attacked us first?

I was surprised to still be capable of coordinated thinking by the time I reached the gravel path again, around the corner from the kitchen toward the den. As I slowed and watched, two more figures slipped into the house via the porch door the first guy had entered through—and I had come outside. It was too dark to see what weapons they were carrying exactly, but they looked at least semi competent, going single-file. Both were tall and bulky—more men, what a surprise.

I was really getting damn tired of being the smallest, slightest player in the game.

No sounds came from inside—at least that I could tell. I waited another moment, but with my pulse still increasing and my body getting ready for a fight, it was hard to lie still. I considered the windows, but I at least hoped the guys had closed them last night, making sure that no zombies could sneak in on us again. Now that, of course, felt like a huge oversight.

Although I was closer to the back entrance, I decided to make my way around to the front. But then I paused. These idiots hadn't kept a lookout for when I'd escaped. It made sense they kept to that. So chances were good that the kitchen was unguarded now.

Gritting my teeth, I realized I should have simply stayed put and could have spared myself some cuts and scrapes.

Just as I rose from the grass, I noticed another hulking shape in the dark, toward the front of the house.

Not a man, but a car. Not ours, because that was halfway down the driveway, left there for a quick exit.

Had we actually been deaf enough to miss them literally driving up right to the house?

Or maybe they had done that after the initial assault, and I'd already been too deaf to hear it. Yeah, that made a lot more sense. Sneaky, coordinated bastards! But then why the bungled drop on us?

I had other things to consider, so I pushed those thoughts out of my mind as I sneaked off toward the car.

I'd expected some kind of assault vehicle, or at least an SUV. Instead, it was a van—large enough for five people, with maybe two more cramped into the back. The doors stood open, leaving me free access to the interior—which included a heap of food wrappers and not much else. No rack full of weapons, or even a pack with spare magazines. That left me with just my trusty knife—which, come to think of it, was more useful, anyway.

How the fuck had I forgotten that I had a five-inch-long knife in my front pocket?

Maybe Jared was right, and I really had to lay off the carb-rich food.

I considered hot-wiring the car and sending it away from the house as a distraction, but that sounded like a needless waste of time. Also, who knew what vehicle might be more useful going forward? Maybe we could trade the van—because the driveways and roads of this country totally weren't well stocked with plenty of vehicles that nobody would ever use again.

A noise coming from inside the house drew my attention, making my idle thoughts grind to a merciful halt as instinct took over.

Without much ado, I made a beeline for the entrance. Sure, we'd barricaded that locked door—but that didn't mean that was still the case.

Even from the corner of the house, I saw that someone had left the door agape—and from the lack of debris, I figured whoever had snuck in elsewhere must have removed the cupboard and chair we'd used to keep it shut.

In hindsight, that had been very much a cartoon-style barrier, but then we'd intended it to keep the undead out. Not people who absolutely knew how to still operate door handles.

The entryway was empty—except for the discarded furniture, almost returned to where we'd found it last night. No debris or dead bodies in sight—moving or on the ground. The crash that I'd heard must have been a substantial one since my ears were still ringing and my balance was slightly off from the aftereffects of the sonic assault.

I felt kind of stupid as I inched forward so I could see into the adjoining rooms, knife in hand but held against my thigh as not to give away the one single advantage I had. Thoughts skittered across my mind about bringing a knife to a gunfight, but if someone happened to be standing stupidly close to one of these doors with their backs turned to me…

Alas, it wasn't so, but my disappointment was minimal. The den was still empty, and at the other end, I could just catch a glimpse of the kitchen, once more vacated from what I could tell but definitely no longer almost pristine. The other room was some kind of library-slash-office, equally abandoned.

I considered hiding in the office for a second, but then decided to check deeper into the house before going upstairs.

I found a body at the bottom of the stairs, the telltale metallic scent of blood heavy in the air letting me know the origin of the puddle still spreading around its head and upper torso. The man was still clutching his rifle in one hand, the sling partially tangled around his neck.

I wondered for a second if I should liberate him of the weapon. It seemed like the obvious choice. Then again, our assailants were easily identifiable by carrying weapons, and I had a good idea who'd literally sliced his throat from ear to ear. Best not to make myself even more of a target than I already was.

But I did slice through that sling and pulled the weapon aside to drop it in the office chair in the next room over. Always best to have a backup solution.

I was just about to step back out of the office when another succession of bangs and thuds came from the hallway, very much a repetition of what had drawn me into the house. When I cautiously glanced outside, I found a second body crumpled on top of the first, still twitching but equally bleeding out all over the terracotta tiles.

Glancing up the stairs, I of course couldn't see Jared smirking down at me since the stairs went around a bend and he wasn't stupid enough to keep himself that exposed, but I had a feeling he was the source of the falling bodies dropping down on me.

A scuffing sound coming from somewhere off to the left—from the den or kitchen—made me duck back into the office, my back pressed against the shelf right next to the door. As I held my breath and listened, I realized I was actually hearing someone move out there again, so at least some of my ear damage must have repaired itself.

Neat!

Not so neat was the low exclamation of a curse that followed, coming from directly outside my door. It sounded very much like it came from a tall, buff guy hellbent on killing me.

The smart thing would have been to remain inside the office. Maybe even to duck under the heavy mahogany desk and find refuge there.

Instead, I quickly chanced a glance around the doorjamb, found the huge, hulking man bent over the two bodies at the bottom of the stairs, and lunged before I could think better of it.

Maybe I wasn't as ruthless or skilled a killer as Jared, but I very much excelled at sneaking up the required five paces and sending my knife into the behemoth's neck, adding a few quick, hard jerking motions at the end for maximum damage.

What didn't work quite that well was that he, of course, wasn't dead immediately; just dying as he quickly bled out, the giant hole in his neck spurting blood everywhere. With one hand, he tried to clutch at the gaping wound, but the other hand was outstretched as he wheeled toward me, throwing one hell of a punch my way.

I barely managed to duck away underneath his fist, but that motion made me too slow to evade his entire body coming crashing down on me, burying me underneath his bulk.

He died with a pained death rattle while his blood sprayed, then soaked me, my feeble attempt to kick him off me for naught.

That was one unfortunate position to find myself in.

And not just because the overwhelming scent of blood really made my mouth water.

Way too late, a wave of disgust slammed into me, giving me that strength and tenacity to first wriggle, then scramble out from underneath the fresh corpse. Not my finest work, I had to admit, as my back slammed into the wall where my mad dash ended, the jarring impact at least punching some sense into me.

That had not been silent or stealthy.

With my pulse still thundering in my ears, I did the next best thing I could think of—I threw myself into the den and onto the black mass of shadows that was the sofa wrapped around the nearby corner. Momentum made me end up on the ground, anyway, painfully but efficiently moving my body out of sight. In all that, I managed to both hold on to the knife and not slice myself up with it somehow.

I didn't have to wait long. A scant five seconds later, I saw a shadow move into the hallway, halting when he saw the bodies.

My lungs screamed for air, but I forced myself to hold my breath, listening intently.

A groaning sound came from somewhere behind me—the kitchen, and it sounded more like floor boards rather than a human making that sound.

I ignored it, my attention remaining on what little I could see of the hallway—mostly the shadows on the ceiling, and in the dim morning light, that wasn't much. But I could hear fabric rustling, as if someone was checking on the bodies.

Should I do something incredibly stupid and sneak back into the hallway to try to get a drop on the investigator? It had worked once. Why not try it a second time?

While I was still debating that, something came zooming past me in exactly that direction.

I had a moment to think to myself, damn, who was faster than me?

Then a soul-piercing scream went up, only to quickly disappear in a gurgling whimper, followed by the unmistakable sounds of... feeding.

Irritation more than fear skipped across my mind. This couldn't be it, right? My danger radar was still completely empty. And yet, that sounded a lot like a zombie feasting.

It actually took me crawling to the end of the sofa closest to the door for me to catch a note of decay over the still-cloying scent of blood that came not just from the two—now three—bodies on the ground but from all over myself.

Right. The downsides of getting drenched in blood.

The fact that I felt irritation more than fear let me know I still wasn't back in normal mental territory.

Since I was already there, I inched forward to get visual confirmation of what my other senses had gathered. Yes, there was a single, somewhat substantial, definitely aggressive zombie having a field day, tearing a fourth body limb from limb, even more blood spurting everywhere.

Following a hunch more than lucid thought, I turned my head back toward the kitchen.

Bingo. Three lurkers were crowded there, holding back, but twitchy with agitation. My guess was that their pack leader didn't tolerate company while feeding, so they'd learned to hang back and wait.

Taking my clue from them, I climbed onto the sofa and slid toward the window behind it instead of trying to inch my way through the door and alongside the corridor wall where I was one swipe of monstrous claws away from death, or at least serious injury.

The window opened without any issues and nary a sound, letting me escape into the morning air, mostly unscathed.

My brief excursion inside had been long enough for daylight to turn from murky to letting me see sharp detail. My sense of smell was still useless since the blood continued to overpower everything, but hunched down below the window, I didn't need it to make sense of the rustling happening in the long grass all over.

A lot of rustling.

I wasted a moment on considering whether I could somehow scale the side of the house.

Then I was sprinting across the lawn, throwing myself at the driver's side door of the van before anything could tackle and take me down.

From the corner of my eye, I saw three shapes converge on the door just as I threw it shut behind me, feeling safe for a second as it closed with a satisfying thud.

Then I realized that the sliding doors in the back were still wide open, making this a very inefficient hiding place.

Fuck.

As I thought that, several bodies slammed against my door. It took them less than five seconds to slide alongside the car and come inside the van—which gave me equal time to slam my fist into the horn of the car, and scramble out the other side of the vehicle.

Sprinting around the corner of the house, elation slammed into me when I realized I made it—only to be met by two men with assault rifles coming around the other corner, looking spooked as hell.

We had a moment of staring stupidly at each other.

They were about to shoot as I threw myself through the front door back into gore central, deciding to chance the possible ire of the pack leader over the guaranteed deadliness of the bullets making my head explode.

The zombie sure looked displeased as he saw me come careening into his territory, but rather than antagonize him, I skipped into the office, going for the chair and the carbine I'd left there. I had just enough time to slide onto the floor on my back, clutching the weapon more or less as I was supposed to and aim it at the open door as the men came barreling into the hallway, their surprised shouts giving me a good sense of their location.

I halted with my finger half pressing the trigger, that fraction of an inch away from pulling it completely.

The zombie came flying past the door, completely ignoring me in favor of the fresh meat right in front of his face. Shots rang out, but far fewer than would have been necessary to stop him for good.

I gave myself another five racing pants with my carbine still training at the door at torso level. Then I scrambled to my feet, trying to keep the weapon steady as I fumbled through the motions, pain pulsing in my ears from the repeat offense of the shots.

I was once more mostly deaf, but that the zombie was feeding was unmistakable. I even saw a few chunks of… some limb or other come flying past the door, toward the other bodies.

Waiting until my breathing had slowed down a little more was taking forever, but was probably closer to a minute.

When still nothing had come tearing into the office, I slowly crept toward the door. Yes, it would have been smarter to try the window exit again, but this time I figured the hallway was the better option since it held more distraction.

As I got close to the door, I could finally hear the zombie tearing into his meal, sounding very industrious about it. Down the hall, I could just make out what remained of the guy I'd killed, currently getting gnawed on by the entourage. Keeping my motions as slow as my nerves could make them—and the rage boiling in my gut would let me—I inched toward the door.

The leader was close, but since his assault had forced the two assholes with guns back against the wall right next to the entrance door, that gave me a leeway of seven feet. I paused for a moment to watch all that tasty, tasty meat go to waste before I forced myself to step out into the hallway with my back pressed against the wall.

The three lurkers had become five by now, but all they did was watch me as they munched on the leftovers. Since that was a full four grown men while their leader savaged two more, there was plenty to keep them occupied for a long, long time. For sure longer than it took me to squeeze past them and make it toward the stairs.

I could have ducked through either of the two doors there, but since they looked like a bathroom and a closet, I instead took my chances and continued up the stairs, trying to make as little sound as possible. The rifle I kept in a secure grip against better judgment, praying that Jared would take a moment to consider my smaller size before he accidentally offed me.

I needn't have worried.

I found him crouching near the top of the stairs where he could see both sections of the staircase, including the last third of the hallway, watching my slow progress up with a hint of his usual smirk on his face. I gave him a silent, baleful glare back for that but kept my attention on what was going on behind me, assuming that the upper level was secure if he dared stay hunkered down half in the open.

That guess confirmed itself when Blake leaned out of the door opposite where Jared was crouching, silently holding out a meaty hand for the carbine.

I gave it up without a comment, happy to be rid of that thing if it meant someone else could use it more efficiently to save my hide.

His grip slipped on the blood my hands had left for a second, making Blake grimace and wipe his hand on his pants before taking professional command of the weapon.

Before I could ask where Axel was, the man in question gestured at me from behind Blake.

Ignoring him, I stepped around Jared instead, hunkering down in the hallway where I wasn't confined to a room but could bolt into any which direction.

And thus we listened—and partly watched—as the zombies continued to feed as the first rays of the morning sun streamed through the windows of one side of the house.

I had to fight the impulse to lick my lips or suck the congealing blood off my hands as I battled the need to hurl myself down the stairs and put that pretender in his place for a good hour. Axel finally put a stop to the first part, at least, when he squeezed past me and returned armed with a pack of wet wipes that he pointedly held out to me until I took the first.

The stench of camomile was absolutely repulsive compared to the sweet, sweet scent of blood, but I forced myself to go through the motions of pretending like it wasn't the wipes that made me gag and want to retch.

Drugs, my ass!

Blake and Jared could continue to cling to their neat little theory all they wanted. I knew what I knew—and that was damn well obvious.

An endless time later, Jared finally got up from his crouch so he could make a quick tour through the upstairs rooms to check through the windows if he could see anything else lurking downstairs. When he came back, he reported in hushed tones that there were a handful of zombies busy by the van, but most of the others must have found their way into the gory hallway below, intent on feasting or dragging away what they could. No sign of any further assailants. If we were smart and crawled out of the house through one of the windows in the back, we could likely avoid drawing attention.

Blake seemed absolutely heartbroken that all he had to show for surviving the ambush was my carbine with its half-full magazine, but he didn't even suggest trying to salvage anything from downstairs.

Before we left, I grabbed yet another change of fresh clothes, peeled off the last of the crusty bandages to reveal virtually unblemished skin, and then we beat it, quite happy to still be alive, if a lot more confused than the day before.

CHAPTER 8

We ended up taking our car, simply because it was easier to get to—and because we trusted it wasn't bugged. Mostly.

"That was an interesting experience," Jared surmised maybe five miles down the road, going almost annoyingly slow today. He didn't exactly look spooked, but his usual cockiness was toned down to a bearable level.

I knew this could only be a matter of a brief time, but that didn't mean I couldn't revel in it at least a little.

Or I would have, if the scent of blood that still clung to me hadn't been too distracting.

"That's one way of putting it," I offered when he was waiting for something. Since the peanut gallery in the back kept silent, it seemed to fall to me to amuse him.

Why didn't that surprise me?

Jared sent me a sidelong glance as he briefly halted at an intersection, choosing the smaller road, far less traveled.

"One thing is for sure," he drawled. "Your danger radar—if it ever existed—is worth shit."

I shrugged, not quite having anything to say to oppose that.

"It seemed to be working well yesterday," I finally offered, far less confrontational than he seemed to have expected. "Not sure what happened between then and this morning." I sent him a sweet smile that he ignored. "Maybe it was all in my head after all."

Blake's low chuckle made me suspect he had changed his mind about that point.

Jared gave me the side eye.

"You are aware that your hair is still completely drenched in blood? And that cleanup job you attempted is a pretty botched one."

I couldn't help but grin, even if the macabre reality of the situation wasn't lost on me.

"Do you like it?" I cooed. "I've been thinking about dying it for a while now. That basic bitch balayage blonde is just too… nice for this world."

Jared's chuckle was very close to a guffaw.

"I say that's exactly why you should keep it. It sure makes for one hell of a surprise when they find out you're more than a young, blonde bimbo."

My smile grew.

"Like you found out?"

He didn't slow down, but took the time to catch my gaze before he replied.

"Darling, I saw the darkness lurking in you from miles away. Why do you think I ever bothered investing any time in getting to know you?"

"Oh, that's what you did when you sent me to my certain death several times over?"

Jared let a derisive snort be his only answer.

With annoyance, I realized I wasn't ready to drop the point yet. Apparently, our little chit-chat over digging out bullets hadn't been enough for me after all.

"You came after me because you thought I was the perfect victim. Nothing more, nothing less."

He smirked. My, that was one loaded smirk. Too bad my fear center was still offline, or that would have made for one uncomfortable moment. He glanced my way, a little disappointed that all I did was stare back.

At least that gave him the opportunity for the perfect delivery, I realized way too late.

"Trust me. Those never last very long. Sure, that was my surface motivation—but I'm starting to realize just how lucky I am that I was wrong."

I honestly didn't know what to say to that, so instead, I stared out into the landscape zooming by, frustrated that I didn't get even a hint of a mental feedback from the three zombies I saw briefly popping out of a ditch ahead of us before they thought better of it.

Much easier to concentrate on that than… the rest.

"That was a pretty neat takedown you did," Jared observed a while later.

I knew exactly what he was talking about but refused to acknowledge his words, mostly because he had that look on his face again. That look from the alley. That seemed to be sneaking into our conversations constantly now, as if he didn't bother hiding it anymore. Which was probably exactly the case. It annoyed the flying fuck out of me, mostly because it still made me feel so damn naive and stupid, although in all honesty, I couldn't exactly beat myself up over this. In this, I was no match for Jared, and we both knew it. All I could hope was for this not to turn into a "fool me twice" situation down the line...

"You know, when you stabbed that asshole in the side of the neck," he offered. "Just after—"

"I know," I acknowledged between gritted teeth. "And you can stop smirking like that. You're not the only one who knows how to use a knife. I think we established that ages ago."

"We did." He smiled, as if that was a fond memory for him— when he'd pretty much provoked Blondie into coming after me at the campsite on the Asheville loot run that had gone sideways in every way possible. Fuck, that seemed like forever ago—and at the same time like just the other day.

I wondered if that was another sign of my deteriorating mental state, or simple stress response.

"You could have easily killed the other asshole, too," he pointed out. "If you'd been faster."

"Or," I pointed out with a pause, "I could have let the undead do it, which spared me lots of danger and possible peril, which I prefer, since I'm not some random homicidal maniac jonesing for his next kill!"

I knew I'd traipsed right into that trap when I practically heard his smirk in his drawled answer.

"Nothing random about that, sweetheart."

"Can you stop it with the fucking terms of endearment?" I complained.

"That's the part you take issue with?" Jared teased. "I'm disappointed."

"No, you're not. That's exactly the point. It's the only part I feel I stand a chance to change. So why bother with the rest?"

Was that frustration crossing his face? Couldn't be.

"So you, what? Just accept me for who I am?" Jared suggested. Definitely disappointed.

I was hard-pressed to roll my eyes but cut down on the impulse, lest he not start calling me a child next.

"I didn't think you needed my approval," I shot back snidely.

He huffed.

"Need? No. Of course not. Don't be ridiculous. But that doesn't mean I don't want it."

I couldn't help but laugh. It had a decidedly hysterical edge to it. At least that part of me was still working.

"Keep on dreaming." When Jared briefly looked my way again, I smiled back sweetly. "I already warned you ages ago that if you piss me off, I'm off on a celibacy bender. I can't help the fact that slicing me up and digging bullets out of my body gives you a hard-on, but I can very well not bring that to the glorious resolution you must be picturing in those long, cold nights alone. You better get used to that if you keep egging me on like this."

I didn't like the considering look settling onto his expression now.

Shit. I couldn't help but feel like I'd just challenged him—and even before becoming aware of his homicidal proclivities, it had been obvious that Jared loved to rise to any challenge he found worthy.

Getting his rocks off—while making me eat my own words—must have counted for that.

At least my mind was mostly back to its full capacity, even if that barely helped keep me out of trouble.

"Maybe it's that."

I turned my head, confused. Had I just said that out loud? No, I was sure I wasn't slipping that much. Not yet. But I could tell that Jared wasn't harping about my threat of celibacy any longer.

"What 'that'?"

"Everything." He vaguely gestured in my direction. "Except for the truly disappointing utter lack of horror at my revelation, you're acting pretty much like your usual charming self. Maybe that's what shut up your zombie radar—"

"If it ever existed," I threw in.

He grinned, since I was making his point for him.

"Last night you were already more normal than when I picked you up in town."

"When I let you catch up to me."

He ignored my point.

"And this morning a little more still."

"Except for inhaling all the food," Blake complained from the back row. "Speaking of which, I'm hungry."

We both ignored him.

Or at least I did.

A smile appeared on Jared's face. "Exactly how distraught are you that you didn't get a single bite from your well-deserved meal?"

That got the glare it deserved—and a very staunch block on the small part of me that wanted to agree with him.

"You can be so funny when you make jokes like that," I harped.

"But it's true, isn't it?" Jared asked, still digging. "If the idiots hadn't made enough noise to literally call the undead down on us, wouldn't you have wanted to take a bite or two? Some spicy liver? Some delicious kidneys? And think of all the subcutaneous fat that one guy must have had, considering all that bulk? Juicy sweet."

It was obvious that I couldn't win with him, so I didn't even try.

I hated how much my silence felt like acquiescence.

"Nothing?" he teased. "Lost yourself in sweet visions of digging your hands deep into that bloody, ripped-apart torso to get to all the good parts?"

I was tempted to ask how I had gotten into a place where the professed sometimes-cannibal was the one making these jokes, but since I wouldn't have liked the answer to that, I refrained. The bad part was, his words didn't horrify me much anymore, and I was definitely salivating now.

And I was getting hungry. Really fucking hungry.

Blake had a point. We were in dire need of some breakfast.

My stomach growled loud enough that Jared noticed, making him frown briefly.

"We really need to get some protein and fat into you," he observed. "Those empty calories just won't cut it."

"Why, getting concerned I get so hungry that suddenly your dick is looking mighty delicious?"

He snorted. "So much for staying celibate."

"For some juicy meat, I might make an exception."

Jared smiled sweetly. Never a good thing.

Well, guess I deserved that one. Any minute now, he was going to crack a joke that would end with "whore."

And yet, that moment never came, although I was sure he was thinking it.

Then it occurred to me he was possibly taking my statement a little too literally, as in, I'd be ready to put out if he provided the right kind and quantities of meat for me.

Worse yet, the idea was somewhat tempting.

My groan had everything to do with my annoyance at myself and very little with the way he kept grinning.

I couldn't believe that we were having this conversation.

What I couldn't believe even more was the fact that I felt completely at ease, sitting here next to him, bantering like that. Almost as if nothing had happened.

I was seriously asking myself what the fuck was wrong with me, and that voice sounded awfully like Osprey's.

With a hint of irritation, I realized I was still somewhat mad at Osprey for pretty much throwing me to the wolves and abandoning me, either to the asshole Marines or Jared's tender care, but my misgivings about that had cooled dramatically over the past days. Well, day, considering I still didn't remember most of what had happened while I hadn't been quite myself.

Just considering what would have happened if I'd flipped with Dharma and Corey and Liam around... or worst of all, Kas. I was seriously hoping that I would have retained enough of myself not to attack any of them—and since my monster seemed to really like Jared, there was hope the same would have been true with them—but the repercussions alone were enough to sober me up once more.

As much as Jared's jokes grated, they were very easy to handle compared to the utmost horror my friends would have displayed—and rightly so.

Fuck. I absolutely hated that everything boiled down to the Asshole being my best bet right now—or possibly ever.

Anything was better than to keep dwelling on that—so I changed the subject, which was long overdue.

"So what's up with those assholes who tried to kill us? Don't get me wrong. It's not like we don't deserve it; some of us more than others. And we absolutely live in a dog-eat-dog world now. But that seemed a little hostile even in the range of what we've seen with the fucktards at the power plant," I surmised.

Jared chuckled. Of course he would.

I was surprised that the answer came from Blake, though—and he didn't even try to deflect that he was a purely angelic creature that had never even thought about harming a fly.

"Not that different from what we've run into, over and over again," he observed. "Or have you forgotten the fuckers at the river who literally shot you in the ass?"

I refrained from pointing out that it had been my thigh instead.

"Nope. And we've had our run-ins with organized groups like the Marines before. Or them several times over. Whatever. But everyone we've met on the road has been at least moderately us-versus-the-undead minded. Not declared open hunting season on us."

"And did it in a manner that got them all killed with barely any action from us required," Jared added.

I was tempted to point out that, between him and me, we had actually killed three of them—and I had no fucking clue how many of them had been there in total. But he kind of had a point in one aspect.

"They kind of looked like an organized operational unit, what with the guns and the van. But why be stupid enough to open fire on us, miss us, and then get chewed up by zombies? Any one part of that could go wrong, but it does sound like a coordinated fumble, in hindsight."

Jared continued to be highly amused.

"Maybe the Marines got tired of getting their asses handed to them by us. Or eaten." And he totally had to cast a sidelong glance my way, because how could he have refrained from that?

I was still silently stewing when Axel spoke up. "It would make sense that they'd sic mercenaries on us, considering our track record."

Why that surprised me, I didn't know. Possibly because I hadn't considered anyone would think me dangerous enough to warrant such actions—but then, considering the company I kept…

"But why now?" I asked when I couldn't come up with a good explanation. "What changed? Because correct me if I'm wrong, but we've been pretty much doing the very same thing since the undead rose. We hop from community to community. I'm sure Jared has been quietly slaughtering his way through them at a steady rate—"

"Sure have," he confirmed with a smirk.

I did my best not to react at all as I resumed.

"They had us at the Enclave, but let us go. I'm not sure they really put a concerted effort into hunting us down at the golf course, after all."

Axel gave a dismal grunt. "Sounds more like they used us for a training exercise—or they would have come after us below the dam. We simply were at the wrong place at the wrong time."

Blake snorted. "We gave them a good lead up for that, with staying at the lake and then heading right into their kill zone."

Hindsight being twenty-twenty and all that…

Typical that none of them sounded like they still felt the emotional sting of being hunted and almost killed that was always raging in the back of my mind.

"Most of the other groups we've met were pretty okay," I noted. "Or at least not directly out to kill us, unprovoked."

Jared, of course, had to open his mouth to that. "Or were too blind and stupid to get the provocation provided."

The fact that he sounded so very proud of himself was making it ten times worse.

I realized I was getting a little jittery with the anger churning in my gut and did my best to think calming thoughts. Not that it worked, but at least I tried.

Sadly, Jared took my momentary muteness as a hint to fill the silence.

"Well, what changed in the meantime is you turning into a zombie and tearing Marines limb from limb. By now, they probably found their missing patrol that you decimated. Sounds like they now have it out for you."

I glared at him. "So now you're suddenly believing me?"

He grinned. "Never not believed you. But I couldn't pass up the chance to get under your skin when you went all pissy at Blake insinuating that you're a poor, sad rape victim rather than a vicious killing machine."

The growl that came out of my throat wasn't quite human, and certainly not intentional, but it definitely was the right response. Also the wrong one, because it broadened Jared's grin, just adding to his amusement.

Fuck, but I really couldn't win with these assholes!

It took me a few minutes to calm down again. Surprisingly, the peanut gallery and Main Asshole even gave me the chance to.

"Do you think they know?" I asked. "And why do they care? I mean, seriously. Except for that first patrol, all their other dead are because they came after us. If they'd simply let us go, they'd all still be alive."

Blake had something to add to that. "Or if they'd used a sniper, you'd be long dead, too."

Jared shrugged as he slowed down at yet another intersection. "The thrill of the hunt, maybe?"

I couldn't help but guffaw. "Yeah, not everyone is as fucked up as you are." I even got a sweet smile for my trouble.

Fuck, but if I ignored the reason my ire was directed at him, he could be almost… charming.

I was so lost, in so many ways.

As much as I wanted to downright ignore this line of reasoning, it wouldn't let me go.

"Think this is it? That they're actively hunting me now? But why? That bitch Kara Mason literally said I was at best one of many, and those asshole doctors in their underground lab were very ready to watch me die for no good reason at all."

Jared shrugged. "Maybe they agree with me. By flipping over, you became a million times more interesting. Maybe even one-of-a-kind interesting."

I really didn't like that idea—both for the assholes in control of the Marines, nor for Jared himself. Although this once, he was the lesser of two evils.

Again. How the fuck had I gotten into this situation?!

Axel cleared his throat, probably guessing what was ramping up in my mind.

"Speculation will only get us so far," he noted. "But I think it's safe to say we should stop traipsing anywhere people can recognize us without a care in the world. If the assholes in charge sent that group after us, they clearly had no issues whatsoever tracking us down and getting a jump on us. We need to be a hell of a lot more careful going forward."

That very idea left a bad taste in my mouth—including because it meant that the beacons of hope that the few towns we'd visited were quickly turning into possible snake pits. And there I'd thought my main reason to stay clear of them would be to not endanger hapless, innocent children!

"Could all still be one hell of a coincidence," Blake offered. When I cast him a doubtful look over my shoulder, he shrugged. "Stranger things have happened. And we had zero chance to go through their gear and vehicle to find possible clues." He chuckled darkly. "Next time maybe leave one of them alive so we can torture some intel out of him?"

Jared managed the feat of looking both annoyed and elated at the prospect. Typical. Axel just made a face, probably because his reasoning ran along the same lines as mine.

Because paranoid complications and threats of torture were exactly what we needed right now!

Ahead of us, a larger stretch of grassland opened up, with several houses scattered in clusters becoming visible. A few looked perfectly normal; others looted for sure, and two even burned to the ground, from what I could tell at a distance. Jared let the car idle to a stop, thinking.

Then he turned to me, flashing me a slightly lopsided smile. "Let's go get breakfast, shall we? You pick. Let's put that supposed danger radar of yours to the test—and check if it gets better the more hungry or annoyed you get, or the more time that has passed since your last meal. Just, you know. Tell me ahead of time before your hankering for juicy steaks turns to my dick."

I glared at him all through the chuckle that followed while I waited for Axel to hand me the binoculars.

Two could play this game—and I was done being the victim and the laughingstock.

And, just maybe, being busy foraging and sneaking into houses would keep my mind occupied enough so it would forget screaming that I'd killed a man in cold blood this morning, and it took until now to realize I should be traumatized and horrified about my actions, even if they had been premeditated self-defense.

CHAPTER 9

No, my danger radar didn't miraculously resurface. We hardly needed it to find an unoccupied house as of yet unraided where we could find some chow, even if it was all canned goods or stuff that needed a thorough soaking or cooking to be edible. As usual, Blake didn't mind going straight for the condiments, which was enough to make my beginning hunger recede somewhat—for all of five minutes.

What took me out of commission for longer was when my lower abdomen suddenly started cramping and hurting like crazy, shooting pains making me pant like I'd gone into labor. Axel looked appropriately concerned as I made a hobbled run for the bathroom while Blake joked about little girls and their modesty. Just as I threw the door shut behind me—more or less vaulting for the porcelain throne—I heard Jared call after me, "And don't forget to keep me updated on how that goes."

To say it wasn't pretty was the understatement of the century.

Considering yesterday had started with a bout of cannibalism, later returned to that, and I'd gone through no less than three major binges of pretty much anything else edible I could cram down my gullet, I kind of got why my digestive tract was upset, but I didn't expect that what finally appeared as my bowels pretty much evacuated themselves with plenty of gas and yet more pain would come out so… identifiable.

It was grotesque enough that I was almost tempted to call Jared in to observe what was left in the soft pink toilet bowl, including the alarming quantities of it. Not everything had quite passed undigested, but I could definitely pick out barely chewed pasta and rice, and bits and pieces of previously super sweet fruit. The weird slush that came with it was likely softer vegetables and crackers, adding an extra level of unappetizing to the mix. The only thing that was missing was bits of meat, and I definitely remembered not chewing much as I'd wolfed down Private Unlucky's innards.

On an intellectual level, I was absolutely horrified, but since that was accounting for maybe one percent of my mental capacity right now—compared to the fifty percent that was simply glad the pain was gone, the literal shit was out of me, and I didn't seem to have torn anything in the process although it still felt like a too-close call—I wasn't exactly exiting the bathroom white-faced when I felt I could trust my legs once more.

The other forty-nine percent of my mind was really intent on finding something to gulp or swallow down to make the increasing gnawing in my stomach stop.

I answered Jared's already present smirk with a deadpan stare as I returned to the kitchen.

"I think I need to re-evaluate my food sources," was what I left it at before making a beeline for the cans of tuna Axel had stacked neatly on the counter to take with us on the road.

No, that was totally not a growl that started up low in my throat when he cast me a reproachful look as I tore open the first can and started digging in, not bothering with cutlery.

Axel quickly backed away and left me to my breakfast, of course with Jared cackling to himself, and Blake complaining about why he couldn't have at least one can to ensure that his muscles weren't going to be wasting away.

Damn, but I would have loved to grab the box of cereal he instead dug into and throw all that down my gullet as well once the fish was gone, but with certain parts of my anatomy still protesting the recent abuse, I didn't dare.

At least my quick healing had kicked in by the time we got back into the car, letting me smile back at Jared when he offered to fetch me a cushion to sit on.

I was sure that he had totally snooped, but at least he kept any and all comments about that to himself. For now.

I was surprised that this time, the men brought all available foodstuffs out to the car, including a weird batter Axel had thrown together using the available flour and some spices. Far was it from me to joke about bread-making in the apocalypse, but that looked a little extreme. We hit two other houses this morning as well—sadly lacking canned protein and fat this time—but at least our rice-and-pasta stores were more than full now. And the condiment box that Blake insisted on. I couldn't quite believe it, but he was absolutely giving me a run for my money in the most-disgusting-eater department still.

So far, the day had gone well—if one ignored the early morning ambush. But that was when we hit a snag.

It was only a tiny speck in the sky as we exited the last of the houses—where we'd finally found a bona fide rain-water barrel I could use to wash my disgustingly gunked-up hair—but from the first second it was obvious that this didn't bode well.

Jared was quick to drive the car into the next available copse of trees, trying to disappear out of sight of the drone. From what we could tell, we easily lost it, but by the time we got near the edge of the forest again to check overhead, six more had joined it.

That, and several plumes of dust in the distance, heralding the passage of vehicles.

"I know it's probably a stupid question, but think they're after us?" I asked.

"Us?" Jared smirked. "No. They're after you."

I grimaced. My stomach rumbled loudly, which made him snort.

I glared at him, hoping against hope that he would keep his trap shut.

"You know, being hunted doesn't have to be a bad thing for you," he pointed out.

I ignored him, instead glaring up at the drones zipping this way and that, seemingly criss-crossing the skies at random.

We were still a good five miles ahead of the closest car—and easily ten or twenty of actual road miles away since we'd stuck to the small roads—but the drones would definitely see us the moment we rolled out from between the trees.

Jared and Axel briefly consulted over the two maps we'd liberated from the Marines before putting them away, gesturing to Blake and me to get our packs.

Not only were we going to leave on foot—but we were going to split up.

What a surprise that I ended up with the Asshole, who was quite amused by my sour face. That even beat Blake's whining over having to leave behind most of our surprisingly impressive arsenal, but when Jared asked him exactly how many carbines and assault rifles at once he intended to use and carry with him, Blake finally shut up. We distributed all the handguns and magazines between us, though, and I pointedly slung my carbine across my chest intended for long-term carrying, not keeping it ready to shoot momentarily.

At least we'd also found some earbuds in the Marines' gear. That would have come in handy this morning, had any of us bothered to keep any in our pockets. Or even don a jacket, in my case.

"If we get separated, we meet up over there, near that small town on that hill to the northwest," Jared said after—reluctantly—entrusting the binoculars into Axel's care. "We hang around for two nights. Who's not there by sunrise the second day gets left behind."

Did he have to look straight at me while saying that? Apparently so.

I ignored him in favor of glaring at the drones some more, then tried to judge the distance to that town. Maybe twenty miles by winding road, just over ten if we could go in a straight line, which seemed inadvisable with the drones in the sky. I had a feeling that we'd either spend the rest of the day wading through underbrush and hiding in the long grass, or waiting for nightfall.

I so didn't look forward to navigating in the dark or running into some lurking undead, but since our trusty car had just become the least useful vehicle around, there was little I could do about that.

At least we still had a full twelve hours of light each day with the fall equinox just past. A month from now, things would get increasingly more uncomfortable—and not just because of the length of the day.

Make that roughly seven hours right now, and those weren't seven hours I was looking forward to.

Axel and Blake set out veering to the right while I followed Jared along the tree line heading left.

It took me all of five minutes to miss the car.

"No chance we could just wait for a couple hours and then take off in a direction that's clear?" I asked as I did my best not to stumble and huff too loudly after Jared.

He paused for a moment, but mostly to watch the progress of the three drones we could currently glimpse through the foliage.

"No deal. We might have had that chance if we'd immediately taken off this morning and driven like the devil was right on our heels—"

"A.k.a. your usual driving speed," I harped.

He flashed me a quick grin. "But that would have had to be in the right direction as well, and I wouldn't be surprised if there's another group already waiting for us right there."

"Isn't that a little paranoid?"

"Not since I noticed several more drones up there to the north and the east." Those overhead had come from the south and the west, mostly.

"So they are really hunting us." I hated how dejected that came out.

"You," Jared told me cheerfully. "They are hunting you."

I knew it was pointless to try to correct him that we still had no way of confirming that, since I had nothing to refute his claim with. It still rankled.

"Does that make you jealous?" I snarked instead.

Petty? Yes. But if that was all that was remaining in my arsenal, I would ride it until Kingdom Come.

Jared sent me a pointed look over his shoulder but didn't deign to stop for that.

I really didn't like the slow smile that was spreading across his face.

"And what do you do if I say yes?" he taunted.

That, at least, I could answer. "Keep ignoring you."

I deserved the chuckle I got for that. "How's that working for you, huh?"

I graced him with a smile of my own. It might have been a slightly toothy one. "How about you ask your blue balls that?"

"Your obsession with my genitals might have bothered a lesser man, but I'm very okay with that," he informed me.

I left it at a loud snapping of my teeth.

Jared laughed. Because he would.

We trudged on in silence for another ten minutes, the going a little easier as we chanced onto a deer track. Then we ran out of forest, forcing us to either wait until the sky cleared up overhead, or we'd have to change directions for at least five to seven miles, from what I could say at a glance.

While Jared studied his map and considered, I tried to catch a glimpse of the others or of our pursuers, but came up blank.

"Why exactly am I stuck with you again?" I asked, more to vent my frustration than expecting an actual answer.

"Because Blake is afraid of you getting a little too chompy," Jared informed me without glancing my way even briefly. "And are you really that pissed off at Axel that you want to see him die? Because you need a heavy hitter at your side, and he simply isn't up for that anymore. I know, I know. His reproachful stares and silences can get annoying. But take some pity on the old man. You've seen nothing yet of how he can get. Now it's still the silences and the looks. Wait until the moralizing starts. 'Oh, no, why did you have to take me literally?' And, 'Can't you see where this is morally wrong?'" Jared chuckled to himself. "Obviously not. Oh, and my all-time favorite is of course, 'Can't you see that you're hurting yourself more than anyone else with this idiocy?' to which my answer has always been and will always be, 'Fuck it—it felt good in the moment. Don't care.'"

His impersonation of Axel's reproachful tone was both comically but tantalizingly good, making me wonder exactly how much I had missed out on—and why he felt like sharing all of a sudden.

"Why exactly do you act like you and I are in the same boat? We are nothing alike."

Now he did glance from his map to me, and I really didn't like the dark amusement in his gaze—among other things. Did he have to look at me as if I'd just suggested getting busy right here behind that tree?

"Oh, but we are," Jared drawled.

"We are not," I insisted.

His mirth only deepened.

"Just because you're not quite ready to admit to yourself that you're a killer doesn't change a thing about the fact that you are." I opened my mouth to protest, but he just kept on talking. "You didn't have to come after the guy with a knife this morning. You could have waited for one of us to kill him. Or for the zombies to get him. But you saw a chance and hesitated all of... how much did you hesitate? Because while I didn't see everything from my perch at the top of the stairs, I saw you moving damn quickly and efficiently. Staying hidden or creeping away would have been the easy things to do. You chose to kill him, sneaking up on him from behind his back. That is the action of a cold-blooded killer. Not a self-defensing, wailing maiden."

I knew that absolutely wasn't what had happened—but for the life of me, I couldn't come up with anything to say to refute his claim.

And damnit, I could already feel his words worm their way into my subconscious where they would take hold and fester to keep me up all night—

Fucking asshole.

Since I couldn't win the conventional way—with arguing and common sense—I didn't even try.

"That's your opinion," I said, maybe a little too defensively. "Still doesn't make it reality."

He turned away with a snort, clearly thinking he'd won that one. "Suit yourself. Keep snuggling with your lies. Eventually, even you will run out of excuses, and I'll still be waiting for you to come crawling back to me then with your tail tucked between your legs."

"I'm so not going to indulge your submissive homicidal furry fantasies," I shot back.

Jared laughed and struck out along the tree line, heading right for the longer diversion I'd hoped we could avoid.

"We'll see," he shot back over his shoulder.

"Don't think I can keep it in my pants for a while? You're in for a rude awakening."

He kept on laughing to himself, and this once, I couldn't even fault him for that.

I absolutely hated how much of me was kind of with him on not quite believing me either.

Pathetic! Just how deep can you sink—

I did my best to keep the self-flagellation to a minimum. I could always be angry at myself for hitting rock bottom after it happened and when we were not in danger of possibly traipsing right to our death. And maybe if that actually happened, I wouldn't have to do that exercise at all?

Always the best of times when you were hoping for a quick, brutal death…

"Don't beat yourself up over it too much," Jared called back from up ahead. "I know I'm irresistible."

It took me a moment to catch on to the meaning of—or rather, the thought process behind—his words. That he thought that was the reason I was grimacing hard enough for my facial muscles to hurt made me want to scream with frustration. For sure, he was the easier target.

It choked me up for a good minute not to offer a snide retort, but eventually, Jared stopped glancing back at me waiting for one. He still looked way too self-satisfied, but there was little I could do about that, I realized.

What rankled was that I still cared. And the bickering back and forth—even if it happened while we were wading through underbrush and high grass, doing our very best to stay out of sight of the open sky—was fun. I was feeling enough like myself now that intellect reigned over my baser nature once more, making it very easy to remember exactly what had gone down in that alley… but it was regret and sadness that made me taste bile rather than anger or fear.

We'd had a good thing going all summer long. I fucking missed that.

Of course, now I knew it had all been just him playing with me; manipulating me, pushing and prodding and pulling me along until he had me right where he wanted me…

That rankled. It was also less of a reality check and more good old, strikingly familiar regret seeping into my very bones.

Why had I been naive enough to think that, this once, things would be different?

And to realize that if I'd just been a little more patient with Osprey and maybe used my words instead of thinking with my vagina—

But no. I was well aware that if I hadn't managed to bungle things myself, Jared would have somehow gotten between us and twisted and manipulated my thoughts until he had me right where he wanted me—

Wasn't that exactly what he had done, in the end? Sure, he couldn't have known about my long history with drugs. Not even after my little word vomit up on the power plant roof. But he must have known what playing on my abandonment issues would make me do. It must have been so easy for him to read the unease on everyone's faces when I'd gotten a little too violent, a little too fast, high out of my mind. I for sure hadn't seen it, but I'd probably lost as soon as I'd trusted him and popped that pill. Everything after that must have been so fucking easy for him…

I hated that it annoyed the living shit out of me it had likely been less about getting into my pants than getting into my head for him. That he'd, of course, done both…

A brief wait followed by a mad dash across a stretch of grassland thankfully made me lose my train of thought. After that, it was skipping across a creek, then some extended crawling through the grass while hoping no drone would come to hover exactly above us. Then another brief walk through the woods before the terrain went from mostly flat to hilly, forcing my body to exert itself.

Before long, I got hungry.

Then I got really hungry, to the point where I felt my concentration slipping.

Like, ravenous.

Not bad enough that I was tempted to start eating grass, but what little provisions we had in our packs were definitely burning a hole into my back. My stomach first growled, then started to cramp, my entire digestive tract soon on the fence. Some of that could still have been from everything else that I'd been stuffing my face with since waking up yesterday morning, but it didn't feel like it.

I also felt myself inching further away from Jared. Not because I was afraid I would literally launch myself at him—in whatever capacity. It took me a while to realize that I was doing it at all, and then a little longer to find out the reason for it.

He didn't smell right.

Not right as in, not the best available food source.

I couldn't help but cackle to myself for a second, glad we were far enough apart that he missed it. That, in turn, made me sad I passed up the chance to crack another innuendo-laced joke about "his meat," but since that just made me salivate—and that in all the wrong ways—it was likely better I didn't. While amusing in part, it all left me feeling vaguely uncomfortable—and that on a much deeper level than stupid jokes or even threats of cannibalism would.

The low rumbling of a car engine in the distance made us halt in our tracks, then retreat deeper into the forest, well out of sight of the road ahead.

While I hunkered down next to him—upwind from Jared as much as I could position myself without him noticing what I was doing—the way he tensed and seemed to vibrate with tension reminded me of when he'd tried sneaking up on the two Marines in the woods by the golf course. Now I could see what had been going on there—and fully appreciate it, as much as that wasn't the case. I'd absolutely cockblocked him back then. Or would that have been slice-blocked?

Whatever.

If I hadn't been so goddamn hungry, I would have found that funny on some level at least.

Now part of me was starting to regret that we were deliberately hanging back.

There was plenty of food in that car, after all—even if they were without provisions.

Fucking stop this!!

I wondered if my hungering for human flesh was actually that, or just my mind being a morbid fucker since all I was dealing with was a fucked-up serial killer who apparently was set on turning me into his cannibal sex doll. And the worst part was that I was mostly opposed to the getting-manipulated-into-having-sex part, far less so the rest.

Not for the first time, I wondered what would have happened had our paths crossed before that fateful cream-cheese-bagel run.

Nothing, obviously, because I would have been a boring worker drone to him, not even worth stalking, least of all killing.

And now everything I did just put me more central in his focus.

The truly fucked-up thing was that if I got even a little distracted, I could feel a smidgen of pride come alive deep inside of me. Or was that affection? Whatever the fuck it was, the fact that what was without a doubt the darkest part of my soul was exactly what drew him to me was… very troublesome, but I would have been lying if I said it didn't affect me on some level.

Fuck.

The car eventually rumbled by—or cars, plural, from what it sounded like. Three, to be precise, but no guessing how large they were and how many people they transported. Less than a minute later, it was quiet again—except that it wasn't.

There was movement going on all around us, enough so to make me antsy and consider grabbing my carbine after all. We didn't have bats right now, but there were plenty of useful branches all around…

Then I smelled the first stronger whiff of decay, making me lunge for the next available branch. It was a little too short and a little too thin for my liking, but for sure better than nothing.

Jared eyed me curiously, but almost immediately, his attention snapped to our surroundings. For once, I wasn't the most interesting thing around.

My joy about that was dubious.

Jared started forward once more—heading straight for the road. At first, I thought he was crazy, but then I realized that wasn't the worst idea. Sure, it exposed us—but mostly to the lurkers, not the drones potentially overhead since we were in a thickly wooded area now, the elevation slowly rising. If they really attacked us on the road, we could at least run. And judging from how easy it had been for us to hide from the cars, it stood to reason the same would be true for the next vehicles we'd encounter.

Being on foot had its advantages.

I was almost annoyed when we finally stepped out onto the road—a small, single-lane one curving gently uphill—and not a single lurker came running for us. Mostly, my annoyance centered on the fact that I still couldn't feel them—or not exactly. Like with that almost unconscious weird vibe I got from Jared, there were… patches all around me that my mind told me to avoid, a few stronger than others. Since today wasn't the day I felt up to experiments, it was easy to decide to follow along with instinct.

So when Jared set out blindly, I followed him, but not without from time to time tapping him on the shoulder to make him switch which side of the road we were kind of avoiding.

Surprisingly, he followed along, but not without the inevitable smirk.

So much for all his protestations about my supposed delusions.

Apparently, he wasn't in the mood to experiment, either.

Ahead, the trees thinned out eventually, making us slip back into full cover. We lost the road eventually but found a different one a while later. Twice we paused for a long stretch to preserve our energy and eat the last of our provisions—which meant mostly Jared ate them while I disdainfully sniffed the can of beans before handing it off to him. My digestion was still upset, but no actions were warranted right now. I was almost hungry enough to say fuck it and down the beans, consequences be damned, but thankfully wised up before that could happen.

I wouldn't starve if I ate nothing more today—certainly not after this morning's haphazard buffet.

It took me until after our second break to realize Jared hadn't even tried to feed me shit that was likely no longer on my menu, meaning he actively tried to starve me... back into full-on attack mode? Or was he just curious if or when my danger radar would return?

A week ago, I would have bet on the latter, but after how he'd been sitting on that log, laughing his ass off over me gorging myself on Private Unlucky's innards, I was pretty convinced it was a heavy dose of the former, if not exclusively that.

What the fuck was I doing here, tagging along with someone who had zero concern about all this was doing to me? Or, worse yet, was happy to put a blow torch directly to the slow-licking flames I tried to control if not douse completely?

I didn't ask him for clarification because I didn't want to know the answer.

As the afternoon slowly turned to evening and my body burned through more and more reserves it no longer had, those concerns slowly disappeared.

The sun eventually set, casting the woods into deeper shadows, almost too dark now to navigate away from another road we were currently following—probably one we'd either passed or already walked along before. There were no convenient houses anywhere close to the road, and as it was, also no stretches of flat ground anywhere near, for that matter. It had been over an hour since we'd seen glimpses of the last drone through the leaves overhead. Soon, it would be getting too dark for them to be of much use.

"How long exactly do you intend to keep going?" I asked Jared eventually when he still showed no signs of slowing down. "I'm kind of not looking forward to pulling an all-nighter."

I got a sidelong smirk for my trouble. "Why, so eager to drag me off to bed?"

I gifted him with a grimace. "I was more thinking alongside the lines of climbing up into a tree, or something."

He snorted. "Your track record of staying up in trees isn't exactly the best."

Which was true.

"Still better than getting eaten by the lurkers."

Jared considered, if only briefly.

"Give me another hour. I think we're close to our waypoint. I remember seeing some houses on the slope nearby. We can crash in one of them—or on some lawn chairs, if you prefer to freeze outside in the cold."

I couldn't help but blink with irritation.

"Why would I want that?"

He grinned. "Well, since all signs point to the fact that you are correct and have cast off the restraints of the completely living, maybe staying cool at night to keep decomposition at bay might be a good idea? I don't mind a little gangrene around the edges, but if you actually start to rot—"

My growl cut him off, but only because he was laughing too hard to continue.

Why had I expected anything else?

Something tickling my nose put an immediate damper on my ire.

"Do you smell that?"

Jared stopped cackling immediately, snapping back to full alertness.

"Decay?"

I shook my head.

"No. Gasoline."

We both listened intently, even going as far as to stop in the middle of the road to keep the sounds of movement to a minimum.

Nothing. I even lost the scent after a moment, the usual odors of nature all that filled my nose.

Jared finally shrugged and started forward again, but I got the sense that he was paying more attention now. Since that also meant he stopped yapping, I was more than okay with that.

Twice more I thought I caught something, but both times yielded the same result. I reasoned that the gasoline was likely from one of the cars hunting us, a few drops spilling on the road earlier today.

We slowly walked around another bend in the road—only to find the road ahead blocked. Well, not technically blocked, but the combination of fresh blood in the air mixed with heavy decay—and at least ten zombies going to town on something already spread out across both lanes—made us halt and then veer off into the underbrush with little coordination between us required. Even this close, they barely made a sound except for low snarls that the wind had carried away and the inevitable cracking of bones and wet rending of flesh.

It was only after I managed to tear my eyes away from the carnage that I realized Jared was staring at me instead, a look of faint amusement on his face.

I silently flipped him off, but the fact that I had to make myself feel revulsion rather than excitement was bad enough.

More rustling coming from around us made it obvious that we were still way too close to the feeding frenzy as it was.

Jared cut right through the trees, with little care how much of a racket he was making—which he was, stepping on branches and rustling through the leaves. I followed him, looking everywhere at once, my back crawling with unease—while my muscles got ready for a good workout, finally!

Ahead, the sky lightened as the canopy of the trees thinned, soon spilling us out into a clearing. It wasn't large—for sure too small for anyone to want to build a house here since it was still deep in the woods with no great vistas opening up anywhere—but at least we could see clearly once more and stopped being so goddamn loud.

My nerves should have calmed down now, but the opposite was the case. As I looked over the small scattering of trees across the clearing—some apple trees, judging from the heavy aroma of overly ripe fruit hanging in the air—I couldn't help but feel the fine hairs all over my arms rise.

Jared turned to me, ready to crack a joke—probably about me salivating over the feeding frenzy; what else?—but his attention immediately snapped to our surroundings when he caught my expression.

The smart thing would have been to retreat into the trees. But the way my skin was suddenly crawling, I felt way more like moving forward rather than back.

Jared cast me a questioning look that I returned with a shrug. When he still didn't move, I stepped toward the haphazard cluster of trees in the middle of the clearing, feeling half-rotten apples crunch and go splat underneath the soles of my sneakers. Several times, I halted and looked back over my shoulder, but as far as I could tell, everything around us was deserted. Up above, the sky was clear, the last colors of the evening slowly fading into night.

With my paranoia ramping up by the moment, I actually checked carefully around the first tree for anything hiding behind it. Of course, there was nothing there. At this distance, I would have been able to tell with virtually all of my senses had that been the case. And yet—

I wasn't sure if it was just my behavior or if anything had tipped Jared off, but he stepped away from me as we spread out underneath the trees, trying to present less of an interesting target. I kept straining my ears, wincing a few times as I heard Jared's footsteps loud in the absolute quiet of the night.

And it was that terrifying, true quiet; no cicadas doing double time, no critters zooming this way and that.

Closing my eyes for a moment, I tried to still my racing thoughts and... sense what was out there, for lack of a better word.

Nothing.

Only that when I snapped them open again, a man was standing in front of me, a little off to the side, his attention centered on Jared as if he hadn't seen me lurking by the trunk of the tree.

He hadn't, I realized, as my breath caught in my throat.

Most of me wanted to snap into panicked alertness, ready to run. But there was also the part of me that wanted to clap her hands with glee, or, better yet, already launch herself at the imbecile.

I was well aware that I was thinking of myself in the third person.

Could this day get any better?

It was for sure about to get much worse, I realized, as I watched the man ready the assault rifle he'd slung across his body, his hands moving in quick, proficient motions. He definitely knew what he was doing—and with Jared standing just over fifty feet away, it was pretty much impossible for him not to hit his target. Never mind that I was less than twenty feet away—close enough to hit well with a pistol.

A pistol that I had safely stashed away in my pack, where it was doing nobody any good.

I considered my options literally at hand—my makeshift branch club, and the carbine partially trapped by my pack after hours of juggling both and honestly being too tired to be prepared to shoot a weapon that would for sure call the undead hordes down on us like nobody's business, a.k.a. my absolute last resort after all other options had been exhausted. And of course my trusty pocket knife that I could pull out and ready blindly with my free hand, no problem.

I tried to assess the man. He was easily a foot taller than me, quite beefy, bordering on fat. That meant his jugular wasn't exactly easily accessible for me if we both were standing on even ground. There was a chance the knife would get caught in the collar of his jacket, or maybe stuck in the tattooed rolls of fat I could see bulging at the back of his neck. With him sitting and me standing, no problem. But I'd have to practically vault onto his back to reach anything critical, and there was always the chance that he would just swat me away if I timed things wrong.

No, this was definitely not a knife-fight kind of situation.

The thing was, I didn't quite trust my skills with the carbine. Sure, on our mad flight from the power plant, I'd done a passingly good job shooting, but that had very much been to deter our pursuers from shooting out our tires and accidentally hitting any of us. And most of the damage I'd done had been wielding that ax, although I had to admit, I could barely remember any of that.

Now, that ax would have come in quite handy—but not eight hours into tramping across the countryside with little rest and by far not enough food.

The carbine it was.

I didn't dare drop my club, so instead, I eased myself down into a crouch, steadying myself on my right knee. Holding my breath as I watched the man finish his preparations, I put the club down and in the same motion pulled the carbine forward on its sling. The weapon briefly caught on my shoulder strap, my jacket and pack threatening to rustle with the strength of a roaring jumbo jet.

I was sure that I was caught—but no; the idiot was still following Jared's slow progress between the trees, now also with the barrel of his rifle.

Clenching my teeth and hoping against all hope that this would work, I gave the sling a hard tug—and the weapon was free, letting me slide it forward into a proper grip. My mind went completely blank with all the motions required to get it to unleash its deadly power, but my fingers were pretty much moving on their own accord, mirroring what the man had done before. Only that I didn't bother with checking on the magazine and shit. That either was ready, or this would become the shortest rescue mission in the history of man.

The last thing I checked was that Jared wasn't in the extended direction of the distance between me and the idiot.

I pulled the trigger, unleashing hell.

Or at least a three-shot version of it, quickly repeated when my finger moved forward and back immediately again.

For how close I was to my target, my aim was pathetic, only a single bullet of the six hitting him from what I could tell—but that was in the back of his neck, not that far from where I would have attacked with my knife. Sure, I'd been aiming for center mass, but it was still a hit!

It was also deafeningly loud, even with the earplugs, the sonic assault hitting my body hard.

The man screamed like a stuck pig, which made me guess it was more surprise and fright than actual pain. Which meant I really hadn't hit him all that much, even if I could smell that siren scent of fresh blood in the air.

Time to finish him off the proper way.

Thankfully, before I could be stupid enough to drop the carbine so I could physically launch myself at the guy, my instinct took over, going for the high-tech solution.

This time when I let out a three-round burst, all of them hit—two high in his torso, and the third somewhere in his lower face. Not that hard since he'd already crossed half the distance between us, his momentum carrying him another three steps that made him go down right in front of my feet.

Oops. That had been a little close.

I stepped back—both to get out of his reach should he be still alive against all odds, but mostly to put physical distance between us so I couldn't get any weird ideas. Then faster when I realized I'd made a lot of noise and remained immobile the entire time. But not too fast, because running away would have likely painted an even larger target on my back.

Casting around, I tried to find Jared, but he was gone, nothing moving even vaguely in the direction where I'd last seen him. Which, to be fair, had been over half a minute ago, before I'd pulled the trigger the first time.

Nothing was moving in the clearing, but all around, I could hear rustling in the underbrush, my sense of unease skyrocketing.

Yeah, so just maybe that hadn't been my brightest moment.

Something moved off to my right, so I immediately corrected course to the left, trying to see exactly what had drawn my attention. I was too slow to bring the muzzle of the carbine along, but by far fast enough to see that the shape was tall, bulky, and pointing a large weapon at me.

Just as he pulled the trigger, I hit the ground, the maneuver less of a graceful action and more of a mad fumble. It was a single shot and sounded very different—definitely a shotgun.

Not what I wanted going off in my face.

I considered trying to crawl away, but that just brought on mental images of slugs making the back of my head explode. So instead, I rolled as much onto my back as I could with the pack on and readied my carbine—

Only that nothing came looming over me to finish me off.

I did hear a suppressed groan, though, seconds before something hit the grass.

Call me jaded, but that had sounded very much like someone else had followed through with my knife idea.

Deciding that crawling away rather than being wrong was the better part of valor, I rolled over and came up into a crouch, then quickly dashed away—only to veer back toward the center of the clearing when the woods up ahead gave me the worst kind of feeling.

Moments after I ducked behind the closest tree, a howl cut through the night as five figures came charging out from exactly where I would have entered the forest, spreading out as several times their numbers followed with little hesitation.

They were on the two downed corpses in no time, zeroing in like sharks in the water on a blood trail.

I was just a little proud of myself that my first reaction was neither wanting to fight them for my kill nor the general urge to join the feeding frenzy that was about to start.

Then I realized I was still only fifteen feet outside of where more and more zombies coalesced, with more and more lurkers now stepping out of the woods—and not all of them from that direction.

A low curse sounded from two trees over, making my head whip around.

True enough, I saw two men crouching there, staring with what I was sure was abject horror at what was happening to their former comrades.

At least I hoped neither of them was Jared when I leveled the barrel of my carbine and sent two quick three-round bursts at them, gravely injuring or killing them in seconds.

I was slinking away by the time the aggressive zombies split off from their secured corpses and went for the new ones, not paying the source of the noise any heed.

My getaway would have been much smoother if I didn't trip—and then fall—over two more corpses, lying in the tall grass just outside the deeper shadow the last of the apple trees cast.

I quickly scrambled back onto my feet, checking that no lurkers were sneaking up on me.

Then I thought better of it, pushed my carbine back on its sling, got out my knife, and went to town, eviscerating both bodies with crude slashes.

No, not to sneak a taste, although the scent of fresh, warm blood hitting my nostrils made it insanely hard not to succumb to the temptation. But to create an even bigger diversion, giving me plenty of time to keep going to the opposite side of the clearing to disappear from sight of the site of carnage.

I didn't even jump when Jared materialized out from between the trees as soon as I was back in moderate safety.

I busied myself with putting away my knife, my hands still sticky with blood.

Oops. Forgot to wipe them.

Jared wordlessly got a bottle out of his pack and helped me clean up—for sure not because of my vanity, but the scent of blood might have drawn exactly the kind of attention we hoped we'd just left behind.

I cast a look back at the clearing, shuddering with the knowledge of what was going on there.

"You can't shoot for shit," Jared whispered from up close, his voice way too intimate for the occasion.

Because of course he would.

I slowly turned my head away from the zombies to face him, our noses almost touching. If I'd wanted to kiss him, it would have been just a slight move forward.

Too bad that was the last thing on my mind, with me having to convulsively swallow twice before I could respond.

"Fuck. You."

He chuckled, the sound perfectly grating down my spine.

"I still killed one more than you," I pointed out.

Jared snickered. "That you know of. Great job literally stumbling over those two by the tree."

I glared at him, then would have loved to glare at myself for being so fucking stupid.

Really? Did I have to play the one-upping game with a fucking serial killer?

Apparently, yes.

Fucking hell, but I was so losing my shit over this. It wasn't funny anymore.

I was sure Jared was still grinning as he slinked away into the forest, leaving behind the zombies—and what would have made a fine dinner for me, my stomach grumbling in protest.

CHAPTER 10

We found refuge for the night in a car left in a small parking area next to the road. Probably not one of the vehicles belonging to the men we had killed since it held zero provisions or gear, but it was there, it was easy to break into, and that was a million times better than climbing up into a tree and falling to my death as soon as I dozed off. We didn't dare try to start the car lest it draw any attention. Since there was little immediate benefit, it was better not to chance it. Not until we'd had time to recover, or at least wait until it got light enough again so we could see where we were going.

I considered claiming the back row—or at least part of it—but then thought better of it, figuring that if I had to bolt, that would work much better from the front. Jared didn't protest when I left the much-less-comfortable driver's side to him, which was just as well. The seats reclined nicely, making this almost a feasible location to spend the night—

Except for the Asshole ending up grinning right in my face, forcing me to either suffer that or start the laborious proceedings of turning over to face the window instead.

A tempting undertaking, but I was too tired and hungry to waste so much energy on nothing.

And yes, it was that stare again—that I'd gotten so used to over the summer months that it had lost a lot of its annoyance potential, but of course now that I knew what lurked behind it…

I flopped onto my back, choosing to glare up at the ceiling of the car instead.

Damn, I was tired. Bone-weary, deep-seated exhaustion, borne of being awake going on forty hours, burning through a hell of a lot of calories fighting, getting shot at, and actually getting shot. And an endless amount of walking and running—no wonder my body felt like it had been on the wrong end of a collision with a speeding train.

Only that, until an hour ago, I'd felt moderately fine. Sure, tired from everything that had been happening over the course of the past two days, but not actually like shit.

Well, that was before you killed several people…

I couldn't help the grimace trying to tear my face apart. Yeah, there was that…

I wondered if it was shock that was doing a number on me. Then again, I knew what that felt like, and for that, my symptoms were way too mild.

If only that gnawing hunger wasn't trying to eat a literal hole into my stomach—

I heard Jared rummage around in his pack before I saw him stretch out on his reclined seat next to mine once more, studying a chocolate bar and a pack of nuts.

"That's all I got left," he declared as he tore open the candy bar wrapper and bit into it, chewing noisily. "I'd offer you some, but considering it would just go to waste—"

My stomach took that opportunity to let out a loud growl that was strong enough that I felt it, making me wince.

"You really should have taken some chunks from the assholes back at the clearing," Jared mused while continuing to chew. Then he laughed, almost delighted. "Or I should have! Since you're obviously not ready to take care of yourself…"

He trailed off there, and I could perfectly feel his attention resting on me once more. Taunting. Teasing. Waiting to get a rise out of me…

"Yes, you probably should have," I told him in the flattest tone I could manage.

Jared chuckled. Yes, he was definitely laughing at me.

Awesome.

Not exactly the first time since we'd reunited but decidedly the first time really meaning it, I asked myself why the fuck I bothered tagging along with him. Being out there on my own couldn't get this bad. And I had about the same amount of blood on my hands, only that now I was fully aware of that, so the benefits were rather debatable.

And I was really fucking hungry. That, I was sure, wouldn't have been an issue if I'd still had my pack with me.

A fleeting thought skipped across my mind that, even now, I could probably find my way back to that clearing and chase away the lurkers to get a few good mouthfuls of meat for myself. I hadn't exactly gotten a good sense of the strong, aggressive ones, but I was sure that I more than measured up to the lurkers…

I wondered where exactly I had gone wrong that my options were now either giving up on humanity and joining the undead, or giving up on humanity and running with the likes of my present company.

There had to be better options out there.

"Exactly how tempted are you to backtrack your way to your rightful kills right now?"

I knew it was a mistake, but I couldn't resist turning my head so I could look at Jared's face as he kept grinning at me, way too self-satisfied with his oh-so-witty remark.

"Twenty percent, maybe," I deadpanned. "But it would be so much more efficient to kill you instead."

He didn't even bat an eyelash.

"Nah, you like me too much to go through with that," he taunted—or teased, really.

"I really don't," I said—and went back to staring at the ceiling, hoping that he couldn't read the lie off my face.

No such luck.

"Liar," he singsonged softly, from way too close for comfort—my own, and the same should have been true for him, seeing as he had seen firsthand what I was capable of when I got hungry.

I pointedly, slowly turned my head back to face him, our noses so close now they were almost touching. I could smell the candy bar on his breath, and it was honestly disgusting.

"Unlike you, I still have integrity left," I let him know—to what end was anyone's guess, but it felt like something worth pointing out. Also something true.

Jared snorted. "And that gets you exactly nowhere in this world. It certainly doesn't get you fed."

My rumbling stomach traitorously agreed.

Fuck.

"Do you really think I couldn't kill you?" I asked, meaning it mostly as a challenge, but then realizing I actually wanted to know the answer.

Jared took a surprisingly long time to respond, but maybe only so he could make me more uncomfortable with his physical closeness—or at least try to.

"If forced? Absolutely, you could," he surmised. "Maybe even in anger, if I really pull out all the stops and lay it on real heavy. Can't say for sure, but from how you acted at the ambush, I'd say once you lose it, all bets are off."

"Which ambush?" There sure was a need to clarify, seeing as there were now three incidents in less than thirty hours.

Jared grinned, as if that was a laughing matter. "The first. When you completely lost it. There was still some of that going on this morning, but none tonight. You really are back to your usual self, even if you really are a crappy shot."

I couldn't help but grimace.

"You actually think I got lots of practice with a rifle?" I taunted. "The cartel goons weren't that stupid. I am a much better shot with a handgun."

"And of course with your knife," he added, as if that needed to be said.

Which was true.

I swallowed the urge to point out that, no, throwing my knife really wasn't that efficient. He would have just made fun of me if I had.

"I killed them in the end," I pointed out—too late realizing that, yet again, I'd played perfectly into his hands.

When I rolled onto my back with a sigh this time, it was because I was sick of his games and annoyed with myself, no longer with everything else.

"You know, it's perfectly normal not to feel bad if you kill someone," he crooned.

My answering laugh was a harsh one.

"Of course you'd say that."

His clothes rustled as he gave a one-shouldered shrug.

"True. But just think about it. All of them were out to kill us. They ambushed us, and would have gone through with it if we hadn't been smarter or at least luckier than them. This is absolutely a kill-or-be-killed world out there. I still don't get how you deluded yourself into believing until now that's not the case, but it is. And the sooner you come to grips with that, the better."

I couldn't help letting out another harsh laugh.

"You mean better for you? So you can get a hard-on, watching me kill?"

"And feast," he added, because of course he had to. When I cast him a caustic glare, he smiled. "What can I say? I admire a predator doing what she does best. It's only natural."

I wondered if I should ask now if he'd be annoyed if one such predator—like a bear or mountain lion—was the one to ultimately end his life. I had a feeling he'd simply state he was happy to contribute to the circle of life.

He'd probably even mean it.

Which begged the question—would his answer still be the same if the predator in question was me?

And why, oh why, was I burning to know the answer to that question on some level I didn't want to acknowledge, let alone explore?

"I'm not a delusional, naive goody-two-shoes," I finally said. "Even if you get off on calling me that. I simply refuse to accept that just because the world went to shit, everything good in it did as well."

His snort spoke volumes of his disagreement.

I hated how much he was right.

And yet—

I just had to cling to that smidgen of hope that was left inside of me. That I hadn't risked my life for nothing, joining the guards at the Enclave. That people like Kas and Dharma—and even somewhat assholes like Osprey—were right, and the reason I had to stand up to what was easier, and more convenient. That just because I ultimately ended up on the side of the strongest and fittest when worse came to worst, I couldn't accept that our cumulative survival was now up to the debatable, charitable feelings of assholes like Jared.

And me. In this, I couldn't count myself among the good anymore. That ship had sailed.

Kas would have been so disappointed in me. Dharma, afraid.

And Ash? Ash would have cried for my soul, knowing that while we all had lost something, this had cost me personally the most.

"Wanna fuck?"

I didn't even glare at Jared, just stared at him flatly.

He evenly held my gaze for a good fifteen seconds—because he would—before he cracked a smile.

"Oh, come on. How long are you going to hold my victimizing you against me?"

"Certainly more than three days," I pointed out. "Besides, we're both indiscriminately splattered with other people's blood."

His silence was poignant before he cracked another smile. "And your point is?"

"You're disgusting."

That could have come out with way more conviction.

"Says the woman who's right now hungering for sinking face-first into someone's chest cavity to tear out their liver."

That the mental image made me shudder—and not with revulsion—was bad.

Of course, he read my reaction perfectly, dipping that smile into a darker register.

"You really think I'm that much of an urge-directed creature that I'd supersede my entire moral code?" I asked, feeling like I was posing a rhetorical question.

Jared put on a mulling expression. Fake, no doubt.

"I was hoping for a 'yes' for sex. Definitely a 'hell, yes' where alternate food sources are concerned."

"Do you see me running back to that clearing, huh?"

His lips pursed.

"But you've thought about doing that," he stated, leaving no room for questions. "Which is only a step away from doing it."

The thought occurred to me that one way to shut him up would be to take him up on his offer—which was exactly what he was pushing for, I was sure.

"What ever happened to you waiting for me to make the first move?" I griped.

I got a long-suffering look for that.

"Oh, come on. You know that every single thing I said was lies to get you exactly where I wanted you."

I had been aware of that. I'd hoped that hearing him admit it would make a difference. It didn't. Part of my body was still very much up for crawling over the center console—or rather, inviting him to come over to me, since the steering wheel digging into my back didn't sound too exciting. That a much bigger part of me was still almost blind with hunger didn't make the situation any easier.

"Would an apology from me help?" Jared suggested, almost sounding sincere.

"A heartfelt one, maybe."

He snorted. "You know me better than to expect that." Then his eyes narrowed. "You don't really want me to continue to lie to you, do you? Because I'm sick of that shit."

"That much is obvious."

His lips curled up into a smile. It would have been a beautiful one under different circumstances.

"I think this is the moment where I confess just how good it feels to truly be myself around you."

I just stared. I mean, what do you say to something like that?

Clearly, sarcasm was the only way forward.

"Yeah, I reckon it must have been truly horrible for you to continually pretend you're someone else."

At least he had the grace to chuckle. That shouldn't have been such an amusing sound by itself.

"What can I say? I got bored."

"Bored," I deadpanned.

"Yes. Bored." He grinned. "One of so many valid reasons to kill."

"I very much disagree with that sentiment."

Another grin. "Duly noted and ignored."

"Obviously."

Now he was laughing for real, if muted, because the last thing we needed was for our nightly hideout to be swarmed because he was making fun of me.

"You don't really think that I'm going to change just because of your disapproval? Hypocritical as it is."

I hated how he was slowly worming his way underneath my skin… again.

"No hypocrisy about that," I offered. "I don't kill for sport."

"Sport is one motive," he pointed out. "I said I was bored. That's another."

"Oh, a convenient kill for any possible emotional state, huh?"

He shrugged, his smile now bordering on self-deprecating. "And wouldn't you know it, plenty of opportunities and people that need to be killed around these days."

The fucked-up thing was, I didn't dare contradict him. From what little he'd told me, it had sounded like he'd mostly been the executing tool, not even the will behind those murders.

"Is that how you justify it? That you're making the world a better place?"

For the first time tonight, Jared actually looked disappointed.

"We've been over this. I don't have a conscience. I can kill a breastfeeding mother or her innocently sleeping child just as easily as the next motherfucker who has it coming. It's all a matter of convenience."

It took me a moment to process that—and extrapolate from there.

I felt more than vaguely sick when the next realization hit me.

"You actually get off on people thanking you for doing it? Like all the sick people who caught the fucking zombie plague? You see yourself as some kind of fucked-up angel of mercy?!"

He was definitely laughing at me inside now.

"Hey, if the shoe fits—"

"You're disgusting!"

"Says the woman who delights in—"

"Yeah, well, at least I don't turn into a fucking cannibalistic monster on purpose!"

The way he regarded me now made me wonder what I'd just said. He looked almost pensive.

"Is that how you see yourself?" Jared eventually asked, his tone strange.

I couldn't help but snort, the need to hug myself incredibly strong.

"What else would you call it?" I was about to pause but then quickly added, "And if you say anything like 'glorious' now, I am going to fucking end you, and not shed a single tear over it!"

Jared remained mute, but it was obvious what he was thinking— and I hated how good it felt that his expression was utterly lacking one thing: judgment.

Until, of course, he had to destroy that beginning of a cozy feeling deep inside of me, because if he could pour salt in my wounds, he was getting ready to dump in an entire pound of that shit.

"I know you're not quite there yet, but here's a lesson for you. You're not going to get far in this world if you keep holding on to Good Girl Callie any longer. You're damn tough, and from what I can tell—particularly after digging literal bullets out of you and watching the wounds practically close up right in front of my eyes—you've become really hard to kill. That leaves a hell of a lot of room for endless pain and suffering. Do you really want to open yourself to that? Because personally, I'd be shying away from that like hell."

His words made my blood run cold, but I couldn't just give in like that.

"You mean, become more like you, huh?"

His shrug was an ambivalent one.

"And why not? The world is much easier to navigate when everyone else but you is like an extra on a movie set."

I fucking hated how familiar that sentiment was. Familiar from a time I'd vowed to barely even remember, let alone let myself devolve into ever again.

It was surprisingly easy to don a sweet smile in response.

"That includes me, huh?"

He smiled, but it didn't reach his eyes as they bored into mine. We were back to that staring again.

"I don't need to tell you that you mean a hell of a lot more to me than that."

The sad thing was, that was true. That lesson I'd learned long ago, and it continued to twist me up with every deeper level of it becoming apparent.

"Is that so bad?" Jared asked when I didn't respond what felt like a small eternity later.

"How could it not be bad?"

Another rhetorical question, of course. Just the same, it was no surprise he still answered.

"As I keep telling you, it's time you let go of all your precious mental wards and routines. We are not living in enlightened, liberated times anymore. It's survival of the fittest out there. Of the strongest. And very much of the biggest motherfuckers around. Your attempts to rise up to that and put yourself like a shield in front of the few surviving vulnerables were valiant, but you saw, yourself—over and over again—how that played out. They picked up your floofball simply because he was associated with you. They fucking murdered Makeup Barbie because she was an easy target—oh, and they would absolutely have let her tear apart Marion and the girls for an even bigger impact if you hadn't launched yourself between them and put her down. Exactly how many times are you going to set yourself up for yet more of a physical and emotional beat down? All you accomplish is hurting yourself deeper and deeper every single time."

He let that sit between us for several seconds.

I had virtually nothing to say to refute a single thing he'd said.

With not just a little satisfaction heavy in his tone, Jared finally went on.

"It is absolutely in your best interest to cut yourself off from all these false beliefs of chivalry and honor, and finally accept that you're safest running with the biggest assholes around. It's simple self-preservation. You're a proficient killer yourself. You surround yourself with others like you. And voila! Suddenly you become borderline invincible, because no other asshole is fucking stupid enough to get anywhere close to you, knowing there is only pain and death waiting for them. The second you become an unstoppable killing machine is actually the moment when you no longer need to be one. Easy peasy."

That statement sucked.

What sucked even more was that I wholeheartedly agreed with him.

And that realization was what broke my back—slowly, silently, and hopefully without a single emotion showing on my face as I kept staring into his eyes, refusing to look away while my soul died another agonizing death.

Because like any other wounded animal in the history of the universe, all I wanted was for the pain to end.

"You say that like it's that easy," I finally got out, my voice flat and hollow. So much for fooling anyone.

Jared shrugged, very much laissez-faire for real.

"It can be. If you just accept it."

I couldn't hold back a snort. "By that calculation, Axel is a fucking security nightmare."

Jared's smirk warned me that I really didn't want to know the cause for it.

"You know, there's a reason why you and he get along so well," he pointed out, then actually leaned even closer to deliver the rest. "And it's not that you're the weak links in our little homicidal quartet, ready to be set up to fall so the rest of us can get away."

I hated hearing that as much as I believed it was true—very much so.

When I said nothing as the minutes ticked by, just kept looking back at Jared, he finally gave a shrug before getting more comfortable on his side, ready to continue staring at me all night long, very much in a suit-yourself kind of way, secure in the knowledge that he'd not just delivered his message but that it had sunk in and taken root inside of me, just as he'd planned.

I was almost glad for the agonizing hunger gnawing away at my stomach. It was a welcome distraction from the much deeper-seated pain in my very soul.

CHAPTER 11

The next day dawned early—or endlessly late, considering I'd barely gotten any rest all night, let alone sleep. Jared hadn't exactly slept like a babe himself but looked much more perky than I felt when utter blackness was finally turning into rancid gray outside, signaling early dawn.

With nothing left for either of us to eat, it was a simple matter of taking another swig from our dwindling water supply and we were off, ready to get to our previously agreed-upon meeting spot.

It was an hour before we saw the first plume of smoke rising somewhere from an early morning fire, and two more when we spied the first drone searching for us. By then, we were in sight of that radio tower, and only two stretches of secure forest away from it.

Things continued to run smoothly and we arrived there mid-morning, only to find Axel and Blake already waiting inside the trees closest to the tower. They both looked slightly worse for wear but uninjured.

Oh, and moving forward was made significantly easier by the fact that my danger radar was active once more, letting us skirt two larger roving packs of zombies and the odd lurkers without getting anywhere near them. While that had been feasible in the car, on foot it was downright easy.

It also made me realize what I should have suspected all along yesterday when Jared and I had barely seen any lurkers at all: just as I could feel them, so could they feel me. And the fact that Jared and I together must have formed quite the footprint, it was easy for the weaker ones to avoid us like hell, and gave the aggressive ones little cause to get stupid, considering there was much easier prey swarming the countryside aplenty at present.

Just how true that sentiment was we saw firsthand when throughout the day, we continued to hear barrages of shots fired, only to come across totaled vehicles amidst carnage later.

The drones continued to patrol, and more than once we had to hide deeper into the trees to let a group of cars pass, but at this rate it was almost too easy to avoid them—provided we were happy to continue on foot, with little chance of finding food.

That third day of our hiding-in-the-woods life, we were still cautious about approaching any buildings. The next morning, I was borderline ravenous and all three men were cranky with hunger, and our guard slipped more and more rather than us letting it down. Any car we saw got thoroughly investigated now, and any building—even if it was a simple barn—was enough to make us veer off our random course in search of food. Between them, the guys found just enough to keep them from starvation to just-hangry mode while there was nothing to be found for me.

That was, until the fourth night, one of the bands hunting us was stupid enough to light a fire too close to the edge of the woods, giving away their position so we could sneak up on them in the dark.

I will spare you the details of how those seven men died.

Suffice it to say, I didn't go hungry that night.

And yes, as revolting as it was to accept it, I let Jared pack me some trail rations—as he put it—drying strips of fatty flesh by a new fire, much better hidden in a pit next to some rocks that shielded it from sight from all angles, just as if we were the fucking Donner Party.

When I voiced that observation, all he did was chuckle. Blake, too, while Axel busied himself whittling away on some figurine made out of a discarded branch.

Ignoring the vehicles of the band of mercenaries, we now were back in business with packs full of food and ammo, and some upgrades for Blake's stupidly large arsenal.

Now the pertinent question was—where to next? We didn't seem to be able to shake the assholes, but avoiding them had turned out to be far easier than expected. It made sense to make plans now.

"We're less than three days away from our summer hideout," Jared pointed out as he and Axel used our newly scavenged GPS to check our position on our old maps. "Just a day if we use the cars, but I don't want to risk it."

My heart soared just a little at the idea of meeting Kay and Oliver again. Not so much the sanctimonious pastor, but in a pinch, I'd be ready to accept his misgiving stares for a day or two.

That was, until I remembered hearing that they had gone dark weeks ago.

"Think anyone is still alive around there?" I asked, not really wanting an answer.

Jared shrugged, as if that was all the same to him. Which it likely was.

"Either someone is still around, or we can scrounge up some provisions from what they left behind. Either from the town, or the lake houses where we moored our boat." He pointedly cast a look my way. "And if you want to, we can stay for a week at our old hideout. We're down to a single bottle of—"

"Fuck you."

He shrugged, still grinning.

"Thought you'd never change your mind!"

We were off with first light again, after I gorged myself once more on the grisly—and increasingly more disgusting—leftovers.

It only took us two and a half days to get back to Lancaster county, reaching the area where the survivors had been from the southeast this time. We didn't exactly shake the drones by then, but it had been an entire day since we'd heard the last shots, and the drones we saw were many miles away, nothing more than indistinct specks in the sky requiring binoculars to identify. I didn't quite allow myself to consider that as us getting away, but we were very close to accomplishing that.

In the late afternoon sunshine, it became clear that Lancaster was deserted—both what remained of the burned-out ruins of the scattered houses where the community had lived during the summer, and the downright war zone that their previous town had turned into, equally or even more so destroyed, from what we could see down the street. We went as far as to check on the church and houses of people we'd personally known, finding little left, certainly no diaries or pinned letters telling us of their whereabouts.

If we hadn't been here six weeks ago, I would have guessed that the damage was from the spring, back when Charlotte had been firebombed.

"When exactly did they go dark?" I asked nobody in particular.

Axel answered. "A little over three weeks ago? When we got to the weirdos before the community before Grace and her people."

That felt like a lifetime ago. Which made a lot of sense, considering recent… happenstance.

The destruction all around us looked a lot older than that.

"Let's check up on the radio station," I suggested.

Jared snickered. "Why? Still hoping that someone's still holed up there? Haven't you gotten enough sanctimonious shit yet?"

I was happy to see Axel make a face at Jared's gripe. Then I remembered that the reason Josh had pretty much kicked us out was that, somehow, some of their teenagers had gotten enough drugs to almost overdose, and other members of their community had suspiciously disappeared without a trace.

It felt stupid to even ask, but I couldn't help comically turning to Jared and staring him down.

He already had a bright if bland grin ready for me that required no questioning.

"You got bored, huh?" I still griped because I couldn't help myself.

It took us a good hour to make it down the road to the radio station that sat much closer to the lake than the scattered-all-over community. Back then, they'd kept some decoy vehicles on the road to make the area look abandoned. All those were burned down as well and had multiplied in number.

Not much was left of the fire station that had housed their radio, but in the ruins, we unearthed three charred skeletons—two larger and one slighter.

I stared at what I presumed were the earthly remains of Josh, Oliver, and Kay, who had either taken refuge here, or, more likely, had made a last stand to get the message out to the world about what was happening to them.

From what little we'd known until getting here, it stood to reason their signal had been jammed, only the absence of updates speaking of their demise.

"Are you done beating yourself up that you couldn't save them yet?" Jared's voice came from behind me where I was still staring at the remains. "You are aware that none of us could have made a difference, right?"

Oh, I knew that well enough. And that thought hadn't even really been on my mind. My mind had only begun to check off three more names from the increasingly small list of people I knew were still alive, let alone cared for.

Looking up and finding Axel and Blake showing at least hints of similar exasperation made me want to wipe that slate clear completely.

"Yeah, all done," I quipped, doing my best to shove the boiling clouds of emotion threatening on the horizon back down. "What do we do next?"

"We left some small caches of provisions at our old place," Blake pointed out. "Why not get our dinner from there, crash for the night in a secure building for once, and decide what to do next in the morning?"

I had the distinct feeling none of that was his idea. It sounded very much like Jared's. Because Blake and leaving behind food? Unheard of.

As if on command, my stomach growled. Because of course it did, empty as it was again. I still had some of my trail rations in my pack, but I'd done my very best to make them last as long as I could possibly stand it. Also because going borderline hungry kept at least a vague sense of that danger radar present, if not good enough to use it to navigate. Right now, it felt as if we were in a dead zone, which wasn't much of a surprise. If anything, the undead must have long ago learned that literal burned earth didn't mean barbecue, but nothing at all for them to eat.

Jared turned with a smirk on his face, without a doubt ready to make fun of my dietary requirements because apparently, that joke still hadn't gotten old. In so doing, his foot slipped on something— maybe what used to be Josh's belly fat and hadn't completely burned up in the fire, because sterile cremation that hadn't been. He staggered, having a hard time catching himself while I was ready to laugh at him—

Only that the laugh caught in my throat when a gunshot went off from somewhere to my right, from the small ridge serving as a natural border of the fire station's parking lot. I didn't exactly see where the bullet ended up biting into the charred ruins, but his stumble might have just saved Jared's life. In the afternoon gloom of the not exactly bright day, the muzzle fire was clearly visible when three more rifles joined in.

I didn't so much consciously seek cover as much as blindly hurled myself at what remained of the back walls of the building, never mind the soot and broken bits of cement and wood that bit into my legs and side. Scrambling behind the wall, I tried to catch a glimpse at what was going on behind me, but more shots—and now coming from three sides—dissuaded me of the notion that this was a situation that we could easily tough out one-on-one.

Looking around through the ruins as much as I could, I realized we'd traipsed into the ideal trap. The fire station sat in a man-made ring of ridges, possibly to keep the area clear of vegetation or for flooding reasons or whatnot. But that meant the only way out of here really was to either scramble up there in full view or to come in from the main road—which was where I saw three vehicles come crawling in, nearly silent except for the crunch of the tires on the gravel road.

The fuckers were using electric cars and driving slowly, meaning virtually no sound for us to catch or dust plumes to track!

Considering that had also been our strategy—albeit on foot— that made me really mad.

Then I caught a larger vehicle following them—a pickup truck towing a medium-sized livestock transport container behind it.

I had a terrible feeling about that, even before it stopped a good distance from the other vehicles, the back of the transporter pointing right at the fire station while none of the cars had spewed out any people yet.

Just as I thought that, the door in the back dropped down to build a ramp onto the ground, a good twenty zombies racing out immediately.

I stared at them, kind of dumbfounded, my brain insisting that I should be able to fucking feel them, particularly so many all at once, and aggressive ones to boot—and yet, it was as if I was watching a herd of sheep.

Well, not quite, since they immediately came running for where the guys were still scrambling out of the way of the bullets and the new threat now, but the point remained the same.

It only took me a moment to shake myself out of my momentary stupor. At least the shooting stopped now that the zombies were swarming the parking lot and ruins. My carbine—strapped to my pack because I'd long gotten tired of it getting in the way or getting caught on random branches—was of zero use to me now. I also had no clue where my latest walking stick had ended up that I must have dropped by the remains.

You'd think this was my absolutely first day of this shit.

At least Jared was sprinting for a different corner from where I was hiding, sparing me a second of his scorn.

Then two of the undead veered away from the others and came right at me, clearly having no issues finding me even where I was mostly hidden behind the warped, crumbling wall.

I didn't exactly freeze, but by the time I whipped around and took off, they had almost reached me, giving chase as I made for the slope behind me.

Sure, because running out in the open, exposed, was such a smart idea. But I kind of hoped our assailants would be stupid and count on their zombies to hunt us down and decide not to waste any more bullets on us than they already had.

The renewed bark of two assault rifles let me know that wasn't so, but while the bullets chewed into the somewhat overgrown ground next to me, none of them hit me. But fear slowed me down, letting the faster of the zombies tackle me to the ground.

I waited for my mind to fold under and for instinct to take over, but just like my extended senses, that didn't happen, either. But damn, that was a hard, brutal fall, and the undead thing trying to claw at my face while the bulk of my pack between us kept it somewhat at bay did not help my situation!

This being a half-zombie really wasn't holding up to my expectations!

On the other hand, what happened very much according to my experience was the second zombie now catching up to the first, and since it was looming above me, it went right for the easy, tall target, which nicely yanked it off me and helped me stagger back onto my feet.

Rather than attack either of them bare-handed, I went for the slope again, only for more bullets to come my way, this time in a longer, more insistent spray. One or two hit my pack—judging from the jerks I felt—but since there was no pain, I figured I was in the clear.

So far.

But that slope was too steep to get up there quickly, and behind me, five more zombies ran right past the fray I'd left behind—coming from a second trailer, I realized, as I madly cast around.

Well, if I couldn't go up, sideways and down it was.

Did it feel insane to run back toward the cars? Absolutely, but since most of the zombies were spread out all across the ruins now and the assholes in the cars made no move to get out, I figured that if I didn't get too close to them, maybe I could escape past them onto the open road.

Return fire coming from the other corner of the ruins made me guess that Blake—and probably Axel—had chosen a different strategy to deal with the issue.

Good. The more we got them to spread out, the better our chances were!

Four against a good fifty zombies and at least twenty armed humans. Easy peasy!

I got a good third of the way before the undead overwhelmed me, pretty much burying me in a pile of stench and body parts.

That did not work out as planned.

Even less when I felt their filthy nails rake scratches into any part of me they could reach, and try as I might to first flail around me, then tuck myself into a tight ball, I felt teeth score my skin.

On a scale of one to complete panic, that sent my heart rate into overdrive, but there was little I could do except pray that I wasn't wrong with all my theories about what the fuck was going on with me—or I wouldn't have that long to regret it because I'd be dead and torn apart long before I could turn.

A shrill whistle cut through the air, the only reason I could hear it the fact that it made the zombies pause. Maybe that was actually the second whistle. While not that loud, it seemed to cut to my very bones, making my teeth ache and my ears feel like they were about to pop. The zombies froze, what I could see of them through the cage of my arms in front of my head still, their heads all turned in the same direction—the direction of the trailers and cars, if I wasn't completely mistaken; like well-trained dogs.

I sure recognized an opportunity when it presented itself.

Springing to my feet, I fought my way through the pack, punching and pushing at anything I could reach until I staggered free. Another whistle followed that almost sent me to my knees, but only almost. Staggering forward, I started running, aiming for the slope right next to the road where the gunmen might hesitate, since they were essentially shooting very close to their friends. Behind me, I heard more than one zombie roar, but for the moment I was free, I was running, and nobody was shooting at me. That was all I cared about.

I didn't look back. I didn't even look over to the vehicles— or at least I tried not to. From the corner of my vision, they were impossible to ignore. The screaming behind me was coming from close enough that I knew very well that I was a single stumble away from being torn down again—and this time, I wouldn't get up again.

As if to cheer me on—or maybe as a deliberate distraction, although I really wasn't sure if I could count on that—gunfire went up from within the ruins, peppering the opposite slope and adjacent territory, making it impossible for the gunmen hidden there to shoot at me.

"Hey! You motherfucking undead assholes! Go after her, not us!" I heard a lone voice coming from the direction of the cars, guessing that someone had gotten out to take a shot at me, only to get a face full of free-running zombie now.

Good. At least their own trap was backfiring on them. As it should be when you were fucked enough in the head to use siccing the undead on someone as a plan.

Going up more or less diagonally, I finally neared the crest of the slope. Twenty feet. Fifteen. Ten, and I tried to gauge how many zombies were still after me. I could still smell them, but that might well be because of necrotic tissue clinging to my clothing and body.

The very idea made me want to shake myself like a dog and hurl myself headfirst into the lake—only that I was actually running away from where I knew said lake was. Which was a good thing because in the water, they would easily see me. But in the surrounding forest outside of the community, I could get lost.

And that was exactly my plan.

I finally reached the top of the slope, ready to hurl myself down the other side, only to realize that it was actually a plateau up here. Fuck. More running. But the least I could do was to minimize my silhouette, so I did my best to bend over as I kept pumping my arms and legs, my entire torso screaming with exertion and my lungs for once doing what they were made for: processing oxygen from the air I gulped in hungrily.

Something in the pattern of the shots changed. Blake running out of ammo, likely. Still no shots reached me, which was a good thing.

There was the tree line, another hundred feet away from me. It felt like I needed to run an entire marathon until I was finally inside the trees, blindly staggering forward, branches slapping at me that I ignored as much as I could.

No more screams behind me—or at least not close.

Making sure that I wasn't about to smack into a tree trunk in front of me, I glanced back, finding the forest deserted. I could still smell their stench, but for now, I was on my own.

Panting heavily, I forced myself to run another minute or two until my lungs threatened to give out. Then I slowed down to a stagger, glancing behind me repeatedly.

Still nothing.

I finally stopped next to where I could scoop up a strategic branch from the ground—the best weapon if I didn't want to draw any more attention. And then I waited, trying to disappear behind bushes and larger trunks.

I hadn't completely shaken the zombies. It took them maybe thirty seconds to come wandering down the path I'd torn through the underbrush, neither stealthy nor coordinated. I could see two in front, with four or five following. Maybe few enough of them that if I was lucky, I could get away, but in a direct fight I still didn't stand a chance.

Too bad that I didn't have my instant-apex-predator mode ready to activate.

I considered ditching my pack, but the residual trauma of the early days where I'd hardly been able to hold on to the clothes on my back was still fresh in my mind. Plus, it was getting cold at night now, and even if I hated those disgusting strips of dried meat, they were my only sustenance. I wondered if I could use them to lure the undead away, but I doubted they'd go for half-dessicated if they could have fresh and juicy. Of course, there was also my carbine and the two pistols inside my pack, but I doubted that, unless I managed a perfect headshot that miraculously scrambled what was left of their brains, a handgun would do much against the undead. Their handlers, sure. But them? Assault rifle rounds hadn't slowed me down when I'd been on that last bender at the Marines' ambush, so I doubted things would work differently now.

Fuck.

I knew exactly when the two lead zombies caught my scent—maybe even literally since I was bleeding from several wounds on my forehead and hands—because they went from looking this way and that to coming straight at me once more. I was ready this time, holding the branch in trembling hands, silently praying to the universe for deliverance.

Like, you know, a bout of super-strength and aggressive attack skills for yours truly?

I fucking remembered tearing into the Marines just like the undead were about to tear into me. Why the hell couldn't I trigger this?

Lacking that, I swung my branch, aiming for the lead zombie's head. My hit even landed well—and thanks to it blindly coming for me, there was some added momentum—but all that did was smash in its already horribly disfigured face. It even staggered back, but that left room for the other to come right for me, and me half unprepared because of the swing that still carried my body.

The zombie smacked into my side, powerful clawed arms closing around me. I tried my best to twist aside and bring up my branch as the easier form of defense. The zombie raised one arm and easily deflected it, jaws snapping shut inches away from my face in anticipation. The other was back, barreling into both of us—and ended up tangled with the other zombie instead of me.

That gave me a moment's respite—that I used to whip around, drop the damn useless branch, and take off running again.

Off to my right, I thought I could see the road through the trees. That was an option to give me more speed for running, but considering the undead didn't tire at the same rate as I did, that was a shit idea. Plus, it gave the assholes in the vehicles a good chance to run me down by car. Ahead, only more woods loomed until I would inevitably stagger out onto the grassland around the burned-down buildings of the community—not a good option, either.

So I zig-zagged to the left, aiming for the lake I knew lay somewhere beyond the trees—and the subdivision of houses that Josh had explained they had cordoned off because everything had been too overrun for them to clear.

Maybe I could hide somewhere in there?

Or at the very least, agitate other undead that might start to fight with my pursuers?

Or, if worse came to worst, I could always jump into the lake, no doubt cold now in early October, even worse since the sun would set in an hour.

I heard rather than saw the snarl of limbs break up behind me. Problem was, I couldn't check on them because now the slightly slower ones were closing in on me, ignoring the other two zombies. I forced a burst of speed out of my body to stay ahead of them, but they made no move to fall back behind me. They actually kept gaining on me, following with single-minded attention that wasn't compromised by all the things that kept distracting me—stumbling over roots, having my face smacked by the odd branch every so often. Compared to me, they were fresh and uninjured—a recipe for disaster.

Suddenly, the ground underneath my sneakers changed. I didn't so much see it since there were fallen leaves everywhere, but I heard and felt gravel crunch where soft earth used to be. Two steps and it was gone, but I hadn't imagined that. Casting around wildly, I tried to find the path again but almost missed it—until I switched directions and happened on it again.

Within seconds, I gained just a little headway, enough to better orient myself. Yes, over there! The terrain was sloping downward, which meant either the road or the lake, and I was pretty sure the road was somewhere else. Dipping into my last reserves, I sprinted toward the dip in the terrain, immediately starting to slip and slide as

I suddenly found myself on a surprisingly steep slope—that dropped down to the fucking golf course!

It was only my mind that ground to a halt while I, of course, kept running for my life, the going actually easier in the long grass that still remembered once having been well-manicured rather than wild undergrowth. Casting back over my shoulder, I spied three—no, make that four—zombies still after me. There was enough adrenaline poisoning my veins that my pulse didn't spike anew at the sight, and there were no energy reserves left to give me a new burst of speed, but of course I kept going ever forward.

But utter confusion set in, and not in a good way—although it was debatable that was even possible, confusion being positive. Even in the expected range, the downright brain fog that crashed through my gray matter was so bad that it almost made my feet stall.

Theoretically, I'd known there was a golf course around. We'd even seen it from the lake, or seen signs for it or… something. I couldn't remember. But it should have been farther to the north, farther inland. I'd been so sure that I was heading for the lake houses, not in this direction.

And what the fuck was it with the entire landscape around the rivers being peppered with golf courses?! No wonder I was starting to mash them all up into one continuous, this-is-so-bad territory.

But even as I looked around wildly, trying to orient myself anew, I had trouble picturing myself relative to the maps and actual terrain I'd been in. I knew where I wanted to be, but couldn't quite figure out where I was. Not even where I should be if I kept going straight, or veered off to the left. Because left was good. Left meant the lake. Because the community—and north of that, the town—were to my right.

Right?

But the entire summer, the lake had been right, and the houses left…

No. That had been looking from where we'd moored our overstuffed boat, and where my makeshift drug laboratory had been. Which was right across the lake from where I should have exited the forest.

I realized it wasn't just lack of access to map-viewing apps for half a year now that scrambled my brain.

Something was wrong with me—something new.

Before even more panic could spread through my brain, I saw something besides the inherently weird topography of the golf course—a road that led to a building with a parking lot. And beyond that, another road that led to yet another... and off there, far to my left, more houses! The subdivision! Terrifyingly uniform McMansions galore!

The sight made my heart soar, almost as much as a buffet table full of meat would have.

Just thinking about that made me salivate and my stomach contract and rumble painfully.

I was a good two hundred feet closer to the road when my mind finally caught up with itself. Why, exactly, was I so happy to see the houses? I'd been repeatedly warned not to go there. That the local survivors went into town rather than here was telling. So why the fuck...

More zombies. Which could be a distraction.

Right.

No, left! Go left!

Even as I kept mulling that over, it made little to no sense to me anymore.

The closer I got to the houses, the less I wanted to be near them.

Glancing back at my pursuers, I wondered if it made any sense to risk getting closer to the subdivision. There were now eight zombies coming from two directions. They didn't give me the best vibes, either, even if I'd managed to put some distance between us in the meantime.

It took me another hundred paces until I realized what those ominous feelings were: my absolutely not-to-be-relied-on danger radar was rearing its head again.

I couldn't remember anymore if I'd felt them at the fire station.

I couldn't remember if anyone had still been shooting when I'd gotten away from there or not.

What I could remember was a lingering sense of unease when I wondered whether I should try to get back to help the guys or not, but I couldn't pinpoint why. It made no sense. After all, being on my own was almost the worst that could happen to me, besides being captured or eaten. But I knew there was a reason.

I just couldn't remember it anymore.

Fuck.

The only vaguely good thing I was aware of was the dash of hope that this meant I was about to flip over into mindless murder zombie mode—which was absolutely a good thing, because otherwise, I didn't stand a chance out here, on my own, without a weapon or pack, against eight of the undead.

Where the fuck had my pack ended up?! This was getting ridiculous.

Still undecided, I kept running ever forward—until a shiny reflection caught my attention.

Seriously? Was my rapidly declining intellect down to "oh, shiny!?"

I'd never live that down if I breathed even a word of that to Jared.

But since we both had to be alive for that to happen—and things didn't look too great in that aspect right now—I felt like this wasn't the most important issue to worry about.

Right. The shiny thing. Or rather, the last rays of the setting sun lighting up the reeds and setting the water of the lake on fire.

The lake! That had been the reason I'd been running in this direction, even if I'd gotten massively off course. Because if I had one advantage over the zombies, it was that I could fucking swim—and use boats, if I happened to find one—while they would drown!

At least I hoped they'd drown instead of getting stuck underwater without air where their decomposition sped up like crazy... but since we hadn't come across any swamp-monster varieties yet, I felt like it was a safe bet that wouldn't happen.

One less thing to worry about...

I tried to judge the distance to the water. Maybe half a mile? A little more than that, I decided, past the swimming pool and tennis courts in the communal area. But I really didn't want to run through there past several rows of houses and no clear way to reach the lake. That seemed like suicide if there were even a handful of zombies hiding in there, let alone possibly hundreds, if not more.

Rather late, I realized that, considering how far in both directions the houses went, the entire first row of them would have lake access. That meant those on the southern edge of the subdivision were the only ones I'd need to run around. It meant I had a longer way to go, but considering the undead often had problems with extrapolating running paths, maybe it wasn't even the worst idea.

I switched routes as soon as that thought cleared in my mind, veering off to the left, almost doubling back on my previous path.

Most of the undead went on running straight ahead, only slowly adjusting to my change in direction.

Not so the foremost two, who I thought had been close to me for the longest time. They actually switched seconds after me, and I lost half of my head start. They also looked more alert and aggressive than the rest.

Shit.

As I kept running, the sun and its reflection were blinding me, making navigating even harder—until I realized that wasn't just a fluke but meant that right fucking now, there was open space directly between me and where the rays hit the water, with no house obstructing the view. From what I could tell, the streets weren't set up in straight lines but rather curved, as if they meandered between the plots.

Without second-guessing my decision, I turned once more, now heading straight into the light. With luck, the zombies would be just as blinded as I was, and twice as confounded by it.

Hair all over my body rose to stand on end, and my gut twisted with a wave of unease that crashed into me. But I did my best to ignore it all, forcing my focus to remain singularly pointed at the water.

Pushing myself for all I was worth, I increased my speed further as my sneakers suddenly hit dirty asphalt, leaving the grass behind.

Only six hundred feet now, give or take.

A single howl rose in the evening stillness, off from somewhere to my right.

I ignored it.

Three more joined in, then many, many more voices picked it up, coming from left, right, in front, but also from behind me.

New fear pushed adrenaline into my veins, but I simply couldn't go any faster. My muscles were burning, my lungs working overdrive for what felt like an eternity already—and not even a flutter of undue aggression stirred deep inside of my heart. Just fear. So much fear.

I had no other option now than to reach the water.

A random thought zoomed through my brain, almost drowned out by the fear.

Is this what turning into one of them feels like?

Forgetting who I am? Forgetting what should be second nature to me?

Very disappointing.

It was very different from what my memory flashes felt like, and waking up in that clearing in a puddle of mud, caked from head to toe in blood.

And, I really expected to go down fighting. Which this was not.

I was still waiting for at least some of that anger to come roaring back, but none of that happened. But spite and defiance? Well, that was something I had going for me in spades.

More and more undead crowded the street ahead. What had been fifty soon doubled to a hundred, with more and more coming from every possible place of hiding.

It was pretty obvious that I had zero chance of making it through or around that crowd.

Not just the setting sun made tears spring into my eyes. This simply wasn't fair! This—

This wasn't the only way to the water, I realized, as my gaze skipped over a group of zombies coming from my left. Right there, behind them, was a gap between one house and the next, a walkway running perpendicular to the road—and right on to a pier leading through the reeds into the lake.

Suddenly, all that stood between me and freedom was a handful of zombies, no longer a town hall full of them.

Too bad that I knew—well, had known—all of them.

Not Kay or Oliver. I was pretty sure that the dirty, crispy, fleshy skeletons we'd found belonged to them. But one of the zombies standing in the middle of that gap I needed to hurtle through was one of the women who'd several times made stew or soup for us. Two of the men next to her I knew from hunting trips I'd opted out of when my leg hadn't quite been up to it yet, and one more was what could be considered a good customer of mine. The same was true for the two teenagers struggling forward behind them.

Wait. Weren't they the people Josh had accused us of making run away or disappear? It was hard to tell, of course, but they didn't look like someone had stuck a knife into the sides of their necks from the distance.

A distance that was rapidly decreasing since I was running straight for them now, weaving and dodging around several more undead who happened to be standing in the way more than coming for me.

From the corner of my eye, I checked in the direction I had previously been running in, looking both ways. My tail was still coming from the buildings but seemed to have lost me. Those aggressive screamers were pushing through the less mobile throngs toward me, but unless one of the lurkers tried to grab me, they wouldn't reach me before I got to the pier—if I managed to somehow get around the knot of former townspeople, that was.

I only had five more seconds to decide what to do.

Make that four. Three. Two—

None of them made a move to get out of my way. They didn't even actually acknowledge me—of course not as in recognizing me, but seeing as something was barreling down on them, you'd have thought that self-preservation—

But the same could have been said for myself. Rather than formulate a plan, I spent those precious seconds staring at them—until it was too late.

I ran smack into the older woman, instinctively going for the softest, weakest target. The impact made her stagger into the side of the house, opening just enough room for me to squeeze through as I staggered on and past the teenagers. At the last second, the boy held out a hand for me, his fingers snagging on the sleeve of my jacket. His fist closed and he pulled, making me stumble as momentum fought inertia—

But then I managed to wrench myself free of my half-unzipped jacket altogether, leaving him behind with the fabric, staring stupidly at his prize. Beyond the group, the aggressive ones howled and descended on them—but by then, I was whipping around and made a last, panting push, gravel underneath my sneakers turning to wood as I reached the pier.

Seven more bounds, and I hurled myself off the pier and into the dark, murky water without a care for my safety.

The idea that the lake might be shallow here didn't even occur to me until my body hit the surface, and a second later, my right ankle gave a twinge as I hit bottom way too soon.

If anything, the lake was waist-deep here, with reeds encroaching the pier now, since nobody had bothered to whack them away in the summer.

The water was cold enough to make breathing hard for a second—besides me being completely out of breath from running for what felt like fucking forever—but it didn't completely numb my brain.

Panic raced up my spine as I realized this was shallow enough that any zombies that came after me would easily be able to stand—and thus pursue me. I hadn't seen that coming.

And probably neither would the zombies, unless I was stupid enough to get up and show them.

It was surprisingly hard to force myself to stay as low in the water as I could make myself, which probably still meant they could easily see my head. So I did the thing my brain screamed the most against and flipped onto my back, letting my clothes drag me down until only parts of my face remained above the waterline.

Between the reeds and the quickly gathering darkness, I figured I stood at least a slim chance of them losing sight of me this way.

Waiting for what was to come was sheer agony. My lungs screamed for me to draw deep, full breaths while every single muscle in my body was poised to fight for my survival, chiefly to trudge away from the shore and swim into deep water. Yet instead, what I did was lock myself down and stay there, water burning in my eyes as I could barely see anything except the changing colors of the evening sky above.

I could hear them, even as muffled as sounds were underwater.

Pounding onto the pier. Screaming in rage as their perceived aggressor-slash-meal was suddenly gone.

My pulse sped up, my ears straining for the only sound I didn't hear—heavy splashing in the water.

I had no idea how long I floated there in the water. Five minutes maybe? It felt closer to five years.

The howls got louder and louder, so close that if they'd articulated actual words, I would have been able to understand them. But then they tapered off, one by one, several starting up anew farther inland—where I presumed other, maybe somewhat less agitated but still hostile zombies were going toe to toe with what used to be my tail.

I forced myself to stay there even as shivers started to overwhelm my body, forcing me to push more of my face up to keep the water from lapping down my nose and mouth.

A spluttering cough was all that might stand between my survival and certain death.

The noise didn't decrease but kept moving farther away from me—not inland, I realized, but at least down the shore. I finally took heart and dared to push enough of my face out of the water to be able to glance up at the pier, maybe eight feet away from me. From what I could tell, it was empty, and I didn't see any lurkers on the sloped lawn leading down to it, either. I still glimpsed something moving up by the houses, but it was getting dark quickly now, and if I moved just slowly enough, I figured I'd look like a log slowly drifting by rather than anything edible.

Hmmm, food.

I could really have done with something juicy, dripping blood—

Cutting down on those thoughts—and everything they entailed—I pushed deeper into the lake until I reached open water, the lake still shallow enough that I was more walking than swimming. Fine with me. Even without my pack and jacket, my body felt laden down with my sodden clothes, weighing a million tons. My legs burned from exertion, and when I finally had to start swimming, my arms and back soon joined in.

It made the most sense to stay in the water, even if I could have traversed the small "finger" I was in and crawled out the other side. It was too dark to see more than shapes now, and all I could make out on the other side was forest. Down the shoreline, at least I had the houses to go by, their lightly painted outsides still distinct from the rest of the world.

Oh, and I could also go by sound, keeping the howls and cries firmly to my right and at a good distance as I took stroke after stroke, slowly making my way deeper into the lake.

They chased me well into the night, only slowly dropping away farther and farther behind me.

CHAPTER 12

I had no idea how long it took me to swim across the lake. Hours. Endless hours. With no way to judge the passage of time, I estimated I needed at least thirty minutes—if not twice that—to make it out of the side arm of the lake and into the main part. There, I rested a while in the shallow waters on the opposite shore of the side arm to catch my breath and try to regain some strength—to no avail. The ice-cold water had by now numbed my fingers and toes well above my wrists and ankles, but I figured as long as I could still swim, sensation would return later if I didn't drown or get eaten. The numbing sensation had spread all across my skin by then, making it impossible to feel the sting of the scratches and bites, but I hadn't forgotten about them.

The way I saw it, I had two options. Either to climb out here and backtrack to the fire station, which was a stupid idea because I had no clue who was lurking in the dark, dead and alive. Or, to swim across the lake and hide in one of the houses we'd stayed in and raided ourselves, where I still remembered the lay of the land, and where very few zombies had been hiding all summer long. Much could have changed about that, of course, but I doubted they'd managed to get into the houses we'd carefully barricaded from the inside and later climbed out of through less obvious doors and windows.

Yes, we had been paranoid fucks, but now I felt like said precaution had absolutely been warranted.

Even if I hated staying hours longer in the water, it was safer to go the direct route than to try to cross via the bridge that might just have been part of the ambush that had almost cost me my life—and maybe the guys hadn't been that lucky.

I didn't really think much as I slowly made my way across the lake, near silent except for when I had to tread water, trying to warm up my frozen muscles to keep going. It wasn't even that long, although all in all, I had twice the distance to go as we'd paddled across many times during the summer in our kayaks because of where I'd jumped into the water. But I was weak, tired, cold, and utterly miserable, and none of that made for great thinking.

Besides the cold, there was only hunger on my mind, which didn't help.

When I finally reached the desired shore, it had started to rain— because I wasn't miserable enough yet.

I didn't bother with one of the few piers reaching into the lake. By then, I neither possessed the strength in my arms and torso to heave myself up out of the water, nor would have been able to perform the fine mechanical manipulations of my digits to wrap them around a ladder rung. The shore was thick with fallen leaves and soaked from the rain, making climbing out an exercise in slipping and sliding and trying very hard not to thrash back into the water. I finally managed, caked with mud and leaves and not giving a single shit about either.

I hadn't thought it possible, but lying there in the cold night air made me shiver even worse, to the point where the clattering of my teeth was alarmingly loud.

I was really getting concerned when some of that went away and a hint of warmth spread through my body.

Shit.

I was too tired to orient myself as I stumbled to my feet, but I could see two houses, so I went to the closer one. No burn marks, and fiddling with the lock on the screen door was quickly solved with the use of a heavy branch. Inside, the air smelled musty but otherwise okay. I made sure to pull the door closed behind me before I trudged into the living room, grabbed a random comforter, and curled up on the couch.

When I still didn't get any warmer a while later, I forced myself to get up and made my way over to the expansive bedroom, stripped, and disappeared into the king-sized bed under all the blankets and comforters I could find on short notice.

I was tired enough that turning over was too much to ask, yet sleep was a long time from coming.

As the cold finally abated into generalized discomfort, the hunger turned into a constant gnawing pain in my middle, keeping me wide awake, staring at the windows, the beautiful vista of the nighttime lake beyond lost on me.

I needed to eat.

I needed to feed.

Anything, right fucking now! Even if it was empty calories that I couldn't very well digest. Anything would have been better than this.

Maybe even the box of tissues on the nightstand.

Problem was, we had been thorough in our raiding all summer long, and I was pretty sure I remembered taking even a rack of spices from this very house, leaving absolutely nothing edible behind.

There was a single exception to the rule—the house right by our mooring point, where I'd established my makeshift lab.

We hadn't left behind much, but I remembered we'd hidden a single meal's worth of food, should we ever choose to return.

That, and a small surprise in the kitchen.

Even ravenous as I was, the idea of getting high now was still met with a shit-ton of resistance, even if I couldn't concentrate on—or remember—why I was so opposed to the idea. I just knew that it was bad.

I tried to wait until first light, but my hunger got the better of me. My skin was still cold to the touch but my hands were no longer quite so useless when I slid out from underneath the covers and blindly went through the cupboards until I had enough dark clothes piled up on the bed to find something that fit me well enough to keep going. Even a fresh, dry pair of sneakers, although I would have to find sturdier ones later since these were more or less glorified house shoes.

Clearly, people who could afford these lake houses hadn't furnished them planning for the apocalypse.

In the darkness outside, I managed to orient myself quickly. If I kept the lake to my right, it was only a matter of how many houses to trudge by until I reached the right one. Outside, it was quiet, but only normal-night quiet, not that deathly quiet that didn't bode well. The air fogged in front of my face, and my still-clammy hair was soon cold as hell once more, my body shivering even as I tried to hide my hands in my sweater's long arms.

I found the house I was looking for easily enough, after having to walk at least a mile north on the shore. I didn't have an accurate map of the area in my head, but this made me guess I'd not swum as straight across the lake as I'd thought but veered south inevitably, maybe because of currents I hadn't really felt that much. But everything was still where I'd expected to find it—the house with the pier and the makeshift lab in the garage.

What was missing was the stash of cans we'd hidden underneath the staircase leading into the upper rooms.

I stared at the discarded box to the side with comprehension only setting in slowly.

Fuck.

I was already walking into the kitchen before my mind caught up to the possible ramifications—besides me going hungry, which was pretty much the only thing on my mind right now and impossible to shut up.

Only four people had known where to look for that box. I was one of them. At least one other of the remaining three must have survived and beaten me here.

I paused as I hovered on the threshold before checking on the screen door opening to the lake. Unlocked, which we'd for sure not left it. That told me little, but it was something.

Cracking the door, I listened outside. Nothing.

Then closed it and listened to the sounds of the house. Still nothing.

Whoever had swung by to grab the food was long gone.

I weighed my options.

No, I absolutely shouldn't try to staunch my raving hunger with what I knew was hidden in here. It might work somewhat as an appetite suppressant, but I had no fucking clue what it would do to my ramped-up metabolism.

Besides, all the scratches and bite marks were still there, no healing having set in whatsoever. The last thing I should add to my metabolism were some heavily modified amphetamines.

And yet, I found myself humming a familiar melody as I traipsed back into the kitchen on autopilot.

Parsley, sage, rosemary, and…

The artisan glass bottles still stood as I had left them when I'd hidden a handful of pills in the one labeled "Thyme" in curly font.

It took way too much willpower not to inhale the contents of the entire bottle—dried herbs included—but to instead dump it all on the counter so I could pick out the pills one by one and make them disappear into a folded-up napkin that I then wrapped in two zip-lock bags before shoving it into the back pocket of my jeans.

That wouldn't survive a dunking in the lake, but a little sweat or rain wouldn't damage the goods.

I took a longing look at the kitchen in general, but I knew all too well that there wasn't even a sachet of artificial sweetener left in here, traded for warm, fresh food to the people across the lake. Like the now undead lady who I'd shoved past to get into the lake.

How some things change…

I tried to remember exactly how far our scavenging trips had ranged. Far, and I didn't exactly know, because most of that had been Axel and Jared alone while Blake and I had been stuck recuperating on the boat. Glancing outside, I didn't see the boat, either, which was a shame but no surprise.

Well, I'd just have to go far enough to get outside the zone they'd checked off and I should be good, even if it meant days more of cramps if all I could find was dry rice and pasta.

I could have killed for some pasta right about now.

Better yet, a steak.

Didn't even have to be cooked.

Raw and bloody and dripping—

I forced my mind to shut the fuck up as I stepped outside onto the dew-slick lawn—and felt something emotionally push me to the south, the opposite direction of where I had been going and intended to go, considering the other side of the lake was full of zombies and assholes that tried to hunt us down in burned-down ruins.

A familiar sensation, that vague sense of aversion.

Averting me from something equally familiar.

Jared.

Looked like my danger radar had sprung to life once more.

Honestly, I wasn't surprised. Not considering how hungry I was, and how fucking hard clear thought was at all right now. I felt somewhat more coherent than when I'd woken up that fateful morning in the woods, but not by much. Also not surprised that he was still alive—cockroaches and all that.

The issue was, I couldn't decide what to do now.

No, that was wrong. The decision was already reached. I was going to find him. The problem was, I wasn't quite so sure whether that was a good idea—for so many reasons, and all of them eluded me right now.

Fuck, but I hated feeling like an oblivious fuckwit!

That—more even than the physical discomfort—made me vow to myself to find something to eat, because this wasn't a state I wanted to stay in a second longer than necessary, even if it had its advantages. But since my fight mode didn't seem to be a reliable one of those, I'd rather ignore all the others as well.

So north it was—which was a grand way of saying that I slowly walked around the side of the house back to the road and kept following it, trying to avoid puddles and patches of dirt and leaves that could make me slip and slide and end up on my ass.

Ask me how I found out about that one.

It took me longer than I had expected to come close to where that vague sense of unease was emanating from. It still wasn't quite that clear blip I'd felt when tracking him down—and consequently avoiding him—in that town, but getting close. I'd expected it to be maybe another mile, two at most. Instead, I walked until the first gray of early morning was showing through the trees and above the lake.

There were no fires or lights or even tracks to guide me, proving that he was still trying not to draw attention. That made sense since not even he could do that much against several container-loads of zombies and unknown numbers of alive humans. Yet when I was close enough to be certain which house he was in—toward the back, close to the lake—I caught a whiff of cigarette smoke in the air.

I couldn't help but frown. It wasn't like any of them to be that careless. Unless, of course, they were sure that I was close—or nobody else was.

Pausing in front of the next house over, I backtracked to the opposite side of the property so that I could cross the lawn with that house in between me and my destination. Not a bad idea, I realized, when I caught yet more smoke, and soon the glimmer of a single cigarette glowing faintly somewhere close to the back. I saw all three of them sitting there, Axel and Jared lounging on chairs while Blake lay stretched out across a bench, the three men sharing a single cigarette—the last one, I presumed, or the only that had survived the torrential rain and possible detours through the lake.

It would have made a lot of sense to simply waltz in there and announce myself—and, much more importantly, the fact that I was really fucking hungry—but something held me back. Maybe it was my innate curiosity, or the utter lack of food scent in the air; I couldn't say. Yet some overgrown hedges right next to a pathway paved with large stones on this property made it downright easy to snoop.

"I'm not sure what got your panties in such a twist," Jared was saying right now as he handed the cancer stick off to Axel. "I'm sure she is fine."

Ah, and there it was, my reason for subterfuge—a chance to pick up something none of them would dare tell me to my face.

Axel's pause likely stemmed from him taking a long drag, or maybe he was simply stalling for time.

"She's tough, I'll give you that. But you saw how many of them took off after her."

Jared's low chuckle answered.

"Yeah, I also heard them shoot at random and shout like stuck pigs. Either she got them, or they ran into the exact same zombies they tried to chase us into. Or their undead sheep turned on them.

You saw yourself how few of them made it back to their cars. They didn't even bother with the trailers."

Blake harrumphed, the sound weirdly satisfied.

It was Axel who replied, though.

"Yes, hours later. That still gave them plenty of time to hunt her down and kill her."

"Nah. I'd know if she was dead."

A stupid chuckle from Blake. I kind of agreed with him there.

"What, you the self-declared zombie chick whisperer now?" the burly mercenary teased.

Jared didn't answer, instead accepting the cigarette from Blake after he'd taken a brief puff.

Axel—ever the contrarian—wasn't ready to drop the point yet.

"Maybe she doesn't want to return to us. To you," he stressed, without a doubt glaring at Jared.

Jared's laugh was a dark one.

"Nah, she'll be here soon enough, if she isn't already lurking in the shadows."

That made me draw up short. Had I somehow given away my position? My stomach was growling loud enough to raise the dead—and I was very much aware of the fact that my lacking mental faculties didn't exactly turn me into a proficient, stealthy hunter. But their conversation had that unguarded air to it that led me to believe that my presence was still a secret.

Blake's answer made me sag in relief.

"You're so full of shit. Anyone ever tell you that?"

Jared chuckled. "Usually not to my face."

"I think you need a reality check."

"Without a doubt," Jared agreed—momentarily. "Then again, you know barely the surface of what she's told me she's done in the past. That is not the kind of woman who can kick all her addictions in one fell swoop. Feel free to call me full of myself, but she's utterly incapable of simply turning her back on me."

Axel let out a guffaw.

"Yeah, because hurling herself out of a speeding car was such a token of appreciation for your company."

"And yet, she came crawling back literally the next day she was mentally capable of."

I hated how fucking self-satisfied Jared sounded, although I got why he felt that way.

On the surface, that had been exactly what I'd done.

And that's not just skin-deep, the nasty voice inside my head cackled.

I would have been annoyed at myself if the topic in general didn't leave me feeling sore all over, even now, over a week later.

Just maybe, I was more of a pushover than I liked to believe. And I fucking hated that about myself.

The men, meanwhile, continued joking, Axel markedly silent. Through the hedge, I didn't get a good look at him, but it was obvious that he wasn't in a mood to play along.

"Maybe she wised up," he pointed out to Jared. "Finally."

The cackle that followed was weird enough to make me want to step out of hiding so I could fully see Jared's face. That wasn't just nasty. It also held a knowing quality that absolutely weirded me out.

"You really bought her good-girl persona, huh?" he asked the older man. "That whole thing where she's blonde and young and perky, so she has to be a good-natured, ditsy little thing? That asinine straight-laced act with her plan to become the most boring, bland individual to ever walk the earth? You disappoint me. You never were stupid enough to be that blind where I am concerned."

"You are a very different kind of beast," Axel pointed out, almost insulted.

"But am I?" Jared singsonged, his voice going up almost an entire octave. "Or am I just really shit about hiding my darkness, while that's her true superpower? Even you must admit, it takes a shitload of guilt and things to atone for to make a woman, of all things, believe she has to go out in this world to help others." He added a pregnant pause, but cut it short with a brief laugh. "That, or you're really itching to kill something and stopped caring whether that's technically still alive or not. But she's not quite there yet, I'll give you that."

Blake chuckled, because of course he would. Axel's long silence weighed on my very soul, and right then I was rather happy about my current very limited emotional range. That unease in my stomach was clearly hunger; nothing else.

When nothing came from Axel, Jared went on, clearly to amuse himself.

"You really have to be more careful about how much of her bullshit you buy, or she will end up sticking a knife into you sooner or later. You actually believe she fell for me? Her one mistake, if I might add. I think she believes it herself. But what that really is—if you cut to the very core of things—is her lapping up every fucking drop of attention she gets. And, lo and behold, from me she's getting all the attention in the world, and not just the pink-hued flavors some fucking pompous MBA asshole would be capable of. That is what she's lapping up like it's the very air she needs to breathe. You think she merely tolerates it? She's fucking addicted to it."

Even half stupid with hunger and a felt IQ of 79 at best, I wanted to balk at that. Not a single fucking word of that was true!

For once, Blake shut up, although I was sure he would easily ignore all the many layers that accusation came with.

Axel—bless his heart—rose to my defense, after two deep inhales before he ground out the cigarette stub.

"And exactly how well did that go when you lavished all that attention on her in that town, huh? That was not the face of a woman who'd just gotten all of her buttons pushed."

That was one way of putting it. I was damn glad he didn't dip into ruder registers, although I might have.

Jared's answer was rather blase. "I may have miscalculated there a bit."

"A bit, huh?" Axel groused.

I personally would have gone for the miscalculated part, but same point, I figured. Only that what he said next was something I hadn't seen coming at all.

"And did you explain to her also that this is one hundred percent your usual MO? And what exactly happens to the girls you do that to? That every fucking last one of them is an exception to your rule of only sticking to the lowlives and those that have it coming? Huh?"

If my ears had had the capability to go up like a dog's, they would have. Because that answer I wouldn't want to miss a single inflection of.

As if to torment me further, Jared took his time providing it. Craning my neck, I tried to get a better look at him where he kept lounging in his chair, staring out across the lake, incredibly relaxed. Which in and of itself was creepy as fucking hell.

"Did you?" Axel repeated his question, hammering down his point.

He finally got a bored, sidelong glance from Jared. "Of course I didn't. I'm not that fucking stupid." His tone was low but incredibly measured. As if he was talking about not being stupid and lying to a cop at a traffic stop. Or always paying for his groceries at the supermarket.

Not about doing... unspeakable things to more than just a few women, if I connected all the many dots.

It was probably stupid but also very understandable that the shudder that ran through me came with the first hint of that very sensation I was starting to recognize—that if I just chased that trail of fear down far enough, my mind would flip away and let pure instinct drop into the driver's seat, shutting off all of my higher, intellectual brain functions.

For the first time, I asked myself: did I actually turn into half a zombie, or was this just the most intense form of a trauma response I'd ever heard of?

Nah, the cannibalism part proved that it was one hundred percent the former. But it dawned on me that the latter might at least be part of what triggered it.

Not even an entire bottle of vodka would have been enough to dull my intellect to let me tackle that topic, that much was for sure.

Leave it to Blake to defuse an otherwise un-defusable situation. He barked out a brief laugh, even if it held an edge. "So I should maybe stop waiting around for your sloppy seconds, huh?"

Jared's chuckle was a nasty one. "Unless you literally want to help dispose of the pieces, that would be wise. That is usually Axel's job, but seeing as I don't have to give a shit about law enforcement anymore, be my guest."

If I'd needed confirmation that the three of them still thought they were on their own, unobserved, this was it. And the fact that, barely missing a beat, they went right back to shooting the shit. Or at least Jared and Blake did. Axel's voice remained markedly absent from their conversation until a good five minutes later, Blake directly involved him, to the point where he had to respond.

All of that washed over me with pretty much the same impact as the early morning wind rustling through the high grass and trees around me, or the fog slowly drifting across the lake.

I knew that it should have been Jared's confession right there at the end of what my brain chose to listen to that should have brought me to a halt. And it had, no doubt. Fact was, I'd kind of suspected something along those lines. It wasn't that much of a stretch that after seeing him get off on scaring me, there was a lot more to exploit down that line—and Jared had never struck me as someone afraid of embracing the unknown.

No, it was what else he'd said. About me.

Not even necessarily about my lies, or lies of omission, or the fact that it was second nature of me to pretend. All that was true. Most of that was even deliberate. Very little of what I could sell as my changes and successes was anything but carefully finding out how society expected me to act, and then to conform. To mold myself into the perfect little cog that fit perfectly into their machine. Conforming meant they left me the fuck alone, and that had been all I really wanted from life. I'd never suffered because I hadn't been able to be honest—completely honest down to the very fibers that made up who I was, mask or not—with anyone. No friend—not even the girls or Ash in particular. No fling or lover. I'd had zero interest in ever telling anyone even half of what I'd breathed to Jared—and I would have been very okay with that going on forever.

Some shit is meant to be buried and forgotten for good.

Yet here he was, dragging it all up into the glaring light of day. Rolling in it, smearing it everywhere so that even if I closed my eyes, I could still smell it.

Okay, that last bit was maybe the result of the unflattering amount of body odor that surrounded me, but the point still stood.

I'd thrived on not just willful but deliberate ignorance. And Jared was all about shoving it all center stage and tearing off any Band-Aids he could find.

That, of course, posed a very important question: was it all about his own morbid fascination to find out just how deep the darkness inside of me went? Or did he think he was actually doing me a favor?

What really sucked was that I was pretty sure he could answer all these questions for me. But because I'd deliberately shied away from doing that very soul delving with him, I simply didn't possess that knowledge. I'd never asked. Never wondered. And now I knew shit, and that rankled.

So fucking much.

I hated that about myself. That I wanted to know him better. Needed to know, on some level.

Right now, without layers of intellectual bullshitting left behind, it was all so simple. Of course I knew he was bad. Evil, probably, although less so in a Machiavellian, all-encompassing way but a very self-centered, selfish level—he was bored, wanted a plaything, and did what he wanted to entertain himself, never mind the horrible fallout for everyone else involved. Even a smidgen of that should have been enough to forever strike him off the list of people I ever wanted to associate with. And I'd been very rigorous about maintaining that list. In college, I hadn't even talked to frat boys who had a certain kind of reputation, and I'd been very discerning about who I let into my pants, even if it had never been to seek or allow any kind of emotional connection.

And in what did that all cumulate now? That I had the serious hots for a self-professed serial killer who loved to torture the women he fucked to death? Because I was pretty sure that was exactly what I'd read between the lines of that conversation.

Any sane person would have run like hell.

Meanwhile, I had to physically hold myself back from strolling right onto their cozy porch and declare, "Well, bring it on!"

Sure, it helped that I was very convinced that I was too emotionally dead inside to actually provide him with what he needed, so he had no reason to push me that far. And was metabolically unhinged enough now to physically stand up to him.

I was oh, so special—and I had a feeling that was exactly what kept drawing him to me like nobody's business.

But why the fuck did that attraction have to be mutual?!

And it was. Damnit, I really didn't want it to be, but it was.

Jared was wrong on so many levels about me in some aspects— like with the drugs. Sure, I'd always be fighting addiction, and withdrawal, and temptation because that was an ingrained part of me now. But I would have forever said no, and I could very well pick up that habit now and die with my liver never having to process any of that chemical shit again. No problem. And as good as sex was with him—and it was, I regretted to say—his dick wasn't magical. I could very well abstain from that, too.

But... and that was a huge but.

I was terrified that he was right when he said I was craving that attention he was lavishing on me like nobody's business.

How had he put it? It felt good to be truly himself around me, now that all cards were on the table? And that he could offer me the one thing nobody else could—because nobody else would, or dared to? Acceptance.

Fucking. Hell.

That temptation was a thousand times stronger than heroin or sugar or any other chemical compound.

Because that shit came from my very soul.

And that was the one thing in my life that I simply couldn't compromise on. That very last shred of my humanity that I had come so, so close to compromising so many times in so many ways... but I just couldn't.

I was well aware that my inner monologue very much resembled that of an overly dramatic young-adult romance heroine, but maybe that was my brain's way of cutting through the layers of shit I'd built up over the years, and my admittedly very lacking intellectual reach at the moment. Proper brain fuel would have done wonders right now.

But none of that changed anything about the truth of the matter.

The fact that if I spent even another minute around Jared, I would inevitably go down the single one road I couldn't allow myself to be on.

I'd rather die. Go insane from hunger, waste away. Get torn apart by animals or the undead. Even if it meant I'd run into the wrong kind of survivors and my life would quickly resemble a living nightmare—all of that was so much better than this.

Literally anything but this.

So instead of waltzing over to the men, I remained crouching where I was. Even when, eventually, they got ready to leave. I did scoot back far enough to remain undetected, but otherwise, I let them pass—and disappear, heading north.

If I closed my eyes, I could feel the blip of awareness that was Jared slowly recede into the distance until I had to strain to remain aware of him—and then I slammed the door on that part of me, forever.

It had been stupid of me to think I could deal with who he was and what he represented. That I could somehow ignore it. That I could pretend like I didn't care. That I could—legit, at times—let instinct rule me and concentrate on the surface-level facts only.

That I could remain fully myself right next to him.

But all of that was, of course, bullshit.

I knew it.

He knew it.

And that was why I needed to get the fuck away from him, and make sure that our paths would never ever cross again—even if I would regret it for the rest of my fucking life.

CHAPTER 13

The list of directions that were off-limits was much longer than the number of options that made sense. I couldn't head north, because I was pretty sure that my danger radar would fail me eventually, and I had a feeling that within a day, I'd run smack into Jared. So following the Catawba River on this side was a no go. Heading across the lake—probably at the bridge to the south we had used so many times—was no better since I didn't trust Jared's observation that the assholes who had ambushed us were gone. Maybe they were about to return to fetch their abandoned gear. Of course, I could have struck out due west, heading deeper into South Carolina, but our little round trek there hadn't really enamored me to the region.

Having no destination at all was also no option.

So what was left were established places—preferably some that still existed—and to where Jared had no reason to return.

It was an even split between heading south to Grace's town, or going northeast to the Enclave.

I wasn't very fond of either option and kind of hoped that on the way there—or maybe just after arriving—I would find something better, but for the time being, that was the best I could come up with.

As I kept mulling that over, I realized it was really just one option since the entire stretch south of here was probably still swarming with assholes searching for me with their drones.

So back to the last place on earth I wanted to go to it was.

This absolutely sounded like a recipe for disaster.

But first things first. I needed to find food, better gear, a pack to carry my shit, and another branch to use as a makeshift club-slash-walking-stick. For all that—except for the stick; that was easy to come by—I would have to head either into a small town, or at least stalk a few single buildings.

Business as usual.

As easy as those tasks sounded, it took me the better part of three days to get it all done.

Step one was to find a way across the river. There was a bridge to the north as well, but I didn't trust that. But I trusted myself to paddle across the lake when I finally found where our old kayaks had washed up and used one of them to make it across, landing in the middle of nowhere. From there, it was relatively easy to sneak north on the eastern side of the lake and later the river, and then follow small roads until I had left the entire burned-to-the-ground Lancaster behind me. The hungrier I got, the more I felt the zombies lurk all around me, which at least made it feasible not to run into them too often.

More than once, I was tempted to turn back and go see if the ambushers had maybe left behind some of their dead.

Was that gruesome? Yes, on all levels, but I was starving to the point where I absolutely stuffed some grass and acorns down my gullet to give my stomach something to work on, with very limited success and some excessive puking involved.

When I finally found some normal-people-food in a house, the results were pretty much the same, leading to some impressive retching that made me almost vow to never try again.

But of course I did, the very next day, when I found some more rice and flour, with exactly the same results.

Two days into this, I stopped sleeping altogether. Ever since waking up in the woods, I'd had trouble staying asleep for long, but now not even dozing worked. All my mind did was think about food, and now it apparently refused to let me rest until I got some food.

On day four, things got so dire that I gave up on searching and went back to some of the tricks I'd learned during all those summers when my mother had been up to no good but I'd been living the hillbilly country life—mainly setting snares and trying to hit birds with stones. Where's the convenient crossbow or composite bow with a full quiver of arrows when you need it? Not fucking available, that's where.

My salvation came because of my nocturnal restlessness, when I happened to stone a dove and catch a rabbit in a snare during the same night.

There was no roasting meat on sticks over the fire. No spices, no making this appetizing and looking like a civilized meal. All I managed was to use my knife to slice up the animals so I could get to their internal organs, and then the feeding frenzy of one commenced.

Few things in my life had tasted so sweet and delicious, and none I'd polished off to the very last scrap of meat I could somehow gnaw off a bone or feathers I could lick clean.

I was almost as ravenous when I was done with my meals as before, but the single-minded brain fog I'd been struggling with lifted exactly enough to make me feel self-conscious about the scene I'd created. As if anyone needed that, of all things. At least I was still aware of the lurkers, far away as they kept hiding from me. That was something, I told myself.

Finding signs of humans was too easy. Right from the get-go, it was all about avoiding them for now.

We'd thought we'd shaken our pursuers until the ambush. I technically still didn't know if they had been part of that group or if we'd just been exceptionally unlucky—or stupid. But whenever I saw plumes of dust from cars or smoke from fires, I stayed the hell away from them. I never got close enough to any of the groups to check if I got any feedback on my radar from them—be it Jared, or simply someone else giving me those special vibes—but I chose to err on the side of caution.

Initially, I'd wanted to stay away from Charlotte, but in the end decided against that. The center and western part of the city might be one eternal black wasteland, but I was certain that something must have survived. Basements, cellars, caved-in buildings—you name it. Food was likely out of the question, but everything else might still be useful.

I very much regretted that decision on the afternoon I tried to make my way closer to the city, but soon gave up and fled, the mental images of hundreds of contorted, scorched bodies forever burned into my memory.

Nobody needs that shit. Fuck basement loot.

I'd been exceptionally wary of crossing the few interstates and larger roads that inevitably stood in my way, but being all on my own and having a certain feeling for what was hiding in between the vehicles made it not easy but manageable to eventually find a stretch out in the open country where I could sneak through, becoming just one of many more lurkers who picked through the rusting wrecks. Summer hadn't been kind to what was left of days gone by, adding layers of dust, grime, and tons of vegetation to everything. Some cars still looked like they just needed a good wash, but a lot of the wrecks were actually destroyed now and looked like they'd never go anywhere ever again. In places, I found clear signs of someone having tried to return somewhere to scavenge, but those were very limited, pretty much about the level I'd been a part of myself with Osprey and the gang.

I spent a lot of time thinking back to those days. I hadn't realized it, but those had definitely been the best times of the end of the world. When it had been only Kas and me, and then us and the handful of other intrepid guards.

And then my path had inevitably crossed Jared's, and he'd thrown me off kilter forever, and all I had to show for it was what I could loot myself.

I didn't have a map, but I also didn't bother finding one, the benefits too small to risk rooting through a car that could easily become a death trap in seconds. I knew more or less where I was headed, and I was certain that when I got close, the signs of people around would become impossible to ignore.

And I was right. A good week after the Charlotte incident—my track getting extended since I took a larger detour around and to the east of the city before finally veering north toward the hills and mountains—the frequency of vehicle-caused dust plumes increased threefold within a single afternoon. I avoided them like the plague at first, but with more wooded areas around as elevation increased, I finally got a few chances to watch them pass undetected.

Most of them were small groups—scavengers, without a doubt. They were all going slow enough to appear cautious, and what I saw of the vehicles, it was obvious that they were filled to the last inch with stuff. A few were less loaded down but usually transported as many people as possible.

It was actually a train of the latter that drew my attention, mostly because the third time I watched it drive past, I recognized it from the previous instances. I still had some severe issues with spatial orientation, even if I managed to catch some food regularly now that my old skills were slowly coming back. At first, I thought I had inevitably crossed into their patrol pattern, but then I realized that made no sense since they were always going in the same direction as me. Unless they were going in circles—which they were, I realized, two days and seven sightings later.

It took me another day and a vantage point up in the trees to find out what—or rather, who—they were circling.

There was a mass of people out there, moving from the low regions of the coast inland, toward the mountains. And from what I could tell, they were still very much alive.

It sounded so ludicrous that it took me another three days of sneaking closer and observing while I remained hidden, to finally accept what I was seeing.

There was a large group of survivors out there, traveling on foot, using a handful of still-functional cars to find the way and keep any attacking zombies at bay.

Well, those few aggressive ones that actually made a run for them. They missed a hell of a lot of lurkers that had also taken interest in them and swarmed their nightly resting places soon after the last weary traveler was out of sight, easily two to three times as strong as the travelers.

Most of them were women and children, a lot sticking together in small groups of families and found families, I figured.

It was the hunger that finally drove me to be stupid and approach them when they made camp—smack in the middle of a meadow a mile away from the next road—one evening. Yes, I'd been able to hunt enough to sustain myself—but barely. And only if narrowly escaping deadly emaciation by a hair was considered feasible. My scratches and bites had finally started to heal, but most were still not completely closed up, disappearing at a much slower rate than would have been normal for any healthy woman my age. And I could feel my body slowly wasting away, my joints constantly complaining now, my muscles getting weaker and weaker at an alarming rate. Back when Kas and I had been stumbling through the aftermath of the zombie rising, I'd been hungry, too, but I'd felt my body recovering from sickness and growing stronger, if only in response to the massive stress of constant movement from sunup to sundown, every single day. Now I could feel the opposite at work—and it was scaring me.

How many more days of lucid, actual thought did I have left?

And, worse yet: how many days until my mind flipped and I would attack exactly the people I was shadowing now, hoping to find a new home with?

Dying of hunger, I could have accepted. But turning into a ravenous zombie? Not on my watch.

"Approach" really was the right term for what I did—at least in my mind. I didn't just step out in front of the next small group of people to dramatically reveal myself, or some shit. If I'd done that, they'd likely killed me on the spot. Some prep work was required, as I realized when last I'd passed a mirror in a house I quickly tore through in search of some canned protein—tuna preferred, but by then, I wouldn't have shied away from cat food, either.

Thanks to my less than civilized eating habits, I'd expected my reflection to look grim, but the hollow-cheeked, dull-eyed creature that stared back at me was almost unrecognizable—and not just because she had plenty of grime smeared all across the lower half of her face.

No wonder a lot of lurkers didn't bother me of late. I looked exactly like them, minus clear signs of decomposition setting in.

Yet.

I really didn't like the fact that my wounds weren't healing as they should, even ignoring how fast the super fast healing had been mere weeks ago. Just how bad that had gotten, I realized when I spent some time washing up and changing into fresh clothes, and I still looked like a haggard, twenty-years older version of myself.

I mean, it did wonders to disguise my real identity, but I could have done without the gut punch to my ego—and without the latent fear of what would happen a week further down the line if things didn't get any better.

Maybe it was sheer random insanity that made me reach for the makeup stored in that bathroom. Maybe it was that hint of panic in my own eyes that reminded me so much of Dharma. Maybe it was the fact that I realized I had something right there that could make me look deliberately thin rather than emaciated. But once I started, I could barely hold back until that face in the mirror was truly no longer myself.

So I'd prettied myself up—although I still drew the line at completely drab and functional clothing—and shadowed the strange traveler group for a good two days before I took heart and stepped out of the ditch beside the road where I'd spent the last thirty minutes watching them pass by while my stomach growled loud enough that I was honestly surprised that nobody had noticed me yet.

And they hadn't, judging from how the entire group of eight people I'd singled out as my target shrank back, if only for the moment it took them to recognize me as like.

Call me jaded, but I'd spent a lot of time watching them, singling this very group out for a reason. It consisted of two mothers with their children—two and four, respectively, all in ages between six and fifteen. Presumably they were their children, or at least now they were, even if their relation hadn't started out by blood. Both women had a tough, no-nonsense air about them, which suited me perfectly. I was sure they would be glad to accept a younger woman ready to lend two hands.

And they were the least likely to rape me.

Yes, that was something that factored into my calculations as well, because, hello? Woman here, lots of frustrated, stronger-than-me men around. Just how much the fact that I hadn't been afraid of that in months rankled right now I couldn't even say, or else I would have started to scream with frustration. By now, I was absolutely desperate enough to accept a bargain where I paid for food with my body. But if there happened to be a chance I didn't have to resort to that yet? And that moms-with-kids group was absolutely my very best bet for that.

Even before I opened my mouth, I saw sympathy and kindness in the women's eyes, which gave me more hope than I'd felt in a long, long time.

"Hi," I said, eloquence incarnate. It came out scratchy and raw—the first sound that had made it past my lips in three weeks that hadn't been a cut-off curse.

My, but I'd really been living rough.

The women just stared. So, just maybe, I had to lay on the charm a little more heavily.

"I'm sorry if I frightened you or your kids," I offered after clearing my throat, sounding just a little more like myself—and weirdly imitating Dharma's accent, I realized. Then again, since I was already borrowing her eyeliner routine, might as well go all the way. "I'm just really desperate, you see. I've been watching your group for a while, and, well, I feel like you're my best chance not to get torn apart and eaten out there. Or raped."

I knew it was a gamble to add the last part—particularly where the children could hear my every word—but I had a feeling these two would understand.

The older one of the pair—a Hispanic woman with laugh lines around her eyes and a scattering of gray hairs in her riot of curls that she kept contained with a folded bandana above her forehead—cracked a smile. It wasn't a one-hundred-percent nice smile, but still held enough warmth to make me want to answer with one in kind.

The fact that my face felt frozen, incapable of doing so, really didn't bode well.

"A lithe, fresh thing like you? I can imagine. I'm not gonna ask how many times you've already had to deal with that BS since the shit hit the fan."

She glanced at her companion, a white woman in her thirties, brown hair gathered in a sensible ponytail, her denim shirt rolled up at the sleeves to reveal faded full tattoo sleeves. If not for that detail, she could have been any suburban soccer mom, complete with her perky twelve-year-old girl and gap-toothed six-year-old boy.

Not-Quite-Soccer-Mom snorted. "You wouldn't believe how quickly some drop the 'young and tight' requirement, though."

Both women chortled, their amusement decidedly on the wry side.

My brain-fog brain had absolutely nothing to contribute to that, so I went with heavily traumatized silence.

Anything to get some food into me, really.

They quieted down way too quickly, but not in a bad way. "I'm Mariana," the Hispanic woman said. "And these are Leon, Theo, Agata, and Ruben."

"Bea," the other woman offered. "And my kids, Sabrina and Darren."

I made a note of remembering the mothers' names. The kids I knew were already a lost cause, although I vowed to try better if they gave me a chance over the next, hopefully many days.

Belatedly, I realized that now it was time for me to introduce myself, and just maybe, Callie wouldn't do with the great lengths I'd gone to already to disguise myself.

Damn, but I really should have thought about that first!

"Dharma" was the first name on my mind, for obvious reasons—and for those exact reasons, I couldn't use it. So I went with the next best thing.

"I'm Ashley. Ash to my friends." I even managed a small smile, mostly because remembering my dear friend always smiling drew one automatically—as a wave of pain almost choked me up at the same time.

"Nice to meet you, Ash," Bea said with a smile that was too knowing, but then again, the fact that she'd went immediately to the "friends" part made me let out a breath that felt like I'd been holding it for days now.

"Absolutely," Mariana said, agreeing with her. The women exchanged another meaningful glance. "We can't exactly offer you much protection, as you can imagine. But if you want to hang around, you're welcome to walk with us. And any help you can offer we'll gladly accept, even if we can't repay you with anything except our scintillating company."

Bea snorted. Several of the kids looked bored and at least vaguely embarrassed by their mothers' interaction.

It was a relief to see such absolutely normal teenage behavior on display.

By now, several other groups had passed by us, curious looks landing on me aplenty, but nobody stopped to inquire. Watching them trudge on, I realized just how tired and numb everyone looked, which wasn't a surprise at all. But all of them looked way better nourished than I was, and that was enough for me right now.

"So what's up with a girl roughing it out there all on her own?" Bea wanted to know. "Lie through your teeth, if that's all you're comfortable with for now." At her gesture, her kids started walking again, Mariana and her bunch quickly falling in line. I remained a little to their right, but from the outside, I was sure I already looked like part of the group.

"No lies required," I, well, lied. "I was part of a group for a while. All summer long, actually. But then shit happened, and here I am, all on my own."

Since they'd lightly cursed before, I didn't think I had to censor my speech much. Neither woman batted so much as an eyelash, which was fine with me. After spending months around Blake, I'd really had to work hard around Grace to clear up my speech, as stupid as that sounded. All things considered, I wasn't sure I could have managed that much now.

Mariana nodded. "Happens to the best of us. I'm sure that if you go up and down our line here, you'll hear the same over and over again."

Bea chuckled. "You'd think that the undead would be enough to unite us survivors, but, noooo." She comically drew out that last word. "But that's actually why we're doing this, if you can believe it. One endless march toward a better future."

I couldn't help but glance ahead, toward the hills and mountains. "Just for the hell of it, or…"

Mariana shook her head. "Hopefully not. I mean, it could still all be a bunch of lies. But there's talk of a group over in the Kentucky—Tennessee area who're calling for other survivors to join them. Apparently, they've been gathering survivors from all around, right up into Arkansas. Some ex-military types but mostly civilians. From what little we know, some of them have been clashing with assorted assholes all year long until they banded together. Now they are promising shelter and security for everyone who dares put up the middle finger to those assholes that want to subjugate us."

All I could do was stare back at her blandly. I just couldn't let my heart flare alive with hope. That sounded too good to be true.

Mariana grinned, echoing my thoughts exactly. "Does sound like a lot of BS? Yes, but apparently, there are some names attached to this group that several of us survivor groups had heard independently of each other. Don't ask me who. The powers that be don't share their eternal wisdom with us lowly moms and providers. But to be honest, I'm desperate enough that strength in numbers is all I can rely on these days, and when our entire community decided to up and move, we just tagged along."

"Exactly," Bea agreed. "We're from the beach colony that made it through the summer right next to Mariana's. Same story here. Some people stayed behind, but I have a ton more faith in those that decided to leave. So we left, too."

The mentioning of beach communities made me perk up.

"Where exactly did you hunker down for the summer?" Grace and her people had lived not exactly at the beach, but close enough that she'd promised to take me there. Of course, before we'd gotten around to that, Jared had to get bored and had gotten stabby, and the rest was history.

Also, if Grace and her people were part of this traveling convoy, my attempts at disguising myself would only land me in hot water.

"Virginia," Bea explained. "Near Norfolk and Virginia Beach originally, although nobody survived there, of course. My kids and I toughed it out north of there on the other side of the bay, near Cape Charles. Having a naval base right in front of your house was both a blessing and a curse." She didn't elaborate, and I wasn't sure I wanted to ask.

"And we're from a couple miles farther north, near the Delaware border," Mariana explained. "Since they cut off the connection to Washington and Baltimore early, and pretty much nuked Wilmington and the surrounding area, that entire peninsula has been mostly cut off from the mainland. We really thought we'd hit the jackpot with that."

She fell silent then, which sounded oddly poignant.

It got even worse when Bea nodded somberly. "Until the last wave hit us six weeks ago. Since then, it turned into a free-for-all. We were lucky that they managed to restore at least parts of the bridge to the south. We still had to swim half the distance across the bay, but with concrete-and-wood islands every few hundred yards where we could rest on, at least we all survived. Then it was just endless miles of trying to get past the infested high-population areas while hiding in the shallow sea near the shore, and voila, here we are now."

One of Mariana's sons—Leon or Theo, if she'd called out their names from oldest to youngest—piped up at that. "Yeah, if I never see the damn ocean again, it will be too soon."

He got a stern look from his mother but also a warm side hug that he tolerated for a moment, but quickly escaped after that.

Bea nodded emphatically. "I've lived near the sea all of my life. Loved almost every second of it. But the kid's right. You spend days on end fighting not to drown in the surf, waiting until the undead fuckers on the beach lose interest in you so you can finally get back onto dry land, and then tell me you ever want to go near a body of water again."

My tongue burned with the comment that Jared had been so enamored with the idea of spending time on the beach, but I quickly swallowed that.

I fucking hated how much I wanted to tell him about their experience and gloat. It rankled to—hopefully!—never get that chance.

"We stuck mostly to rivers," I explained when it felt like they were waiting for something from me. "Great way to put some distance between you and whatever's coming for you in a pinch. And lots of deserted lake houses. For a while."

Remembering swimming across that lake—almost drowning while freezing to death—made me shudder. Yeah, that had done a number on my fond summer memories, back when I'd had enough to eat to actually gain a little weight for once. Of course, I'd needed nobody else but Jared to destroy the warm glow of that, although the mercenaries that had hunted us had helped.

Oh, what great times we were living in.

Bea and Mariana quickly changed the topic, and after that had gone stale, they did it again. They were both very fond of chatting and recounting stories to me I was sure they had told a million times already, but I was happy to be the newbie around who they could relate it all to one more time. It was enough if I added the odd sentence or observation, making it easy not to get caught in my web of lies that I was still trying to build inside my head. I was mostly failing, so I tried to stick to the truth mostly with omitted details. That worked well, as I knew it would.

Old dogs, old tricks, and all that shit.

By noon, we'd fallen into a comfortable pattern, and by afternoon, I was sure that I'd completely disappeared in the anonymous mass of people slowly trudging their way forward.

Perfect.

Well, in all but what was the most important and constant thing on my mind: food.

The caravan didn't stop for noon, lunch, or anything close to that, but the different small groups did, often congregating into knots of up to fifty people. Why, I learned when it was finally time for our group to take a break. The cars that I'd seen coming and going a few times didn't just drop by to unload their family members to spend time together. They also carried what food and other stuff the caravan had—and presumably collected ahead of where the mass of people was trudging through the wilderness.

There was hoping they wouldn't notice—or mind—another mouth to feed.

That was, of course, not the case.

The two men distributing boxes, cases, and Tupperware containers from the back of their pickup truck singled me out immediately, even when I didn't approach their vehicle but tried to hide in the gaggle of kids while Mariana and Bea went to fetch lunch. I didn't hear what exactly was said, but snippets like "picked up another stray" and "not gonna get a bite extra" easily filtered across the distance.

I knew I should have felt bad for the women and their kids, but I was so beyond hungry that I simply couldn't.

I was still surprised when they returned and started handing out things, already mixing and matching what each of them had gotten and then distributing it in what seemed to accommodate everyone's preferences as much as possible—including me. And not a single one of the kids spoke up, although I was sure they knew exactly that because of me, their portions had been cut short.

I didn't dare voice my thoughts that the crackers Bea shoved at me were absolutely wasted on me, but was insanely grateful for the can of sardines they came with.

By far not enough to fill me up, but easy, nutritious food nevertheless.

I thanked them profoundly—including so I would be busy a moment longer—before I inhaled my food, crackers included. It was something to fill my stomach, and for now, that took priority over actual nutrition.

That I would have terrible digestive issues was literally tomorrow's problem.

I also got to know some of the other people that were loosely connected with Mariana and Bea—some because they'd been traveling together for a while, some because they also had kids. While I had been watching the caravan for a while, it had never been enough to really puzzle out the detailed dynamics. I got a crash course in that now. While Bea in particularly seemed ready to already call me family, a lot of the others kept looking at me sideways—something I couldn't hold against them.

We were getting ready to set out again—after a round of ducking behind some convenient trees by the road that someone had previously double checked weren't infested with lurkers—when one of the other women approached me. Her sour expression already told me what was about to come.

"The last thing we need is fucking whores," she almost spat in my direction.

I didn't even blink with the irritation that raced up my spine.

"Yeah? Well, the last thing I need is to be a whore, so sounds like we'll get along splendidly."

Her eyes narrowed. Apparently, my snippy response had been the wrong thing to say.

"Listen, Missy." She even went as far as to push her fists into her sides. "I know exactly how it is with you young things. You smile brightly when you beg for scraps. You promise the world. And the second a good, hard-working woman turns her back, you go jumping her husband and sons, making them do all number of ungodly things—"

I was honestly tempted to let her prattle on, only that Bea's daughter was standing close enough to hear, and the way she was scrunching up her face, it made me wonder if she was checking if these accusations might apply to me—or maybe to herself, seeing as she was almost one of those young women.

It was mostly my annoyance that made me cut her off, not a noble attempt to keep the girl's innocence intact another day—if there even was something like that still existing.

"Well, you're in luck then," I told the outraged hag. "Because I'm gay as fuck. I'd much rather dive into your bush than even look at your husband and precious sons. Well, obviously not you yourself because I can see that you're a God fearing, straight-as-a-stick woman. But chances are, not everyone's as straight-laced as you." That shut her up with a gulp, which was the perfect opportunity to add, "Besides, I'd much rather work for my food and upkeep, thank you very much. I'm sure that with so many people around, there must be something for me to do to prove myself useful—that doesn't include me on my back, spreading my legs. Or ass cheeks. I'm sure you know how some men are."

Crude? Yes. But also effective, as it made the woman turn on her heel and march off. I was surprised literal steam wasn't coming out of her ears.

When I turned back around myself—admittedly, with a sarcastic twist to my lips—I found myself face to face with Bea's daughter. She scrutinized me with an expression that I couldn't quite place. Something between a smidgen of hopefulness but also a lot of suppressed emotion. And she was absolutely trying not to laugh her ass off. That much was obvious.

"Is that true what you just said?" she asked me once the hag was out of earshot. "That you're into girls, you know?"

Damn you, consequences of my own actions…

Trying to respond as quickly as possible as not to—again—give anyone reason to wonder whether I was lying, I shrugged.

"I'm really not into hooking up with some random guys right now, if that's what you're asking." Which she wasn't, but I fucking hated how utterly honest that statement had been. Not random or pretty much any guys, except for a single one that my damn heart—and other places—wouldn't stop missing, even if my intellect kept going to town on the rest with a sledgehammer of righteousness. Because, obviously, I was a lost cause.

The girl scrunched up her face further, pretty much telling me she was disappointed in my response.

Me, too, girl. Me, too.

"I'm just asking because…" She trailed off there, briefly gnawing on her bottom lip.

Fuck. This wasn't going to end in a damn confession, now, was it? I'd been with them all of two hours. The end times made people move fast, but she looked like she'd barely hit puberty. Eleven, twelve, maybe? And even on the parallel tangent—that she wasn't into me personally but exploring her own sexuality… Again, two fucking hours!

"It's because Mom… before things got bad, she had a girlfriend," she finally hedged. "Who never got home when the riots began. So… just so you know."

That… was a much better explanation than what my addled—and apparently quite egotistical!—brain had jumped to.

Only why was she now giving me those weird puppy dog eyes?

"How old are you exactly, uh, Sabrina was it, right?"

"Thirteen," she offered. When I kept looking at her, she rolled her eyes. "Okay. Twelve. But I will be thirteen in five weeks from now. Besides, the last six months haven't exactly kept me thinking like a kid."

I nodded, giving her that.

"Almost thirteen. And yes, very mature for your age, without a doubt. So this is not us having the 'are you going to be my second mommy now' conversation, right?"

She looked at me like I was crazy—something we could agree on—before she burst out laughing. It lasted just a second, but it nevertheless happened and left a weirdly warm glow inside my chest. Sabrina herself ended up grinning, even if it was mostly in a "you adults are so stupid" kind of way.

"Ah, no. Not that I have a clue whether she'd be into you or not. I really can't say. I'm also not sure she's generally thinking about anything else right now except for how to feed us. What I was going to say—before you started spouting ridiculous stuff—is that we're not a bunch of bigots. And we're also not automatically thinking the worst of you, just because you look like you've been through some really bad shit. You can be one hundred percent yourself around us. You're safe with us. Maybe not from the zombies eating you, but from anyone leaving you behind because you're queer, or expecting you to… you know. Things like that. Mila's a bitch. Mom caught her stealing from us last week but let it go. She told me Mila's worse off now because two of her sons died, and she's grieving. You should never act like that to another person just because of your own pain."

I wished I had the mental capacity to say something wise in response. Since I didn't, I left it at a nod—and then gave the girl a sideways hug as I started steering us back toward her family.

"Your mom sounds like an awesome person," I told her. "But I'm still not going to become your second mommy."

"You're way too skinny to be a mom," Sabrina joked as she lingered a moment longer at my side before she extricated herself from my loose grasp. "I mean, seriously. You look like a model, particularly with that makeup on. Like you stepped out of some distressed, post-apocalyptic shoot."

I couldn't help but chuckle. It wasn't a happy sound. But for probably the first time, her accidental gut punch didn't even land, which was a weird sensation.

"Yeah, that's what weeks of terrible hunger do to you. Can't recommend it, though. Particularly if you want to keep your boobs."

She glanced at my chest, then quickly back up to my face.

"Yup, that used to be more," I joked. "But that's pretty much the first fat your body will burn up. Long before belly or thighs, even if the fitness industry will sell you plenty of shit that's supposed to target those areas first. Guess none of us has to worry about that anymore going forward."

The girl glanced down at her own chest—pretty much on par with me—definitely uncomfortable now.

"You don't think I'll stay this flat forever, right?"

I couldn't help but snicker, but quickly shut up and explained.

"Theoretically, bad malnutrition can halt development. But from what I saw, you're all still getting plenty of food. I've really hit a rough patch. Like, exceptionally hard. Until a few weeks ago, I never had that issue, not even when it felt like I was constantly running for my life. You'll be okay. Besides, if I look at your mom's rack and butt… nah, you'll be okay."

As I'd intended, the girl was grinning from ear to ear now.

"You totally just checked her out!"

I left it at a conspiratorial eye roll.

No, I wasn't going to tell the girl that when looking at her mother's assets, a part of me was tallying up calories, and a much larger part of me was in full-on salivation mode over all that juicy sub-cutaneous fat.

Hiding in plain sight among the humans would take some getting used to, for sure.

"Your secret's safe with me," Sabrina enthused, sounding almost giddy.

I gave her a grateful nod, because what else was there to do? I was just glad my aggression level remained low, particularly since the growling of my stomach still hadn't quite stopped. Those sardines had been nice, but by far not enough to fill me up.

I felt even worse when, a few minutes after we started walking again, Sabrina sidled up to me and pressed a candy bar into my hand. She was gone before I could protest. I let it disappear inside my jacket pocket, not wanting to insult the girl by not appreciating it now but also getting ready to throw it away. I was sure that later I would find a deserving recipient for it—either her little brother, or her herself, pretending I'd found a new one somewhere in a day or two.

CHAPTER 14

The question of how I could help was soon answered, and I didn't even have to drop any hints about what I thought would make the most sense. Once the entire caravan of people stopped for the night—in the middle of a wide-open swath of land, when it got too dark to comfortably see where we were going—one of the men who returned to drop off some food and a few blankets accosted me outright.

"Hey, Blondie," he called out to me after giving Bea her share. "You up to earning your keep, or you going to take literal food from the babes' mouths?"

Never before had I been more inclined to debate the use of the term "literally" over "figuratively," but instead, I shut up and nodded as I walked up to him.

"You need help with looting, I presume?" I could have voiced that differently, but since he was an asshole, I was ready to be one back.

He snorted, but it had a good-natured ring to it.

"Do we ever. Guards, too, but no offense. A heavy gust of wind is all it takes to knock you over. But yes, we always need extra hands who help us bring what we need back to the people. You can ride with the cars and distribute things all day, or do a four-hour shift going into houses and bringing everything back that might be useful. Your choice."

I had a feeling that either Bea or Mariana had already insisted that no lewd suggestions in my direction would fly, or that guy really was one of the few good ones.

"I'll take a looting shift, if you don't mind," I said, offering my hand. "I'm Ash."

"Jerry," he shot back, his handshake firm. "And if you're not too beat up, I'd say come along with us right away. Unless you're afraid of the dark, or what a bunch of grisly men might do to you away from camp."

I didn't go as far as to pat my pocket with my current trusty knife, but something about my smile might have tipped him off that I wasn't quite the defenseless waif he had pretty much accused me of being. In jest.

"Lead the way, old, grizzled man," I told him.

He was still grinning as he helped me up on the pickup's bed and told me to hold on tight.

I was surprised when I realized just how literal—actually— Jerry had been. The group of men I set out with was mostly indeed grizzled—as in, most of the men were in their sixties and seventies, and the handful of younger ones were sixteen maximum, their manhood status quite questionable. It was then that I realized what my brain must have registered and catalogued for days already— there were hardly any young, fit men around. The only demographic that fit that age range were women, and usually carrying or caring for a bunch of children. It was easy, of course, to guess what had happened to those men now missing.

And no, I wasn't jaded enough to believe they'd all up and abandoned their wives, kids, and parents.

For the first time since I'd gotten sick, I realized just how exceptionally lucky I'd been both at the Enclave but also later falling in with Jared and his gang. And all of us were still alive and kicking— presumably. Except those outright murdered. We'd had the best cards where survival was concerned, but you only get so many chances to escape the inevitable. And it looked like this group of survivors was all out of those who'd run out of chances.

Being back to what I was now actually proficient at—looting— was a strange comfort. With over twenty people in and on four vehicles, things actually progressed well, even cursing and stumbling in the dark. Even if most were too young or too old to be in their physical prime, strength in numbers was a thing—which I'd been sorely missing over the past three weeks.

It felt good to be able to tackle houses that looked promising but were also infested.

My danger radar was still going strong, making me reluctant to follow Jerry's lead into the first two houses. He noticed, particularly when I was a little too quick to duck into the third that was obviously clear. When he accosted me because of that, I tried to lie to him, insisting that I had a particularly strong sense of smell.

He looked doubtful, but let me bet him a double ration of canned protein if I was right two out of three times for the rest of our shift.

I was, of course, right three out of three, and even managed to make the entire group avoid a larger cluster of houses that might very well have killed all of us.

He was happy to give me three extra cans of tuna, and I was happy to wolf them down before he dropped me off with Bea and Mariana again, smirking at my lack of manners but not speaking up in protest.

The next morning, the women got nine full rations rather than eight, and I was more than happy to join Jerry's gang at noon for the next loot run when we got close to some vacation homes in a scenic spot that we simply couldn't pass up.

Nobody questioned my "special zombie sense" after that first night of scavenging. Also because I was smart enough only to say something when the odds were overwhelming, not when there was a single lurker or two to stir up and either chase away or kill pretty quickly. And while a few men—mostly boys—looked my way a little too long a little too quizzically, that was easy to ignore.

All that almost made me feel like I'd been needlessly paranoid over exactly nothing!

That was, until on day four of running with the group, the outer patrols returned when an unfamiliar train of cars approached our drawn-out column.

Outer patrols? Something nobody had bothered to explain to me. As it turned out, there were in fact some young, fit men still around, but they spent their entire time forging ahead, either finding clear ways or making them clear with the use of all kinds of possible weapons in their arsenals, but preferably those that were silent. They also did their best to keep any ranging bands of assholes away from the camp, although mostly from the provisions and women.

Mostly the women, I realized, when Jerry pulled me away before the incoming cars were converging on us, and told me to hide under a thick blanket in the cabin of his truck, where Sabrina was already waiting, her wide-eyed stare making me guess that at least once, Jerry had been too slow with that maneuver. Sabrina came with us on the following looting trip, as did Leon and Theo—Mariana's teenage boys. That meant we also had to make sure nothing happened to them, but they were pretty okay with playing packing Tetris with the loot we brought to the vehicles while the rest of us did the actual looting.

When we finally returned to the caravan late in the evening, my suspicions of why that trip had run extra late proved itself all too true—but not in the way I had expected. Which was a welcome surprise to the never-ending tsunami of crap that had almost driven me to the point of believing that all that was left of us were human shit stains.

Although, what we returned to was bad enough.

A lot of the few things that the survivor train had been carrying with them were gone—packs, tents, sturdy clothes and gear that were already needed when the nights got cold and would be vital for survival in the coming winter months. Not a scrap of food was left, which was why they were insanely happy to see us trundle back into camp. Our forward defenders were gone, but from muttered comments I picked up from all around, that was a good thing because they had proven to be next to useless when the raiders had come in and demanded their picks of the goods provided.

But, yeah, at least they hadn't sunk as low as to trade the women for some extra boxes of ammo.

Watching a lot of the parents go hungry tonight so at least their kids could eat made me unbelievably angry—and not just because I felt like crap for already eating my protein rations today and what little I had to give up was stuff I wouldn't have wanted to eat, anyway.

Even if nobody had gotten raped, there must have been struggles, because several of the survivors sported bruises now that hadn't been there this morning. Including some of the kids.

I didn't ask who exactly had been responsible for this and in what capacity, but I hadn't expected to be missing Jared because of his proclivities this early in our eternal separation.

My, but he would have had a field day or two over this—and I couldn't even swear with a straight face that I wouldn't have offered to lend a hand.

This wasn't the only issue the next day that eventually forced us to seek shelter in the woods. It wasn't just raining; it was pouring down, the winds bad enough that I was seriously afraid this was going to end in a hurricane. So far, the season had been a rather mild one—or at least, the parts I'd been in all summer and fall hadn't been hit hard, and the signs of destruction could have come from a lot of things. But this day was simply miserable, too bad to be out and about.

And yet, people had to eat.

Or as Jerry put it, jarringly frank: "We only have food for everyone for two more days. If it gets worse than this tomorrow, we're fucked."

So looting we went. We didn't find much that day, but it was better than nothing. Including what blankets and clothing we brought back to make up for the stolen gear.

What we did find—or at least I noticed—was a signpost leading to Lake Norman, thirty miles this way. I realized we must be getting close to that damn interstate again.

Maybe the storms were good for one thing and made passing possible now.

The weather did get worse the next day, yet after some heavy debate in the morning, it was decided that we had to move on. I was on looting duty right from the morning on, only returning briefly to drop off some food at noon, and then again to pick up some injured people who had slipped and fallen in the sludge that the world had turned into.

I was still afraid of crossing the interstate when a different kind of danger reared its ugly head, one not entirely disconnected from said fear.

Every single house we tried now had already been looted, often down to what furniture could be carried away.

We finally reached and crossed the interstate at a point someone had apparently declared as safe.

I was baffled when I realized they had been right. There were still lurkers around, but nowhere near what we'd happened upon every single time we'd gotten close to that damn highway. Maybe the undead had had time to wander off, and whatever had made them congregate there was no longer happening? Maybe my wild theories at seeing those masses in Asheville were all completely wrong?

North of the interstate, it took us a single day to walk up to the first house with a red, spray-painted X on its door—exactly how Osprey and the gang had marked up their looted houses.

I didn't know for sure, but I had a feeling that we'd reached the southernmost border of what used to be the Enclave's borders.

I hadn't asked about them. Hadn't even breathed a single word, too afraid of anyone connecting me with or even recognizing me from there. I'd also not wanted to hear the truth if it ended with, "… and everyone is dead." But now I was getting close enough that if I took off once everyone tucked in at night, I might make it to the Enclave proper by morning.

The question remained, was this a viable option? And, more poignantly, was it the better option?

As I spent another night huddled under a tarp-covered blanket with Bea and her kids, it was really hard not to want to be in the climate-controlled environment of a mine.

But I'd already been there, done that, gotten kicked out after my friends had been brutally murdered, right? And there was the added fact of someone being after us—Jared, Blake, Axel, and me—who might very well be content if only they got their grubby hands on yours truly. Then again, they might have better food options, and if they knew about the changes in my physiology, maybe they were ready to accommodate that.

Why not spend eternity locked in a glass box, provided with all the juicy meat I could possibly gorge myself on?

Yeah, even cold, wet, and hungry as fuck, that idea haunted me.

Even crawling back to Jared on my hands and knees would be preferable to that. At least after some gloating, he'd help provide for my meals, and I'd be almost free to do as I pleased. If not for the fallout of when he got bored...

Sitting between a rock and a hard place wasn't exactly a comfortable existence—but it made it a million times easier to choose sticking with Bea and Mariana, and hoping for the best.

If worse came to worst and we ended up bogged down in the mountains like some modern day twisted version of the Donner Party, at least I would have something to eat.

And yes, my mind kept flipping back to that subject way too often for me to be completely comfortable about sticking with them, day in, day out. I would have loved to swear that, if worse came to worst, I'd simply waste away and die—and probably as one of the first ones to go—but I had the sneaking suspicion that long before that happened, my mind would finally flip again and put a very bloody conclusion to those pipe dreams.

But as long as we still found something to eat, I should be good.

Damn, but it wasn't fun to feel like I'd turned into a ticking time bomb.

We traversed the former Enclave territory east to west without altercations and very little incidents once the storm finally eased up again. The going remained slow, mostly due to the damage nature had inflicted on what used to be rock-solid infrastructure—but also because now we finally ran into some solid undead opposition. The mobs I so clearly remembered from early summer may have dispersed, but a lot of the undead were still lurking in the foothills.

A lot, a lot, as we had to admit, as with every day that led us further northwest, the more attacks happened, to the point that—again!—I couldn't sleep at night because my danger radar kept going off at all times now. What used to be a drawn-out column of people turned into a solid mass now, with everyone capable of holding a stick to whack something hard on rotating duty to keep those who couldn't safe in the middle.

Looting got harder and harder, and finally ground to a halt when we simply couldn't afford to leave the main group for long anymore. Besides, fuel was running low, with wrecks everywhere around us siphoned dry months ago. One by one, the cars and trucks broke down, making going forward even harder, since now everyone had to carry what little gear we'd managed to scrounge up since the last raid.

Then things got even worse when we finally had no other option than to head into the mountains, following the twisting roads I was familiar with from earlier in the year. Whoever was in charge knew about the state of Asheville and the surrounding area from summer and did their very best to avoid running into that.

Famished, sleep deprived, and feeling like my body was about to give out very soon, the fucking pills I still carried in a pouch haphazardly sewn into the lining of my jacket burned a hole into my back that got harder and harder to ignore with each passing day.

Why was I even resisting?

I knew they'd make me feel good—and relief for even a couple of hours sounded better and better each day. They'd likely curb my hunger, and give me the energy to go faster, farther, to find the food we all so direly needed.

There was virtually no reason not to take them—except for my very soul and sanity.

Not that there was much left of either, and the needs for both became more questionable with each passing day.

And yes, I was well aware that I was turning incredibly morose and dramatic, but having to keep a straight, positive face every single day to lie to the kids that soon, things would be better was making it impossible for my inner monologue not to flip into that.

Shit, but I really missed Jared. And Axel and Blake as well, but they weren't quite on the same level of contention he posed. I was sure that he would never have gotten into a situation like this, and gotten stuck in it no less.

I knew this was likely just a phase, but I started really regretting my choice to strike out on my own.

Just look how well that was playing out for me.

But, of course, things could always get worse—and the next morning, it did.

I knew something was wrong when, instead of starting into another dreary, endless day, people remained where they had slept. Then a knot of people gathered, agitation running through the entire camp in waves.

Bea and I shared a glance. Without a word, I got up to find out what was going on, surprised to see that she was coming along after telling her kids to stay with Mariana for now.

I didn't recognize half the men milling around, but I didn't need Jerry's whispered comment when we joined him to know who they were. Our entire forward defense was in camp—something that barely ever happened.

"We need to decide what to do next," one of them said as he looked around, speaking up so at least the people in his direct vicinity could understand. "Every group will designate a leader who'll cast a vote, and then we go with what the majority decides."

Very democratic on the outside. I just wasn't too sure what he considered as a group, and how smart it really was to give everyone a voice. Yes, shocking indeed, but the idea that someone like Sanctimonious Mila could decide my fate wasn't exactly leaving me feeling confident in democracy anymore.

Oh, Jared would have had a field day with that as well!

"This issue at hand is the following," the guy explained after murmurs had finally quieted down. "As you can all tell, we're kind of stuck in the middle of the mountains. Not stuck in place, but every which way we go from here, we still have mountains we need to get over before we're across the Appalachians."

That part was glaringly obvious, as I was sure all our legs could attest to. Going uphill wasn't even the worst part, really. It was standing on a ridge and seeing exactly how far into the next valley you had to drop so you could climb back up again on the other side that was killing me—and everyone else around, I was sure.

A few of the onlookers called out so, some even managing a pained smile in return.

The speaker was unperturbed, going on as he kept looking around.

"We have several options of where exactly we cut through the mountains. The quickest, shortest way would be to head for Tennessee." Some appreciative murmurs rose. "But as far as our scouts could tell, that route is also the one most infested with the undead." The murmurs quickly died.

"So what's the alternative?" an older woman close by called out the obvious question.

"We think we found a route that might work better, but it adds up to a week to our journey. Which isn't necessarily that bad," he added when sounds of annoyance immediately rose. "It's a detour heading almost straight north, and then cutting through West Virginia and on into Kentucky. We have a couple of locals among us, and they've assured me that there's a good chance that the looting stopped somewhere near the border. So once we get to West Virginia, we might have a much easier time finding food and might be meeting with a lot less resistance." He paused. "We might even get some help from the locals, although nobody has a fucking clue if anyone's still alive up here. But even so, that sounds like the more feasible option."

Murmurs rose again, the vibes mostly positive.

Until Bea next to me called out, "And exactly what's the catch? Because we wouldn't be standing here, discussing, if it was that easy. We'd already be heading that way, right?"

The man inclined his head, as if to silently salute her.

"The issue is, there's a three-pronged valley about two to three days from here that we have to cross. It's full of aggressive undead fuckers, and no, there's no way we can get around that, unless we want to get out the climbing gear—that we don't have. If we try a detour east, it will cost us another week, and chances are good that first snow will absolutely devastate us if it hits us there. Think, people freezing to death in droves."

It hurt on an almost physical level to see the hope die on Bea's face, although she tried to conceal it well.

"So why even suggest that?" she finally asked.

"Because it's a grim outlook, but we think it's possible to cross that valley." The man paused. "If we find enough volunteers who go ahead, physically beat back the undead that are lurking in the pass to let us into the valley, clean up the way to the bottom, and then keep those at bay streaming in from the west to join the feeding frenzy while the rest of the people escape to the northeast. I say we need at least sixty to seventy men to form and hold up a human barrier, and everyone else will have to do a forced march past them that will probably be two nights and an entire day in between until they reach the next pass where they can form a chokepoint and hold it with maybe ten people strong. We'll use up all our ammo that we have, but it can be done."

He didn't need to add a tally of the lives lost that plan required— including a lot of non-combatants, I was sure.

It was an absolute Hail Mary maneuver, but considering how the last days had been shaping up, that sounded better than to simply keep slogging on—and be eaten with very little to be torn from our bones left.

Silence spread through the masses after the first few murmurs died away when those in front relayed the gist of it to those in the back. Nobody seemed to want to be the first to speak up, until the guy eventually did.

"Food for thought. Go back to your friends and families. Discuss what you want to do. We can only attempt this if most of us are on board. And there is, of course, a chance that our scouts missed some vital intel and we're all going to die in that valley. No guarantees but death in the end. But me and all the other guards are for it. We just need another twenty volunteers, and everyone else needs to know that they will be running for their lives. We'll have to leave behind almost everything that we can't eat the day before, and then it's all about speed and stamina. I'm really sorry that it's coming to this, but unless you want to disperse and try to sneak through the mountains back to the coast, this is it."

I was left standing there with Bea for only a few moments. The tides of people pushing every which way easily carried us back to Mariana and the kids. I was surprised when I found Jerry tagging along behind us, his closed-off expression already telling me what he was about to say.

His truck had broken down two days ago. Since then, he'd helped the two women carry some of their things, but more often than not, both mothers had relieved him of his burdens soon after our noon break.

Mariana already knew what was going on, with the news spreading like wildfire. Even as we waited until everyone had gathered around—including a few other families, like Mila's—I saw several people disappear into the woods around, awkwardly trying not to look back.

I had a feeling the decision would be unanimous because by the time it was reached, nobody who was against it was still sticking around.

This was definitely what Jared would have done—and likely carried me, kicking and screaming, off with him. Not quite unlike how we'd left the Enclave that last time.

Maybe I should have checked up on them after all when we'd passed by last week.

Hell, the way things were shaping up, even that damn mountain lab might have been favorable to this.

Yet I strangely lacked both fear and reluctance. All I felt was relief. There was a solution, and a way out for the mothers and their kids. And a way for me to sell my life as dearly as I could, without having to fear flipping one agonizingly ravenous night and killing them all before someone put me down with a well-placed shot to the back of my head.

People still seemed to waffle about starting the conversation long overdue, so I took it upon myself to break the stalemate—very much unlike I'd tried to blend into the background all this time.

"I'm volunteering," I said, content that my voice was firm and full of conviction. "If I can do anything to help get the kids to safety, I will."

Mariana looked devastated, Bea stricken, but it took both of them a full ten seconds to voice their token protest. In that space, Jerry and five other men—four of them over the age of seventy, the last barely seventeen—had also spoken their piece. That was already a fourth of the extra strength required. With that, we would give the others a literal fighting chance.

Bea finally found her voice, reaching one hand out to grasp mine as she pleaded with me.

"You don't have to," she pointed out. "And we need you." Because, obviously, she knew me well enough that one argument would work much better than the other. "What if one of us falls or gets injured? We will need an extra pair of hands to help all of us get through this!" That she was clearly excluding Jerry ate her up, I could tell, but she knew better than to reason with the grizzly old man.

I hated to do this, but she needed another reality check.

"Bea, whoever gets injured is already dead," I stressed. "You break a leg, you're dead. You sprain an ankle, you're dead. You pick up your child and try to carry them? You're both dead because you will fall behind and be too slow, and they will pick you off one by one when that happens. I know it's scary, but you will be on your own once we make it past that pass. I can't help you, even if I stick by your side every single minute. But I can make a difference if I help the others form that barricade. That way, I can buy you maybe ten seconds—or possibly two hours—to make it through that valley." I knew that still wasn't cutting it, so I went with what I knew would work—straight-up lying to her. "Plus, I can't run for two nights and a day. I have this lung thing. I'd slow you down in no time, and even if you tried to help, I'd just fall behind and get you all killed. I'd much rather choose not to end my life this way."

The relief—brief, and almost immediately replaced by guilt—that hit them was almost comical to observe.

I didn't even feel bad about lying. In fact, my lungs were the only parts of my body that still did exactly what they were supposed to do. It was much more likely that my strength would fail me long before that—or my mind would decide to flip and forever go into standby mode. But so long as that happened where I wouldn't tear into the kids and feast on their livers, I was surprisingly okay with that.

Lack of food was turning me into a suicidal heroine. Interesting.

Jared would have so laughed his ass off over that. I could even imagine the insults he'd hurl my way in between bouts of laughter.

The very idea brought a smile to my face—possibly the first in weeks.

Fucking hell, but I really needed to get on with this quickly!

Nothing quick happened, of course. It took everyone hours of debate until they were finally ready to accept the inevitable. By the time the official vote was cast, there were only thirty people represented in the "against" faction, and a good ten of them ended up also joining the human shield brigade. The drain I'd noticed starting immediately when discussions began had robbed us of a good two hundred people, but I was ready to call good riddance to them. With luck, some were just hiding and would later join the runners, anyway. And those that didn't might become zombie food that kept lurkers occupied and thus uninterested in joining the hunt. Or maybe one of them would be the only one who survived the next handful of days and got to tell someone else how almost a thousand people had died for nothing.

My declaration—as the only woman, what a surprise—to help with the offense was met with equal resistance as Bea and Mariana had shown, although I got the sense that nobody took my offer seriously, not even Jerry. I accepted that and trudged on with the rest, doing my very best not to feel too bad as I tried to squirrel away any and all useful protein I could get my hands on to give myself a fighting chance later.

Two more days of climbing through the wooded mountains. Two more nights spent wide awake because I was too hungry to fall asleep, my body wired with the need to go out there and hunt for sustenance. Then half a day more of hiking that brought us into sight of that mountain pass behind which the valley lay. We would rest until full dark, then set out to clear the pass so that, come midnight, the main body of the group could start their grueling trek, meeting up with us one last time before we went to close off the valley to the west so they could make a run for it.

I hugged everyone one last time when dusk fell over the camp, answering all their well-wishes with silent smiles.

No, I was absolutely not feeling as serene as I might have looked on the outside, but I was quite frankly too hungry to trust myself any longer around them.

I was met with quite a lot of dismissive disdain as I joined the men, and everyone but Jerry soon ignored me as they talked strategy. Or what little strategy there actually was to talk. The entire plan hinged on the hope that we would be able to clear the pass and later form and hold a line down in the valley. If the undead ate us all right up on that mountain… well, then I wouldn't be alive to regret my decision, anyway.

There was a small part of me that still hoped things would work out differently. Or—hilariously—that as we trudged up toward the pass, a certain Asshole would suddenly step out of the gloom and yank me behind a tree, feed me enough meat that I wised up and would no longer be hell-bent on ending my life like this, and we could all slink off into the sunset.

I was clearly delusional because that would never have happened. But realizing that made the whole situation almost bearable.

There were a good one hundred and fifty of us, hopefully enough for the plan to work. Because that was still too many to coordinate, we were split into groups of fifteen. Jerry stuck with me still, which I didn't exactly appreciate. I'd kind of counted on the fact that I wouldn't know anyone around me when it was time to either die or hulk out. The old man's presence kind of cramped my style.

We reached the pass a little ahead of time.

There were fewer undead around than predicted, but that still meant we had a lot of work to do to cull the herd and chase down the stragglers before starting down the other side.

We were working in thirty-minute rotations, two groups going side by side.

Before morning light started to filter through heavy clouds, I'd bashed in skulls and destroyed joints for what felt like forever. But that was okay. That was hardly scratching the surface of the mass that was trailing through the valley—and lots more hiding behind the bend in the road that had become our destination for the chokepoint. Even so, we'd lost a good twenty percent of manpower—most to injuries, but a couple were dead for good. The injured decided to remain where they couldn't move on anymore, trying to help the runners once they came along here later in the morning.

I was by far not the only one of the fighters who was moving on autopilot by then. Also not the only one appearing on my danger radar. None of them gave me appraising looks even though a few seemed surprised that I was still alive, so I was still kind of unique, even around them. The closer we sneaked toward the would-be chokepoint, the harder it got for me to track them. Not because they died, or I miraculously found some meat. But there was so much background noise all over that it became hard to concentrate on that and keep the aggressive ones that attacked us at bay.

We got to the halfway point just as a poetic ray of glaringly bright sunshine cut through the clouds, illuminating the way ahead of us like a beacon sent by some cruel god of war.

That was where those that had guns got them out and readied them, and phase two of our plan began: to clear out the valley behind us so the runners had a chance.

Because why else would we have switched from bashing heads in to shooting at them, the sudden shock of sound reverberating from mountains all around us like crazy?

That was also the last time I had time to think and look around before utter chaos buried us under an avalanche of undead, zombies coming screaming at us from all sides while we still tried to keep moving forward, toward our destination. Because if we didn't manage to get there in time and plug it up, it would all be for naught.

I was hungry, thirsty, and desperately needed to relieve myself. I was hurting all over, just from the strain of moving, and constantly hitting things and ducking out of the way didn't positively add to that.

Just concentrating on any one thing became impossible.

And still, my damn mind refused to flip, leaving me stewing in my miserable, consciousness-driven existence.

I may have blacked out a time or two, but that was mostly from overwhelming exhaustion—nothing more, nothing less.

A small eternity later—hours after that single barrage of shots that we'd used to attract the undead from all over—a series of shouts went up from the men in front of me.

We had arrived at the point where we would make our last stand.

I'd expected that realization to come with a hint of triumph, at least. All I felt right now was bone-deep weariness, my arms so heavy I could barely keep the branch up that I'd been using for a bat since the last one had splintered spectacularly.

Looking up, I realized we were standing in a narrow ravine. The road brushed a steep cliff to my left, and to the right a river gurgled through the gorge, too deep and fast that I would have dared to try to cross it—for sure a natural barrier for the undead. And right beyond the river was the other cliff face, almost as steep as the first. An accomplished climber might have made it up there, but none of the undead had shown that alacrity.

There were fewer of us left than I would have liked. Thirty, maybe, although several men were still lagging behind.

Not Jerry, I realized. I didn't remember when I'd last seen him. Hours ago. Fuck.

It didn't really matter. Even now, we barely had time to shout a few orders. Then the next wave of undead was on us, likely drawn by the shout.

A while later, I came up for air once more in a momentary lull of the onslaught. A lot of the men were switching to their guns now, deciding to use what ammo we had left since dying with it unspent made absolutely no sense.

Craning my neck, I looked back and up toward the road leading from the pass.

It was full of people now, moving in discolored clusters wherever the trees would let me catch a glimpse at them.

I knew Mariana, Bea, and the kids were somewhere up there. Maybe already closer to the valley floor. They were all healthy and still had enough energy to make it through the day.

They would absolutely make it.

Rather than relief, I felt a wave of bitterness slam through me that choked me up.

I was almost glad when the next zombie forced me to put my branch to some more good use.

I don't want to die.

I don't deserve to die.

I fucking deserve to live!

Well, now was way too late for all of those mad thoughts zooming through my mind. I'd made my bed, and all I could do was lie in it.

Who were these people to me that I even considered laying my life down for them, let alone going through with it?

Why hadn't I slunk off, like the rest of the deserters?

Why the fuck didn't I slink off now?

The last question I could answer, at least. I was sure that the hard-eyed geezer next to me would have shot me in the back if I'd even tried to jump into the river.

So… I just have to hold out until all of them are dead, and then I can slink off?

I didn't seriously intend to do that. But it was a thought, and one that refused to leave me. It was about all my tired, addled brain could still compute, getting stuck there like a mantra.

Time went on. Our numbers dwindled. Less so because men were torn apart by zombies. More because they dropped from exhaustion, too weak to keep defending themselves and the men next to them. If someone was close by who could close ranks around them, they sometimes managed to get back on their feet. But most didn't. Most just remained where they fell, whether a bunch of undead came to pull them away and tear them apart or simply ignored them in favor of making life harder for us.

The entire ravine stank to the high heavens, blood mixing with urine and feces, and over all that, the overpowering stench of decay.

I had indeed chosen a great place to die.

"Something's wrong," the guy to my left grated out, even going as far as to turn so he could look behind us.

I wasn't stupid enough to fall for that, instead waiting for the next zombie to come for me. Or us, since I now had to have that idiot's back as well. It only took thirty seconds for that to happen. And then fifty more for the next.

"There are none coming from behind us anymore," he muttered when I didn't respond.

With dull acceptance, I waited for my next target—only that none came. Forcing myself to focus, I looked farther ahead. There were three more coming, but they were more hesitant; less aggressive. With so many dead around lying on the ground, they got distracted easily.

And damn if they didn't all look more fleshy than my bony torso felt whenever I lay down to sleep and felt something poking into me, only to realize those were my own ribs.

I finally allowed myself to glance at the guy, and then on to where he was still staring. I could easily tell where our line had wavered over and over, us getting pushed back, then us doing the pushing. Because of where the corpses were, including those of our fallen comrades. But as far as I could see—which was a full three hundred feet until a bend in the road obscured what lay behind it—it was indeed clear.

I looked from the road back to the four undead. They were still advancing, but slowly. Meanwhile, two of the survivors broke formation and came to meet them, putting an end to them. Farther down the road, a new cluster appeared, but they were even slower, half of them already descending on the fresh corpses.

Corpses that had been living humans only hours ago.

That were still warm, and rigor mortis hadn't set in yet.

That weren't infected—or not full of the same bacterial load as the undead.

That hadn't started to rot and fall apart.

I really didn't like where my mind was going.

"You complaining about that?" one of the other men called over.

I had a hard time making sense of his words before I realized it had been in response to our opposition tapering off.

"Fat chance! But it's weird. Didn't Budd say there was no way in hell we'd make it through this alive?"

A pause.

"Yeah. I did." I presumed that was Budd. When I craned my neck, I realized it was the guy who had started all this. So he was still alive.

Looking up and down the line, I realized that all of us—all fifteen of us—had one thing in common. Well, two. We were the young, initially fit and healthy ones—and none of us likely had kids who we'd given our food to, instead eating our full shares. And maybe even pilfered the good stuff before rations were distributed whenever we could.

Huh. Survival of the Assholes.

It all made sense now.

"Looks like you were wrong," the guy next to me harangued, sounding wickedly pleased.

Budd let out a snort. "Sucks, doesn't it?" He got serious then. "I was scouting ahead for days with Tom and Aaron. This is nowhere near the amount of the zombies we saw when we were trying to find a way across the valley. This is half, at max. Maybe even less, particularly farther up the valley." Meaning behind us, where our friends and families were hopefully soon done running for their lives.

Or wearily walking, if he was right, and the undead had suddenly all gone poof!

That sounded really unlikely.

And yet, when I tried to cast around with my sixth sense, I got… not a lot of blips coming from either direction.

"Maybe they didn't like the bad weather?" I called out—why, I couldn't say. Weariness was clearly making me stupid.

The guy next to me laughed. The next one over snorted. "More like a possible mud slide cut off the ravine farther to the west. Would explain why they were all bunched up in here, just waiting for us to take them down. They had nowhere else to go when we cut them off from behind."

That… made sense. Also, it could easily have happened last night while we were fighting our way up the pass. Or the day before, since I had no idea when their last scouting trip had been.

Nature for once working in our favor? I was so up for that.

Only that it was barely an extension on life support, as it was.

There was nothing left in my energy tanks. And no food waiting for us with the families, because they'd already eaten the rest so they wouldn't have to carry it. Nobody had been around to find more and bring it back. So either I died here this afternoon—or possibly later tonight, when my body finally gave out after what felt like months of severe starvation.

My eyes fell on one of my dead compatriots once again.

Nobody would miss him. Nobody would bury him. He'd get torn apart and eaten by scavengers as soon as we were gone. So why shouldn't I—

"Shall we check what's further down the road?" another of the men asked, sounding very unenthusiastic about his own idea.

Budd gave it some thought.

"Let's wait another twenty minutes here. Rest up a little. Get our breath back. And if there are no more of them coming, we go back down that road until where it merges with the other one, and follow our people. Even if we go slow, we should make it out of the valley sometime during the night."

That… was the best news I'd ever heard.

Except that I didn't have until sometime during that night.

I wasn't sure if I even had until sunset, although part of me was loath not to see one last day end in a glorious wash of colors one last time. The sky was still overcast, but maybe if I made it deeper into the valley where the mountainsides weren't that close…

My feet gave out from underneath me with little command needed from my brain. It was more a matter of no longer forcing my body to keep itself upright.

Two or three heads turned, but nobody made a move to come over and help me.

Which made sense.

Nobody could have carried me out of here.

You get injured—you get too weak—you die.

It was only inevitable.

They didn't wait twenty minutes, in the end. After barely five minutes had passed, Budd turned around and started trudging back up the road without another word, or even a glance in my direction. A few of the men did look, but none of them offered me a hand up. I didn't even need to pretend to be dead. Just lying there, on my side, letting them pass was all it took for them to abandon me.

After I'd watched the last one disappear around the bend of the road, I waited another—endless—five minutes before I sat up and took a look around before I staggered to my feet, getting a better look at my surroundings.

First, to check that not too many undead had started coming closer, which barely any had.

But really, so I could have a bird eye view of the men that had gotten killed.

They were easy to pick out from in between the undead-turned-dead. Their blood was bright and fresh, their clothes mostly intact.

I waited for a mental block to appear in my mind and give me grief—so much grief.

All I felt was the gnawing hunger deep inside my stomach, all-encompassing now.

I pulled out my knife from my pocket and flipped it open, staring at the clean—pristine—blade for a second.

And then I went to work.

CHAPTER 15

Butchering human beings is hard work.

Not just because of the mental implications, although they are not to be ignored. It helps a lot when you're a half-zombie, and the last time you've eaten until you were full was weeks ago, while some asshole kept cracking Donner Party jokes while roasting yet more meat cut into neat strips near a fire.

Or so I kept telling myself as I did my very best to imitate the cuts that I—exceptionally vaguely—remembered from that incident with Private Unlucky.

Old, emaciated corpses weren't exactly great produce. Particularly not the first I tried, who already looked skeletal, and when I finally managed to get his abdomen open, I caught a look at the bottom of his lung that looked exactly as black with tar as what those weird pictures in no-smoking campaigns depicted.

That weirded me out more than the grisly task at hand.

And his liver tasted like ass.

I couldn't make myself spit out the chunk I was chewing on, but dropped the rest and moved on to the next corpse, getting a little more selective this time.

There had been, what? Over forty guards in the ravine? Fourteen had survived. There should have been one or two around that hadn't gotten too badly savaged yet—because if I could avoid rooting around a corpse already full of zombie saliva, I'd gladly spend more time looking.

It took me a while to find one, but then I hit the jackpot—one guard, and the seventeen-year-old who had volunteered with me.

I knew I should have felt bad, but my mind was all calculations that younger bodies meant less damage and more subcutaneous fat, and that was pretty much the intellectual horizon I was capable of right then.

It got a little better after eating some of the internal organs of those two corpses. Better yet when I added some muscle, just for the fun of it. Since the boy's skull was already cracked, I took a poke at his brain, knowing fully well that was pretty much all fat—but that was one thing I simply couldn't stomach. It kind of had a weird... spongy... texture to it that made me spit out that first bite without even swallowing it. It also had a weird color, kind of pinkish. Shouldn't that have been gray? Wasn't that why they called it gray matter and all that?

No brains, then. Lesson learned.

I was feeling better already. Still exhausted, but more like I'd spent the entire day bashing in zombie skulls only, not like I was literally on death's doorstep. Stronger, too, which made dragging the next corpse out from underneath a heap of zombie corpses much easier. I went for his liver as well, but then paused to take another look around, doing a quick tally on the corpses I could easily find and that were worth my time—which wasn't all that many more. Three, to be exact.

I took their livers as well, to the point of having to fight to swallow those last few bites.

Apparently, my stomach was now full.

I was still hungry to the point of going insane after eating pretty much pure protein with just a hint of fat, which should have made all satiety signals fire on full.

Looked like that feedback loop no longer worked.

I tried to sum up how many calories I'd just consumed, and how many more my body was still lacking after how I'd abused it over the past several weeks.

Yeah, that wasn't happening. I almost needed to count my bodies using my fingers. Math beyond that wasn't on the menu.

Speaking of which, I should maybe pack provisions. I had a feeling this was the only meal I would get if I chose to stick with Bea and Mariana a while longer—and maybe even if I decided to strike out on my own. Because those zombie corpses were all way more repulsive than the boy's brain, so unless I happened to be involved in another fatal standoff like this one, I was out of luck.

Maybe a few more would die of exhaustion in the coming days. I didn't particularly look forward to becoming that kind of a grave robber, but feeling like myself for the first time in fucking forever made me realize just how damn miserable my existence had been of late.

Existence. Not life. Mere existence.

That was not what I had signed up for and worked so hard to maintain.

I should really pack some trail rations, just to be sure.

One of the men had been wearing a thick flannel under his jacket. That was, of course, not leakproof, but it served well enough as a makeshift bundle I could fill, knot up, and then carry with me as I started walking down the road with something close to a spring in my step.

Oh, I was sure that I was still several more days like this one away from getting my C-cups back, but it was a start.

I took one last look around—kind of glad to see the first intrepid lurkers making their way over to the butchered mess I had left behind, to obscure it all within moments—before I turned my back on the slaughter and started making my way down the road to look for the other survivors.

Part of me waited for my conscience—not intellect, but the thing inside my head that was ready to wield guilt and reproach like a sledgehammer—to come roaring back, but when a while later I felt like I could stomach some more meat, I had zero qualms to untie my grisly package and cut off some more slices of spleen, chewing meditatively as I rested sitting on a bolder. The blood still mostly filling the organs helped slake my insane thirst, but when I saw some rain water had gathered in a small crevice in the rock wall by my side, I greedily sucked it up. As I wiped the moisture off my face, the back of my hand came away stained red—liquid red, which was visible against the deeply encrusted blackish-red already on my skin.

Just maybe I should find a way to wash up, I realized.

A lot of the grime covering me head to toe was easily explained away by what I had been doing all day, but probably not the deep-red stains covering the bottom half of my face and neck.

What could I say? I really was a messy eater.

My heart gave a painful twinge when no, "Yes, you absolutely are," came from behind me, delivered with a dark chuckle.

When I had eaten as much as I could, I packed up my bundle and continued down the road, managing an even but god-awfully slow pace.

At this rate, it would be dark long before I left the floor of the valley, and likely morning by the time I reached the pass up on the mountain. Not that I was on a schedule here, but at this rate, I wouldn't be able to catch up with even the stragglers, and I had no clue where they would head after making it out of this field of slaughter.

Not that several hundred people could pass through anywhere without leaving plenty of traces, but no clue in what mental state I would be when I got there, and how much sense of that I would be able to make.

Because even just an hour or two into recovery, I could already tell that my mental faculties right now were sharper than they had been in two weeks, easily.

Fucking rice and pasta! Who could sustain themselves, running on that crap?!

The very idea of those sorry excuses for food made me sick, although thankfully not in the sense of my gorge actually rising. My body was way too fond of the first-rate sustenance I had filled it with to give up even a single barely chewed and hastily swallowed bite.

Good. I really needed every ounce of strength I'd get from that.

Over the course of the next two hours, I found plenty more places to sit down and keep eating, and enough water that I didn't feel like a dried-out husk anymore. I also found a few more recently dead corpses, but all of them were already about to get picked clean by the army of lurkers coming out of hiding from everywhere. I maybe could have chased them off, but they'd already gobbled up the good parts, and my aversion to their saliva only increased, if anything.

That made me wonder if that wasn't some kind of innate instinct, brought along by my recent changes. That somehow, my brain knew what to stay clear of if it wanted to keep working a while longer.

Like the boy's weirdly colored and weirdly textured brain.

Huh. I would have loved to puzzle that out, but no brain power for that. Not yet.

Still needed more quality food to recover.

And to find shelter, and safety, back with the group of survivors, to hide in their midst like a wolf in sheep's clothing.

I should maybe also find new pants and a new jacket, because mine were torn and caked in blood, and no match for the winter, should it come early this year. While I wasn't averse to flashing a little skin, I had a feeling my metabolism wasn't above frostbite.

It was on my next-to-last lunch break that the sun set—barely visible behind the almost complete cloud cover, making for a really shitty last sunset that made me glad I'd get many more chances to try for a better one—and I saw the first survivors struggling along the road leading up toward the pass. Or last, I maybe should have said. They were easily two to three hours ahead of me up there, and that was hoping that I wouldn't slow down now that I was almost out of fresh sustenance.

I idly wondered if anyone would notice if the very last of them disappeared, but only a passing consideration of that was enough to slam the door closed on that very idea.

So apparently I hadn't completely switched over into murderous-monster territory yet. Just opportunistic cannibal. Good to know.

The cackle that left my throat was a nasty sound, making me cut off immediately.

Sanity might have been overrated, but I'd have to show at least a semblance of it if I wanted to stick around humans. For whatever reason, they kind of required that.

That made me miss Jared even more. I had a feeling he wouldn't have minded.

I made one last stop when the last tones of gray faded into black and deeper shades of black and the last bites of my trail rations were gone. I even tried sucking some more blood out of the flannel, but all I got from that was a nasty taste of cotton and man stink in my mouth. Rain had set in some fifteen minutes ago, which made me feel a little miserable but also meant I could just roll up some leaves by the side of the road, wait for a minute, and then have a fresh, cool drink. It would also wash my hands and face clean, so no extra cleanup required.

Climbing up the road was exhausting. Way more exhausting than just following the other one on the valley floor. Obviously, but I hadn't counted on just how much harder it would actually be. It wasn't like I was about to fall over and die. I was a million miles away from that. But my muscles were sore and protested this continued abuse, and my lungs labored somewhat awfully.

If I'd just had something to give my metabolism a good kick that let me ignore all those things and power through, even if that meant I'd pay for it later—when I was safe with my group where someone else could easily pick up my slack…

And it so happened that I had such a miracle thing right there in my pocket…

There wasn't even a hint of intellectual resistance as I rooted around the back of my jacket until I managed to tear open the secret pocket holding my happy pills. I stared at the bundle for a second, then opened it, ignored the vile scent of thyme, and popped two into my mouth.

You only live once… or maybe I was on life one and a half now, technically, but I wasn't going to be splitting hairs over this.

The relief wasn't instant, of course. I'd have to liquefy them and inject them for that to happen. But already, my next steps were easier, and the ones after that even more, and half an hour later I felt like I was actually making some progress, lumbering up the mountain.

It sure helped when, all of a sudden, three lurkers came at me, forcing me to put my walking stick to good use that I'd mindlessly picked up along the way.

Well, maybe not quite that mindless since my instinct was working on full capacity once more. It was just my higher intellectual functions that were still severely impaired.

And obviously, the flake that was my danger radar was getting incredibly patchy all over again.

That same instinct that had made me pick up the stick noted that it was about time that I learned to use that thing, and fine-tune the point where I lost it.

Gorging on meat? Definitely made me lose it. Check.

I knew I should maybe have proceeded with more caution now, but just as I thought that, I heard voices ahead of me. Low, murmuring; not shouting loudly. They weren't that stupid, even if they weren't cautious enough.

Sounded like I'd caught up to the stragglers.

It took me another thirty minutes or so to actually see them ahead of me, and an hour in total to catch up to them—and that mostly because they stopped for a brief rest in a series of switchback turns in the road that gave them the illusion of safety, or whatever.

Nine dirty, haggard male faces stared at me as if they'd seen a ghost as I walked up to them, stopping in the middle of the road—close enough to converse relatively safely, but at enough of a distance that I would be able to get my stick up should I need it.

Not that I would. I was sure that they would have shot me if killing me had been their intent.

Not that they could have had many bullets left. Or maybe even weapons. Among them, I saw only a single pack, everything else that they didn't absolutely have to carry discarded.

"You're still alive," one of them murmured—Budd, if I wasn't completely mistaken.

I flashed him a grin that I wasn't sure he'd even see in the darkness. "Surprise!"

I'd meant to let that come out as a neutral statement. It sounded both accusatory and exceptionally hyper—very much as if I was riding the methamphetamine high for all it was worth.

Which I kind of was, but since my body was running just shy of empty and all I could do was trudge up that mountain, it didn't really show. Except for the fact that I was still able to move, and at a good extra ten percent faster than the men who had left me behind to die.

No, I wasn't bitter at all.

Really not, because if just one of them had lingered, I couldn't have followed through with my… harvesting.

But they didn't know that, and if their guilt might come with an advantage in the form of them going the extra mile to protect me better now, I was going to ride that bitch to kingdom come.

Fuck, but I'd missed Meth-Brain Callie! She sure as fuck wouldn't have looked forward to joining a fucking suicide run!

The realization that being high as fuck actually did wonders for my chance of survival was not lost on me, and I celebrated it with a low chuckle.

This would have been another perfect moment for Jared to step out of the gloom and join me. I didn't think I would have even grimaced for a second if I'd watched him knife all those assholes in the back right now.

Yeah, I'd missed that righteous anger as well. Who even was I when that was gone? A pathetic wash rag, ready to be abused—and oh, all these fine people had done plenty of that!

I knew some of that scorn was unwarranted. Jerry had done his very best to keep me safe from the raiders, and he'd never protested, although he must have noticed me stealing food before handing the rest over to be shared among everyone else. And I could tell that both Bea and Mariana genuinely cared for me.

It was mostly that almost all of them were pathetic losers.

Maybe not Budd. Budd hadn't even blinked as he'd left me to die.

Yeah, Budd was one of the good ones. Useful ones. But I still wouldn't have moved a muscle to defend him because he had left me to die, so there.

I really fucking hoped I didn't breathe a word of that.

"You… look pretty energetic for someone who couldn't even keep herself upright all of four hours ago," one of the other men observed. I thought I recognized him as the one who'd done most of the talking down in the ravine; the one who'd been standing and fighting next to me. I didn't really care who he was. It was all the same to me, really, because there was no Jared lurking anywhere around here.

Too bad.

I scrutinized his face, but any possible emotions on his expression were completely lost in the darkness.

Whatever.

No, not whatever. Had that been an accusation?

Was that fucker actually on to me, very much aware that I had torn open and gorged myself on the organs of his friends?

No. Just the meth paranoia talking.

Bad Callie. No cookie. And sure as fuck no more meth for the foreseeable future—at least until my current dose wore off.

I realized I'd been staring at him too long—and that while likely grinning maniacally.

"All thanks to the powers of good old methamphetamine and neighboring substances," I told him succinctly.

So, there. I'd spoken one hundred percent truth. And without telling him I had zero inhibitions tearing his face off with my teeth if he kept staring back at me like that.

Some of that unspoken threat must have translated into my tone or posture since he dropped his gaze and then even turned his head away.

And no, I for sure hadn't voiced any of that aloud.

Budd chuckled darkly. "Where you get that from?"

I shrugged, trying to appear casual.

"Found it in a house I was looting. Before I found your group."

"And you just knew what it was on sight only, huh?"

I gave him the incredulous stare that deserved.

"Fuck, no. Of course I popped one of the pills. Figured it would be painkillers if I was lucky. Turned out it was something entirely different. I've been hogging them ever since, not quite sure what to do with them. When you left me to die and I still wasn't dead ten minutes later, I figured, might as well go out with a bang. Which obviously didn't happen since here I am!"

It was damn hard to stop rambling once I was on a roll.

The men all just stared at me.

"Want some?" I asked. "I still have enough left for each one of you… seeing as you're several men short from when you left me. To die."

Yeah, so maybe I should stop beating that dead horse.

The mental image of that made me chuckle.

I quickly shut myself up when that came out too shrill. And way too loud.

Everyone cast around, just waiting for the lurkers to come running now, but nothing happened. So I turned back to Budd.

"What do you say? We're at least another two to three hours behind the rest, and we're not getting any faster, with the mountain being fucking high and all of us running on empty." Well, except for me, of course. "It's not like they didn't specifically make that shit for situations exactly like this. It's how the Nazis won the first waves of World War Two. And how fighter pilots fly mission after mission with just enough time to refuel their jets." That was probably the better selling point. Just because Jared and I had bonded over our shared historical knowledge didn't mean the same would work for these assholes.

Damn, but I really missed my Asshole!

I fucking hated how true that damn proverb was. How did it go? Absence makes the heart grow fonder?

It didn't even rankle that I knew he knew. He'd said so himself on that morning at the lake when I'd been eavesdropping on the guys before being stupid and setting out all by my lonesome self.

My one single mistake was that I'd let myself fall for him. Now that it had happened, there was no sense in crying over spilled rice. Particularly since that shit was fucking vile.

Yeah, I was about done resting up, or any moment now, some of that bullshit would spill over my lips, and there was no accounting for where that would lead.

"So? Want some?"

The words weren't even fully out of my mouth when every single man was nodding.

Nobody commented on the thyme scent or questioned my incredibly stupid story of how I'd come to have that shit on me. Maybe they were really too fucking tired to care.

I made a mental note that over the coming days, I'd have to check up on if that remained true.

I had been a hunted woman, after all. And that right there was very incriminating evidence of my identity. But for any of that to become an issue, we'd first have to survive, and my own chances of making it to tomorrow had just risen exponentially.

That, and just maybe the meth burnout would be enough to kill them all once we reached the other survivors and the issue would resolve itself. I doubted I could pull the very same stunt with hanging back and harvesting a second time, but even so, I figured I was good for the time being.

And everything else was literally tomorrow's problem.

We made surprisingly good time as we set out again, walking in a somewhat drawn-out line that might be less noticeable than a bulk of people. Once the meth kicked in, the men turned a little livelier, which just meant less like walking corpses and more like bone-weary, at-the-end-of-their-rope humans.

It took us another two hours—give or take—to catch up to the last of the stragglers from the main group. And two more after that—together with several more that we collected on the way to the top—to reach the mountain pass. Where an entire bunch of people were waiting for us, anxiously looking in all directions.

Bea was among them, coming at me to envelop me in a bone-crushing hug while my addled brain still tried to make sense of what I was seeing.

"I knew you'd make it!" she whispered into my ear, sounding like she would have loved to belt it across the mountains, but of course didn't. Sound carried way too much up here, even with all that vegetation and rain that should have dampened it.

For a second, I was afraid she would kiss me when she let go, but held me at arm's length, studying me closely.

"Not a scratch on me," I joked—then winced when I shifted and my right thigh let me know it was about done taking the abuse. "Well, lots of scratches and bruises, actually. But no bites. All things considered, I got away clear."

She hugged me again, never mind my completely drenched, torn jacket. It actually squelched as she squeezed me. Only then did she seem to notice in just how bad a shape we all were.

"Come on. We have a camp not far from here. There's little food left and no fire or warm, dry clothes, but at least you can sit down and rest until we go on come morning."

I didn't protest and let her lead me away.

The men stayed with the guards up at the pass, working on rolling boulders and dragging logs from a nearby logging site across the narrow road to block it. It wasn't enough to actually keep anyone from climbing over that block, but it might deter lurkers if they didn't see what was beyond it.

And it only had to hold them off until the morning, when all of us would be gone.

Bea kept holding on to me as she walked me to the camp. It took me a while to realize she wasn't getting overly affectionate but actually was supporting me—and I kind of needed it.

Half of the kids were asleep, but the rest and Mariana were equally ecstatic to see me limping over to them. Nobody had a fresh jacket, of course, but they kept shoving several long-sleeved shirts at me that, layered, were way warmer than my torn clothes. Huddling together hip to shoulder also helped, as did the logs we were sitting on that at least kept our asses off the cold, sodden muck.

As I changed into my fresh clothes, I noticed that the bite marks on my arms that had refused to completely heal were gone now, and barely a new scratch was still visible. Only plenty of bruises, but I was sure that, come morning, they would start to clear up as well.

And almost all was well with the world again.

CHAPTER 16

The aftermath of the valley crossing became obvious in the gray-purplish light of early morning.

Less than half of the survivors had made it. The guards and generally capable people were reduced to less than twenty. The number of orphaned children had tripled—but at least most of them were still alive. So was Mila, and I got another baleful volley of glares from her because I was still alive, and she was now a mother of only two small daughters, the entire rest of her family wiped out.

I knew I should have felt bad for her, but all I could think of was that weird, spongy texture of her son's brain on my tongue.

And no, I didn't tell her that, even if a twisted part of me wanted to—and get really fucking descriptive.

The meth took a while to wear off, but kept me going well through the next day that was spent getting off that mountain and into the lower plateau beyond it. There were still plenty of lurkers around that forced us to move slowly enough so the tired guards could get the job done, but we surprisingly didn't lose a single person that day—after another twenty hadn't made it through the night.

I mostly helped with chasing away—and when I got a chance, killing—zombies that got a little too curious while walking with my two families plus the inevitable extra tail they had adopted, now that half the people were either injured, too exhausted to move at a normal pace, too famished to pay enough attention, or overloaded dealing with those that were thus affected. I was probably the only one in the entire exhausted caravan not getting ravaged with hunger, although I really could have done with some bloody steaks.

It was during a brief mid-afternoon rest that Bea sat down heavily on a boulder next to me, and she leaned against my shoulder for support—maybe only to catch her balance for a moment. Either way, I was too slow to cut down on the impulse to stiffen—because my brain and entire skin felt on fire because drugs, because beginning hangover, because I didn't want her to injure herself falling over, and just a tiny hint of "oh, wrong person I really want to get up close and personal with!"

No wonder it was the last part she caught on to, answering that with a wry chuckle as she straightened herself outside of my personal space.

"You know, Ash, I'm really not that desperate or into you that I'd use the old accidental-fall bit to charm my way into your panties."

At least my answering—equally wry—smile was a real one. Ah, it was good to have my range of emotions back, even if they were out of whack and running a lot darker than any of these fine people could ever know.

"I know you well enough to realize you'd go for a full-frontal, no-guessing-required assault," I shot back.

She smiled—and yet, there was a level of reservation in there that hit me the wrong way.

What the fuck had I just done wrong? Had she actually tried to be cute? Or was it something else…

At least she did me the favor of not stringing me along, getting right to the point—after looking around to make sure it was just the two of us, with Mariana and the kids still a ways behind where we were waiting for them to catch up.

"I didn't want to say something for the longest time because we all deserve our privacy. But Ash… why don't you tell me your real name? Nobody cares, promise. That you lied to us, I mean. But then you can finally stop being so confused who we are all talking to before you remember that's supposed to be you."

I was ready to let her know that my state of confusion usually stemmed from me first having to cut down on the impulse to analyze how well she would taste—and not in the sapphic way—before I could manage a more civilized response but decided to roll with the punch since it was so very convenient.

"I don't think that's a good idea," I told her, hoping the smile I offered was apologetic. "Things are… were complicated. You're probably right. I think it's been weeks since I left all that behind. But I thought I was safe once before—" That made me cut off to guffaw. "Several times before. And each and every time things got turned on their head, and when the shit hit the fan, I escaped by the skin of my teeth. I can't risk you or the kids getting caught up in any of my shit." I gave her another long look, considering—and decided to make another thing very clear. "Bea, I really like you. And while I've very much all my life been pointing in one corner of the spectrum, we are definitely living in a world where I'm desperate enough for creature comforts like safety and plain human warmth to override all of these settings—you don't want me in your family's lives in that capacity. I know a hundred percent that I'm missing out, but I can't do that to you."

Her smile was a brave one—but also held a certain lopsided quality. Almost a smirk, but considering who that reminded me of, she didn't even come close.

"Because you're such a burden, huh?" she teased.

I was very tempted to tell her that yes, I was, because there was a good chance that she'd have to point-blank execute me to save her kids one day, and I honestly didn't think she was capable of that. I really didn't want to have that blood—literal and figurative—on my hands.

"I also lost my heart to someone else. And brain. And increasingly more my moral code," I admitted. "I know you believe I'm being dramatic. I'm not. I'm nothing if not very much aware of who and what I am. And that's not good company in the long run."

"And yet, you risked your life for—"

Thankfully, the kids coming running for us cut her off there and made it easy for me to duck out of our conversation.

Well, I tried. Now it was up to her to be smart.

I really hoped she would wise up since it didn't look like anyone was going to whisk me away, fairy-tale style... Although that would have made for one morbid story. Or a very regular one, considering what all the tales of old entailed.

I didn't even know if I missed Jared himself all that much, or simply the air of safety his readiness to procure food for me wherever he could provided.

There was a thought.

But not in a good way, I realized, when half an hour into us setting up our camp for the evening—still without food or shelter available—and someone did step out of the undergrowth.

Several someones.

A lot of someones, clad in camouflage fatigues and heavily armed.

And I was—again!—the only fucking one smart enough to be fucking alarmed because some fucking military guys had snuck up on us, compared to the fucking sheeple all around me, already baah-ing their happiness at "being found!!"

Just my luck that I was too lazy—and hadn't found a good spot to slink away, smack in the middle of too many people, but not enough that my disappearance could have gone unnoticed.

Fuck.

While I wanted to scurry off and run, what I did instead was remain sitting on the cold boulder I'd chosen for the occasion, very, very still as I watched the men—and a handful of women—in combat gear swarm the camp.

I was honestly surprised that in the first five minutes, nobody had pointed one of their nifty assault rifles at me and shot me in the face yet. But that didn't happen. Instead, packs were slung off buff shoulders and food and water bottles were distributed. No, thermos flasks full of hot tea—and hot chocolate for the kids. The food was fresh, mostly ration bars... but also some jerky of questionable origin.

Or so my mind griped. Because after all, we were living in the times of zombie sex dolls. Who said that wasn't dried human flesh? Or, worse yet, dried zombie flesh that would make every single one of us convert? Well, except for me, so I might as well have some.

Yeah, I was still rocking the paranoia heavily—and aware of it enough to keep my mouth shut and watch the proceedings rather than butt heads with anyone, which might have actually gotten someone suspicious of me, this becoming a self-fulfilling prophecy.

Lo and behold, nobody cared about yet another young, scrawny woman that sat in a gaggle of kids who were all torn between traumatizing fear and really needing more hot chocolate!

Still, I couldn't quite curb that paranoia, and remain completely silent. Leaning over to Sabrina, I whispered to her, "If anyone asks,

I'm your aunt. Make that your mom's sister. We're close enough in coloring that we could be related."

Bea's daughter gave me a weird look but then flashed me a—hot-chocolate stained—grin. "Sure! Aunt Ash."

Before I could even think about warning her to keep this on the down low, she'd already scurried off, likely to inform her brother and mother, but also Mariana and her bunch of my upgrade. Bea gave me a meaningful look while Mariana flashed me a quick thumbs-up. I had a feeling both women understood, if for the wrong reasons.

Unattached single women might soon become very interesting for a special kind of male asshole, but at least some of them wouldn't be that stupid if she had a bunch of very loving blood relatives sitting right there who would immediately notice her disappearance, or if she suddenly started sporting all kinds of bruises.

Call me paranoid, but this wasn't actually the meth talking.

It took rather long until all the provisions the soldiers had brought along were distributed, and even longer before one among them—sporting a single bar on a patch on the front of his combat uniform—stepped away from the others, in a very important fashion.

"If you could listen to me for a sec?" he called out—loud enough to carry, but low enough not to attract attention beyond our camp, hopefully. "I'm Lieutenant Peter Barnes. I—and the men and women under my command—are part of the Army reserve. We'll bring you to our base, which is a few hours' walk from here. All downhill, so no worries. You absolutely have the worst behind you. We'll keep you safe. Tonight, you'll sleep in warm, heated, closed-off quarters, with lots more food waiting for you there. We only have field cots, I'm afraid, but those make way better beds than bare rock out in the freezing rain."

Some even laughed at that lame joke.

Everyone was ecstatic.

All I heard was that they would put me in yet another cage.

Awesome.

But at least they'd clothe and feed me. And likely not make me continually overdose on drugs. That was some kind of improvement, right?

As they started rounding us up—well, herding us toward wherever, really, if one was nit-picky—I couldn't help it when I just so happened to end up rocking to a halt next to the head honcho.

"Let me guess. You're not giving us the option of, I don't know. Just staying up here in the mountains?" I asked. Because clearly, I'd gone insane. But judging from the perimeter they were establishing around the group, there really was no sneaking off.

He gave me a look as if I'd suddenly sprouted a second head.

"You... want to stay here? We're expecting the first snow in a week or two, judging from the current weather patterns."

That made me do an involuntary double-take.

"You still have weather data?"

He cracked an involuntary smile that easily ripped ten years off his age. Damn, that guy was hardly any older than me.

"Yes, ma'am."

I frowned.

He gave me a self-conscious smile. Make that almost self-deprecating smile.

"I got nothing else to call you, so I have to ma'am you," he let me know.

"Ashley," I offered.

Mariana—hanging around closely, likely to make sure nothing untoward happened to me—added a sweet, "Ash to her friends."

I got a knowing—and again kind of cutesy—smile from him.

"Ashley," he acknowledged, actually offering me his hand to shake. "Peter."

"I know. You just told us."

He gave me a quizzical look, clearly at odds with himself about where to go from there.

I would have loved to leave him hanging with that—but the issue was, that was very much a Callie move. Add some more staring, and it would have been a Jared's Callie move. Since I had no clue where these people got their intel from, it was safer to err on the side of caution.

Cracking the most ditsy smile I could manage—which I hoped didn't look too much like a grimace—I shook his hand. "Nice to meet you, Peter. And yes, you can call me Ash."

And that was the beginning of a never-ending love story!

Or so one might have thought from the stupid grin he kept sporting all the way back to their base.

Fucking hell. The curse of being a young, at least moderately attractive woman.

Or simply having female-presenting genitalia that weren't completely shriveled up in this day and age.

I had to admit, a lot of that was my own projection. Lt. Barnes—Peter—did a good job of bringing us safely to their hideout. As did his people. Soon, half of them were ranging farther from the group while a lot of the others were carrying kids on their backs or helping injured people move forward, sometimes almost carrying them as well. The general air of utter relief was infectious, also including the soldiers, as if they hadn't expected to find much more than a handful of starved, maybe even dying survivors, and instead they could usher several hundred people to perceived safety.

Or likely, real safety, as they thought of it.

I sure as hell seemed to be the only one taking every step with trepidation.

I really should have kept my mouth shut, because once the base came into view—illuminated by only a few, dark-red outside lights, but still a beacon of illumination in the otherwise pitch-black night—I found Peter sidling up to me.

"Any specific reason you didn't want to come with us?" he asked, some of his previous enthusiasm gone now—but maybe that was simple exhaustion. I had a feeling they must have set out much sooner and been searching for us, likely all day. How they had even known we were in the area was something I still needed to find out.

"I didn't say that," I pointed out, unsure what exactly I had actually said. "It was a mere question."

"The reason I'm asking is, I can assure you that you're all safe with us. Every single man, woman, and child. But also, you personally."

I must have given him too much of a pointed look that even in the scattered light of the soldiers' flashlights, he caught it, offering a low chuckle.

"Trust me, we've heard all the stories. About supposed authoritarian fascist military types locking up survivors and doing unspeakable things to them."

"Wouldn't that be exactly what a member of said authoritarian fascist military group would say?" I hedged.

He pursed his lips.

"Maybe. What's the worst thing you heard?"

Oh, did I have a list to choose from.

Remembering Kay's delight—and feeling only a light pulse of pain inside my chest at the memory of her—I went right for the bull's eye.

"Some assholes making their new recruits fuck zombie sex dolls and laugh while they slowly convert so they can then stash them a hundred zombies to a lot in tight maintenance spaces?"

Peter actually missed a step, almost sliding on some wet leaves. For a second, that made suspicion rise inside of me, until I caught his wide grin.

"Okay. I have to admit, if you heard that, I get why you'd be wary of coming with us. I figured it was something closer to you being afraid someone would rape you or threaten to hurt your niece and nephew if you didn't comply."

I gave him a surprisingly easy shrug.

"Well, that's what happened before we had the damn zombie plague to deal with already. Don't need any imagination for that."

My words shut him up for a second—but only that long.

"You do know it's anthrax, right?" He actually sounded cautious about that.

"Yeah. Obviously." I paused. "Does anyone not know by now?"

He gave me an uneasy look.

"Know? Probably. But there are plenty of groups that declare otherwise. You know, running the entire gamut of conspiracy theories. That it's an engineered disease. That it was the political elites. A military coup to make a grab for control. The Illuminati. Some hippy eco-freaks. Vegans, because obviously zombies are meat-eaters, and this is our just punishment for our sins. Plenty of quasi-religious theories, too. But deliberate conversion via zombie sex dolls? Didn't hear that before."

I hated how much fun it was teasing him.

"Why? Too out there? You forgot aliens."

"Sorry. Of course aliens, too. Right in the top three." He paused, giving me a meaningful look. "I was just surprised because that one's actually true."

My turn to almost suffocate on a mouthful of spit and fall to my death when my heel slipped on a loose pebble all at once. Thankfully, Peter was right there to grab my arm and steady me.

"Excuse me?" I said when I had finally straightened myself, not believing for a second he hadn't taken that for exactly what it had been.

He grinned. "It's true that they tell that myth," he iterated. "No clue if it actually happened, but we've been hearing the same story for months, coming from all over, mostly propagated by the radio network but of late also by what few travelers there are still out there. No clue where that originated, but it's a settled urban myth now. But without the conversion part."

I knew I should have kept my trap shut, but since his tone was completely guileless, I just had to dig deeper.

"Oconee power station, actually. That's where it supposedly happened. No idea where it came from, but I first heard it in a community down in South Carolina."

Oh, he tried hard to hide it, but Peter's expression briefly closed off, telling me a lot more than he'd likely intended to.

Except that after a sidelong glance—and to make sure no kids were hanging around close by—he leaned closer and went on.

"Actually, that place exists, and there have been a series of incidents related to that. Not this specifically, but… things got bad there before help arrived and they got better. No reason for you to be afraid now." He paused, slightly conflicted, but then went on. "If you want to know more, we can talk about that later. But first, we need to get you all safely squared away at our base where the worst that can happen is you getting frightened from yet more unsubstantiated rumors."

My, wasn't he full of surprises?

Or had that just been an invitation for a booty call?

I really couldn't say. He looked so damn sincere with that young, slightly freckled face and those honest, bright eyes. But then, so could I, I knew very well. And the two of us would have made really cute children—if that in any way or form had been on the menu. Which it of course wasn't, for all the reasons in the world.

And yet… maybe I could play this to my advantage? Some women wanted roses or jewelry. I wouldn't have objected to a bouquet of steaks and sausages. That hint of bashfulness that clung to him made me guess I might even badger him into courting me and then get away without rubbing myself all over his… sausage.

"I might just do that," I promised him. "After a long, hot shower, some bacon and eggs for breakfast, and snuggling up in cozy clothes in my own bed."

I'd been joking, but he actually flashed me a grin. "No bacon, but we have eggs and dairy at the base. And while there's not enough hot water to luxuriate in for long, we can warm up plenty of buckets so you can absolutely clean up. It's not perfect, but you'll see, compared to how you've been living for way too long, it's like a little slice of paradise."

I found myself smiling, even if the no bacon part was a let-down. Dairy meant cows, so maybe steak was actually on the menu? Best news in a long time, indeed!

Since we were getting close to base, Peter had orders to bark and stragglers to guard, leaving me with a promise of making sure to check up on those eggs as soon as we were all squared away.

I found Mariana smiling almost insipidly at me, doing my best to ignore her.

The all-too-familiar uneasy feeling of knowing I was going to disappoint a hell of a lot of people washed through me, but it was very easy to ignore.

Kind of their fault for being so gullible, right?

I absolutely heard Jared cackling gleefully in the back of my mind for thinking that—and meaning it.

Yes, I was honestly and truly fucked.

CHAPTER 17

It was almost disappointing how close to Peter's promises reality turned out to be. And the most severe letdown was that no, he didn't personally deliver scrambled eggs to me at three in the morning, but that had to wait until we were shown into the base mess hall after the personnel were done eating five hours later. In the meantime, we were provided with places to sleep, new clothes, plenty of warm water to wash up, a handful of nurses to check injuries and other ailments, and plenty of packaged food and snacks to eat until our first official meal on base.

While it all had a simple, industrial feel and efficiency to it, it was miles better than anything I'd gotten in… forever. Easily since the Enclave, but in all honesty, even farther back. Since I'd gotten sick. It lacked the freedom and abundance of choice of the summer, but not having to carry every damn pack full of stale food back to the boat came with a lot of comfort.

And the fact that the base could easily house five hundred extra people added yet another layer of comfort to it all.

We were told that there were already other survivors living here, but it would be a few days until we could mingle with them.

For infection control reasons, obviously.

At least whoever was in command wasn't stupid, and the fact that they didn't actually segregate us but simply let us have an entire wing made up of close to twenty rooms with bathrooms aplenty and a small kitchen made it all feel… tantalizingly normal.

I didn't get to luxuriate under a hot shower, but getting provided with hot water aplenty and all the soap, shampoo, and soft towels imaginable was the next best thing to it. After pretty much getting used to personal hygiene mostly consisting of dumping myself into the next—more often than not ice-cold—body of running water, this was good.

So, so good.

Even spending the night on my cot without a second of downtime—let alone sleep—was… nice.

The next morning, I got up extra early to return to the washroom and its bank of mirrors to do something incredibly out of character. Me, Callie, that was. But since now I was Aunt Ash, I had different priorities. Like making sure that I resembled the image once more these fine people had cultivated of me before things had gotten too dire that even this ditsy girl had ditched her makeup in the constant downpours.

I would have loved to claim that the haggard, emaciated woman with the dark circles underneath her sunken yet somehow still too-bright eyes was a stranger, but she was not. Older, yes. Definitely not wiser, if I looked at my track record of the past months. Depending on the cut-off date of that, things were even worse.

I'd tried—so fucking hard—to do better.

And where exactly had that gotten me?

It was much easier to ignore those thoughts in favor of mindless beautification to make myself disappear before my very eyes.

How a tube of mascara, an eyeliner pencil, and some lipstick that now had to double for blush as well had survived in my jacket, I had no damn idea, but since I had managed to hold on to it, I might as well put it to good use.

It sure distracted me from my stomach once more complaining bitterly of its utterly empty status.

It also provided me with quite a lot of mirth when, not five minutes after I'd taken over the empty bathroom, Sabrina slipped in to watch me with rapt attention.

"War paint," I explained to her.

She grinned and gave me two thumbs up.

A brief while later, Mila traipsed in, took one look at my—admittedly somewhat overdone—creation, and left again, muttering something about "whores painting themselves like circus clowns" under her breath, loud enough that the entire base must have heard it.

I was tempted to wad up some toilet paper after that to pad my almost non-existent cleavage, but since I was wearing enough layers to hide the desired effect, I went without that special kind of torture. Really, eating lipstick for the foreseeable time was bad enough.

It was all such an utterly normal, entirely human moment that the insane stress of the last two weeks felt almost surreal.

When I got back to the others, we heard that breakfast was ready, my mouth immediately watering.

It was almost too good to believe. Which I was one thousand percent certain was the case. Obviously.

And no, that wasn't the drugs talking.

But damn, those scrambled eggs were good! And real coffee with real milk! And cheese!

And there was hoping that my digestion would do well with all that, because I was really anxious about that first… thing to leave my body at the other end.

Nobody seemed to notice that I stuck to animal products only, but then it was heartwarming to watch the kids go nuts on applesauce and pie.

I knew it was probably a stupid thing to do—definitely stupid, no question—when I saw Peter making a beeline for our table after getting accosted by profound and heartfelt thank-yous aplenty, and my opening line was, "Exactly what do you have in mind that you are fattening us up for like this?"

In the light of day, he looked maybe a little older, and maybe a little more rough around the edges than last night, but his smile was still dazzling—and real.

I batted my fake-blackened eyelashes at him—and judging how long he stared at my face before he seemed to notice anything else, my efforts seemed to be working.

Fuck me. I was so going to hell.

"You all really need it," he said, smoothly passing by any innuendo awfulness. "And we needed to make the most of the apples before they go bad. So indulge while stores still last!"

Nobody but me seemed up to protesting that point. If they pigged out on the apples, good. That left more of the eggs for me.

The scarce light of the new day—still as dreary and damp as the last—revealed what the night had hidden from us. The "base" wasn't actually a military base. Or maybe it was now, by right of declaring it so. But until recently, it must have been some kind of school complex, explaining why there were plenty of rooms of curious sizes that worked well to house families of up to twenty people easily. Looking outside, I saw a huge parking lot, and on the other side, some hastily erected barns and tents for storage. Everything was surrounded by sturdy fences that were well-patrolled, and in places, more sturdy barricades made up of concrete blocks and plenty of wood were still being worked on.

It was likely not a bad place to spend the winter, but mere hours in, it gave me that claustrophobic pressure on my very soul of knowing that I was locked in rather than being kept safely stashed away.

"How many people are there, all across the compound?" I asked Peter, who seemed happy to play tour guide for now. Several more men under his command had come into the mess hall, happy to chat and explain—and probably keep an eye on us.

"Before the addition of your people, our head count was at just shy of thirteen hundred. Only around a tenth of us were active military, but we've been working all year to build up proficiencies in pretty much everything we need. We're in close contact with three towns farther down the mountains toward the plains. You can all stay here, if you'd like, but we would normally try to distribute you between them."

"Normally?"

He gave me a slight smile.

"If we weren't about to maybe get snowed in soon, or you all didn't obviously need a few weeks of solid three hot meals to regain some of what you've lost. The towns have food aplenty, but ditching hundreds of malnourished, hungry people on them would be stressful for everyone. So the plan is to do that in phases, as the weather allows and as people request it."

That surprised me.

"So we could just up and leave?"

He gave me a quizzical look.

"Nobody's locking you up here," he explained, a weird tone in his voice. "The only reason why you're segregated right now is so we can make sure that nobody's infected, but as you very well know yourself, that's just a matter of days and an issue that resolves itself."

I didn't tell him that I'd actually gotten through the entire apocalypse so far without watching anyone turn, if I ignored my experience of waking up in the quarantine tent. Everyone who'd gotten injured and bitten had always died of their injuries—and yes, it didn't get past me that, likely, Jared'd had a hand in that as well.

Kas and Dharma didn't count.

I also suddenly remembered Kara Mason—that bitch—screeching that we, the guards at the Enclave, had all been infected, whatever the fuck she'd meant with that. Probably just an excuse so they could justify slaughtering us one by one, thus robbing the Enclave of the last line of defense—or resistance—it still had. It turned out Jared had negotiated us a way out of that, although it was debatable if anyone else but the four of us had survived.

It was probably just the talk of infection that made me remember that.

Right.

I did my very best to hide the grim sense of unease that threatened to tank my already not exactly bright mood this morning. Which had nothing to do with my last experience at a military installation whatsoever. Of course not.

"You're not going to test us, or something?"

Peter gave me a quizzical look.

"We might have—if we'd had enough material. Which hasn't been the case in months. If we get new recruits, we put them through a mandatory physical—which is actually just a nurse making them strip and checking them for bites. That's about as high-tech as it gets around here. Sorry if you expected something more sophisticated."

That was actually a relief.

"Not going to do that with five hundred civilians, half of them kids? Too many snotty noses?" I joked.

He flashed me a quick grin. "Something like that. We also strongly believe in people being smart, and particularly in a community like yours where you've been fighting for your very survival for weeks together, that people would self-report if they got bitten, and if they consequently felt ill. Or, at the very least, that when they start showing symptoms, someone around them will report them. Just as you must have handled that—day in, day out—for yourselves until now. Only that now you have the benefits of our med station where we can treat at least your garden variety ailments and set bones and stitch up wounds. But we're pretty much down to what a world-war-two-era combat medic could have pulled off."

I nodded and gave him what I hoped was a gracious smile while my mind kept roiling in the background.

As we'd been handling ourselves, he'd said.

Exactly how fucking oblivious had I been since I'd joined the caravan?

Yes, of course. People had gotten injured, and some had died. Several heart attacks and strokes, most happening during the night but not always silent and peaceful in someone's sleep. Three times that many dead from zombie attacks at the same time before we'd started for the first mountain pass, but most of that had happened outside of the main body of the caravan. I must have gotten lucky with my looting parties as well, since we'd all always come back whole, if sometimes a little winded from having to run away or dispose of some lurkers.

But there had been no dramatic "we need to put you down before you eat us," moments.

Or had there been, and I'd just not noticed? Exactly how out of it had I been?

It made a lot more sense that I was oblivious because I'd been sticking around six children almost night and day, and everyone would have made sure to keep that brutal fact of our lives from us.

I'd also not seen anything like that happen in the many towns we'd visited during the summer and early fall. Or at the Enclave. Then again, they had locked me away and then exiled me to the Militia camp.

All valid explanations. And yet, something about it grated along the very outer limits of my awareness like chalk on a board.

Crossing that valley, we'd had to slaughter a hell of a lot of zombies. And the families'd had to run from many more. Plenty had died—but more had survived.

Exactly how likely was it they had all—to a woman and child—gotten away clear?

Unbidden, my attention wandered to the soldiers that sat around the mess hall, chatting idly with everyone.

"Exactly how many days is that quarantine going to be?"

Peter gave me a shrewd look that made me wonder if I should maybe shut up soon or pretend to be way more of an airhead than I could convincingly act like.

"Five days is standard. And yes, as you probably already noticed, me and my men, we're quarantining with you. We're staying in the barracks just outside your wing, doing a three-shift rotation so everyone gets some downtime after the ordeal of the last three days."

I kept staring at him, trying to make it as bland as possible.

"That's how long you were trying to find us?"

He snorted. "That's how long our op took to annihilate as many of the undead as possible when we saw you were heading into our designated kill chute. And then one extra day of finding and bringing you back to base, yes."

My memories from before I'd been done with the third corpse harvest were sketchy, but I remembered something about someone saying that there were fewer undead than expected—the reason some of us had made it at all. And why the stream of zombies had dwindled as we'd kept fighting them.

"I guess we owe you our lives in more sense than simply getting us warm and fed, huh?"

Peter shrugged as if it was nothing, but I could tell that he was trying not to preen under my attention.

"Just doing our duty, ma'am," he playfully quipped back.

And now they were watching us.

I hadn't missed the fact that he'd never answered my very direct question about if we could leave. I had a feeling that meant the answer was "no."

Since the mess hall was on a rotating schedule now as well, we eventually had to vacate it, but were not only allowed but encouraged to take all the food with us back to our quarters. Probably because it was now considered contaminated—and really, nobody wanted it to go to waste. Back in our wing, Peter and his men continued to play hosts, organizing games for the kids, bringing in coloring books, and setting up several TV sets all over the place, both to the kids' and adults' delight.

I did what I always did—stayed glued to either Bea, Mariana, or watched their kids. Even with several of the soldiers checking me out, that made me borderline invisible. Just the young aunt who maybe was a little too vain for her own good but had her heart in the right place.

And was certainly not using helping the kids to the bathroom to case the joint and familiarize herself with the entire layout of the wing, counting steps silently to commit distances to memory.

Peter was back to chatting with me over dinner—which came with some beef, but sadly buried in a nasty stew full of all kinds of roots and potatoes. With everyone watching, I couldn't very well just pick out the pieces and leave the rest untouched. I almost threw up several times, not even washing it all down with milk helping. Add to that the light but constant scrutiny of my new best friend, and I was ready to go hunting for some canned tuna later.

"I've been asking around about you," Peter informed me, dropping that bomb casually after ten minutes of non-stop prattling over how he'd failed to learn to water ski on his last vacation two years ago in California.

One more reason to choke on the borderline inedible stew, but at least by then I'd almost gotten used to that.

"You did, huh? Why not come to the source herself? I'm nothing if not an open book. If you ask me nicely." I added an actual wink to that, hoping he'd fall for it.

His smile told me he did, but I wasn't completely buying it yet. That probably depended on what he'd heard.

"That was very brave of you," he offered.

I blinked in confusion. Yeah, trying to flirt while you're struggling not to barf all over yourself because you're an obligatory carnivore now did require guts. Clearly, he was talking about something else.

"Joining the men to hold the line so the kids could escape?" he explained, his eyes crinkling at the corners. "Because five men swore up and down that was you, and from one nasty woman's slander, I got the same drift."

"Ah. That." And the Oscar goes to… I did my very best to put on a serious face. "What do they say? If you want something done right, do it yourself? I knew I wasn't going to be any extra help to get my sister, niece, and nephew out of this, and Mariana and her kids on top of that if I stayed with them. But I could maybe buy them some extra minutes if I joined the line." I couldn't help but smirk. "Plus, when they saw that I signed up, several of the men couldn't not sign up as well. You know how it goes. That was very likely what actually saved them—and those of us that survived, too. And of course what you and your people did, although we didn't know that at the time."

He still didn't volunteer that intel, but his proud smile from earlier was back.

"We didn't have the time or resources to reach you for direct support," he explained—which gave me absolutely nothing. "Even if you don't see it, what you did was exceptional. It's my job to, if worse comes to worst, use my own body as a shield to defend the vulnerable. You didn't have to, and yet, you did."

Something else occurred to me.

"Are you trying to recruit me or something?" I teased. Because his attempt at flattery was obvious.

He actually looked slightly guilty. "No. At least not right now. I know that the kids—and your sister and her friend—need you. Guess what I'm saying is once you're all settled somewhere safe and eventually you get bored… we will need more people to help rebuild next year. I'm not asking you to pick up a gun and go zombie hunting. But you're tough and resourceful, and that's something you can teach others. That, and from the way your sister is staring at me, sometimes I get the feeling if I did offer you a gun, she'd take it and clobber me over the head with it."

I couldn't help but cast Bea a sidelong glance. She caught it and widened her eyes, trying to look innocent. But I didn't miss her cautious frown following that.

Oh, she hadn't forgotten our little talk back there, and I had a feeling that—unlike Peter himself—I wasn't fooling her about why I was cozying up to the young lieutenant.

I really needed to get the fuck away from here before my web of lies was going to get me caught in it. The fallout wouldn't be pretty.

And yet, it seemed like the easiest way to accomplish this was to keep my head down, wait for the quarantine to end, and then let myself get shuffled along with the families to wherever they wanted to—or were supposed to—spend the winter. Simply disappearing into the woods on the road wasn't that hard.

If worse came to worst, I could always jump out of a speeding car. Again. That had worked so well last time.

"So, how are we doing for quarantine so far?" I asked, changing the topic. We'd been here for almost a day. Three days since the valley. Even if infection maybe spread more slowly in older people, they should have come down with the cold of the century by now—and I barely heard anyone clearing their throats, let alone cough.

"Good," Peter offered. "Not a single incident yet."

I couldn't help but chuckle. "I think I would have noticed someone turning into a zombie in our very midst."

He hesitated for just a moment before he cracked a smile at my joke, but it was way too long for me to ignore.

Either this quarantine story was complete bullshit—or I was missing some truly vital part.

I was almost choking with the need to ask, but instead forced another bite of stew down. Better not ingrain myself in his memory as the capable, super inquisitive girl. Capable was already bad enough.

We kept playing that same game over the next two days. Pleasant conversation, sharing some—in my case all completely made up—anecdotes interspersed with some light needling and fishing for information. The only thing that changed was my digestive issues that really gave me a run for my money—and way too much in the literal sense. One night it was so bad that I was afraid someone would start suggesting I was infected any day now, but when I washed my face in the mirror afterward, I noticed that my skin was that perfect, normal temperature, and any clamminess was simply from the recent strenuous exertion. All cuts were now old, white scars, and the bruises had completely disappeared. Thanks to the base being heated mostly by our body warmth, I was wearing long-sleeved shirts all the time, leaving no one the wiser about how mottled my entire skin had been after the fighting—and how much that had changed.

My face looked a little less gaunt now, but the feverish glint in my eyes had increased.

The next morning, I realized that the latent agitation that wouldn't leave my body—previously chalked up to very understandable jumpiness resulting from recent trauma—had turned into full-on fidgeting around the clock. It took actual effort to sit still long enough to eat, and even that I only managed because I jumped up and went to fetch something each and every time one of the kids wanted something.

If Bea or Mariana noticed, they didn't comment, both just happy to be safe and well-cared for.

By the next evening, it had gotten so bad that I could hardly lie down at all. Ten minutes later—or hours, as it felt like—I was up again, trolling the corridors for something to take my mind off with… or, lacking that, finding where the smokers among the soldiers were taking their breaks so I could bum a cigarette.

Like all people heavily reliant on their nicotine hits, it took me exactly two tries to find the right door—close to the exit of our wing, and right by the barracks.

That should have been my first guess, really.

I almost ducked immediately back inside when I found Peter lounging outside in the cold, the collar of his parka turned up against the cold while he was leaning casually against the side of the building, staring into the pitch-black night, illuminated only by the stars since none of the red-light lamps was anywhere near here. I had a feeling that door was supposed to be locked at all times, but of course as the man in charge, he had a key.

Without having to be asked, he offered me a pack of cigarettes and a lighter, watching with faint amusement as I lit up before hastily burying my hands in the opposite armpits. Unlike him, I was just in my two layers of thermals over a tight tank top, and sorely regretting that decision now.

But at least I got my first cigarette in fucking forever.

It tasted exactly as vile and delicious as I'd expected.

"Didn't think you were a smoker," he remarked as he put away his paraphernalia.

I couldn't help but smirk around the—brief—object of my salvation.

"Why is that? Because I'm a girl and smoking ages the skin? I think I can risk a few wrinkles, considering the state of the world. Gotta stay alive long enough to grow old."

Peter shrugged, not protesting.

"It's more that you appear so damn responsible, pardon my French. Helping your sister with the kids. Sacrificing yourself for the greater good. Doesn't quite go with possibly giving someone second-hand-smoke cancer."

I had to bite the inside of my cheek to keep from laughing hysterically. Yeah, because nicotine was my biggest vice… but good to know that I was fooling him. While he was definitely teasing me right now, I could tell he really believed that.

Oh, what a disgustingly gullible fool.

And yes, that had definitely whispered through my mind in Jared's voice.

"Everyone needs a break from time to time. Even heroes." I took a long drag, inclining my head in a way to signal I was referring to him.

He ignored it, but couldn't quite hide a smile.

Good. Crisis hopefully averted.

Except that I didn't have a clue how I'd spend the other eight endless hours of the night once I was done with this cigarette.

As much as I had vowed to myself to lie low, talking was, of course, a good way to waste some time.

None of this would have been an issue with Jared around. Starting with the fact that around him, I wouldn't have had to watch myself. We also wouldn't have been talking, and neither of us would have been sober. And I fucking hated that my mind had only two modes right now: hunger, and failing the Bechdel test almost nonstop. Then again, eating meat was still by far my number one priority and something I couldn't do anything about right now, and Jared was just kind of another addiction in quite a list of overlapping ones, so maybe that made some sense.

"Two more days of quarantine, huh? You must be happy to be let out into the general population of the base again," I noted.

Peter gave me a slow smile. "Actually, this is kind of a babysitting vacation for us. Wouldn't mind doing this another week or two. And the company's better than in the general barracks over there." He nodded across the parking lot to the barn-like structure.

"I thought you were housed in the main building?"

An innocent question, I figured, until I saw him pause.

I really didn't like where this was going all of a sudden. But I still had half my cigarette, and I was going to enjoy every damn inhale, so help me God!

Peter hedged a second longer, but the momentary tension quickly drained from him again.

"We have two barracks," he clarified. "One for those on sortie rotation, who are usually out there most days and do the perimeter watch. The inner barracks are for when we need to be out of rotation like recovery from injury, or what counts for leave here these days. And of course, the small barracks in the wards… Err, wings, like this one. As you know, because that's where you've watched us come and go for days now, pretending very much not to."

I gave him a pointed glance, trying very hard not to look guilty. And get paranoid as hell.

"Not to sound ungrateful," I offered. "But days can get boring pretty quickly when you're locked in here with nothing more to do than eat and sleep. Even if that's amazing in and of itself and I wouldn't want to change it for the world—particularly not after how the days before that were. Don't take this the wrong way, but watching the guard rotations has been the most interesting thing that happens outside of breakfast, lunch, and dinner calls."

He smiled—but it didn't quite reach his eyes.

"I've been watching you, too," he admitted—confessed, almost.

"What, me, specifically?"

Uh huh.

His mouth twisted, making me very much want to jump into a defensive stance—but then ended up in a broad grin.

"I know you keep sneaking things out of the mess hall," he said, laughter ringing in his tone. "I just haven't quite figured out what yet. Candy bars for the kids? Just tell me how many more you want and I'll personally drop them off tomorrow morning. No need for subterfuge."

That... was a damn good explanation. Really, it had been canned fish and meat—borderline inedible because of oil and additives, but still a lot closer to what I could stomach than what they usually made of it. Except for maybe the eggs, but they didn't hold a candle to a raw steak...

"Guilty as charged." I faked a laugh, raising both hands for a moment before taking another drag. "I'm sorry for being so stupid. I just didn't want to be a bother. That's why I didn't ask. I've been siphoning off small treats for them for weeks. We all have. Usually they've come directly from our rations. And suddenly, there are boxes and boxes of everything here..." I dramatically trailed off. "They're smart kids. They've watched us all drop weight like nobody's business. Eventually, they'll figure out where their extra treats have come from. I'd very much like that day not to be in the near future where food scarcity might be around the next corner all too soon if anything happens."

He actually looked guilty, as if it was his fault that some parents were worth being called that designation. It also made me feel weird because I was well aware that my stealing had been virtually all selfish self-preservation only, and I knew that wasn't a white lie I'd just told him.

But the hunger. And the meat. And the fact that I wasn't about to flip a switch and eat someone's face should have counted for something as well.

It took me a few seconds to realize he didn't immediately contradict me about that last part. Then a few more to read the unease—and warring with himself—in his body language.

"I'm not delusional," I told him in a low voice. "I know this is like paradise now. But nothing is certain. Nobody takes any of that for granted anymore, even if they maybe sound a little too joyful and naive."

Peter paused, still considering. Then took another deep inhale from his cigarette and put it out, completely burned down to the filter as it was. When he finally turned back to me, I could tell that something had changed about him.

"Do you want the answer I'm supposed to give you, or the one that might give you a better chance of survival?"

Oh, now we were talking!

I really wanted to go for the former, but of course that wasn't what I told him.

"Ask me about that power plant again."

That wasn't what I'd expected. Not at all. And I really didn't like where this was going.

"Why? What didn't you tell me?"

He exhaled slowly, searching for words, and only found them after lighting another cigarette.

"I wasn't there when the clean-up crews arrived, but let's just say that those who were unanimously said that things were bad. And a lot closer to the rumors you heard than anyone will officially acknowledge."

He paused, gauging my reaction. I just stared back and gestured for him to continue.

"The zombie-sex-dolls part is obviously fake." He chuckled. "And I don't think they ever actually actively infected anyone deliberately. But yes, we found zombies stashed away in maintenance hallways. And even worse, they weren't the only infected that we found."

It was hard not to give away just how much I knew, so I had to fake my horror—which was mostly real, anyway. And one hundred percent true for what followed.

"What do you mean, infected?"

Peter slowly let out a cloud of smoke.

"Did you hear about the waves yet?"

"Waves?" That sounded ludicrous in any context that I could think of. "What waves?"

He shook his head, chuckling softly. It was far from a happy sound.

"The zombies, as we know them—and whatever your people call them—are virtually all victims of the official first wave. Some people claim it wasn't the first, but it sure was a world-changing event that's a good point to count from. Obviously, you know the drill. People got sick. People died. People got up again and started attacking and eating anything alive they could get their slowly decomposing hands on. We all know they're infectious. Something in their saliva, but it usually needs to get into the bloodstream to actually infect and convert someone. Timelines vary, but all three times that I've seen it happen, it was pretty quick. Hours quick. A buddy of mine got badly wounded on a sortie in the morning. He was running a high fever by noon, and he died and almost immediately came back before dinnertime." He paused so he could catch his breath. "That is not the kind of infection we are checking your people for, because you all would have noticed, and it would have happened days ago. It's also pretty rare because usually, when they get close enough that they can take a bite out of you, you're very likely gravely injured to start with."

I stared at him for several seconds straight, my mind oddly blank.

I wished I could have said that this was all news, but it had an awful vibe of familiarity to it.

"So what you're saying is that there's… more?"

He nodded.

"The bacteria… the pathogen… whatever it is, it mutated. I've heard some doctors call it attenuation to the host environment, and whatnot. I'm not a scientist. Don't quote me on any of that. But what we saw—and not just in one community, or one place of origin—is that people continued to get sick. Like in the first wave. Only that now, most didn't get quite that sick. Some maybe not even at all. Or it was easy to mistake the symptoms. I don't need to tell you that yourself. You run for your life. Maybe you even have to fight. You're starved and malnourished. You don't feel your best, right? But you have an entire laundry list of explanations, and the least of which is that you caught second or third wave anthrax, right?"

"You don't mean that like me, specifically, right?"

It was a valid question. Particularly as my brain was now starting to put pieces together that had previously looked like they had belonged to entirely different universes, let alone parts of the same puzzle.

Peter was quick to shake his head, even going so far as to raise both hands.

"No, no! Of course not! But that was exactly why I asked around about you." When he caught my frown, he did his best to smile, quickly going on. "Your behavior. Let's ignore misogynist BS, but as a woman to go for the aggressive, maybe even borderline suicidal stance? Could be the hallmark of a mother-bear instinct, or plain being a kick-ass, strong individual. But it's exactly the same behavior we've seen in way too many of those late-wave infected. They are aggressive. They lose their moral compass. They do things they would have never done previously, or allow them to happen unchecked and unchallenged. That was exactly what happened at Oconee station. Some turned into sadistic assholes. A lot of the others just plain ignored them, either because they couldn't find it in themselves to stop what was going on, or because they didn't care. From what we sorted out from those who got there later, it got worse and worse, almost in…"

He paused, then deflated a little.

"In waves. But different. It's a progressive thing. It was also spreading through the population. Maybe even mutating inside that community, although we've seen it several times over to the point where our scientists say it's part of the life cycle. In the initial outbreak, the fallout was the worst, but it wasn't a smart strategy for the pathogen. It killed the hosts immediately, and they can rarely propagate it. But in the second, third, fourth wave? Very few died, and the infected changed their behaviors in ways that let them spread it more easily. And we still don't fucking know exactly how it spreads. Because by now, we're down to maybe twenty scientists in the entire country who are still alive and have access to labs to test and develop theories. So far, what has worked best is to shoot everyone up with the conventional anthrax vaccine that we've had for a long time, but that only halts the deterioration for a while. It's like once you're infected, your body gains the ability to overload the system and break whatever limitations the shots introduce. They're working on attenuated versions and apparently, some show promising results, but as far as we know, the ugly truth is still the same: once you get infected, you're on the road to becoming a brain-dead, mindless killer. Some just take a while longer to get there."

I stared at Peter, what was left of my cigarette long forgotten.

Then I remembered where I'd heard that thing about the waves. Bea—or Mariana—had mentioned something like that. Before they'd had to flee. What had caused them to flee from their walled-off, previously safe peninsula.

And it fit like a glove on the slow but continuous erosion I had gone through all year long.

So much for Jared, playing his mind games. Playing me perfectly.

There was very little satisfaction in getting presented with the excuse that, maybe, I simply couldn't help myself because I was sick.

It would also explain a lot of his proclivities.

Except that I was pretty sure he had been doing this since way longer than this plague had started up, even if it had existed before May this year.

And the very same was true for my behavior as well.

But it did explain my recent flips—complete or the slow, sliding scale I was on right now. And it wasn't like I wasn't intimately familiar with how it would end.

It did make me wonder what would have happened with me had they given us the shots in that laboratory rather than turn us into their next batch of lab rats. But maybe that was why they had been able to act as they did, convinced that we were already lost causes. And Kara Mason had screeched so as well. All of them, infected!

Huh.

An awful stench tickled my nose, making me realize my cigarette had burned down to the filter. I quickly dropped it and stomped it out, happy to have something to do to distract myself.

"I'm sorry. I scared you, huh?"

Glancing up at Peter, I had a hard time hiding my real emotions. Fear wasn't one of them—or at least not in the sense he believed.

"Well, this sure isn't a comforting good-night story that'll help me sleep easier," I said, deliberately making my voice thin and shaky. Then I narrowed my eyes at him. "And you think that some of us... they're like that?"

"That's why we keep watch over you," Peter hedged. "And why we chat a lot with people in hopes of them opening up so something will slip out."

"If there is something like that."

"Exactly." He paused. "Honestly? I think you all went through so much, the infection would have taken over long ago. We've seen that happen as well. That stress can trigger changes. And what gets more stressful than having to run or fight for your lives while almost at the point of starvation? We're just making sure you're all clean, so that when we merge you with our resident civilians, they won't catch anything. Same with the towns we have already cleared up. Who have been incident-free for weeks or even months, and who are running similar quarantine protocols."

That made a lot of sense—only that, apparently, I'd quite successfully ducked around all that since it got implemented, and without even trying hard.

"What happens with the infected?" I finally asked. "You said the vaccine helps staunch the progression? What happens when it fails? Or when they never get it?"

Peter held my gaze evenly, but then had to look away, briefly scratching the back of his head.

"Another urban myth confirmed. One you might not have heard, or at least haven't mentioned yet. They convert. But they are different. Like the wild phenotype—the initial zombies—some are more placid, others get really aggressive. But these, they are smarter. They can tell each other apart, particularly from us. They attack each other only for territorial or hierarchy fights. And yes, they build hierarchies. Like pack animals. They know who's infected and who isn't. They don't eat their own, not even when you starve them. That means you can actually lock them up, particularly if you separate the most aggressive ones. Smart fuckers, all of them. I've heard that some even managed to instigate breakouts. So, yeah. A fucked-up solution, but we lock them up. Try to keep them fed, if possible, hoping that before they're completely gone, we will have a cure. And those who are on the way there but who the shots helped slow it down? They get to guard them. And help with base defense, culling the undead hordes already out there, things like that. You wouldn't believe what some people are prepared to do when they are too stubborn to give up on hope yet."

Oh, did I have an idea of that.

My gaze drifted over to the barn-barracks across the lot.

"That's them in there? Your fellow soldiers who might soon be on death's door but haven't given up yet?"

He slowly nodded.

"Those were the guys and gals we sent in to try to thin out the horde you and your people ran into. Only we couldn't risk them infecting you, so they couldn't get too close. My team and I, we set out immediately to rendezvous with you, but it all happened too fast. They only became aware of you after your scouts had already started their harebrained assault plan, and until intel reached the base here, all we could do was set out to come rescue whoever survived."

"And now you're checking if any of us will get a personal invitation to join their ranks?"

He nodded slowly.

"As grim as it sounds, if you talk to them, most don't see it as horribly as it sounds to you. Many lost everyone they cared about, and their will to live. Now, they have a new purpose. And we already have medicines to slow down their deterioration. Before long, we might have a complete cure. A lot of them don't really care, as long as they stay sane enough that they can fight and follow orders. Not that different from when you volunteered to die to give your family a fighting chance, right? You'd rather do something—and accomplish something good—than not do anything at all."

It was all very touching.

It also explained why the fuck we kept running into locked-up zombies that were—for whatever fucking reason—behaving ever so slightly differently. It also explained how anyone would be so fucking stupid as to become their handlers.

It did not explain why they had been hunting us, each and every time.

Or why I—a first-wave survivor, as he likely would call me—had only started to deteriorate now.

Maybe it was as easy as a recent secondary infection.

That I probably caught from Josh, Oliver, and Kay, who had been so very, very welcoming at first… until their entire community had gotten aggressive and paranoid. And then someone else had nuked them off the side of the planet.

"How exactly do you determine if someone's infected?" I asked. "Just acting like a jack-ass, or are there some tests?"

He shrugged. "Some pretty much self-identify. If they're willing, we send them straight to the barracks. That's seventy to eighty percent of them. If they still have friends, they don't want to risk infecting them, too. And if that already happened—well, at least they are going down fighting together. But there are some tests we can run. Only what I said days earlier is true. We are running out of everything, including materials for those test kits. We have a doctor on staff who can run them, but that's only happening in very few cases. Like, when we can't stress-test a possible candidate."

"Stress-test them?"

He winced.

"If it's a strong, healthy male? We absolutely beat them up and see what happens. Less so with women, but a lot of them are sensible enough to choose other means themselves—like physical exertion to exhaustion, sleep deprivation, things like that. It's mostly the kids where we use the test kits. Because that's a line not even most of the confirmed cases would cross."

My mind was still spinning from all that new information—and five days of clean and plentiful food, not exactly running at peak performance. And that—like no other statement of our entire conversation—was a good point to end things on.

Particularly since this supposed small break had given me a hell of a lot to think about.

"That absolutely sucks," I said, figuring that was the only thing to say. "But it's good that people are working on a solution."

"It is," he agreed. "It really is. It goes without saying, we all, always, risk our lives when we head out there. Now you have that added layer of shit to worry about, huh?"

I couldn't help but snort, then quickly turned it into what I hoped was a charming smile.

"Well, I have you to protect me from that, right? If some of us really are infected, like that. You'll find them, and you'll make sure they don't turn into those monsters."

He nodded, showing way more confidence than I knew could be real.

"Exactly. And no, I'm not going to insult you by saying something stupid now, like you don't need to worry your pretty little head. Actually, please let me know if you notice something. Even if it's just a stupid fight that breaks out because someone was an idiot, or people were scared. We absolutely do not beat up anyone on principle. Most are glad we pick them out because if they actually still do have families, none of them want to infect their spouse and kids. Just... let me know. I'll pay you with an extra box of candy bars."

It was hard to smile through that, but somehow I managed.

"Will do. Promise."

He nodded.

The moment turned predictably awkward.

I was very glad he didn't do anything stupid like try to lean in and kiss me, because right now I didn't have the emotional bandwidth to field that—and neither fucking him nor tearing his head off sounded like a smart idea. Although both would have scratched certain itches that got increasingly harder to ignore.

Damnit, but I needed more fucking food!

"Night," I whispered as I stepped back into the dark hallway, escaping in what felt like just in the nick of time.

CHAPTER 18

Exactly how fucked was I?

That question wouldn't leave my mind as I returned to my cot by the door of the smallish room I shared with the two families. I almost fell over Leon's shape, curled up directly on the floor, inside the door, before carefully stepping over him. Then I thought better of it, climbed over the too frail, too light body once more and slinked down the hallway to the bathroom, hoping some of the water would still be warm.

Half a thermos bottle was left, the water lukewarm but more than enough for what I had in mind.

Only that when I caught my own gaze in the mirror, I froze, the water all but forgotten.

Was this the mad stare of a mindless killer?

Of an infected?

Or was my mind simply playing tricks on me? Was it all coincidence? Excuses, even?

My intent had been to wash the makeup off; become myself again. But who was this person, this self? I'd really wanted to believe that it was Callie. I'd given her a lot of strengths and very few vices. Maybe boring, but who needed excitement, anyway?

And then came the anthrax apocalypse and washed it all down the drain.

How much of her was still left in me? How much did I really want to be her, anymore? How much of that doubt was my own, how much was Jared's manipulations, and how much was my eternal flaw of needing to conform to what felt like the way of least resistance?

I'd almost died from famine—or flipping and getting put down—and what I worried about now was that I hadn't managed to not take drugs for a single month? Then again, who cared? I'd almost fucking died, and yet, here I was, staring at myself, having some kind of meltdown over… nothing?

Who the fuck am I?

And who the fuck do I want to be?

Playing bullshit bingo with my options was easier than answering those questions.

I was absolutely the woman who had—repeatedly—risked her life for others. Mostly because it was The Right Thing To Do. Also, because their lives were more valuable than my own. That was a one hundred percent emotional calculation. I couldn't have kids, and I was only so dependable. The handful of people who would even notice that I was gone were tantalizingly close to zero. And if I was honest, I couldn't remember the last time I'd actually liked myself. Plenty of therapists had tried to jump into that breach and tackle those demons, but in my entire life, nobody had given me a reason to see myself as valuable. Just look at my track record. A complete waste of space was very much what I usually felt like. I had very little to show for myself, and what there was usually ended up in the dog-shit pile.

In that aspect, Jared had been a hundred percent right. There was a part inside of me—buried underneath all those many intellectual layers—that got off massively on the attention he so loved to dump on me, however I tried to avoid it. Not that much trying had been involved of late. Or at all, if I was honest. And the fucking asshole appreciated the damn things about me that, at best, made me want to scream with shame if not outright guilt. He easily had enough self-esteem for the both of us, and I couldn't see him letting me give up on myself. Unless, of course, it came in the sense of becoming a pious, chaste, moral woman, and proving myself impenetrable to his manipulations. That was probably the only way to make him run for the hills and never look back—and I wouldn't even have to be afraid he'd kill me out of retaliation, because he'd consider letting me suffer forever in that existence my just punishment. Which it absolutely would have been.

And with him, I'd probably never get as hungry as I was at this damn moment, let alone what I'd recently bounced back from.

Damn it! That couldn't really be my deciding factor! I was so much more than a constant need for food—and sex, and drugs, and attention, and being seen and valued as the person I was instead of the ideals I had been striving for so long…

As I kept staring deep into my eyes, I realized just how fucking sick I was of Callie. She was abso-fucking-lutely boring to the bone. An eternal pushover. A turn-the-other-cheek muppet. The sheer amount of people I had deliberately let walk over me and abuse me in the past four years was mind-boggling—and I was fucking sick of it! Of her!

Jared was absolutely right, laughing in my face whenever he could at the very idea that this was the template for myself that I had put on a pedestal.

But in no shape or form was he ever the good, healthy, and least of all sane choice.

Yes, he accepted me for who I really was. Embraced it even, including my recent changes. But none of that was healthy. None of that was good—for me, or for anyone else. I mean, he would have egged me on to feast on my fallen comrades, so freshly killed that their insides were still warm—something I had done, completely out of my mind with hunger and the will to survive that had suddenly flared alive again. And I had yet to feel even a shred of guilt over it. If anything, the only negative emotion connected to that remained my aversion to the boy's brain.

That was not the hallmark of...

I didn't even know of what. Anything, really. Civilization. Strength of character. Goodness.

If I breathed a word of what I had done—and why, and how—to anyone here, they would be right to put me down like a dog! Not even charge me with crimes against humanity or whatnot—just go straight to execution. And done. All that would be left of me was a tale of caution, and rightly so.

But yes, Jared would absolutely provide for me.

That thought drew a wry chuckle out of the depths of my chest.

Where the fuck had things gone so wrong? It was so easy to blame him for everything—and he certainly deserved his fair share of it—but my current situation wasn't because of the machinations of a single man. I had very much played along, and more often than not, it had been my own actions and choices that had sent me on the trajectories that had gotten me to where I was now.

Looking back, what absolutely did make me want to writhe in shame was my behavior at the Enclave. Being so resentful and sullen. Pretty much foisting myself at Osprey, then whipping around and sulking like a little girl—and having nothing but haughty bullshit for him when he pointed out my behavior to me. Worse yet, if I ran into him now, he'd be disappointed at how low I had sunk, and very actively so. And yet, I was pretty sure that he would be the first to lend me a hand and help me drag myself out of this shit of my own making.

Was that the solution I was looking for?

I was almost a hundred percent certain that Osprey was still alive. Of course I couldn't know—and I didn't believe in that woo-woo shit that I'd somehow have felt it had he died—but he was a damn resourceful guy. A lot more so than he'd shown in the brief time we had been working together, I was sure. It had been very convenient to say he'd abandoned me and opened all doors for Jared, but thinking back now with a lot less emotion involved, he had absolutely done the right thing. The smart thing. Put your own oxygen mask on so you can help others. He'd up and disappeared so he wouldn't be shot, locked in, or whatnot. So he could regroup, do recon, formulate a plan, and then act.

Not on a moment's whim, which was pretty much as far as Jared seemed capable of planning into the future. Was it an option and sounded like fun? He was already doing it, and damn the consequences—particularly for everyone else.

Osprey was a true team player. A damn good leader, if a reluctant one, but for him that was one hundred percent not just a cliché, but the truth. Yes, he'd used me, too—because a good leader knew the worth of their people and set them to do the tasks they could do best.

Not simply mainline all the serotonin and dopamine possible, and damn the consequences.

But damn, I missed that rush!

I also missed Osprey, I realized—my friend. Who—like I—had lost two good friends in Dharma and Kas; Dharma arguably worse for him than me since they'd been thick as thieves for… weeks. Like me and Kas. Only that I had done a much shittier job being a good friend to Kas, trying to pawn him off to the next capable person immediately so I would have nobody depending on me for once in my life, because, oh, the horror! How could I keep existing now that, for once, I really had to show up for someone?

Now there was the guilt that had been so absent from my thinking of late, hitting me like a sledgehammer to the gut.

But only for a few moments, because whatever it was in my blood—or brain, or wherever—that drove me to rip out mens' livers and gorge myself on them thirty minutes after they'd had my back and I'd had theirs wasn't big on letting me wallow in what it considered useless anguish. Only the good anguish prevailed—hunger.

So much fucking hunger.

Screwing my eyes shut for a moment, I tried to think clearly.

How would Osprey deal with me as I was now?

It wasn't like I had to sustain myself on human flesh alone. I hadn't had much chance to test it out, but from what I could tell, my body didn't differentiate between the source of my protein and fat, as long as it was animal based, and the rawer, the better. I had a sneaking suspicion that dairy wasn't my friend, so that meant absolutely only eggs and meat—but that still left plenty of sources. Chickens, pigs, sheep, goats, cows... everything on Old McDonald's farm! There had to be farmers left. Sure, their herds must have suffered over the summer—and the coming winter would be its own circle of hell—but come spring, I was certain that enough people had caught enough escaped animals to once more tend to them, and gather around more people to defend them all. A lot fewer humans meant far fewer animals needed. And even if that didn't play out well, I was sure that cows would soon remember that they had once been proud, indomitable herd animals, just like wild boar were a true menace. And yet, humans had hunted them successfully since we'd learned to put sharp pieces of rock onto long sticks. Sure, it would require effort, but Osprey was exactly the kind of guy who would rise to that challenge.

Unlike Jared, who actually got off on watching me tear myself apart over not wanting to eat the damn human remains he sliced up for me but eventually caved because I wanted to go back to mindless monster mode even less.

Or, you know... you don't have to constantly attach yourself to a man just because you grew up without any in your life.

You can be literally anyone—be someone. On your own.

There was a thought.

It had literally taken me five minutes of thinking and a handful of makeup and a lie to become Aunt Ashley. That I was capable of shedding good parts of my personality—and identity—like a snake sheds her skin I'd proven time and time again. I hadn't really paid that much attention to it, so that was why my mask had slipped a few times, alerting Bea to the fact that I was using a name that wasn't mine.

But neither was Callie, if anyone wanted to be particularly nit-picky.

Callie had died in that triage tent, next to her friends, who had, for years, been the pillars that held up her identity.

The woman who had woken up, crawled out of that tent, and made it out of that city hadn't really been her anymore. Too much of my old self had bled through the cracks. Sure, that had been vital for my survival, and I didn't regret it. Well, not most of it. But then I'd met Jared and let him take what could have been Callie version 2.0 and twist and turn it into... something else.

Something I wasn't happy with.

Something I downright loathed, I had to admit, as I stared straight into her eyes again—and watched her smirk back at me.

Fuck. No.

This was stopping. Tonight. Right here, right now.

What better place for a complete reset than when you're safe, well cared for, and still locked in quarantine until you get the all-clear that none of you are sleeper-cell zombies-to-be?

Because, let's face it—I had no fucking clue if anything that Peter had told me was pertinent to me. The more I thought about it, the less sense it made... for me, personally. I didn't doubt the truth of his words, but I definitely had something else going on. Including what the fuck was wrong with me that I could honestly consider staying with Jared, even though every single detail I learned about him just made him into a bigger monster. The sad fact was, those were all flaws that I had come with—or that trauma had forever fused into my very soul. It wasn't something that any mutating bacteria could unleash inside of me. It would have been such a convenient excuse... but I already knew it was just that. An excuse. Just like he'd been a psychopathic murderer before getting infected.

Whatever we were, we were different kinds of monsters than those Peter and his people were looking out for.

Or that's what the infection-caused insanity is making you believe...

There was still that possibility. But since there was absolutely nothing I could do about that, I chose to ignore that option.

Except, maybe that wasn't true.

Peter had mentioned that they had a doctor on base who knew about all this shit. Who was clearly running out of chemicals and kits, but I didn't necessarily need to see some lines on some graph for any kind of confirmation. I was more than happy to just... talk to someone more intelligent and knowledgeable than me and then listen to their opinion.

And, just maybe, whatever the fuck was wrong with me—meaning, slowly turning me into a zombie but then letting me skip back over the line to human again—might be of use to them. Maybe I was unique. Or maybe I was just the only individual like that who'd ever shown up in a lab and told them about what was going on with her. Even so, maybe it was connected to what was going on with the later-wave infected—or could be connectable, by someone intelligent and knowledgeable.

Going to them and letting them know that, just maybe, my body harbored a possible component of a cure would be something Aunt Ash would do.

Problem was, I'd never really been enamored with going to see health professionals, and my recent experiences had for sure not changed that for the better.

I didn't think it likely to happen, but the paranoid part of me immediately thought about being locked in yet another cage, getting vivisected. Because that was the kind of trust issues that drugs give you—and being strapped to a gurney while they give you zombie-goo infusions.

And there was the latent resentment that, if things had been different in so many ways, maybe I would have been that doctor working on finding that cure, of course in a completely ethical, morally blindingly white way. I sure had the smarts. Life simply conspired—again and again—against me getting on that track and staying there.

Pushing away from the sink, I started pacing, trying to come up with a solution. Staring at myself sure didn't help with that right now.

I could talk to Peter. Maybe not start with "oh, by the way, I'm a zombie sometimes and eat the organs of my compatriots." But I could explain that I'd had symptoms—but different from what he was looking for. Hence why he'd completely discounted me already. Sure, there was the danger that they would isolate me—or at least no longer let me hang out with Bea, Mariana, and her kids—but that was something I could deal with. As much as I liked them—or maybe just loved what they saw in me—most of my possible plans already involved leaving them to fend for themselves... now that there hopefully wasn't any more physical fending involved. Every which way considered, they were exactly why the rest of us went out there and gave danger the middle finger—the next generation, and those who could, in a pinch, still provide yet more of said next generation. Even if I hated the inherent misogyny of "women and children first," they were exactly why that existed—and prevailed. They would do just as well—if not better—without me.

And if there was that last smidgen of a possibility left that I was actually contagious in any way and could infect them, all the better if someone took that possibility away from me.

I considered that course of action some more, but it didn't... feel right. Not in a morally objectionable way—although I didn't look forward to confessing to someone I liked that yet again, I had lied and deceived my way into their good graces. As much as that rankled, I would have done it in a pinch if that was it. But there was something that rubbed me the wrong way there, so I decided to leave that for a last option I could later fall back to.

What else was there?

Directly speaking to the doctor was one option. But also the most risky option, obviously. I really didn't like that.

As I kept pacing, my gaze flitted over the clock on the wall.

2:30 a.m.

I hadn't realized it had gotten that late.

Just how much time had I spent staring at myself in that damn mirror? Or maybe I had actually slept some before sneaking out of our room, and my semi-clandestine smoke break with Peter had happened way after midnight rather than just after curfew.

The very possibility that I was losing time—again!—wasn't the most comforting thought, so I ignored it.

Nobody would be in that lab at this time of the night. Even if that doctor was a true workaholic—and why wouldn't they be? Being the last line of defense humanity had against the zombie plague would do that to anyone tenacious enough to go that route under normal conditions. But any brain needed rest, particularly a brain that had been running in overdrive for months and months. There was still a slim chance that insomnia got them to return to their work, but I doubted that would happen in the lab. More like wearily reading notes in their personal quarters, or maybe chatting with the night-shift soldiers over coffee or a smoke.

That opened up a slew of tantalizing possibilities.

One—and probably the most important one—I could simply sneak in there, leave a sample of my blood in the fridge, write a long note explaining everything, and then slink back into complete anonymity. No way they could run a DNA test to identify me. Even if they figured it was someone from our group—and doing sex chromosome typing to realize the sample was from a woman was much easier—that still left a good hundred possible candidates. I hadn't dazzled anyone with my bright mind and scientific knowledge this time around, so I was likely the very last in that already impossibly long line of suspects.

Two—I might not be able to talk to the doc, but there was a good chance that there were notes lying around everywhere, maybe even some kind of typed-up summary—on a computer that I could more quickly and intelligibly sift through. After all, we were on a military base here. It made sense that whoever was in command asked for regular updates. Those notes would be in a language I could more easily read than scientific jargon, too.

Three—I couldn't really think of any other options. One and two were already more than enough for me, and they ran very little personal risk. Even if I managed to get caught, what was the worst that could happen to me?

Cage and vivisection, my paranoid mind roared.

I ignored it.

Likely that they would detain me until a very disappointed Peter came to fetch me so we could have that very uncomfortable but probably harmless conversation I had already considered.

Or I could bullshit him into believing I'd been trying to score something for my raging addictions.

Or pain meds, for the kids, or the women, or someone else, instantly putting a halo around my lying head. After all, he'd already promised me candy bars. Why not add a box of tampons, some condoms, hormonal contraceptives, Plan B, and some Tylenol to that?

That sounded very much like an Aunt Ash move. Including that she wouldn't think twice and already be on her sneaking way without properly thinking about the consequences first—including to herself. After all, she was a brave, brave heroine.

I caught my own smirk at myself as I tried hard—and failed—to hold back a cackle.

Sneaky-sneak it was!

I made sure to silently step out of the bathroom before I could wise up or think better of it. The time for thinking was over. Now it was time for action.

CHAPTER 19

I had no clue where the lab was situated but trusted one thing: military people were sticklers for protocol, and I was sure that someone had been through their freshly converted base putting up signs before even assigning personnel quarters. And since nothing Peter had told me made me think the lab was a clandestine operation, I figured that would be the case.

My first obstacle was how to get out of the wing—which was literally as easy as pausing for a few seconds, checking that there was nobody currently watching the connective hallway over to the main building where the mess hall was situated, and squeezing myself through the unlocked door. I didn't even need my makeshift lock picks, filched days ago from general supplies, simply because I was a paranoid fuck.

Then it was a matter of being exceptionally silent, so I could hear boots—lightly—pounding the ground as a patrol of two very bored soldiers made their rounds and find a room I could duck into well ahead of them seeing me. There were plenty of—mostly unlocked—doors everywhere, and I probably could have hidden behind a column or boxes that were neatly stacked everywhere at random intervals.

Since I had another three and a half hours until the official morning roll-call came, I could take my time and not attract the least bit of attention.

It also gave me another chance to snoop around and get a better picture of the institution here and the people who were living in and running it.

Call me jaded, but just because Peter seemed to be a good egg, I didn't necessarily buy that on face value. I had been burned too badly too many times too often of late not to keep my guard up at least somewhat.

What I found was a lot of inconspicuous shit, but also some shelves with cans and cans of tuna, sardines—and chicken! I'd never thought this was possible, but I almost broke out into a little happy dance as I grabbed some of that, tore it open, and gobbled white, usually bland to the point of tastelessness chicken meat down! It sure was a hell of a lot tastier than I remembered, but since for a while, I'd literally chewed and eaten grass and acorns to keep my stomach from digesting itself…

My sneaky trip having already paid for itself, I continued on my silent way down the many, many hallways.

Twice, I encountered more than the two-person patrols, but those groups were easy to avoid since I heard them from several turns away already. All men, but that wasn't that much of a surprise on a military base. And they were wearing fatigues, for the most part. All rowdy and drunk, or under the influence of something else—but who was I to judge? I had no reason to square off with them, and as long as they kept being so easy to avoid…

I did more or less a complete search of the main building, then only a cursory glance into the back wing, where I found the civilian living quarters. They were very much like ours, although everyone was better fed here—no surprise, but a welcome confirmation of what Peter had told me before.

I also quickly discarded that part of the base because it was where the main, non-infected barracks were, and I figured that was where I might find the most awake and alert people who could get in my way because of their constant shift changes. Even if you were off duty, you'd be playing cards or chatting with friends now when you were used to sleeping during the day if you just came off a night-shift rotation. I had no reason to be there, and it made little sense for the lab to be in that part, so I left it as soon as the patrols let me.

When I started for the other side wing, I had to dodge yet another of those drunk, loud groups. I still wasn't interested in where they came from—presumably exactly where I had just been. Only that while I was hiding from them behind some boxes now because there had been no convenient door nearby, a cold gust of wind blew down the corridor that made me peek.

I watched the five soldiers step out into the ice-cold night, the corridor falling silent as soon as the door closed behind them.

Hesitating only for a second, I sneaked forward to the next window overlooking the parking lot.

In the scant, red illumination, I could easily follow their progress to the barn.

What were a bunch of infected doing in here, drunk no less?

Then again, if they had places to be—like being allowed in the mess hall, or maybe a gym I hadn't yet stumbled on—it made a lot of sense to allow them access only when everyone else was asleep, and knew well to leave them the fuck alone.

That also explained the patrolling guards—who were likely not on the lookout for a zombie incursion but trying to keep people like me from being stupid and accidentally getting infected by the, well, infected.

Not me, personally, I was sure, since I doubted they could give me anything that literal zombie bites hadn't already, but still…

If one wasn't a paranoid fuck, it all made perfect sense.

Since I wasn't supposed to be here at all—let alone in the middle of the night—it made perfect sense that nobody had warned me about this.

I realized I was finally on the right track when the first few rooms I checked in this part of the building were all maintenance stuff. And storage, lots and lots of storage. The same was also true for the corridors in general. They were still tidy going on immaculate where the cleanliness of the floor was concerned, but a lot of the available space was filled with tidily stacked everything.

That was why when yet another group of loud, lewdly joking soldiers appeared, I simply ducked behind some stacked tables and chairs and waited for them to walk past my hiding spot.

What exactly were they doing here? Moving boxes at 4:30 in the morning, or some shit?

Then a different reason came to mind—a rather obvious one.

It made sense that if they got regular checkups by the doctor—and they absolutely would—that this happened also outside of the time where most other people on the base were up and about.

It also made sense that the medical station—or whatnot—was in a part of the base that was also accessible from the outside, and because of quarantine reasons not directly next to the living quarters. And the lab was likely right next to it.

So much for happening upon an empty, deserted lab for snooping around.

Then again, with morning approaching, it was likely that the doc would soon be done, disinfect the station—and then catch some more sleep while I could snoop around with actual daylight that let me read notes that the scant night-time illumination made next to impossible. I doubted anyone would immediately miss me, and even if this made sneaking back harder, I wasn't that afraid of being accosted.

And with daylight outside, I might even dare sneak across the parking lot and make a direct run for our wing, hoping that the perimeter guards were all busy watching outside rather than what was naturally going on across the base.

Or just walk casually with purpose, which was ten times less suspicious.

With that settled—and the soldiers out of earshot—I continued my routine, if at a much more casual level. Maybe I'd return later to root through some of the storage rooms, but it wasn't exactly like I needed anything stashed away there—that Peter and his men wouldn't happily bring over if requested. The only two things I could really think of were a fitting sports bra for Callie or a push-up bra if I actually decided to go down the Aunt Ash route. Right now, I could do very well without either.

Hearing voices—low, male voices—ahead, I paused next to a stairwell. The med station was likely up ahead. If I hadn't gotten terribly turned around, I must be nearing the last third of the ground level tract. Upstairs, another two levels waited for my perusal where I wasn't about to turn a corner and run into someone—so that was exactly where I went.

More rooms full of everything a base housing several thousand people potentially needed, plus lots and lots of stuff more suited for rebuilding civilization. Nothing useful since food was stored elsewhere. Also no bras—but again, not an issue.

The third level was mostly empty, offering yet more space that I was sure would eventually get filled up as well.

I returned to that stairwell when I was done and figured the six or seven soldiers I'd seen had had enough time to get their checkups.

I was greeted with welcome silence, but just to be sure, I sat down on the top of the stairs at level two—well out of sight of the ground floor—and waited some more. Then I got up, went over to the windows facing the parking lot, and checked up on the barracks. It was still dark outside but no longer pitch black—which just meant it was probably one more incredibly overcast, dreary day and would take a good two hours for actual daylight to start. I saw no movement anywhere, and the barn looked as locked up as usual.

I figured the good doctor was done, and maybe even already headed to catch some well-deserved rack time.

The smell of bleach—or some other disinfectant—tickled my nose before I saw the med station as it was: several rooms, sparsely furnished except for exam tables, a couple chairs and desks, and locked cupboards full of medical supplies. Judging from the stench, someone had very recently cleaned up here and left the doors open to air everything out.

The central corridor went on past that point, the same low illumination barely lighting it up as the rest of the hallways in here.

Bingo.

Even though I guessed I was on my own now, I still didn't want to jinx it and did my best to keep my guard up. Gorging myself on the canned chicken seemed to have helped in that department, since I felt a lot more alert and less easily distracted—although I could have wolfed down half a cow, as always.

Up ahead, there was another bend in the corridor, signaling the very end of the wing, if it was built remotely like the floors above. Approaching cautiously, I found several closely spaced doors, and yet another bend in the corridor.

Something in the air changed. Maybe it was just that my nose was finally done working through the bleach fumes? I kept marveling about that as I reached the next bend and glanced around the corner.

One last stretch of corridor, with doors only leading away to the right.

On the left, I saw a bank of windows, only that they weren't opening to the outside. Some kind of seminar room must have been behind there, before. It was mostly dark inside, but up ahead, brighter lights shone from a door coming from the seminar-room side that must have been around yet another corner. Because whoever had built this had really been averse to long, straight lines of sight.

As I approached the windows, I stopped to catch a glance inside. Most of the light spilled into the corridor, so I actually had to shade my eyes to see.

Lab equipment. Lots of overstuffed benches, racks, and cupboards, most even looking like actual lab equipment, not just repurposed office furniture like in most of the rooms of the med station that weren't the clearly medical purpose equipment.

Bingo.

A few steps further down the corridor, I stopped, finally realizing what it was about the air here.

It smelled clean.

Not disinfected, strongly like chemicals. Also not like the mountain air outside. Just clean. Something few people would notice—let alone negatively. And maybe it was mostly because the storage rooms had been kind of musty. But this was different.

I knew that scent all too well, because back in the day, I'd been spending a lot of time in a room that smelled exactly like this—after Anita'd had an HVAC installed in my then no-longer-makeshift drug kitchen.

Lab, really. It had all been lab equipment, just like what I saw everywhere here.

Sure enough, when I looked back, I realized that after the final bend in the corridor, those were heavy fire doors, just as one might install in tandem with first-rate air filtration systems.

Which I figured made sense, if this had been some kind of seminar space where lots and lots of people gathered regularly, and nobody wanted to return home every single time, sick with con crud.

I started forward again—and stopped.

I was having a really bad feeling about this.

Huh.

I listened for a few moments and tried to… sense… with my danger radar, but clearly, that had been offline since we came to the base, if not before. Or else, I would have fucking felt who—and what—was lurking in that barn. At the least, I would have felt those drunk soldiers move past me in the corridor when they had been close enough that I could have reached out and grabbed one of them. I'd legit felt nothing, which I only realized now that I thought about it.

And yet…

Something was setting me off.

Which of course had nothing to do with labs and zombie goo and having to listen to my best friend die a horrible death before almost becoming the instrument of my equally horrible but even more brutal impending demise.

Exhaling slowly, I told myself to calm down.

Not that this had ever worked, for anyone, in the history of human nervous systems going into overdrive.

Gritting my teeth, I forced myself to keep going forward, even if it happened at a snail's pace and with my entire back crawling with unseen eyes watching me. I even paused again to inhale deeply, trying my very best to scent the air.

Not even a hint of decay anywhere—yet my unease kept increasing.

I even tried one of the doors, but they were locked—and like the fire door in the corridor, those were sturdy security doors. Of course I could have—eventually—gotten through those locks, but it really wasn't worth the bother and time that would waste.

Telling myself again to stop being so damn paranoid, I finally made it to the end of the corridor.

Around the corner, there were two doors—the one to the lab I had just passed, cracked a few inches to let the residual light spill in. And opposite of it, the wide-open door to a second, similar room, also offset to my left. Because of that architectural feature, I could only see a sliver of the room, but it was clearly another lab. It was brightly lit—the source of the illumination I'd been following for the past couple of minutes.

And it was clearly occupied as the sound of a female voice muttering under her breath gave away.

I paused right at the corner to listen, since me not being able to see inside also meant that whoever was in there wouldn't see me as long as I remained lurking in the corridor.

"Really, they could have cleaned you up better," I heard her mutter, a distracted kind of anger clear in her voice.

Was she one of those weirdo doctors who talked to their equipment? Stranger things had happened. Including in labs like this.

No wonder my nervous system was freaking out, with my mind constantly jumping back to the zombie goo!

"Damn neanderthals! I swear, if this wasn't for science, I would…" A pause. "Never mind."

Something bumped into something, causing a small crashing sound. More cursing followed.

"Hold still, damnit! I swear, for something so braindead, you get utterly jumpy sometimes." Another pause. "Here. Get up. No, stop! Bend over. I need to check—" More muttering that I didn't catch. "Well, at least they did what they were supposed to, I guess. Stay! Damnit, I still need to plug you up before all that gunk comes seeping out! I swear, if this wasn't a million times more efficient and solving two problems at the same time, I'd go for insemination with a turkey baster and even do it myself! This shit is making you way too jumpy."

What the ever-loving fuck was I listening to?

I knew what my brain was immediately jumping to, but that had to be from yet more out-of-this-world weird experiences like with the zombie sex dolls. Also, it absolutely sounded like there was only a single person in the room. I heard her clothes rustling as she moved, following where the displaced voice was coming from, plus some clanking and other sounds of someone putting shit away and getting more shit from somewhere else. Normal people moving sounds, in short.

It was likely something completely innocuous. Like, I didn't know. Maybe the doc was also a botanist, trying to... do whatever shit botanists did to propagate plants. Just using weirdly inappropriate mammal terms that made it sound terribly rapey. I had to admit, it was totally something I might have done, overworked, sleep-deprived, puttering away on some passion project at five in the morning, trusting that she was unobserved and all on her own. To amuse herself, or maybe just to keep herself awake.

And yet...

I knew that fucking voice.

Because it was burned forever into my brain, putting the name and face belonging to that bitch right at the fucking top of the very short shit list I constantly carried with me.

Maybe that had been what set me off. Before I'd consciously picked up her muttering, my subconscious had already heard and recognized that voice, and slammed down everything available on my internal red-alert button.

I wasn't exactly moving without conscious thought—and exceptionally slowly and carefully—but my mind was kind of blank as I slowly inched my way toward the door, craning my neck to catch a glimpse at where I heard that bitch rooting around, off to the left side of the room.

Bingo.

Slim build, not that many years older than me, blonde hair in a boring ponytail at the back of her head, black-rimmed glasses on her too-thin nose.

Felicity Irons. A.k.a. The Bitch That Killed Kas.

I didn't freeze. That would have been a defensive reaction. Instead, I tensed, my mind already sending signals to my body to slam into fight mode before any intellectual thought had time to form. Thankfully, I wasn't quite that close to operating on a hairline trigger, letting me stay poised to jump, but not actually doing anything yet as I watched and listened to Felicity puttering away with whatever she was doing.

"Where the fuck did I put—" she muttered, then straightened with a triumphant shout, actually holding up something to the bright ceiling lights that looked a lot like a white, round sponge. "Here we go."

She whipped around and pranced back the way she must have come.

If she'd looked at the door and beyond into the corridor, she would have seen me standing there, but she didn't.

As she skipped out of view, I slowly shifted to the side so I could see into the right side of the room, where she had been when I'd first heard her.

Slowly, a table with a single chair came into view. It looked out of place—normal furniture, not lab stuff. And it was painted in bright colors—pink, yellow, and blue—which put it at a stark contrast with the omnipresent gray of the lab benches.

A woman stood at the table, bent over at the waist, her backside facing me. That made it exceptionally easy to tell that it was, in fact, a woman. Also, because she was naked from the waist down, only wearing one of those open-backed, flimsy hospital gowns from what I could tell, but most of that was hidden from view by her position. Her incredibly pale skin was mottled with bruises, only a few patches mid-calf giving away the fact that she was Caucasian.

And because we were one thousand percent living in the garbage-people-only timeline, that sponge went exactly where my mind had immediately gone but my intellect had refused to accept. Because of course it did. And Felicity didn't have a hard time getting it in, making terms like "well used" giving me the fucking creeps.

"That's much better," the bitch muttered as she straightened once more and grabbed something from the table—a pair of white grandma panties that she then coaxed the woman to step into, which involved a series of mostly ignored commands and ended with Felicity physically grabbing her ankles and raising her legs one by one so she could shove the panties up the woman's legs.

"Now, sit down," Felicity ordered.

The woman's legs buckled, making her lie down on her torso on the table before she started to slide backward onto the floor.

"No! You fucking cow—"

Felicity ran to her, ready to catch her before she could spill onto the floor, but at the last second stopped herself when it must have occurred to her that she was too late—or might have injured herself, getting between the body and gravity.

The woman flopped onto the floor without trying to catch herself, not making a single sound as she hit the ground. She also didn't try to roll over, simply remaining where she had fallen in what looked like a really uncomfortable heap, long, oily blonde hair spilling across her shoulders and head.

Felicity stood there for a second, staring down at the woman's body, her expression blank. Then anger twisted her features into a scowl.

"Did you just break your wrist again? What the fuck is wrong with you? Not even an ounce of self-preservation… and now I have to heave you up all on my own because it will be hours until I can call for one of these goons to help! You know, I should just let you lie there where you crap and piss yourself, you useless piece of—"

And yet, she was already bending down, rolling the woman over onto her back so she could pull her into a stretched-out position, yet from the careless way she was handling her, she still didn't seem to care about her injured hand.

A last heave got the woman to flop onto her back, her hair no longer obscuring her face—

And my breath caught in my throat.

Ash.

A visceral shudder ran through me, an intense spike of emotion cutting right through the red haze of rage omnipresent inside of me.

I blinked hard and pinched my thigh, hoping that would chase away the ghosts of my past.

To no avail.

That, lying right there, was Ashley. My friend and roommate through almost four years of college. Funny, happy Ash, who could often be so very silly but was really sharp as a whip underneath.

Ash, who had died in the bed right next to mine in that damn quarantine tent.

It was really her, not just a woman vaguely resembling her. Because that thing that looked like a bruise on her left ankle was really a unicorn tattoo—a souvenir from one of the skiing trips we'd taken thanks to our friends' well-off parents.

And no—Ashley was definitely no longer alive.

Yet, when Felicity finally managed to get her arm slung over her shoulder so she could pull up the younger woman and heave her onto the chair, she moved along well enough, once her body was close enough to the furniture, leaving her sitting in a weird but well-balanced position.

In many ways, that was even worse. For one, because it quenched that flicker of hope that I got to see my friend again. See her? Yes. But I already knew there would be no recognition in her dully staring eyes because that was, at best, my friend's body, her mind long gone.

And thank fuck.

Felicity puttered off out of sight once more, leaving me plenty of time to stand there and stare until I finally managed to pull myself together once more.

Disturbed didn't begin to cover what I was feeling. Not even close. Just how—

Before I could even think that question, I already had my answer. She must have revived—or whatever you wanted to call it—in the quarantine tent. Someone must have recognized her—not her, Ashley, my friend. But the young woman who had been used as a human guinea pig, getting similar experimental treatment as they'd given me. And somehow, she'd ended up here. Considering what I already knew Felicity and the other asshole scientists were up to, that part was less of a surprise, particularly considering that Kara Mason had also immediately recognized me. There had still been military present on site before things had really gotten bad. Maybe more had rounded back and picked up what... specimens were interesting to them? I had to admit, I hardly remembered anything from that day. Except, of course, that Jared had almost fucking shot me!

Just how close had I come to sharing Ashley's fate? Being fully conscious, one might have hoped that wouldn't have involved... getting repeatedly gang-raped to get impregnated by infected soldiers? What the fuck was up with that?

Honestly, I didn't want to know. Absolutely not. None of that was important. It also didn't change the situation at all. Not even if Felicity could have sworn up and down that it was the literal cure for the zombie plague.

One thing was for sure. I couldn't just turn around and walk out of here.

Not because of Ash—and for sure not because of Felicity.

Since I already knew what I needed to do next, there was no sense in postponing the inevitable. So I stepped into the seventh circle of hell, still whisper silent but no longer thrumming with tension.

The cold-blooded need to murder someone will do that to you.

If anything, getting my first full view of the lab just strengthened my resolve.

By a thousand.

Because really? What exactly was it with that bitch and needing to trigger every single one of my Go-To-Hell buttons?

Well, not every single one. One body I might have expected after seeing what was in a tank-like cage on the other side of the room was missing: Dharma.

But that was definitely Kas in that tube.

Or what was left of him. Which was a lot less than was the case with Ash, who—all trauma signs aside—seemed to be physically intact.

Kas? Not so much.

It actually would have been easier not to think of that thing that my mind had severe issues cataloging as what was left of my friend, but that was something I forced my mind to do. Gone were his limbs—one arm completely, the other ended in a ragged stump just below his shoulder. Both legs as well, ending mid-thighs. Not much was left of his muscles, his trunk completely emaciated—and also missing several chunks. His dark skin hid some discolorations, but it was obvious that his entire body was not just in the first stages of decomposition.

I'd seen enough zombies in the last six months to categorize what was going on with Ash and him.

Ash had been well-fed. Kas? Not at all. And considering that I'd witnessed first-hand what a glorious, terrifying weapon of mass destruction he had converted into, that had been deliberate.

Fuck.

What the fuck had these motherfuckers been doing to my friends?!

Besides that, the lab was empty of other horrors, but that was by far enough to give me nightmares well into my next lifetime.

Felicity still hadn't noticed me, but then I was lurking—soundlessly—right inside the door at the other side of the room. She was putting things away, then leaning over some spread-out notes on one of the workbenches, right next to Kas's cage. I realized the reason why it was likely made of glass was to contain the immense stench. There were some hoses attached to the top of the cage, probably to let in some oxygen or whatnot.

It was still almost impossible for me to tear my eyes away from him, but I knew I needed to focus.

"You know, it would be so much easier if I could just milk you, or something," Felicity muttered.

Uhm, what?

Oh, she was talking to Kas—as was evident when she paused, looked up at him, actually smiled and affectionately patted the outside of the tube, close to his admittedly—

No, not going to see that!

My mind was maybe more flexible than other people's, but even I had my limits.

Avert thy gaze, oh maiden with murder on your mind…

I almost laughed at my own silliness. But of course didn't, because stealth was one advantage I wasn't giving up freely, even though I was pretty sure I could take Felicity even if I was drunk and had one arm bound behind my back.

The rage was back. That rage. That had let me flip without even a conscious thought when the Marines had ambushed us. I could feel it roiling low in my stomach, easily chasing away even the ever-present hunger. The temptation to let it take over was there—and strong.

Instant absolution of guilt.

Instant forgetting what I had seen happening in here—at least for the time being.

And, who knew? Maybe I wouldn't automatically snap out of it again. Maybe I could deliberately keep it up—until that option to stop slowly faded away…

But no.

I may have been half numb with pain and three quarters ready to call myself insane with the tsunami of revulsion that threatened to overwhelm me, but this? This I would do with my eyes open and my actions one hundred percent coldly planned and executed.

And I would fucking walk away from this, not giving the bitch the satisfaction that her people would continue their "research," or whatever they called it—and certainly not on me.

There was a tray with surgical tools on a bench nearby. Look, this insane bitch even offered me a knife on a literal silver platter. Who was I to deny her that?

I could have been completely quiet, but I picked up the scalpel, deliberately rattling the tray, half hiding it with my body as I dropped my right hand, wielding it at my side. My eyes remained glued to my target—after I made sure not to make the same mistake as her and glanced out into the corridor one last time.

Still empty.

Felicity paused, but only for a moment. She didn't turn, and then went right back to her scribbling.

Somehow, that infuriated me even more.

Ash didn't even have some kind of muzzle or leash. Did she really trust a fucking zombie to just sit there, docile as hell—

Obviously, she did. And that made what they had done to my friend a million times worse. Even if that was only her body. Whatever. Still. Didn't change a fucking thing.

Not having that same level of stupid confidence, I couldn't help but glance over to Ash to check that she was still sitting at the table, staring straight ahead. Right by the table was a large cabinet with glass doors, letting me see the vacant stare in her eyes in the reflection. Nobody home there—

Not even when I waved my right hand slightly, hoping the motion would draw her attention since she must be seeing it…

Nothing.

What had I expected? That after—clearly—being unresponsive to the point that she dropped to the floor when someone gave her an insufficient command, she would suddenly react to me, just because we were friends? Or—unlike me—her inner radar must be firing at full strength because a fucking apex predator was lurking not five feet behind her?

And that this was a thing I could tell was still going on I realized when I took another step toward Kas, and he suddenly went berserk.

I hadn't been sure if he'd been aware of me before, but as soon as I got into the twenty-foot range, his entire body started to move, tensing and straining—not that it really could, considering there wasn't much left of it anymore.

Felicity noted that, but the fact that she didn't immediately connect the dots and whip around almost made me reveal myself all over again with another pressed laugh.

"Really, sometimes I don't know what gets into you," she muttered absentmindedly, then paused to stare up at him, watching him with a look of rapt attention on her face. "I know you're not reacting to her. That part of your brain is completely useless now. Thank the universe, really, although it would make my job so much easier. I know you don't see her as food, either. And she's not even doing anything right now. And yet, from time to time, you go completely bonkers, out of the blue. It just makes no sense!"

I figured I wouldn't get a better opening.

Fuck stealth. That bitch was getting her oh, so smart intellect handed to her before I made her regret she'd ever even considered going into science.

"It's not Ash he's reacting to. It's me."

Oh, I loved how my voice sounded. Cool, but with just a hint of fire in it to make it menacing.

Measured, calm, dripping with arrogance.

Deadly.

Felicity didn't still, but her motions were almost comically slow as she swiveled on her chair until she faced me, her expression strained. Her eyes went wide, then wider as recognition set it. No half-smudged mascara was fooling her, it seemed.

"You," she breathed.

I wasn't sure if she meant that as in me, showing up here, or in response to my words.

"Yes, me," I confirmed both. "Because unlike you, dumb bitch, he recognizes death when it comes knocking."

So maybe I was being a little dramatic. Sue me! I'd spent so many nights cursing this woman. So many sleepless hours tossing and turning, imagining what I would be doing to her if I ever got my hands around her neck—

Or that was like the cold wrath seething through me felt like. I'd actually done none of these things, although sleep had been hard to come by at times. But I would have done so, had I expected to ever see her again in a million years…

Felicity gave me a weird look that I likely deserved. Oh well. It wasn't like anyone but me would ever remember this conversation, anyway.

"Like all the smart ones, he recognizes the other equally smart, aggressive ones," I told her. "Because correct me if I'm wrong, but considering how he tore through your little guards as if they were made of cardboard, he is definitely one of the smart, aggressive ones. And I'm, well. How should I put this? If I flip the switch, I become the kind of apex predator that makes those like him my bitch. They all have that innate sense of hierarchies. So my guess is, if he got triggered like that in the past, it must have been when one of your rape brigade was getting close to converting into an equally strong one. Of course he doesn't react to Ash. She's—at best—like one of the smart lurkers. Smart enough not to get in between the aggressive ones fighting it out, for sure."

The look of rapt attention on Felicity's face—and utter lack of fear—was weirding me out, but I did a good job suppressing that emotion. Empathy might have come riding piggyback with that, and I couldn't risk that happening.

"We weren't sure until now that actually worked out like that," she mused. "Fascinating." Then her light eyebrows drew together. "So you can control it? That's a first. It will be so interesting to learn more about that."

Since I wasn't hiding anymore, I could let out the bark of laughter that drew from me.

"You will learn exactly nothing new from me. Except how it feels to die, and you won't get a chance to make notes on that. I'm more merciful than that."

A hint of disappointment crossed her face. I couldn't tell whether she was annoyed that I didn't agree to play her game, or if it was at the idea that she wouldn't be able to continue her fucked-up excuse for research.

What the fuck was wrong with these people?!

"Did you understand what I just said?" I asked her.

"Yes, yes," she said, making a throwaway gesture. "You threatened to kill me. How pedestrian." She paused. "That means—"

"I know what that fucking means!" I shouted—not shrilly, but with more emotion than I'd wanted to show. That somehow helped me get a grip on myself again.

"That's a really stupid thing of you to do," Felicity pointed out. "It just means your friends died in vain. And the world would lose one of the last remaining people who are able to save it. Exactly what gives you the right to commit genocide?"

That was reaching a little far, even from what little expectations of her morals I'd harbored before.

"I'm afraid personal revenge will have to take precedence over world peace today," I harped, loving the sarcastic note in my voice.

Felicity gave a small huff—and swiveled back to face her workbench.

"Please, go ahead. Murder me in cold blood, as you apparently came here to do. Someone else will pick up where I have left off. All my research is stored in the cloud and across several hard-copy drives. You'll only slow us down for a week or two." She then shot me a look over her shoulder. "But please. Go ahead and have your useless revenge."

I wondered if Jared ever felt that twisted mix of disappointment and frustration.

This was not how this was supposed to play out!

This was likely how I'd made him feel when I'd come back, going all "yes, yes, sure. You had your fun but look, I don't care, there's something more important on my mind than your stupid games," on him.

He'd been awfully quick to pivot and deal with that, come to think of it.

If he could do that, so could I.

While I was still considering that, Felicity turned back to me, clearly expecting that, somehow, her huffy statement had changed my mind.

"Or, you know. You could actively contribute to science," she suggested.

"Been there. Done that. Didn't really enjoy having an itchy neck for two days. Oh, and watching you kill my friend!"

She briefly glanced at Kas.

"Oh, he's magnificent, isn't he? Too bad he was a little too aggressive. We couldn't tame him, and when we tried to integrate him into one of our packs, he kept starting fights he couldn't end. Hence his sustained injuries. But he's been like that for three months now, and look how he's still going strong! And all that on a protein-fat slurry we feed directly into his stomach. It's remarkable."

As if I needed any more reasons to kill her...

"Why do you keep him underfed?"

Her brows rose. "Oh, he's not. We give him exactly what he needs, calculated for his current weight—"

"He's obviously completely emaciated," I pointed out, narrowing my eyes at her. "Don't you know they have an insanely elevated metabolic rate? You should see what insane amounts of food I can churn through if I have access to it. Easily two to three times what I used to be able to polish off. And I absolutely need it, or I get really fucking stupid really fast. It's a requirement if I want to hang on to my mind."

Her face scrunched up.

"See what I mean? Five minutes of light banter with you, and I've learned more than in two months of grueling research almost round the clock! If you could just see how asinine your undertaking is…"

She trailed off with a sigh.

"First off, not insulting me might be a good idea," I suggested.

Felicity's face lit up as if that had been actual advice coming from me.

"Well. That's going to be hard, but I think I could manage for a while. After all, you can't know that many more things we're not already privy to."

Maybe I was a bigger sadist than I'd known, because I asked, "Why, what would you need from me?"

"Your blood," she gushed with zero hesitation. "Tissue samples, too. But let's be real here for a sec. I'm not delusional. I know very well that if I ask to do biopsies, you'll just get angry again and keep waving that scalpel around. Please don't. I already have plenty of bodily fluids to clean up between those two. I don't need anything extra."

"Why? What would you think to find in my blood? You've had plenty of samples before. Your friend, Kara Mason, was quite fond of sticking needles into my veins." Among other things, elsewhere, from what I'd learned in the meantime.

Felicity rolled her eyes. "Yes. Before. When you were a semi-failed experiment. But not since you progressed to the next stage. Which reminds me—when exactly did that happen? When did you first change, or felt any symptoms?"

I kept my lips compressed, feeling some fleeting petty satisfaction when that made her frown.

"Not being cooperative doesn't solve our issues, either," she let me know.

"But it feels damn good."

She sighed, clearly resigned to her fate.

"Good. Be like that. In the end, it's the same to me. I only trust hard evidence. Which I will get from your blood, whether you want to give it to me or not."

I actually tensed, expecting someone to grab me the next moment. Yet when I turned, nobody was there, except for Ashley, of course.

When I turned back, I found Felicity on her feet, reaching for a pack of sterile syringes still encased in plastic.

"I'll need at least half a liter," she let me know. "A little much for a normal human, but we both know that's not what you are, anyway. I've given way more than that at blood drives in the past. You'll be fine."

I stared at her as if she'd gone insane.

She couldn't be expecting me to just let her draw my blood, right?

And then what? I'd just… leave? Go back to my quarters? Wait for her flunkies to come pick me up and throw me into the next cage?

The woman was completely delusional.

Well, might as well satisfy my curiosity since we were already talking nonsense.

"Why are you trying to knock up a zombie?"

She paused, halfway done assembling the blood-draw gear.

"Technically, she's not really one. Maybe even less one than you are, but to judge that, I'd have to examine you more closely."

"She's just another failed experiment, huh?"

Felicity gave me a quizzical look. It took me a moment to realize that she meant that in an agreeing way.

"Our fault, I guess. Casually racist bias, as it so often happens in science, know what I mean? Of course you don't. Let me explain. We had four doses of the monoclonal antibodies left. Two of the attenuating ones—furthering chances of survival. And two of the recombinant ones that we figured would mess with the pathogen and inactivate it. We—wrongfully—thought we'd give the recombinant ones to the two white girls, seeing as statistically, women of Caucasian background always have the best survival chances everywhere, so we could take things a step further. Your friends we gave the attenuating ones, hoping they would boost their overall survival chances. As you know, the exact opposite was true. One of them simply died, even ahead of the expected window. And while the other technically revived, she was useless to us since she turned into one of the super aggressive ones and we lost her because she got killed for good before we could pick her up. Ashley never completely died—from what we can tell—but her body remains in this half-in, half-out state. She still has a completely working metabolism, including her reproductive organs. And what works should be put to good use, right? There's a good chance the fetus could contain entire sets of vital antibodies since it has to fight off its mother's infection to be able to grow. At least the first five did."

I couldn't help but stare at her—and not just because of the endless info dump.

"She was already pregnant?"

Felicity nodded enthusiastically.

"As I said, five times. All natural abortions, I'm afraid. We are still working on fine-tuning the cocktail required to let a viable fetus grow to full term. We've made great progress. The last one actually went to week fifteen—twice of what the one before managed. I only just got her ovulating again. Hence, you know. Why I need to keep her filled to the brim with sperm at all times to maximize the chance of conception."

I only had a single, slow blink for that.

"You mean have her raped nonstop."

Felicity wrinkled her nose. "Is it really rape if you can't actually give consent anymore?"

I was very much tempted to tell her to ask the parents of daughters in nursing homes that had gotten knocked up by asshole male nurses raping them what they thought about the topic.

That was obviously pointless.

I was just wasting my time here. Not that I could stop myself, it seemed.

"And you're using the infected soldiers for that because of the different waves that infected them? Kind of, double whammy chance for glorious outcomes?"

"Exactly!" she crooned. "Oh, and so they don't get infected. There are actually viral particles in the vaginal secretions, too. And in her blood, of course. Tears sometimes happen, even if I keep telling them to be gentle with her. I don't want to use too much lube because it could reduce sperm viability."

None of the conversations I'd ever had with Jared came anywhere close to this—and that included the one in that alley.

I had nothing more to say to this. Or any other topic, really. The more we talked, the more disgust settled over me like an oily film that would never go away ever again.

"Anything you can tell me about my own state?" I asked. "Like, why and how? And are there any more like me out there?"

A shrewd look crossed her expression. This woman really was a shitty actress.

"I'll happily tell you everything—after I get your blood. Fair is fair, right?"

I stared at her before I slowly nodded, once.

A look of glee appeared on her face while I felt my own freeze.

She went back to fiddling with her bag, line, and syringe.

The scalpel was steady in my right hand as I raised my left arm and shoved up my sleeve, briefly glancing down at the exposed skin, criss-crossed by so many parallel scars.

I brought the scalpel down perpendicular to all the scars and sliced my arm up from my wrist to almost my elbow.

"Hey, what… what are you doing?" Felicity screeched. "The blood! You're doing this all wrong! You'll have bled out before I get enough—"

I was already moving while she was still shouting. Dropping the knife, I grabbed her and spun her around, still perched on her damn chair. The back of her head hit my sternum as I raised my left arm that was gushing blood like mad and pressed her mouth directly into the cut as I leaned further over her. It took some fiddling to find her nose and pinch it shut, using my entire body to keep her in place.

She tried to wail and flail around, but she really wasn't a match for me. Particularly not when I let go of the usual restraint I kept on my body, easily doubling my strength.

"Choke on this, bitch," I whispered into her hair as I kept holding on, even long after I felt her stop to resist and go limp.

I felt just a little lightheaded when, eventually, I let go of her and shoved her away, her lifeless body toppling off the chair just as Ash's had before.

I stared at what used to be Felicity, feeling absolutely nothing.

Exhaling slowly, I considered for a moment, but then bent over, picked up the fire extinguisher from where it hung at the end of a nearby bench, and bashed her head in until I was sure there was no brain left to convert or revive anything.

And for good measure, I grabbed some ninety-six percent ethanol off the bench and poured it over all the blood that had run down her chin onto her chest, just to make it a little harder for the motherfuckers to get their damn sample.

I still felt absolutely nothing as I checked that the cut was already healing—it was—before I turned to face Kas.

"I'm sorry," I told the still trying-to-rampage-ing zombie. "You deserved so much better."

I picked up the same fire extinguisher to shatter his cage so I could sever his spinal cord with my pocket knife. It was hard work—particularly since I didn't stop there but worked completely through his entire neck—but as soon as the thick bundle of nerves was cut, the life went out of his eyes and he quieted down quickly.

Ash was much easier, only requiring a quick slice through the thick veins and arteries in her neck, although I decapitated her as well, just to be sure.

I wish I could have wept into her hair as I did so, but I was too emotionally dead inside to manage.

Then I turned toward the door and stepped out of the lab without a single look at anything else.

I'd found way more in here than I had bargained for—and I couldn't even begin to imagine what I had lost.

CHAPTER 20

There was a lone figure lurking in the corridor outside, after the double bend outside the fire doors. Casually leaning against the wall was more like it, which was probably the only reason why my instinct didn't immediately fly off the handle into nuclear mode. This way, I got a split second to decide what to do while my brain kicked into working mode again.

Recognition set in a moment later.

Jared.

Of all the people in the world, in all the possible places…

But of course he was here. Because.

All I did for a second was stand there and stare at him.

He took his time and pushed off the wall, sauntering three steps forward where one of the scant, low lights in the corridor illuminated us both. His gaze—as always intent on my face as if he could read my very thoughts this way—dropped down to where my hands hung at ease at my sides.

"Callie, what did you do?" he asked, his voice casually teasing.

I simply stared back at him, feeling a last rivulet of blood run down my left arm, right to my fingers before a drop fell off and onto the floor. Jared followed its way, weirdly transfixed. Then his eyes skipped back up to meet mine.

"Dig the blood," he observed.

"Dig the man bun." Pause. "What happened that you cut off most of your hair?" Because that was what was important right now.

Jared smiled. It wasn't pleasant. "Long story, actually. I'll fill you in later. But from my own, recent experience, I can tell you, consider getting some hair ties for your mane. Not much fun when someone grabs you there and you have to chop it all off to break free. Blake threatened me with a buzz cut for two days. Axel finally had enough of it and cut it properly for me, but he bitched me out the entire time. You know how he gets." He flashed me a quick grin. "Glad you like it."

He fell silent. We kept staring at each other.

"You done?" he asked, again glancing down.

No more fresh liquid followed, the last of the cut finally closed up for good.

I blindly shoved down my sleeve, the cotton coarse against the still-sensitive new scar.

"You're late," I let him know. "If you'd been a little earlier, you wouldn't have missed out on this."

He offered me a lazy grin, very much like a cat that just licked the cream.

"Actually, I've been here for a good ten minutes or so. Checked in with you. Saw you were busy. Figured you needed to have a moment to yourself. Get shit done, as they say."

Which meant that had likely happened before I'd made Felicity drown on my blood.

I wondered if I should be irritated with him, but my mind remained completely calm. Too calm, but that was nothing new.

So much for wondering what to do now.

Not that there was much wondering involved. I'd more than proven to myself that I couldn't hack it on my own. And in no way, shape, or form would Osprey have ever accepted me after this.

And yet, I didn't regret a single second of it.

Not yet. Not ever.

While I was still standing there, Jared pulled something out of his pocket—a folded piece of paper. He showed it to me—some kind of wanted poster. An actual "wanted" stamped on top, with four more or less atrocious character sketches on it. Even so, I recognized them.

Us.

"You are a wanted woman," he declared, his smile bright. "Well, of course you are. You know that. You'll always be wanted by me. But looks like others are slowly catching on. This is the reason those assholes started coming after us, with the drones. You remember? Where I dried up a bunch of jerky, just for you?"

I stared at him flatly.

"Of course I still remember."

He snorted, chortling to himself. "Of course you do." He paused. "Your danger radar's off again, huh? You really seemed surprised to see me standing here. For just a second, I thought you were about to come for me with that knife of yours."

"That's because I was." I let that sink in, not that it had any effect on him. Of course it didn't. "Ate too much. Earlier today. And seven days ago. Also a long story, probably not one I'm going to share with you. It's dormant right now, but give me a couple more hours to digest and it might just reappear. It kind of comes and goes. Haven't really found the perfect balance yet."

He nodded, as if that made any sense, then gave me the first real once-over.

"You deliberately going for that heroin chic look nowadays, or did someone go through some moral quandaries about keeping herself well fed, huh?"

"Almost starved to death, but not because I was a picky eater." I flashed him a quick grin. It felt like a twisted grimace. "But let's just say that's one lesson I learned. I'm not doing that again if I can help it."

He looked way too gleeful about the news. Of course he would.

"Why exactly are you here?" I asked what should have probably been my first question.

"Why, to find you, of course!" Jared crooned. "I figured I'd give you some time to cool off and come to your senses. Then it became obvious that something was wrong. We started looking for you. Had to kill a bunch of assholes until we found someone who gave us the vaguest of leads. But he's also the one who had this atrocious piece of art in his pocket, so there's that. We skipped ahead and started checking up on the bounty collection spots. Third time's the charm, as they say. Here I am, and so are you."

I had a feeling that he'd left out a lot.

"Did you kill anyone getting in here?" Probably a stupid question, but our next steps might depend on his answer.

"Regretfully not yet," he joked—completely serious, of course. "Why? Someone around here you got your eyes on? Someone I need to kill because he dared try to charm your pants off?"

I gave him the flat stare that deserved, the lick of ire up my spine making me feel just a little more like myself.

"No, asshole! But there's an entire wing of people in this facility who I've bled with and almost died for. I can't let you go around undoing all my good work now."

Jared gave me a weird look, but then dropped the point.

"You ready to go now? We can continue playing this game where you pretend to have higher morals than I do, which simply provokes me into pushing you into a situation where you have to go real low just to survive to make you see the error in your ways and that you hopefully come to your senses eventually and come crawling back to me—"

"I think I already told you I'll literally never fucking crawl back to you," I hissed.

He flashed me a bright grin.

"Now there she is, the Callisto we all know and love."

This once, I followed the temptation to roll my eyes at him. But then I nodded.

"Blake and Axel around here, too?"

"Waiting outside. I actually did the sneaking around all on my own, kind of hoping I'd find you first and we'd still have some time for a heartfelt reunion. You know, like in—"

"You providing me with some clean, delicious meat to chew on?"

He chuckled, dropping the point.

I maybe should update him one of these days exactly how bad my hunger was getting of late. That joke still hadn't gotten old.

Jared checked his watch.

"Half an hour until daylight starts to intrude on this clandestine business. Guards aren't really doing their thing, so we might make it out before anyone sees us. Not that I'm opposed to the whole killing-my-way-out business, but odds of one thousand five hundred to four aren't exactly my idea of a good time."

That made me snort.

"At least half of them are civilians. Then again, that barn out there? That's full of soldiers that are infected and more or less on the fast track to conversion. Like me, just without the super awesome control."

"That gotten any better of late?"

I shook my head. "Haven't flipped once since I decided I'd rather starve to death than let you corrupt me and turn me into your twisted little murder sex slave."

Jared had a hard time not bursting out laughing.

"But who would want to do that? I very much value your strong spirit and thriving for independence."

"Since when?"

He shrugged.

"Already told you so. Since I realized there are a million women out there who I could literally scare to death, but none of them would give me even a tenth of the satisfaction that you give me, and that's just us standing here, talking. No sex or drugs involved."

My. What a declaration of love.

"Are you really here? Not just a figment of my imagination because my mind broke just a little in there?"

Jared snorted. "One hundred percent me." He took a step forward, then another, which put him firmly in my personal space. Still holding my gaze, he reached for my left hand, taking my wrist in a borderline gentle grasp and raised it to his lips—before licking a wet line up as far as he could easily bunch up my sleeve, moving even closer. When he raised his head once more, his face was close enough to mine that I could feel his breath across my cheek as he exhaled. "That real enough for you?"

The smile I gave him was almost genuine.

Inside, my heart still felt like a field of broken glass, but at least my sense of humor was rearing its ugly head again.

"I would have preferred a cigarette, honestly. Or something stronger."

His brow furrowed.

"I thought you were done with that? At least you gave me that speech twice, if I remember correctly."

"Yeah, I also thought I could get by without ripping anyone's liver out, but clearly, I was wrong."

"That's my girl." He smirked. "Woman."

I couldn't help but snort.

"I really didn't think I'd say that, but I'm fucking glad to see you."

His turn to scoff, if gently. "What, your new soldier boy not cutting it in the sack?"

My eyes narrowed. "Exactly how long have you been lurking around the base?"

"Long enough to see you eye fuck him for a cigarette."

"And he's still alive?"

"Oh, please. I'm not the jealous type. Either you choose me, or you deserve to be bored out of your fucking mind, stuck with what's beneath what I'd consider my competition."

The bad thing was, I actually believed that.

Just one more thing. Well, two.

"Promise me you didn't somehow microchip me like a dog, and that's how you found me."

He gave me a weird look, but not a hint of concern in his eyes.

"Dig the paranoia, but no. Would I do such a thing? Maybe, but as you might have noticed, we're running short on equipment, so that makes undertakings like that very much non-feasible. We lost our last can opener last week, so it was all knife skills from here on out. You would have loved it."

I doubted that slicing up cans was on the same level of fun as slicing up people, but what did I know?

"Promise me you didn't spend the last month somehow following me, just outside my line of sight and sense, constantly watching what I would do next and how soon I would break. Because I am well aware that is exactly what you would do, and not swoop in at the last possible moment to save me. You'd wait until I somehow got through this, against all odds, and then come casually strolling in several days later and try to sell this to me as my own, if incredibly dumb, victory."

He snorted. When I glared at him, he actually chuckled.

"What, you're serious? I mean, would I do that? Absolutely. I won't lie. I see you've inflicted some first-class anguish on yourself by stupidly setting out on your own to prove something to… us both, I guess? You've clearly paid the price, and the only reason I'm not gloating about that now is because we are kind of on a schedule, and I'd very much like to get laid before I next antagonize you to the point where you clam up and get all prudish on me again. But have you met me? Do I strike you as capable of holding back for days, let alone weeks of depriving myself?"

There was that.

I was kind of glad my mind was still too far gone to dissect all that.

I was sure I would have plenty of time to do that later.

"Let's go. I think I've by far overstayed my welcome."

"Anyone you still want to say goodbye to?"

I shook my head.

"Nah." Not that I didn't want to. But I'd have to clean up and likely find fresh clothes, too. Leaving bloody smears all over the kids when I hugged them one last time seemed like a terrible idea. "I'm ready to get the fuck out of here."

A hint of surprise crossed his features, but far was it from Jared to object.

"Then let's go. I've told the others to meet me by the main gate just before daylight breaks." He checked his watch again. "Which is in seventeen minutes from now, give or take Blake running into anything interesting he thinks he needs to either have or destroy."

"This really is the third base you've been searching for me?"

Jared shrugged. "Why would I lie to you?"

"Because that's absolutely something you do. All the time."

"Usually by omission, and even I wouldn't know how to go about this with something as obvious as that."

A good point.

"Were the other bases also full of starved refugees and borderline raving mad soldiers ostracized from the others?"

"Now that you mention it, we were wondering why they kept the rowdy bunch separate, but then, if you remember, so did the fine people of your beloved Enclave as well…"

He trailed off there with a smirk.

I was sure he'd intended to make a different point.

Something clicked in my head, making me damn uncomfortable.

"Exactly whose idea was it to make that forward outpost up in the middle of the cliffs the Militia camp, anyway?"

Jared caught on after only a second.

"Why, the Colonel offered it to us graciously, pretending to do so after seeing a lot of us more than uneasy to disappear into that infested rat warren he called his castle. But now that you mention it, I think Kara Mason suggested it. Who, as you will remember, was with the Militia before she conveniently let herself be invited into the very heart of the Enclave."

We really didn't have time to chew on this now, but just thinking about this gave me a really bad feeling. And not just because I hated that woman from my very heart. I still remembered all too well the many dead bodies we'd had to step over in our failed rescue attempt, many of them slight and small.

Utterly dispensable, though, if they were already infected. They were useless as guards, and a cure was still miles down the road.

I was thrilled to get moving and try my very best to ignore those thoughts for now.

I fully expected Jared to lead me back through the corridors I'd sneaked down on my way to the lab, but he was a lot more pragmatic—by opening the first window that led out onto the almost-dark parking lot and climbing through.

Yeah, just maybe my mind really wasn't up to snuff this early morning.

Having to kill not one but two of your friends—again!—will do that to the best of us.

So far, the good news.

The bad news was that, for whatever reason, there were plenty of people already out and about, getting a bunch of trucks ready. The commotion in general was not the issue. That might have aided us in getting away. But there were guards aplenty out and about, actually doing some guarding thing—likely because they were supervising what the others did, and those looked like the rough bunch from the barn.

Hiding behind some bushes, Jared got out his binoculars and scanned the yard. That explained how he must have seen me chatting with Peter—what felt like half a lifetime ago.

"Give me that," I said after waiting impatiently for half a minute next to him.

Jared paused, gave me a pointed look—and then handed over the binoculars without further comment.

I pushed away the hint of surprise as I got myself a better picture of the situation.

The swarming of people really didn't make our situation any better, but when I checked the guardhouse by the secondary gate—the one we had walked in through on foot that was farther away from the commotion—I let out a low chuckle.

"That's our way out," I told him, handing back his toy.

Jared frowned.

"Why exactly is that? It's closed, we have no idea how to open it, and it's several hundred yards out of the way of where Blake and Axel must be getting bored right now."

"And it's currently manned by a guy I know who I think I can talk to rationally who will see sense in simply letting us sneak out." Or so I hoped. "And if not, it's only three guards there. Those odds too steep for you?"

Jared's smile shouldn't have been that joyous.

"We can collect the others after we've secured our exit."

"Think your lover boy will spring for a ride, too? Because we've been woefully under-motorized of late."

That could be a problem, but I would take that one issue at a time.

"He's not my—" I cut myself off when I caught Jared's satisfied smirk. No, I would not stroke his ego by explaining to him now that my mind had—for whatever fucked-up reason—decided ages ago that he wasn't replaceable in that aspect.

The way to the secondary gate was actually longer, but since that part of the former recreational whatever-this-had-been hadn't really gotten converted into an actual base, there was plenty of shrubbery and stuff to hide behind as we made our way there. I knew we must have gone over Jared's deadline by now, but it was still miserably dark all around, so I figured it was all the same. Nothing had exploded yet toward the main gate, so I figured Blake was still biding his time.

When we reached the last hedge before the gate, Jared made as if to start sneaking forward, but I held him back.

"Let me handle this."

His eyes narrowed.

"But you'll cost us the element of surprise if you walk up there and fucking talk," he said—no, whined.

"Are you for real?!"

He gave me a pout, followed by a near-silent snarl.

Oh my God, he was literally about to have a tantrum like a small child because there was a chance I was—again!—taking what he probably thought of as a deserved kill from him?

We were going to have a long and thorough talk in the very near future! But not now!

"I'll handle this," I told him in no uncertain terms. "If that fails, please, go ahead and murder them. But first, let me try this."

Jared gave me a look of utter discontent—very much like a dog denied his favorite treat—but then shrugged and gave me a go-ahead gesture.

This man was so going to be the end of me!

Rather than continue my proficient sneaking routine, I made sure to be very obvious as I half-walked, half-ran up to the guard post. It was more of an open lean-to that was just large enough to house a table, two chairs, and kept all that out of the rain and worst of the winds. Peter and the two soldiers by his side saw me coming easily, the two men already sharing joking remarks behind his back, while Peter looked my way with mounting concern.

I paused just outside the post, as if I was still undecided what I was even doing here.

"Peter?" I whisper-called, as if there was any chance that it would only alert him, not the other two. "Are you in there? One of your men said I'd find you here."

I didn't quite catch the remarks between the soldiers, but they were definitely lewd, and Peter told them to shut the fuck up before stepping outside close to where I was hovering.

"Ash, what are you doing here?"

I hoped that what little light spilled out of the post let him see the conflicted expression I tried to put on my face as I stepped back, gesturing him to follow me.

"Do you have a minute to talk?"

He seemed irritated for a moment, making my stomach sink— and me seriously question my people skills of late—but then he sighed, and with a look of utter annoyance turned to his men. "Jenkins, Anderson, beat it. When I come by for your quarters inspection in fifteen minutes from now, they'd better be spotless."

Rather than get annoyed, one of the soldiers chuckled.

"Take an extra twenty, Lt. We'll hold down the fort while you're busy."

I heard them snicker their way back to our wing until they were out of earshot, kind of hoping that Jared wouldn't get too impatient, but not devastated if that happened to be the case.

"I'm sorry for that," Peter told me as he turned back to me. "They're a bunch of immature idiots, but they're the best we have left right now."

He probably expected me to joke with him. Instead, I did my best to appear uncomfortable but imploring.

"Peter, I need your help."

He drew up short, if ever so slightly, putting on his serious face. Was that a hint of disappointment that this wasn't actually a booty call?

Sigh. Men.

"Sure. What can I do for you?"

I thought about going about this the sneaky way, but my emotional range wasn't coming back any minute now, so I went with blunt honesty instead.

"I need you to open that gate. I'm leaving. And if you could spare a car, that would be real nice. Doesn't need to be fully fueled, but enough gas for a hundred miles would be great."

A light frown appeared on his forehead. "You're leaving?" The way he said that made it sound like he hadn't even considered that possibility.

"Are you going to stop me?"

He paused—which very much made me tighten my grip around the knife I was still carrying in my right hand, which only just occurred to me. At least I'd been smart enough to keep that hand pressed against my thigh, mostly hiding it from view.

Yup, definitely not at my A-game right now.

"Peter?"

"No, no. Of course not. But why, all of a sudden? And what about your sister and the kids? Are they going, too?"

I was tempted to lie, but then dropped that idea. I didn't know why, but I felt like I owed him the truth. Also, because I'd always gotten the sense from him that he valued honesty over nice tales.

"There's nothing for me here. I'd rather find my luck elsewhere."

His frown deepened.

"Is this because of what we talked about earlier? You don't need to be afraid of the infected. They aren't contagious themselves, unless maybe their saliva, but likely not even that. Yes, we think they caught it from inhaling spores, but that happened weeks ago. And we keep them well under wraps. They won't get anywhere near you, don't worry. And even if; they are all still human. They don't act like animals."

Unless prompted otherwise, as I'd pretty much witnessed tonight—or almost. I'd certainly seen the aftermath of it. And damn, I wished I'd known what was going on in there sooner because then I could have stuck each and every one of them like the pigs that they were—

It took me way too much effort not to let that anger show on my face as I tried to push it away once more.

"It's not that. It's—" I paused, then sighed, giving up on that charade.

I could tell Peter picked up on the change in my body language as I straightened, dropping that last bit of that slightly fawning, nice-girl facade that I'd kept up around him very much since the mountain rescue.

"Peter, let's get real here. You have no fucking clue who I am. And that's the only thing that's keeping you alive right now. We can do this the easy way, or the way that ends with you bleeding out in that ditch over there. I'm asking you—nicely—again. Please open that gate, and yes, I'd very much still like that ride, but if that's more than you can procure in a pinch, the open gate will more than suffice. Don't be stupid. Don't play the hero over something you're not even beginning to understand—and which, quite frankly, is none of your business. I get the feeling you actually are one of the good guys, and all those people back there in that wing need someone like you to help them. But I'm not one of them."

Jared's words, pouring out of my mouth. Or close enough not to sit right with me.

Peter stared at me, not comprehending—until something clicked. He didn't outright go for his gun, but his entire body language turned… a little hostile, for lack of a better word.

Good. At least not all was lost. Even if that made things slightly more inconvenient for me.

But damn, it felt good not to be wearing a mask anymore.

Just how much of a relief that was should have told me that my moral quandaries about who to be and how to live my life had been kind of moot. Not that reality had left me to indulge my delusions for long, anyway.

"So that really is you. On the bounty posters."

I was a little surprised he made that connection—and so quickly.

"Those are really bad renditions. Don't you people have security cameras anywhere you can get actual pictures from? I wouldn't have recognized myself from that… sketch."

I got a rather flat stare from him.

"Let me guess. Your friends are here, too? Finally caught up with you, huh? Smart idea to try to throw us off your course by splitting up and hiding among the women and children. You really had me fooled there."

I shrugged, hating that his hit actually landed.

"I wasn't really trying to deceive anyone. Believe it or not, I was having a crisis of faith. Kind of. And just for the record, I really did put my ass on the line for them. I almost got killed several times over, and if I wasn't who I actually am, I would have died like so many others. Sure, your efforts to help—if you want to call it that—culled the herd, but that still left hundreds dead. Hundreds. So, yes. Please give me some grief for actually trying to help. I can't wait to be out of here where you people keep foisting absolutely indigestible shit down my throat."

So just maybe that had come out a little more angry than intended.

Another light bulb went off in Peter's head, and I could tell that now he really was considering drawing his pistol.

"And yes. I'm not alone." I smiled sweetly at him. "Pull that gun, and you'll choke on your own blood in ten seconds flat."

Ten for Jared. Probably less than five for me.

Peter hesitated before he pointedly raised both hands a little, showing me his empty palms. He kind of deflated, maybe realizing that his life was actually hanging in the balance right now—and trying very hard to make peace with that.

Exhaling forcefully, I tried to clear my head and make sure this situation wasn't escalating any more.

"Look. I know you're one of the good guys. Or at least, I very much hope so, and your actions so far speak one hundred percent for you. That's an incredibly hard thing to come by these days—capable men who are not assholes who are actively trying to fend for the vulnerable and not take whatever they can grab by all means possible. You almost got my belief in humanity restored for a second."

He looked conflicted, as if he didn't quite trust my praise—or where this was leading. Smart man.

"What trashed it again?"

I allowed myself a small chuckle. It really came out as a nasty guffaw.

"Oh, just the simple fact that your dear doctor there kept two zombies in her lab, one of which she regularly lets your infected soldiers rape to knock her up. Yeah, I don't quite get how that still works, but she rambled enough about that to make me believe her. Oh, and did I mention, those two used to be two of my best friends? My first fucking zombie apocalypse buddy—who, admittedly, wasn't a great fighter, and I sometimes got really annoyed because, every single fucking time, the damn undead would come for me and leave him completely untouched, but that was okay. I can take it. More than anyone else in this fucking apocalypse, he kept me on the straight and narrow. And that fucking bitch had to pump him full of fucking zombie goo just because there was a hint of a chance that I was rubbing off on him, or some shit! And then she kept him around for I don't even know what purposes. To amuse herself? To stare at his undead, flaccid zombie dick? Kas deserved so much fucking better! And do not get me started on Ash! Yeah, exactly. That Ash. Whose name I picked up, because when I ran into Bea, Mariana, and their kids, half crazed from being starved almost beyond my limits,

I thought to myself, how would a nice, normal person act, she was the one who came to my mind! My roommate for four fucking years! Who's never done a single bad thing to anyone in the entire fucking world! She always overtipped everyone, even a food delivery driver who was two hours late and had obviously eaten that one sandwich that was missing from our order!"

I needed a few angry breaths to calm down again after that.

Peter kept staring at me as if he was watching a mad dog perform a surprising trick—but not trusting it at all not to bite him the next moment.

I hated how damn accurate that assessment felt.

Calming myself once more, I did my best to go for a measured poise—only to fly right off the handle again.

Just maybe, the stress of the last two weeks had worn down my defenses a lot more than I'd thought.

"And just so you know, the whole shit with the zombie sex dolls? It's all true. Because unlike you, I was there, in that fucking power plant. I had to watch them lie to one of our guys, and as some fucked-up kind of hazing ritual, they made him mouth-rape one of the female zombies they had rigged up—put them in stocks, hacked off their limbs so all that was left was a light, easily maneuverable head and torso in a damn sex swing. They even told him it was safe because they'd pulled out all her teeth. I don't need to tell you what their saliva does, huh? Bite or no bite. Took all of seven minutes for the damn idiot to turn into a brainless husk. While they drank and watched and cheered him the fuck on! And then stashed him with all the others. If you ask me, not a single person in that entire damn power plant deserved to live because they were all complicit. They all fucking knew what was going on, and they damn well let it happen. They didn't warn us. They only told us the bare gist of it later when we were already on the run. And the only reason why we managed to get out of there was because a fucking psychopath managed to stash away two pills of meth and had the brilliant idea to give one to the biggest, strongest brute around, and the other to the small, easy-to-dismiss girl. He couldn't have known that I actually know how to fight back then. That we actually pulled it off was sheer luck."

I wasn't even surprised when I heard Jared pipe up from behind the hedge at my back.

"You need to begin giving yourself more credit than that! You're a damn magnificent force of nature when you let loose!"

My grunt of annoyance was real.

"See what I need to put up with?!" I whispered to Peter. "Day in, day out. It's like his purpose in life is to wear down what little human decency I'm managing to still cling to. But I would manage, you know? If you fucking assholes would stop to fucking rape every single woman out there, dead or alive! And fucking stop killing every damn friend I've ever made since I woke up in that quarantine tent!"

Just maybe, the last part of that came out almost as a shout.

Peter said nothing in response, but his eyes had gotten continually wider, particularly when Jared interjected. He waited for me to go on with my rant, not relaxing when nothing more came.

I sighed again, regaining part of my composure.

"I'm just a little stressed out right now. Sorry." That last bit was a lie, but it would have been the decent thing to add, so that was what I did. "Fact is, we are leaving. With your help, or without. Your choice entirely. Do with what I just told you as you see fit. I hope I'm right with my assessment of who you are, and you make damn sure that nothing happens to those women and children in there. Because there's a damn chance that if you funnel them into that very same meat grinder that already killed most of my friends, I will come for you, even if I might not intend to. This shit keeps happening. I can't control it. As much as I'd like to say it's the Asshole's fault, I think all he really wants to do is indulge in his urges once in a while, and be left in fucking peace for the most time. Which right fucking now is already playing whack-a-mole with opportunities where we have to damn well kill our way out of traps and situations way beyond our control, way too often. Be the better man. Affect change. Protect those women and kids. And, yeah, also the old geezers, because most of them are decent guys, too. Okay?"

Again he waited for more before he finally nodded. Slowly. Carefully.

"Sure. You can go. I sure as hell won't stand in your way. The switch for the gate is right there, at the back wall. If you need a car, don't go to the main lot. They're right now getting ready for the next sortie. You'll stand out in your civilian clothes."

He glanced down my body—and finally saw my left hand, completely covered in blood, and my right, not much cleaner, still clutching the knife.

Peter swallowed thickly and went on, his eyes once more trained on my face, and very much trying not to look anywhere else again.

"There's a shed with several more cars about a hundred yards from here, right along the fence. If the door is closed, the code to the keypad is zero-one-two-three."

"Seriously?"

He shrugged. "We are dealing with a bunch of jarheads here, and I'm not even sure the half-brain-dead ones are the issue." He paused. "Nobody'll hold you up, but I can stay here and guard the gate, if you want—"

I shook my head. He immediately shut up.

"Go back inside. Deal with your men. If you like for them to live a little longer, don't sic them on our trail."

He nodded slowly. "Nobody's going to come after you. At least not because of me. You didn't want to come here in the first place, I now realize. You point-blank asked me about leaving several times. I thought I was being chivalrous, disbanding your unfounded fears. Teaches me not to be such a fucking sap from now on."

I couldn't quite hold in a chuckle.

"Oh, your instincts were good. Just wasted on the wrong woman."

He didn't protest, but that was probably for the best.

I made a throwaway gesture with my knife, signaling him to beat it. Judging from the feeling of... vague emptiness behind me, I was certain Jared was already halfway to those cars.

Peter hesitated for another moment.

"Why are you running with those assholes?" he finally asked, probably reasoning the same about us likely being on our own for the moment. "Is it because you're in love with one of those fucking monsters? Please. You can do so much better than that."

I couldn't help but frown—both because that was definitely a question I had more than once asked myself, but mostly because Peter couldn't know the slightest thing about what kind of person Jared was.

"Why? What do you actually know about them?" I asked. "And why is it that there's a fucking bounty on our heads? We didn't exactly leave a trail of dead bodies behind. More like we're kind of fucking shit magnets." Which wasn't quite true—but true enough—since Jared had been pretty careful about hiding the signs.

Peter looked almost offended, but then something in his expression changed. As if something I'd said was making him rethink what he'd thought were known facts.

"Actually, I can't answer that last part. We got the intel in a briefing early in July, I think. It came from the science division."

Of course it did—but I didn't interrupt Peter to add that.

"No idea where they got it from, but part of the package were some witness testimonies. Some survivors of your purported atrocities, but my captain himself said most of that didn't sound like reliable statements. One of them had apparently been very close to raving mad, and he kept stressing how much of a bitch you are with that damn knife—a direct quote, not my words."

The mix of guilt and caution on his face made me smile—as did the realization that followed.

"Oh, nice. Blondie did make it out alive. We had no idea what happened to them after we split off from them after they kicked us out of the Enclave."

Peter didn't add any details, but I was sure he was filing all of that away.

"They kept updating the intel," he went on. "Details about how you apparently killed off entire towns. Most of that seemed overdone or downright fantastical, but we found an entire group slaughtered off, and that was when my captain said to better be safe than sorry."

I was ready to dismiss that—when I remembered.

"Was that close to two bends in the Catawba River, a little north of some of the lakes?" I really couldn't remember most of their names anymore. "South of Lake Wylie?"

Peter nodded slowly. "Yeah, around there."

I scoffed.

"Those fucking assholes had it coming. They shot at us while we were simply drifting by in boats! It took me three damn weeks until the wound in my leg healed! The blood clots alone still give me nightmares."

He didn't comment on that, but instead went on.

"They also said you were responsible for infecting the entire community in Lancaster county. They had to send in the cavalry to burn it all to the ground because there were too many bat-shit crazy, half-turned infected there to contain them."

I shook my head, feeling physically sick for a moment. Those skeletons would haunt me for a while yet.

"Not us. I mean, yeah. We spent some time close by. But we got into trouble with one of their leaders because we were giving their young people drugs. Nobody infected anyone with anything beyond good old addiction to illicit substance abuse."

I got another one of those disbelieving stares from him—until I drew up short.

"They were acting weirdly paranoid, though," I mused. "At the end, when we decided we'd overstayed our welcome. So maybe that was one of those waves you mentioned. But that wasn't us."

He thought about that for a moment, but then nodded.

"That was kind of our working theory, too. Pinning it on four people who we had about a zero chance of ever finding sounded like a very convenient use of scapegoats."

"But why lie?"

He shrugged.

"You realize what happens when we are honest with the survivors and tell them that while we can keep them safe from zombie bites, none of us knows what to do about waves of spores in the air?" He paused to let me consider that. "Besides, the waves theory is just that—a theory."

"You know that's what scientists call what the rest of us would already consider hard facts? It's just science lingo."

He shrugged. "Doesn't exactly make it better, right?"

No, it didn't.

Behind him, I heard the engine of a single car approaching.

"Looks like my ride is here," I told him.

Peter just stared back at me, possibly waiting for me to go back on my word and execute him on the spot.

Which probably would have been the smart thing, to hide our tracks and all that.

Instead, I gestured for him to go, again.

"Take care of Bea, Mariana, and the kids for me, will you? Unlike me, they deserve it."

Peter paused—and cracked a small smile. "Yes, ma'am." And with that, he was gone, running back to our wing at an easy lope, as if he was catching up with his people after some fun time in the bushes.

I wasn't surprised to find Blake and Axel already in the back row, both cautiously happy about seeing me.

I more fell than climbed into the front passenger seat, buckling myself in immediately because Jared was—of course—already flooring it, sending the car down a half washed away gravel mountain road without lights on in the early morning gloom.

It took me a good ten minutes of sitting there in silence before I was ready to put away my knife—and only did so with reluctance.

"You need some baby wipes to clean up?" Axel offered from behind me.

I stared at my blood-encrusted hands, nearly black in the scant illumination from the dashboard. Nothing short of a long soak in hot water would get rid of that—and that was just the physical stains.

Nothing could wipe away the mental ones.

"Yeah, hand me a pack of them," I finally said, forcing myself to pull out of that momentary funk.

Jared kept on driving in silence while he kept glancing my way, probably fucking disappointed he couldn't... I didn't know what. Gnaw off the flakes of that from my bare skin later, or some shit. Who knew with him?

When I was finally done—and my hands were by no means clean—he finally spoke up.

"So, what do you wanna do next? We have the entire fucking world out there for us to explore."

That was—in so many ways—way beyond the scope of what I was able to consider right then.

"For now? After we've gotten far enough away from here to be damn sure they're not after us..."

"Naturally."

I let my head lull to the side, watching Jared's profile for a while as I kept thinking.

"Right now? I want to eat enough meat that I'm bursting. Then I want some booze, enough drugs to wipe my mind clean, and I want you to fuck me into oblivion. That sound about right?"

The corner of his mouth twisted into his usual smirk while it was impossible to miss Axel's exasperated—and very much tired from already having given up on us—sigh.

"I think that can be arranged. Provided you don't change your mind again and jump out of yet another speeding car. Was fun the first time, but everything gets annoying when you do it too many times. Except for sex and drugs. Those just keep getting better."

I didn't try to hide my annoyance as I grunted, flopping back over so that I was facing the road.

"Been there. Done that. Can't really recommend it."

"See, I knew you would come to your senses eventually."

That made me eye the car door critically.

"What do they say? Third time's the charm? That means I still have two more tries."

Jared laughed—and pointedly engaged the central locking mechanism.

I allowed myself a small smile—particularly when Blake said from the back, "There's some booze under your seat. And some food. Mostly kibble, because that was the only pure-protein shit we found on the quick, but Jared said it would be fine."

I laughed—and then dug in.

While a little bland, it really wasn't so bad. For sure, a million times better than what they'd been feeding me at the base. Not as tasty as the dried trail rations, but I wasn't quite ready to admit that yet—out loud or to myself. Washing it all down with moonshine strong enough to make my eyes water sure helped.

And thus, we drove into the dreary, gray sunrise, free and united again.

TO BE CONTINUED IN SEDITION
WORLD OF ANTHRAX BOOK 6

ACKNOWLEDGMENTS

Ah, writing this book was a lot of fun!

What was going on in my life in the meantime, not so much, but by the time you're reading this, the worst is hopefully behind me, and I can soon shelf this entire experience as "did not need that to happen but, oh, well."

It certainly helped having this wonderful story to get lost in as a distraction - and I can't wait to write the last two remaining books in the series!

My eternal thanks go to the great people who helped make this book into what it is:

My amazing beta readers—Jackie, Tracy, and Connie. You're the best!

My wonderful editor—an absolute joy to work with, as always!

And last but not least, the man in my life. Just because.

ABOUT THE AUTHOR

Adrienne Lecter has a background in Biochemistry and Molecular Biology, loves ranting at inaccuracies in movies, and spends increasingly more time on the shooting range. She lives with the man and cat of her life in Vienna, and is working on the next post-apocalyptic books.

You can sign up for Adrienne's newsletter to never miss a release and be the first to know what other shenanigans she gets up to: http://www.adriennelecter.com

THANK YOU

Hey, you! Yes, you, who just spent a helluva lot of time reading this book! You just made my day! Thanks!

Want to be notified of new releases, giveaways and updates? Sign up for my newsletter:
www.adriennelecter.com

If you enjoyed reading the book and have a moment to spare, I would really appreciate a short, honest review on the site you purchased it from and on goodreads. Reviews make a huge difference in helping new readers find the series.

Or if you'd like to drop me a note, or chat a but, feel free to email me or hit me up on social media. I'll try to respond as quickly as possible! If you'd like to report an error or wrong detail, I've set up a separate space on my website for that, too.

Email: adrienne@adriennelecter.com
Website: adriennelecter.com
Twitter: @adriennelecter
Facebook: facebook.com/adriennelecter

BOOKS PUBLISHED

Green Fields
#1: Incubation
#2: Outbreak
#3: Escalation
#4: Extinction
#5: Resurgence
#6: Unity
#7: Affliction
#8: Catharsis
#9: Exodus
#10: Uprising
#11: Retribution
#12: Annihilation

Beyond Green Fields
short story collections
Omnibus #1
Ombinus #2

World of Anthrax
#1: Survival
#2: Collapse
#3: Desolation
#4: Defiance
#5: Attrition
#6: Sedition
(coming fall 2023)

Made in United States
North Haven, CT
04 August 2023

39944979R10228